The Dove in the Eagle's Nest

Charlotte M. Yonge

Table of Contents

The Dove in the Eagle's Nest..1
    Charlotte M. Yonge..1
    INTRODUCTION..1
    CHAPTER I: MASTER GOTTFRIED'S WORKSHOP...3
    CHAPTER II: THE EYRIE..13
    CHAPTER III: THE FLOTSAM AND JETSAM OF THE DEBATEABLE FORD...........20
    CHAPTER IV: SNOW-WREATHS WHEN 'TIS THAW..25
    CHAPTER V: THE YOUNG FREIHERR..29
    CHAPTER VI: THE BLESSED FRIEDMUND'S WAKE...32
    CHAPTER VII: THE SCHNEIDERLEIN'S RETURN..39
    CHAPTER VIII: PASSING THE OUBLIETTE...43
    CHAPTER IX: THE EAGLETS...50
    CHAPTER X: THE EAGLE'S PREY...54
    CHAPTER XI: THE CHOICE IN LIFE..59
    CHAPTER XII: BACK TO THE DOVECOTE...65
    CHAPTER XIII: THE EAGLETS IN THE CITY...71
    CHAPTER XIV: THE DOUBLE-HEADED EAGLE...77
    CHAPTER XV: THE RIVAL EYRIE...87
    CHAPTER XVI: THE EAGLE AND THE SNAKE...94
    CHAPTER XVII: BRIDGING THE FORD...99
    CHAPTER XVIII: FRIEDMUND IN THE CLOUDS..105
    CHAPTER XIX: THE FIGHT AT THE FORD...109
    CHAPTER XX: THE WOUNDED EAGLE...114
    CHAPTER XXI: RITTER THEURDANK...120
    CHAPTER XXII: PEACE...124
    CHAPTER XXIII: THE ALTAR OF PEACE..130
    CHAPTER XXIV: OLD IRON AND NEW STEEL..135
    CHAPTER XXV: THE STAR AND THE SPARK..146

The Dove in the Eagle's Nest

Charlotte M. Yonge

Kessinger Publishing reprints thousands of hard-to-find books!

Visit us at http://www.kessinger.net

INTRODUCTION

In sending forth this little book, I am inclined to add a few explanatory words as to the use I have made of historical personages. The origin of the whole story was probably Freytag's first series of pictures of German Life: probably, I say, for its first commencement was a dream, dreamt some weeks after reading that most interesting collection of sketches. The return of the squire with the tidings of the death of the two knights was vividly depicted in sleep; and, though without local habitation or name, the scene was most likely to have been a reflection from the wild scenes so lately read of.

In fact, waking thoughts decided that such a catastrophe could hardly have happened anywhere but in Germany, or in Scotland; and the contrast between the cultivation in the free cities and the savagery of the independent barons made the former the more suitable region for the adventures. The time could only be before the taming and bringing into order of the empire, when the Imperial cities were in their greatest splendour, the last free nobles in course of being reduced from their lawless liberty, and the House of Austria beginning to acquire its preponderance over the other princely families.

M. Freytag's books, and Hegewisch's History of Maximilian, will, I think, be found fully to bear out the picture I have tried to give of the state of things in the reign of the Emperor Friedrich III., when, for want of any other law, Faust recht, or fist right, ruled; i.e. an offended nobleman, having once sent a Fehde-brief to his adversary, was thenceforth at liberty to revenge himself by a private war, in which, for the wrong inflicted, no justice was exacted.

Hegewisch remarks that the only benefit of this custom was, that the honour of subscribing a feud-brief was so highly esteemed that it induced the nobles to learn to write! The League of St. George and the Swabian League were the means of gradually putting down this authorized condition of deadly feud.

This was in the days of Maximilian's youth. He is a prince who seems to have been almost as inferior in his foreign to what he was in his domestic policy as was Queen Elizabeth. He is chiefly familiar to us as failing to keep up his authority in Flanders after the death of Mary of Burgundy, as lingering to fulfil his engagement with Anne of Brittany till he lost her and her duchy, as incurring ridicule by his ill-managed schemes in Italy, and the vast projects that he was always forming without either means or steadiness to carry them out, by his perpetual impecuniosity and slippery dealing; and in his old age he has become rather the laughing-stock of historians.

But there is much that is melancholy in the sight of a man endowed with genius, unbalanced by the force of character that secures success, and with an ardent nature whose intention overleapt obstacles that in practice he found insuperable. At home Maximilian raised the Imperial power from a mere cipher to considerable weight. We judge him as if he had been born in the purple and succeeded to a defined power like his descendants. We forget that the head of the Holy Roman Empire had been, ever since the extinction of the Swabian line, a mere mark for ambitious princes to shoot at, with everything expected from him, and no means to do anything. Maximilian's own father was an avaricious, undignified old man, not until near his death Archduke of even all Austria, and with anarchy prevailing everywhere under his nominal rule. It was in the time of Maximilian that the Empire became as compact and united a body as could be hoped of anything so unwieldy, that law was at least acknowledged, Faust recht for ever abolished, and the Emperor became once more a real power.

The Dove in the Eagle's Nest

The man under whom all this was effected could have been no fool; yet, as he said himself, he reigned over a nation of kings, who each chose to rule for himself; and the uncertainty of supplies of men or money to be gained from them made him so often fail necessarily in his engagements, that he acquired a shiftiness and callousness to breaches of promise, which became the worst flaw in his character. But of the fascination of his manner there can be no doubt. Even Henry VIII.'s English ambassadors, when forced to own how little they could depend on him, and how dangerous it was to let subsidies pass through his fingers, still show themselves under a sort of enchantment of devotion to his person, and this in his old age, and when his conduct was most inexcusable and provoking.

His variety of powers was wonderful. He was learned in many languages—in all those of his empire or hereditary states, and in many besides; and he had an ardent love of books, both classical and modern. He delighted in music, painting, architecture, and many arts of a more mechanical description; wrote treatises on all these, and on other subjects, especially gardening and gunnery. He was the inventor of an improved lock to the arquebus, and first divined how to adapt the disposition of his troops to the use of the newly- discovered fire-arms. And in all these things his versatile head and ready hand were personally employed, not by deputy; while coupled with so much artistic taste was a violent passion for hunting, which carried him through many hairbreadth 'scapes. "It was plain," he used to say, "that God Almighty ruled the world, or how could things go on with a rogue like Alexander VI. at the head of the Church, and a mere huntsman like himself at the head of the Empire." His bon- mots are numerous, all thoroughly characteristic, and showing that brilliancy in conversation must have been one of his greatest charms. It seems as if only self-control and resolution were wanting to have made him a Charles, or an Alfred, the Great.

The romance of his marriage with the heiress of Burgundy is one of the best known parts of his life. He was scarcely two-and-twenty when he lost her, who perhaps would have given him the stability he wanted; but his tender hove for her endured through life. It is not improbable that it was this still abiding attachment that made him slack in overcoming difficulties in the way of other contracts, and that he may have hoped that his engagement to Bianca Sforza would come to nothing, like so many others.

The most curious record of him is, however, in two books, the materials for which he furnished, and whose composition and illustration he superintended, Der Weise King, and Theurdank, of both of which he is well known to be the hero. The White, or the Wise King, it is uncertain which, is a history of his education and exploits, in prose. Every alternate page has its engraving, showing how the Young White King obtains instruction in painting, architecture, language, and all arts and sciences, the latter including magic—which he learns of an old woman with a long-tailed demon sitting, like Mother Hubbard's cat, on her shoulder—and astrology. In the illustration of this study an extraordinary figure of a cross within a circle appears in the sky, which probably has some connection with his scheme of nativity, for it also appears on the breast of Ehrenhold, his constant companion in the metrical history of his career, under the name of Theurdank.

The poetry of Theurdank was composed by Maximilian's old writing- master, Melchior Pfinznig; but the adventures were the Kaisar's own, communicated by himself, and he superintended the wood-cuts. The name is explained to mean "craving glory,"—Gloriaememor. The Germans laugh to scorn a French translator, who rendered it "Chermerci." It was annotated very soon after its publication, and each exploit explained and accounted for. It is remarkable and touching in a man who married at eighteen, and was a widower at twenty-two, that, in both books, the happy union with his lady love is placed at the end—not at the beginning of the book; and in Theurdank, at least, the eternal reunion is clearly meant.

In this curious book, Konig Romreich, by whom every contemporary understood poor Charles of Burgundy—thus posthumously made King of Rome by Maximilian, as the only honour in his power, betroths his daughter Ehrenreich (rich in honour) to the Ritter Theurdank. Soon after, by a most mild version of Duke Charles's frightful end, Konig Romreich is seen on his back dying in a garden, and Ehrenreich (as Mary really did) despatches a ring to summon her betrothed.

But here Theurdank returns for answer that he means first to win honour by his exploits, and sets out with his comrade, Ehrenhold, in search thereof. Ehrenhold never appears of the smallest use to him in any of the dire adventures into which he falls, but only stands complacently by, and in effect may represent Fame, or perhaps that literary sage whom Don Quixote always supposed to be at hand to record his deeds of prowess.

Next we are presented with the German impersonation of Satan as a wise old magician, only with claws instead of feet, commissioning his three captains (hauptleutern), Furwitz, Umfallo, and Neidelhard, to beset and ruin Theurdank. They are interpreted as the dangers of youth, middle life, and old age—Rashness, Disaster, and Distress (or Envy). One at a time they encounter him,—not once, but again and again; and he has ranged under each head, in entire contempt of real order of time, the perils he thinks owing to each foe. Furwitz most justly gets the credit of Maximilian's perils on the steeple of Ulm, though, unfortunately, the artist has represented the daring climber as standing not much above the shoulders of Furwitz and Ehrenhold; and although the annotation tells us that his "hinder half foot" overhung the scaffold, the danger in the print is not appalling. Furwitz likewise inveigles him into putting the point (schnabel) of his shoe into the wheel of a mill for turning stone balls, where he certainly hardly deserved to lose nothing but the beak of his shoe. This enemy also brings him into numerous unpleasant predicaments on precipices, where he hangs by one hand; while the chamois stand delighted on every available peak, Furwitz grins malevolently, and Ehrenhold stands pointing at him over his shoulder. Time and place are given in the notes for all these escapes. After some twenty adventures Furwitz is beaten off, and Umfallo tries his powers. Here the misadventures do not involve so much folly on the hero's part— though, to be sure, he ventures into a lion's den unarmed, and has to beat off the inmates with a shovel. But the other adventures are more rational. He catches a jester—of admirably foolish expression- -putting a match to a powder-magazine; he is wonderfully preserved in mountain avalanches and hurricanes; reins up his horse on the verge of an abyss; falls through ice in Holland and shows nothing but his head above it; cures himself of a fever by draughts of water, to the great disgust of his physicians, and escapes a fire bursting out of a tall stove.

Neidelhard brings his real battles and perils. From this last he is in danger of shipwreck, of assassination, of poison, in single combat, or in battle; tumults of the people beset him; he is imprisoned as at Ghent. But finally Neidelhard is beaten back; and the hero is presented to Ehrenreich. Ehrenhold recounts his triumphs, and accuses the three captains. One is hung, another beheaded, the third thrown headlong from a tower, and a guardian angel then summons Theurdank to his union with his Queen. No doubt this reunion was the life-dream of the harassed, busy, inconsistent man, who flashed through the turmoils of the early sixteenth century.

The adventures of Maximilian which have been adverted to in the story are all to be found in Theurdank, and in his early life he was probably the brilliant eager person we have tried in some degree to describe. In his latter years it is well known that he was much struck by Luther's arguments; and, indeed, he had long been conscious of need of Church reform, though his plans took the grotesque form of getting himself made Pope, and taking all into his own hands.

Perhaps it was unwise to have ever so faintly sketched Ebbo's career through the ensuing troubles; but the history of the star and of the spark in the stubble seemed to need completion; and the working out of the character of the survivor was unfinished till his course had been thought over from the dawn of the Wittenberg teaching, which must have seemed no novelty to an heir of the doctrine of Tauler, and of the veritably Catholic divines of old times. The idea is of the supposed course of a thoughtful, refined, conscientious man through the earlier times of the Reformation, glad of the hope of cleansing the Church, but hoping to cleanse, not to break away from her—a hope that Luther himself long cherished, and which was not entirely frustrated till the re-assembly at Trent in the next generation. Justice has never been done to the men who feared to loose their hold on the Church Catholic as the one body to which the promises were made. Their loyalty has been treated as blindness, timidity, or superstition; but that there were many such persons, and those among the very highest minds of their time, no one can have any doubt after reading such lives as those of Friedrich the Wise of Saxony, of Erasmus, of Vittoria Colonna, or of Cardinal Giustiniani.

April 9, 1836.

CHAPTER I: MASTER GOTTFRIED'S WORKSHOP

The upper lattices of a tall, narrow window were open, and admitted the view, of first some richly-tinted vine leaves and purpling grapes, then, in dazzling freshness of new white stone, the lacework fabric of a half-built minster spire, with a mason's crane on the summit, bending as though craving for a further supply of materials; and beyond, peeping through every crevice of the exquisite open fretwork, was the intensely blue sky of early autumn.

The lower longer panes of the window were closed, and the glass, divided into circles and quarrels, made the scene less distinct; but still the huge stone tower was traceable, and, farther off, the slope of a gently-rising hill, clothed with vineyards blushing into autumn richness. Below, the view was closed by the gray wall of a court- yard, laden with fruit-trees in full bearing, and inclosing paved paths that radiated from a central fountain, and left spaces between, where a few summer flowers still lingered, and the remains of others showed what their past glory had been.

The interior of the room was wainscoted, the floor paved with bright red and cream-coloured tiles, and the tall stove in one corner decorated with the same. The eastern end of the apartment was adorned with an exquisite small group carved in oak, representing the carpenter's shop at Nazareth, with the Holy Child instructed by Joseph in the use of tools, and the Mother sitting with her book, "pondering these things in her heart." All around were blocks of wood and carvings in varying states of progress—some scarcely shaped out, and others in perfect completion. And the subjects were equally various. Here was an adoring angel with folded wings, clasped hands, and rapt face; here a majestic head of an apostle or prophet; here a lovely virgin saint, seeming to play smilingly with the instrument of her martyrdom; here a grotesque miserere group, illustrating a fairy tale, or caricaturing a popular fable here a beauteous festoon of flowers and fruit, emulating nature in all save colour; and on the work-table itself, growing under the master's hand, was a long wreath, entirely composed of leaves and seed-vessels in their quaint and beauteous forms—the heart-shaped shepherd's purse, the mask-like skull-cap, and the crowned urn of the henbane. The starred cap of the poppy was actually being shaped under the tool, copied from a green capsule, surmounted with purple velvety rays, which, together with its rough and wavy leaf, was held in the hand of a young maiden who knelt by the table, watching the work with eager interest.

She was not a beautiful girl—not one of those whose "bright eyes rain influence, and judge the prize." She was too small, too slight, too retiring for such a position. If there was something lily-like in her drooping grace, it was not the queen-lily of the garden that she resembled, but the retiring lily of the valley—so purely, transparently white was her skin, scarcely tinted by a roseate blush on the cheek, so tender and modest the whole effect of her slender figure, and the soft, downcast, pensive brown eyes, utterly dissimilar in hue from those of all her friends and kindred, except perhaps the bright, quick ones of her uncle, the master-carver. Otherwise, his portly form, open visage, and good-natured stateliness, as well as his furred cap and gold chain, were thoroughly those of the German burgomaster of the fifteenth century; but those glittering black eyes had not ceased to betray their French, or rather Walloon, origin, though for several generations back the family had been settled at Ulm. Perhaps, too, it was Walloon quickness and readiness of wit that had made them, so soon as they became affiliated, so prominent in all the councils of the good free city, and so noted for excellence in art and learning. Indeed the present head of the family, Master Gottfried Sorel, was so much esteemed for his learning that he had once had serious thoughts of terming himself Magister Gothofredus Oxalicus, and might have carried it out but for the very decided objections of his wife, Dame Johanna, and his little niece, Christina, to being dubbed by any such surname.

Master Gottfried had had a scapegrace younger brother named Hugh, who had scorned both books and tools, had been the plague of the workshop, and, instead of coming back from his wandering year of improvement, had joined a band of roving Lanzknechts. No more had been heard of him for a dozen or fifteen years, when he suddenly arrived at the paternal mansion at Ulm, half dead with intermittent fever, and with a young, broken-hearted, and nearly expiring wife, his spoil in his Italian campaigns. His rude affection had utterly failed to console her for her desolated home and slaughtered kindred, and it had so soon turned to brutality that, when brought to comparative peace and rest in his brother's home, there was nothing left for the poor Italian but to lie down and die, commending her babe in broken German to Hausfrau Johanna, and blessing Master Gottfried for his flowing Latin assurances that the child should be to them even as the little maiden who was lying in the God's acre upon the hillside

And verily the little Christina had been a precious gift to the bereaved couple. Her father had no sooner recovered than he returned to his roving life, and, except for a report that he had been seen among the retainers of one of the robber barons of the Swabian Alps, nothing had been heard of him; and Master Gottfried only hoped to be spared the actual pain and scandal of knowing when his eyes were blinded and his head swept off at a blow, or when he was tumbled headlong into a moat, suspended from a tree, or broken on the wheel: a choice of fates that was sure sooner or later to befall him.

The Dove in the Eagle's Nest

Meantime, both the burgomeister and burgomeisterinn did their utmost to forget that the gentle little girl was not their own; they set all their hopes and joys on her, and, making her supply the place at once of son and daughter, they bred her up in all the refinements and accomplishments in which the free citizens of Germany took the lead in the middle and latter part of the fifteenth century. To aid her aunt in all house-wifely arts, to prepare dainty food and varied liquors, and to spin, weave, and broider, was only a part of Christina's training; her uncle likewise set great store by her sweet Italian voice, and caused her to be carefully taught to sing and play on the lute, and he likewise delighted in hearing her read aloud to him from the hereditary store of MSS. and from the dark volumes that began to proceed from the press. Nay, Master Gottfried had made experiments in printing and wood-engraving on his own account, and had found no head so intelligent, no hand so desirous to aid him, as his little Christina's, who, in all that needed taste and skill rather than strength, was worth all his prentices and journeymen together. Some fine bold wood-cuts had been produced by their joint efforts; but these less important occupations had of late been set aside by the engrossing interest of the interior fittings of the great "Dome Kirk," which for nearly a century had been rising by the united exertions of the burghers, without any assistance from without. The foundation had been laid in 1377; and at length, in the year of grace 1472, the crown of the apse had been closed in, and matters were so forward that Master Gottfried's stall work was already in requisition for the choir.

"Three cubits more," he reckoned. "Child, hast thou found me fruits enough for the completing of this border?"

"O yes, mine uncle. I have the wild rosehip, and the flat shield of the moonwort, and a pea-pod, and more whose names I know not. But should they all be seed and fruit?"

"Yea, truly, my Stina, for this wreath shall speak of the goodly fruits of a completed life."

"Even as that which you carved in spring told of the blossom and fair promise of youth," returned the maiden. "Methinks the one is the most beautiful, as it ought to be;" then, after a little pause, and some reckoning, "I have scarce seed-pods enough in store, uncle; might we not seek some rarer shapes in the herb-garden of Master Gerhard, the physician? He, too, might tell me the names of some of these."

"True, child; or we might ride into the country beyond the walls, and seek them. What, little one, wouldst thou not?"

"So we go not far," faltered Christina, colouring.

"Ha, thou hast not forgotten the fright thy companions had from the Schlangenwald reitern when gathering Maydew? Fear not, little coward; if we go beyond the suburbs we will take Hans and Peter with their halberts. But I believe thy silly little heart can scarce be free for enjoyment if it can fancy a Reiter within a dozen leagues of thee."

"At your side I would not fear. That is, I would not vex thee by my folly, and I might forget it," replied Christina, looking down.

"My gentle child!" the old man said approvingly. "Moreover, if our good Raiser has his way, we shall soon be free of the reitern of Schlangenwald, and Adlerstein, and all the rest of the mouse-trap barons. He is hoping to form a league of us free imperial cities with all the more reasonable and honest nobles, to preserve the peace of the country. Even now a letter from him was read in the Town Hall to that effect; and, when all are united against them, my lords- mousers must needs become pledged to the league, or go down before it."

"Ah! that will be well," cried Christina. "Then will our wagons be no longer set upon at the Debateable Ford by Schlangenwald or Adlerstein; and our wares will come safely, and there will be wealth enough to raise our spire! O uncle, what a day of joy will that be when Our Lady's great statue will be set on the summit!"

"A day that I shall scarce see, and it will be well if thou dost," returned her uncle, "unless the hearts of the burghers of Ulm return to the liberality of their fathers, who devised that spire! But what trampling do I hear?"

The Dove in the Eagle's Nest

There was indeed a sudden confusion in the house, and, before the uncle and niece could rise, the door was opened by a prosperous apple-faced dame, exclaiming in a hasty whisper, "Housefather, O Housefather, there are a troop of reitern at the door, dismounting already;" and, as the master came forward, brushing from his furred vest the shavings and dust of his work, she added in a more furtive, startled accent, "and, if I mistake not, one is thy brother!"

"He is welcome," replied Master Gottfried, in his cheery fearless voice; "he brought us a choice gift last time he came; and it may be he is ready to seek peace among us after his wanderings. Come hither, Christina, my little one; it is well to be abashed, but thou art not a child who need fear to meet a father."

Christina's extreme timidity, however, made her pale and crimson by turns, perhaps by the infection of anxiety from her aunt, who could not conceal a certain dissatisfaction and alarm, as the maiden, led on either side by her adopted parents, thus advanced from the little studio into a handsomely-carved wooden gallery, projecting into a great wainscoted room, with a broad carved stair leading down into it. Down this stair the three proceeded, and reached the stone hall that lay beyond it, just as there entered from the trellised porch, that covered the steps into the street, a thin wiry man, in a worn and greasy buff suit, guarded on the breast and arms with rusty steel, and a battered helmet with the vizor up, disclosing a weather-beaten bronzed face, with somewhat wild dark eyes, and a huge grizzled moustache forming a straight line over his lips. Altogether he was a complete model of the lawless Reiter or Lanzknecht, the terror of Swabia, and the bugbear of Christina's imagination. The poor child's heart died within her as she perceived the mutual recognition between her uncle and the new comer; and, while Master Gottfried held out his hands with a cordial greeting of "Welcome, home, brother Hugh," she trembled from head to foot, as she sank on her knees, and murmured, "Your blessing, honoured father."

"Ha? What, this is my girl? What says she? My blessing, eh? There then, thou hast it, child, such as I have to give, though they'll tell thee at Adlerstein that I am more wont to give the other sort of blessing! Now, give me a kiss, girl, and let me see thee! How now!" as he folded her in his rough arms; "thou art a mere feather, as slight as our sick Jungfrau herself." And then, regarding her, as she stood drooping, "Thou art not half the woman thy mother was—she was stately and straight as a column, and tall withal."

"True!" replied Hausfrau Johanna, in a marked tone; "but both she and her poor babe had been so harassed and wasted with long journeys and hardships, that with all our care of our Christina, she has never been strong or well-grown. The marvel is that she lived at all."

"Our Christina is not beautiful, we know," added her uncle, reassuringly taking her hand; "but she is a good and meek maiden."

"Well, well," returned the Lanzknecht, "she will answer the purpose well enough, or better than if she were fair enough to set all our fellows together by the ears for her. Camilla, I say—no, what's her name, Christina?—put up thy gear and be ready to start with me to-morrow morning for Adlerstein."

"For Adlerstein?" re-echoed the housemother, in a tone of horrified dismay; and Christina would have dropped on the floor but for her uncle's sustaining hand, and the cheering glance with which he met her imploring look.

"Let us come up to the gallery, and understand what you desire, brother," said Master Gottfried, gravely. "Fill the cup of greeting, Hans. Your followers shall be entertained in the hall," he added.

"Ay, ay," quoth Hugh, "I will show you reason over a goblet of the old Rosenburg. Is it all gone yet, brother Goetz? No? I reckon there would not be the scouring of a glass left of it in a week if it were at Adlerstein."

So saying, the trooper crossed the lower room, which contained a huge tiled baking oven, various brilliantly-burnished cooking utensils, and a great carved cupboard like a wooden bedstead, and, passing the door of the bathroom, clanked up the oaken stairs to the gallery, the reception-room of the house. It had tapestry hangings to the wall, and cushions both to the carved chairs and deep windows, which looked out into the street, the whole storey projecting into close proximity with the corresponding apartment of the Syndic Moritz, the goldsmith on the opposite side. An oaken table stood in the centre, and the gallery was adorned with a dresser, displaying not only bright pewter, but goblets and drinking cups of beautifully-shaped and coloured glass, and saltcellars, tankards, of gold and silver.

"Just as it was in the old man's time," said the soldier, throwing himself into the housefather's chair. "A handful of Lanzknechts would make short work with your pots and pans, good sister Johanna."

"Heaven forbid!" said poor Johanna under her breath. "Much good they do you, up in a row there, making you a slave to furbishing them. There's more sense in a chair like this—that does rest a man's bones. Here, Camilla, girl, unlace my helmet! What, know'st not how? What is a woman made for but to let a soldier free of his trappings? Thou hast done it! There! Now my boots," stretching out his legs.

"Hans shall draw off your boots, fair brother," began the dame; but poor Christina, the more anxious to propitiate him in little things, because of the horror and dread with which his main purpose inspired her, was already on her knees, pulling with her small quivering hands at the long steel-guarded boot—a task to which she would have been utterly inadequate, but for some lazy assistance from her father's other foot. She further brought a pair of her uncle's furred slippers, while Reiter Hugh proceeded to dangle one of the boots in the air, expatiating on its frail condition, and expressing his intention of getting a new pair from Master Matthias, the sutor, ere he should leave Ulm on the morrow. Then, again, came the dreaded subject; his daughter must go with him.

"What would you with Christina, brother?" gravely asked Master Gottfried, seating himself on the opposite side of the stove, while out of sight the frightened girl herself knelt on the floor, her head on her aunt's knees, trying to derive comfort from Dame Johanna's clasping hands, and vehement murmurs that they would not let their child be taken from them. Alas! these assurances were little in accordance with Hugh's rough reply, "And what is it to you what I do with mine own?"

"Only this, that, having bred her up as my child and intended heiress, I might have some voice."

"Oh! in choosing her mate! Some mincing artificer, I trow, fiddling away with wood and wire to make gauds for the fair-day! Hast got him here? If I like him, and she likes him, I'll bring her back when her work is done."

"There is no such person as yet in the case," said Gottfried. "Christina is not yet seventeen, and I would take my time to find an honest, pious burgher, who will value this precious jewel of mine."

"And let her polish his flagons to the end of her days," laughed Hugh grimly, but manifestly somewhat influenced by the notion of his brother's wealth. "What, hast no child of thine own?" he added.

"None, save in Paradise," answered Gottfried, crossing himself. "And thus, if Christina should remain with me, and be such as I would have her, then, brother, my wealth, after myself and my good housewife, shall be hers, with due provision for thee, if thou shouldst weary of thy wild life. Otherwise," he added, looking down, and speaking in an under tone, "my poor savings should go to the completion of the Dome Kirk."

"And who told thee, Goetz, that I would do ought with the girl that should hinder her from being the very same fat, sourkrout-cooking, pewter-scrubbing housewife of thy mind's eye?"

"I have heard nothing of thy designs as yet, brother Hugh, save that thou wouldst take her to Adlerstein, which men greatly belie if it be not a nest of robbers."

"Aha! thou hast heard of Adlerstein! We have made the backs of your jolly merchants tingle as well as they could through their well-lined doublets! Ulm knows of Adlerstein, and the Debateable Ford!"

The Dove in the Eagle's Nest

"It knows little to its credit," said Gottfried, gravely; "and it knows also that the Emperor is about to make a combination against all the Swabian robber-holds, and that such as join not in it will fare the worse."

"Let Kaiser Fritz catch his bear ere he sells its hide! He has never tried to mount the Eagle's Ladder! Why, man, Adlerstein might be held against five hundred men by sister Johanna with her rock and spindle! 'Tis a free barony, Master Gottfried, I tell thee—has never sworn allegiance to Kaiser or Duke of Swabia either! Freiherr Eberhard is as much a king on his own rock as Kaiser Fritz ever was of the Romans, and more too, for I never could find out that they thought much of our king at Rome; and, as to gainsaying our old Freiherr, one might as well leap over the abyss at once."

"Yes, those old free barons are pitiless tyrants," said Gottfried, "and I scarce think I can understand thee aright when I hear thee say thou wouldst carry thy daughter to such an abode."

"It is the Freiherr's command," returned Hugh. "Look you, they have had wondrous ill-luck with their children; the Freiherrinn Kunigunde has had a dozen at least, and only two are alive, my young Freiherr and my young Lady Ermentrude; and no wonder, you would say, if you could see the gracious Freiherrinn, for surely Dame Holda made a blunder when she fished her out of the fountain woman instead of man. She is Adlerstein herself by birth, married her cousin, and is prouder and more dour than our old Freiherr himself—fitter far to handle shield than swaddled babe. And now our Jungfrau has fallen into a pining waste, that 'tis a pity to see how her cheeks have fallen away, and how she mopes and fades. Now, the old Freiherr and her brother, they both dote on her, and would do anything for her. They thought she was bewitched, so we took old Mother Ilsebill and tried her with the ordeal of water; but, look you, she sank as innocent as a puppy dog, and Ursel was at fault to fix on any one else. Then one day, when I looked into the chamber, I saw the poor maiden sitting, with her head hanging down, as if 'twas too heavy for her, on a high-backed chair, no rest for her feet, and the wind blowing keen all round her, and nothing to taste but scorched beef, or black bread and sour wine, and her mother rating her for foolish fancies that gave trouble. And, when my young Freiherr was bemoaning himself that we could not hear of a Jew physician passing our way to catch and bring up to cure her, I said to him at last that no doctor could do for her what gentle tendance and nursing would, for what the poor maiden needed was to be cosseted and laid down softly, and fed with broths and possets, and all that women know how to do with one another. A proper scowl and hard words I got from my gracious Lady, for wanting to put burgher softness into an Adlerstein; but my old lord and his son opened on the scent at once. 'Thou hast a daughter?' quoth the Freiherr. 'So please your gracious lordship,' quoth I; 'that is, if she still lives, for I left her a puny infant.' 'Well,' said my lord, 'if thou wilt bring her here, and her care restores my daughter to health and strength, then will I make thee my body squire, with a right to a fourth part of all the spoil, and feed for two horses in my stable.' And young Freiherr Eberhard gave his word upon it."

Gottfried suggested that a sick nurse was the person required rather than a child like Christina; but, as Hugh truly observed, no nurse would voluntarily go to Adlerstein, and it was no use to wait for the hopes of capturing one by raid or foray. His daughter was at his own disposal, and her services would be repaid by personal advantages to himself which he was not disposed to forego; in effect these were the only means that the baron had of requiting any attendance upon his daughter.

The citizens of old Germany had the strongest and most stringent ideas of parental authority, and regarded daughters as absolute chattels of their father; and Master Gottfried Sorel, though he alone had done the part of a parent to his niece, felt entirely unable to withstand the nearer claim, except by representations; and these fell utterly disregarded, as in truth every counsel had hitherto done, upon the ears of Reiter Hugh, ever since he had emerged from his swaddling clothes. The plentiful supper, full cup of wine, the confections, the soft chair, together perhaps with his brother's grave speech, soon, however, had the effect of sending him into a doze, whence he started to accept civilly the proposal of being installed in the stranger's room, where he was speedily snoring between two feather beds.

Then there could be freedom of speech in the gallery, where the uncle and aunt held anxious counsel over the poor little dark-tressed head that still lay upon good Johanna's knees. The dame was indignant and resolute: "Take the child back with him into a very nest of robbers!—her own innocent dove whom they had shielded from all evil like a very nun in a cloister! She should as soon think of yielding her up to be borne off by the great Satan himself with his horns and hoofs."

The Dove in the Eagle's Nest

"Hugh is her father, housewife," said the master-carver.

"The right of parents is with those that have done the duty of parents," returned Johanna. "What said the kid in the fable to the goat that claimed her from the sheep that bred her up? I am ashamed of you, housefather, for not better loving your own niece."

"Heaven knows how I love her," said Gottfried, as the sweet face was raised up to him with a look acquitting him of the charge, and he bent to smooth back the silken hair, and kiss the ivory brow; "but Heaven also knows that I see no means of withholding her from one whose claim is closer than my own—none save one; and to that even thou, housemother, wouldst not have me resort."

"What is it?" asked the dame, sharply, yet with some fear.

"To denounce him to the burgomasters as one of the Adlerstein retainers who robbed Philipp der Schmidt, and have him fast laid by the heels."

Christina shuddered, and Dame Johanna herself recoiled; but presently exclaimed, "Nay, you could not do that, good man, but wherefore not threaten him therewith? Stand at his bedside in early dawn, and tell him that, if he be not off ere daylight with both his cut-throats, the halberdiers will be upon him."

"Threaten what I neither could nor would perform, mother? That were a shrewish resource."

"Yet would it save the child," muttered Johanna. But, in the meantime, Christina was rising from the floor, and stood before them with loose hair, tearful eyes, and wet, flushed cheeks. "It must be thus," she said, in a low, but not unsteady voice. "I can bear it better since I have heard of the poor young lady, sick and with none to care for her. I will go with my father; it is my duty. I will do my best; but oh! uncle, so work with him that he may bring me back again."

"This from thee, Stina!" exclaimed her aunt; "from thee who art sick for fear of a lanzknecht!"

"The saints will be with me, and you will pray for me," said Christina, still trembling.

"I tell thee, child, thou knowst not what these vile dens are. Heaven forfend thou shouldst!" exclaimed her aunt. "Go only to Father Balthazar, housefather, and see if he doth not call it a sending of a lamb among wolves."

"Mind'st thou the carving I did for Father Balthazar's own oratory?" replied Master Gottfried.

"I talk not of carving! I talk of our child!" said the dame, petulantly.

"Ut agnus inter lupos," softly said Gottfried, looking tenderly, though sadly, at his niece, who not only understood the quotation, but well remembered the carving of the cross-marked lamb going forth from its fold among the howling wolves.

"Alas! I am not an apostle," said she.

"Nay, but, in the path of duty, 'tis the same hand that sends thee forth," answered her uncle, "and the same will guard thee."

"Duty, indeed!" exclaimed Johanna. "As if any duty could lead that silly helpless child among that herd of evil men, and women yet worse, with a good-for-nothing father, who would sell her for a good horse to the first dissolute Junker who fell in his way."

The Dove in the Eagle's Nest

"I will take care that he knows it is worth his while to restore her safe to us. Nor do I think so ill of Hugh as thou dost, mother. And, for the rest, Heaven and the saints and her own discretion must be her guard till she shall return to us."

"How can Heaven be expected to protect her when you are flying in its face by not taking counsel with Father Balthazar?"

"That shalt thou do," replied Gottfried, readily, secure that Father Balthazar would see the matter in the same light as himself, and tranquillize the good woman. It was not yet so late but that a servant could be despatched with a request that Father Balthazar, who lived not many houses off in the same street, would favour the Burgomeisterinn Sorel by coming to speak with her. In a few minutes he appeared,—an aged man, with a sensible face, of the fresh pure bloom preserved by a temperate life. He was a secular parish–priest, and, as well as his friend Master Gottfried, held greatly by the views left by the famous Strasburg preacher, Master John Tauler. After the good housemother had, in strong terms, laid the case before him, she expected a trenchant decision on her own side, but, to her surprise and disappointment, he declared that Master Gottfried was right, and that, unless Hugh Sorel demanded anything absolutely sinful of his daughter, it was needful that she should submit. He repeated, in stronger terms, the assurance that she would be protected in the endeavour to do right, and the Divine promises which he quoted from the Latin Scriptures gave some comfort to the niece, who understood them, while they impressed the aunt, who did not. There was always the hope that, whether the young lady died or recovered, the conclusion of her illness would be the term of Christina's stay at Adlerstein, and with this trust Johanna must content herself. The priest took leave, after appointing with Christina to meet her in the confessional early in the morning before mass; and half the night was spent by the aunt and niece in preparing Christina's wardrobe for her sudden journey.

Many a tear was shed over the tokens of the little services she was wont to render, her half–done works, and pleasant studies so suddenly broken off, and all the time Hausfrau Johanna was running on with a lecture on the diligent preservation of her maiden discretion, with plentiful warnings against swaggering men–at–arms, drunken lanzknechts, and, above all, against young barons, who most assuredly could mean no good by any burgher maiden. The good aunt blessed the saints that her Stina was likely only to be lovely in affectionate home eyes; but, for that matter, idle men, shut up in a castle, with nothing but mischief to think of, would be dangerous to Little Three Eyes herself, and Christina had best never stir a yard from her lady's chair, when forced to meet them. All this was interspersed with motherly advice how to treat the sick lady, and receipts for cordials and possets; for Johanna began to regard the case as a sort of second–hand one of her own. Nay, she even turned it over in her mind whether she should not offer herself as the Lady Ermentrude's sick–nurse, as being a less dangerous commodity than her little niece: but fears for the well–being of the master–carver, and his Wirthschaft, and still more the notion of gossip Gertrude Grundt hearing that she had ridden off with a wild lanzknecht, made her at once reject the plan, without even mentioning it to her husband or his niece.

By the time Hugh Sorel rolled out from between his feather beds, and was about to don his greasy buff, a handsome new suit, finished point device, and a pair of huge boots to correspond, had been laid by his bedside.

"Ho, ho! Master Goetz," said he, as he stumbled into the Stube, "I see thy game. Thou wouldst make it worth my while to visit the father–house at Ulm?"

"It shall be worth thy while, indeed, if thou bringest me back my white dove," was Gottfried's answer.

"And how if I bring her back with a strapping reiter son–in–law?" laughed Hugh. "What welcome should the fellow receive?"

"That would depend on what he might be," replied Gottfried; and Hugh, his love of tormenting a little allayed by satisfaction in his buff suit, and by an eye to a heavy purse that lay by his brother's hand on the table, added, "Little fear of that. Our fellows would look for lustier brides than yon little pale face. 'Tis whiter than ever this morning,—but no tears. That is my brave girl."

"Yes, father, I am ready to do your bidding," replied Christina, meekly.

The Dove in the Eagle's Nest

"That is well, child. Mark me, no tears. Thy mother wept day and night, and, when she had wept out her tears, she was sullen, when I would have been friendly towards her. It was the worse for her. But, so long as thou art good daughter to me, thou shalt find me good father to thee;" and for a moment there was a kindliness in his eye which made it sufficiently like that of his brother to give some consolation to the shrinking heart that he was rending from all it loved; and she steadied her voice for another gentle profession of obedience, for which she felt strengthened by the morning's orisons.

"Well said, child. Now canst sit on old Nibelung's croup? His back- bone is somewhat sharper than if he had battened in a citizen's stall; but, if thine aunt can find thee some sort of pillion, I'll promise thee the best ride thou hast had since we came from Innspruck, ere thou canst remember."

"Christina has her own mule," replied her uncle, "without troubling Nibelung to carry double."

"Ho! her own! An overfed burgomaster sort of a beast, that will turn restive at the first sight of the Eagle's Ladder! However, he may carry her so far, and, if we cannot get him up the mountain, I shall know what to do with him," he muttered to himself.

But Hugh, like many a gentleman after him, was recusant at the sight of his daughter's luggage; and yet it only loaded one sumpter mule, besides forming a few bundles which could be easily bestowed upon the saddles of his two knappen, while her lute hung by a silken string on her arm. Both she and her aunt thought she had been extremely moderate; but his cry was, What could she want with so much? Her mother had never been allowed more than would go into a pair of saddle-bags; and his own Jungfrau—she had never seen so much gear together in her life; he would be laughed to scorn for his presumption in bringing such a fine lady into the castle; it would be well if Freiherr Eberhard's bride brought half as much.

Still he had a certain pride in it—he was, after all, by birth and breeding a burgher—and there had been evidently a softening and civilizing influence in the night spent beneath his paternal roof, and old habits, and perhaps likewise in the submission he had met with from his daughter. The attendants, too, who had been pleased with their quarters, readily undertook to carry their share of the burthen, and, though he growled and muttered a little, he at length was won over to consent, chiefly, as it seemed, by Christina's obliging readiness to leave behind the bundle that contained her holiday kirtle.

He had been spared all needless irritation. Before his waking, Christina had been at the priest's cell, and had received his last blessings and counsels, and she had, on the way back, exchanged her farewells and tears with her two dearest friends, Barbara Schmidt, and Regina Grundt, confiding to the former her cage of doves, and to the latter the myrtle, which, like every German maiden, she cherished in her window, to supply her future bridal wreath. Now pale as death, but so resolutely composed as to be almost disappointing to her demonstrative aunt, she quietly went through her home partings; while Hausfrau Johanna adjured her father by all that was sacred to be a true guardian and protector of the child, and he could not forbear from a few tormenting auguries about the lanzknecht son-in- law. Their effect was to make the good dame more passionate in her embraces and admonitions to Christina to take care of herself. She would have a mass said every day that Heaven might have a care of her!

Master Gottfried was going to ride as far as the confines of the free city's territory, and his round, sleek, cream-coloured palfrey, used to ambling in civic processions, was as great a contrast to raw- boned, wild-eyed Nibelung, all dappled with misty grey, as was the stately, substantial burgher to his lean, hungry-looking brother, or Dame Johanna's dignified, curled, white poodle, which was forcibly withheld from following Christina, to the coarse-bristled, wolfish- looking hound who glared at the household pet with angry and contemptuous eyes, and made poor Christina's heart throb with terror whenever it bounded near her.

Close to her uncle she kept, as beneath the trellised porches that came down from the projecting gables of the burghers' houses many a well-known face gazed and nodded, as they took their way through the crooked streets, many a beggar or poor widow waved her a blessing. Out into the market-place, with its clear fountain adorned with arches and statues, past

The Dove in the Eagle's Nest

the rising Dome Kirk, where the swarms of workmen unbonneted to the master-carver, and the reiter paused with an irreverent sneer at the small progress made since he could first remember the building. How poor little Christina's soul clung to every cusp of the lacework spire, every arch of the window, each of which she had hailed as an achievement! The tears had well-nigh blinded her in a gush of feeling that came on her unawares, and her mule had his own way as he carried her under the arch of the tall and beautifully-sculptured bridge tower, and over the noble bridge across the Danube.

Her uncle spoke much, low and earnestly, to his brother. She knew it was in commendation of her to his care, and an endeavour to impress him with a sense of the kind of protection she would require, and she kept out of earshot. It was enough for her to see her uncle still, and feel that his tenderness was with her, and around her. But at last he drew his rein. "And now, my little one, the daughter of my heart, I must bid thee farewell," he said.

Christina could not be restrained from springing from her mule, and kneeling on the grass to receive his blessing, her face hidden in her hands, that her father might not see her tears.

"The good God bless thee, my child," said Gottfried, who seldom invoked the saints; "bless thee, and bring thee back in His own good time. Thou hast been a good child to us; be so to thine own father. Do thy work, and come back to us again."

The tears rained down his cheeks, as Christina's head lay on his bosom, and then with a last kiss he lifted her again on her mule, mounted his horse, and turned back to the city, with his servant.

Hugh was merciful enough to let his daughter gaze long after the retreating figure ere he summoned her on. All day they rode, at first through meadow lands and then through more broken, open ground, where at mid-day they halted, and dined upon the plentiful fare with which the housemother had provided them, over which Hugh smacked his lips, and owned that they did live well in the old town! Could Christina make such sausages?

"Not as well as my aunt."

"Well, do thy best, and thou wilt win favour with the baron."

The evening began to advance, and Christina was very weary, as the purple mountains that she had long watched with a mixture of fear and hope began to look more distinct, and the ground was often in abrupt ascents. Her father, without giving space for complaints, hurried her on. He must reach the Debateable Ford ere dark. It was, however, twilight when they came to an open space, where, at the foot of thickly forest-clad rising ground, lay an expanse of turf and rich grass, through which a stream made its way, standing in a wide tranquil pool as if to rest after its rough course from the mountains. Above rose, like a dark wall, crag upon crag, peak on peak, in purple masses, blending with the sky; and Hugh, pointing upwards to a turreted point, apparently close above their heads, where a star of light was burning, told her that there was Adlerstein, and this was the Debateable Ford.

In fact, as he explained, while splashing through the shallow expanse, the stream had changed its course. It was the boundary between the lands of Schlangenwald and Adlerstein, but it had within the last sixty years burst forth in a flood, and had then declined to return to its own bed, but had flowed in a fresh channel to the right of the former one. The Freiherren von Adlerstein claimed the ground to the old channel, the Graffen von Schlangenwald held that the river was the landmark; and the dispute had a greater importance than seemed explained from the worth of the rushy space of ground in question, for this was the passage of the Italian merchants on their way from Constance, and every load that was overthrown in the river was regarded as the lawful prey of the noble on whose banks the catastrophe befell.

Any freight of goods was anxiously watched by both nobles, and it was not their fault if no disaster befell the travellers. Hugh talked of the Schlangenwald marauders with the bitterness of a deadly feud, but manifestly did not breathe freely till his whole convoy were safe across both the wet and the dry channel.

The Dove in the Eagle's Nest

Christina supposed they should now ascend to the castle; but her father laughed, saying that the castle was not such a step off as she fancied, and that they must have daylight for the Eagle's Stairs. He led the way through the trees, up ground that she thought mountain already, and finally arrived at a miserable little hut, which served the purpose of an inn.

He was received there with much obsequiousness, and was plainly a great authority there. Christina, weary and frightened, descended from her mule, and was put under the protection of a wild, rough— looking peasant woman, who stared at her like something from another world, but at length showed her a nook behind a mud partition, where she could spread her mantle, and at least lie down, and tell her beads unseen, if she could not sleep in the stifling, smoky atmosphere, amid the sounds of carousal among her father and his fellows.

The great hound came up and smelt to her. His outline was so— wolfish, that she had nearly screamed: but, more in terror at the men who might have helped her than even at the beast, she tried to smooth him with her trembling hand, whispered his name of "Festhold," and found him licking her hand, and wagging his long rough tail. And he finally lay down at her feet, as though to protect her.

"Is it a sign that good angels will not let me be hurt?" she thought, and, wearied out, she slept.

CHAPTER II: THE EYRIE

Christina Sorel awoke to a scene most unlike that which had been wont to meet her eyes in her own little wainscoted chamber high in the gabled front of her uncle's house. It was a time when the imperial free towns of Germany had advanced nearly as far as those of Italy in civilization, and had reached a point whence they retrograded grievously during the Thirty Years' War, even to an extent that they have never entirely recovered. The country immediately around them shared the benefits of their civilization, and the free peasant— proprietors lived in great ease and prosperity, in beautiful and picturesque farmsteads, enjoying a careless abundance, and keeping numerous rural or religious feasts, where old Teutonic mythological observances had received a Christian colouring and adaptation.

In the mountains, or around the castles, it was usually very different. The elective constitution of the empire, the frequent change of dynasty, the many disputed successions, had combined to render the sovereign authority uncertain and feeble, and it was seldom really felt save in the hereditary dominions of the Kaiser for the time being. Thus, while the cities advanced in the power of self—government, and the education it conveyed, the nobles, especially those whose abodes were not easily accessible, were often practically under no government at all, and felt themselves accountable to no man. The old wild freedom of the Suevi, and other Teutonic tribes, still technically, and in many cases practically, existed. The Heretogen, Heerzogen, or, as we call them, Dukes, had indeed accepted employment from the Kaiser as his generals, and had received rewards from him; the Gerefen, or Graffen, of all kinds were his judges, the titles of both being proofs of their holding commissions from, and being thus dependent on, the court. But the Freiherren, a word very inadequately represented by our French term of baron, were absolutely free, "never in bondage to any man," holding their own, and owing no duty, no office; poorer, because unendowed by the royal authority, but holding themselves infinitely higher, than the pensioners of the court. Left behind, however, by their neighbours, who did their part by society, and advanced with it, the Freiherren had been for the most part obliged to give up their independence and fall into the system, but so far in the rear, that they ranked, like the barons of France and England, as the last order of nobility.

Still, however, in the wilder and more mountainous parts of the country, some of the old families of unreduced, truly free Freiherren lingered, their hand against every man, every man's hand against them, and ever becoming more savage, both positively and still more proportionately, as their isolation and the general progress around them became greater. The House of Austria, by gradually absorbing hereditary states into its own possessions, was, however, in the fifteenth century, acquiring a preponderance that rendered its possession of the imperial throne almost a matter of inheritance, and moreover rendered the supreme power far more effective than it had ever previously been. Freidrich III. a man still in full vigour, and with an able and enterprising son already elected to the succession, was making his rule felt, and it was fast becoming apparent that the days of the independent baronies were numbered, and that the only choice that would soon be left them would be between making terms and being forcibly reduced. Von Adlerstein was one of the oldest of these free families. If the lords of the Eagle's Stone had ever followed the great Konrads and Freidrichs of Swabia in their imperial days, their descendants had taken care to forget the weakness, and believed themselves absolutely free from all allegiance.

And the wildness of their territory was what might be expected from their hostility to all outward influences. The hostel, if it deserved the name, was little more than a charcoal-burner's hut, hidden in the woods at the foot of the mountain, serving as a halting-place for the Freiherren's retainers ere they attempted the ascent. The inhabitants were allowed to ply their trade of charring wood in the forest on condition of supplying the castle with charcoal, and of affording a lodging to the followers on occasions like the present.

Grimy, half-clad, and brawny, with the whites of his eyes gleaming out of his black face, Jobst the Kohler startled Christina terribly when she came into the outer room, and met him returning from his night's work, with his long stoking-pole in his hand. Her father shouted with laughter at her alarm.

"Thou thinkest thyself in the land of the kobolds and dwarfs, my girl! Never mind, thou wilt see worse than honest Jobst before thou hast done. Now, eat a morsel and be ready—mountain air will make thee hungry ere thou art at the castle. And, hark thee, Jobst, thou must give stable-room to yon sumpter-mule for the present, and let some of my daughter's gear lie in the shed."

"O father!" exclaimed Christina, in dismay.

"We'll bring it up, child, by piecemeal," he said in a low voice, "as we can; but if such a freight came to the castle at once, my lady would have her claws on it, and little more wouldst thou ever see thereof. Moreover, I shall have enough to do to look after thee up the ascent, without another of these city-bred beasts."

"I hope the poor mule will be well cared for. I can pay for—" began Christina; but her father squeezed her arm, and drowned her soft voice in his loud tones.

"Jobst will take care of the beast, as belonging to me. Woe betide him, if I find it the worse!"—and his added imprecations seemed unnecessary, so earnest were the asseverations of both the man and his wife that the animal should be well cared for.

"Look you, Christina," said Hugh Sorel, as soon as he had placed her on her mule, and led her out of hearing, "if thou hast any gold about thee, let it be the last thing thou ownest to any living creature up there." Then, as she was about to speak—"Do not even tell me. I WILL not know." The caution did not add much to Christina's comfort; but she presently asked, "Where is thy steed, father?"

"I sent him up to the castle with the Schneiderlein and Yellow Lorentz," answered the father. "I shall have ado enough on foot with thee before we are up the Ladder."

The father and daughter were meantime proceeding along a dark path through oak and birch woods, constantly ascending, until the oak grew stunted and disappeared, and the opening glades showed steep, stony, torrent-furrowed ramparts of hillside above them, looking to Christina's eyes as if she were set to climb up the cathedral side like a snail or a fly. She quite gasped for breath at the very sight, and was told in return to wait and see what she would yet say to the Adlerstreppe, or Eagle's Ladder. Poor child! she had no raptures for romantic scenery; she knew that jagged peaks made very pretty backgrounds in illuminations, but she had much rather have been in the smooth meadows of the environs of Ulm. The Danube looked much more agreeable to her, silver-winding between its green banks, than did the same waters leaping down with noisy voices in their stony, worn beds to feed the river that she only knew in his grave breadth and majesty. Yet, alarmed as she was, there was something in the exhilaration and elasticity of the mountain air that gave her an entirely new sensation of enjoyment and life, and seemed to brace her limbs and spirits for whatever might be before her; and, willing to show herself ready to be gratified, she observed on the freshness and sweetness of the air.

The Dove in the Eagle's Nest

"Thou find'st it out, child? Ay, 'tis worth all the feather-beds and pouncet-boxes in Ulm; is it not? That accursed Italian fever never left me till I came up here. A man can scarce draw breath in your foggy meadows below there. Now then, here is the view open. What think you of the Eagle's Nest?"

For, having passed beyond the region of wood they had come forth upon the mountain-side. A not immoderately steep slope of boggy, mossy- looking ground covered with bilberries, cranberries, and with bare rocks here and there rising, went away above out of her ken; but the path she was upon turned round the shoulder of the mountain, and to the left, on a ledge of rock cut off apparently on their side by a deep ravine, and with a sheer precipice above and below it, stood a red stone pile, with one turret far above the rest.

"And this is Schloss Adlerstein?" she exclaimed.

"That is Schloss Adlerstein; and there shalt thou be in two hours' time, unless the devil be more than usually busy, or thou mak'st a fool of thyself. If so, not Satan himself could save thee."

It was well that Christina had resolution to prevent her making a fool of herself on the spot, for the thought of the pathway turned her so dizzy that she could only shut her eyes, trusting that her father did not see her terror. Soon the turn round to the side of the mountain was made, and the road became a mere track worn out on the turf on the hillside, with an abyss beneath, close to the edge of which the mule, of course, walked.

When she ventured to look again, she perceived that the ravine was like an enormous crack open on the mountain-side, and that the stream that formed the Debateable Ford flowed down the bottom of it. The ravine itself went probably all the way up the mountain, growing shallower as it ascended higher; but here, where Christina beheld it, it was extremely deep, and savagely desolate and bare. She now saw that the Eagle's Ladder was a succession of bare gigantic terraces of rock, of which the opposite side of the ravine was composed, and on one of which stood the castle. It was no small mystery to her how it had ever been built, or how she was ever to get there. She saw in the opening of the ravine the green meadows and woods far below; and, when her father pointed out to her the Debateable Ford, apparently much nearer to the castle than they themselves were at present, she asked why they had so far overpassed the castle, and come by this circuitous course.

"Because," said Hugh, "we are not eagles outright. Seest thou not, just beyond the castle court, this whole crag of ours breaks off short, falls like the town wall straight down into the plain? Even this cleft that we are crossing by, the only road a horse can pass, breaks off short and sudden too, so that the river is obliged to take leaps which nought else but a chamois could compass. A footpath there is, and Freiherr Eberhard takes it at all times, being born to it; but even I am too stiff for the like. Ha! ha! Thy uncle may talk of the Kaiser and his League, but he would change his note if we had him here."

"Yet castles have been taken by hunger," said Christina.

"What, knowest thou so much?—True! But look you," pointing to a white foamy thread that descended the opposite steeps, "yonder beck dashes through the castle court, and it never dries; and see you the ledge the castle stands on? It winds on out of your sight, and forms a path which leads to the village of Adlerstein, out on the other slope of the mountains; and ill were it for the serfs if they victualled not the castle well."

The fearful steepness of the ground absorbed all Christina's attention. The road, or rather stairs, came down to the stream at the bottom of the fissure, and then went again on the other side up still more tremendous steeps, which Hugh climbed with a staff, sometimes with his hand on the bridle, but more often only keeping a watchful eye on the sure-footed mule, and an arm to steady his daughter in the saddle when she grew absolutely faint with giddiness at the abyss around her. She was too much in awe of him to utter cry or complaint, and, when he saw her effort to subdue her mortal terror, he was far from unkind, and let her feel his protecting strength.

Presently a voice was heard above—"What, Sorel, hast brought her! Trudchen is wearying for her."

The Dove in the Eagle's Nest

The words were in the most boorish dialect and pronunciation, the stranger to Christina's ears, because intercourse with foreign merchants, and a growing affectation of Latinism, had much refined the city language to which she was accustomed; and she was surprised to perceive by her father's gesture and address that the speaker must be one of the lords of the castle. She looked up, and saw on the pathway above her a tall, large-framed young man, his skin dyed red with sun and wind, in odd contrast with his pale shaggy hair, moustache, and beard, as though the weather had tanned the one and bleached the other. His dress was a still shabbier buff suit than her father had worn, but with a richly-embroidered belt sustaining a hunting-horn with finely-chased ornaments of tarnished silver, and an eagle's plume was fastened into his cap with a large gold Italian coin. He stared hard at the maiden, but vouchsafed her no token of greeting—only distressed her considerably by distracting her father's attention from her mule by his questions about the journey, all in the same rude, coarse tone and phraseology. Some amount of illusion was dispelled. Christina was quite prepared to find the mountain lords dangerous ruffians, but she had expected the graces of courtesy and high birth; but, though there was certainly an air of command and freedom of bearing about the present specimen, his manners and speech were more uncouth than those of any newly-caught apprentice of her uncle, and she could not help thinking that her good aunt Johanna need not have troubled herself about the danger of her taking a liking to any such young Freiherr as she here beheld.

By this time a last effort of the mule had climbed to the level of the castle. As her father had shown her, there was precipice on two sides of the building; on the third, a sheer wall of rock going up to a huge height before it reached another of the Eagle's Steps; and on the fourth, where the gateway was, the little beck had been made to flow in a deep channel that had been hollowed out to serve as a moat, before it bounded down to swell the larger water-course in the ravine. A temporary bridge had been laid across; the drawbridge was out of order, and part of Hugh's business had been to procure materials for mending its apparatus. Christina was told to dismount and cross on foot. The unrailed board, so close to the abyss, and with the wild water foaming above and below, was dreadful to her; and, though she durst not speak, she hung back with an involuntary shudder, as her father, occupied with the mule, did not think of giving her a hand. The young baron burst out into an unrestrained laugh—a still greater shock to her feelings; but at the same time he roughly took her hand, and almost dragged her across, saying, "City bred—ho, ho!" "Thanks, sir," she strove to say, but she was very near weeping with the terror and strangeness of all around.

The low-browed gateway, barely high enough to admit a man on horseback, opened before her, almost to her feelings like the gate of the grave, and she could not help crossing herself, with a silent prayer for protection, as she stepped under it, and came into the castle court—not such a court as gave its name to fair courtesy, but, if truth must be told, far more resembling an ill-kept, ill-savoured stable-yard, with the piggeries opening into it. In unpleasantly close quarters, the Schneiderlein, or little tailor, i.e. the biggest and fiercest of all the knappen, was grooming Nibelung; three long-backed, long-legged, frightful swine were grubbing in a heap of refuse; four or five gaunt ferocious-looking dogs came bounding up to greet their comrade Festhold; and a great old long-bearded goat stood on the top of the mixen, looking much disposed to butt at any newcomer. The Sorel family had brought cleanliness from Flanders, and Hausfrau Johanna was scrupulously dainty in all her appointments. Christina scarcely knew how she conveyed herself and her blue kirtle across the bemired stones to the next and still darker portal, under which a wide but rough ill-hewn stair ascended. The stables, in fact, occupied the lower floor of the main building, and not till these stairs had ascended above them did they lead out into the castle hall. Here were voices—voices rude and harsh, like those Christina had shrunk from in passing drinking booths. There was a long table, with rough men-at-arms lounging about, and staring rudely at her; and at the upper end, by a great open chimney, sat, half-dozing, an elderly man, more rugged in feature than his son; and yet, when he roused himself and spoke to Hugh, there was a shade more of breeding, and less of clownishness in his voice and deportment, as if he had been less entirely devoid of training. A tall darkly-robed woman stood beside him—it was her harsh tone of reproof and command that had so startled Christina as she entered—and her huge towering cap made her look gigantic in the dim light of the smoky hall. Her features had been handsome, but had become hardened into a grim wooden aspect; and with sinking spirits Christina paused at the step of the dais, and made her reverence, wishing she could sink beneath the stones of the pavement out of sight of these terrible personages.

"So that's the wench you have taken all this trouble for," was Freiherrinn Kunigunde's greeting. "She looks like another sick baby to nurse; but I'll have no trouble about her;—that is all. Take her up to Ermentrude; and thou, girl, have a care thou dost her will, and puttest none of thy city fancies into her head."

"And hark thee, girl," added the old Freiherr, sitting up. "So thou canst nurse her well, thou shalt have a new gown and a stout husband."

"That way," pointed the lady towards one of the four corner towers; and Christina moved doubtfully towards it, reluctant to quit her father, her only protector, and afraid to introduce herself. The younger Freiherr, however, stepped before her, went striding two or three steps at a time up the turret stair, and, before Christina had wound her way up, she heard a thin, impatient voice say, "Thou saidst she was come, Ebbo."

"Yes, even so," she heard Freiherr Eberhard return; "but she is slow and town-bred. She was afraid of crossing the moat." And then both laughed, so that Christina's cheeks tingled as she emerged from the turret into another vaulted room. "Here she is," quoth the brother; "now will she make thee quite well."

It was a very bare and desolate room, with no hangings to the rough stone walls, and scarcely any furniture, except a great carved bedstead, one wooden chair, a table, and some stools. On the bare floor, in front of the fire, her arm under her head, and a profusion of long hair falling round her like flax from a distaff, lay wearily a little figure, beside whom Sir Eberhard was kneeling on one knee.

"Here is my sisterling," said he, looking up to the newcomer. "They say you burgher women have ways of healing the sick. Look at her. Think you you can heal her?"

In an excess of dumb shyness Ermentrude half rose, and effectually hindered any observations on her looks by hiding her face away upon her brother's knee. It was the gesture of a child of five years old, but Ermentrude's length of limb forbade Christina to suppose her less than fourteen or fifteen. "What, wilt not look at her?" he said, trying to raise her head; and then, holding out one of her wasted, feverish hands to Christina, he again asked, with a wistfulness that had a strange effect from the large, tall man, almost ten years her elder, "Canst thou cure her, maiden?"

"I am no doctor, sir," replied Christina; "but I could, at least, make her more comfortable. The stone is too hard for her."

"I will not go away; I want the fire," murmured the sick girl, holding out her hands towards it, and shivering.

Christina quickly took off her own thick cloth mantle, well lined with dressed lambskins, laid it on the floor, rolled the collar of it over a small log of wood—the only substitute she could see for a pillow—and showed an inviting couch in an instant. Ermentrude let her brother lay her down, and then was covered with the ample fold. She smiled as she turned up her thin, wasted face, faded into the same whitey-brown tint as her hair. "That is good," she said, but without thanks; and, feeling the soft lambswool: "Is that what you burgher-women wear? Father is to give me a furred mantle, if only some court dame would pass the Debateable Ford. But the Schlangenwaldern got the last before ever we could get down. Jobst was so stupid. He did not give us warning in time; but he is to be hanged next time if he does not."

Christina's blood curdled as she heard this speech in a weak little complaining tone, that otherwise put her sadly in mind of Barbara Schmidt's little sister, who had pined and wasted to death. "Never mind, Trudchen," answered the brother kindly; "meantime I have kept all the wild catskins for thee, and may be this—this—SHE could sew them up into a mantle for thee."

"O let me see," cried the young lady eagerly; and Sir Eberhard, walking off, presently returned with an armful of the beautiful brindled furs of the mountain cat, reminding Christina of her aunt's gentle domestic favourite. Ermentrude sat up, and regarded the placing out of them with great interest; and thus her brother left her employed, and so much delighted that she had not flagged, when a great bell proclaimed that it was the time for the noontide meal, for which Christina, in spite of all her fears of the company below stairs, had been constrained by mountain air to look forward with satisfaction.

The Dove in the Eagle's Nest

Ermentrude, she found, meant to go down, but with no notion of the personal arrangements that Christina had been wont to think a needful preliminary. With all her hair streaming, down she went, and was so gladly welcomed by her father that it was plain that her presence was regarded as an unusual advance towards recovery, and Christina feared lest he might already be looking out for the stout husband. She had much to tell him about the catskin cloak, and then she was seized with eager curiosity at the sight of Christina's bundles, and especially at her lute, which she must hear at once.

"Not now," said her mother, "there will be jangling and jingling enough by and by—meat now."

The whole establishment were taking their places—or rather tumbling into them. A battered, shapeless metal vessel seemed to represent the salt-cellar, and next to it Hugh Sorel seated himself, and kept a place for her beside him. Otherwise she would hardly have had seat or food.' She was now able to survey the inmates of the castle. Besides the family themselves, there were about a dozen men, all ruffianly-looking, and of much lower grade than her father, and three women. One, old Ursel, the wife of Hatto the forester, was a bent, worn, but not ill-looking woman, with a motherly face; the younger ones were hard, bold creatures, from whom Christina felt a shrinking recoil. The meal was dressed by Ursel and her kitchen boy. From a great cauldron, goat's flesh and broth together were ladled out into wooden bowls. That every one provided their own spoon and knife—no fork—was only what Christina was used to in the most refined society, and she had the implements in a pouch hanging to her girdle; but she was not prepared for the unwashed condition of the bowls, nor for being obliged to share that of her father—far less for the absence of all blessing on the meal, and the coarse boisterousness of manners prevailing thereat. Hungry as she was, she did not find it easy to take food under these circumstances, and she was relieved when Ermentrude, overcome by the turmoil, grew giddy, and was carried upstairs by her father, who laid her down upon her great bed, and left her to the attendance of Christina. Ursel had followed, but was petulantly repulsed by her young lady in favour of the newcomer, and went away grumbling.

Nestled on her bed, Ermentrude insisted on hearing the lute, and Christina had to creep down to fetch it, with some other of her goods, in trembling haste, and redoubled disgust at the aspect of the meal, which looked even more repulsive in this later stage, and to one who was no longer partaking of it.

Low and softly, with a voice whence she could scarcely banish tears, and in dread of attracting attention, Christina sung to the sick girl, who listened with a sort of rude wonder, and finally was lulled to sleep. Christina ventured to lay down her instrument and move towards the window, heavily mullioned with stone, barred with iron, and glazed with thick glass; being in fact the only glazed window in the castle. To her great satisfaction it did not look out over the loathsome court, but over the opening of the ravine. The apartment occupied the whole floor of the keep; it was stone-paved, but the roof was boarded, and there was a round turret at each angle. One contained the staircase, and was that which ran up above the keep, served as a watch-tower, and supported the Eagle banner. The other three were empty, and one of these, which had a strong door, and a long loophole window looking out over the open country, Christina hoped that she might appropriate. The turret was immediately over the perpendicular cliff that descended into the plain. A stone thrown from the window would have gone straight down, she knew not where. Close to her ears rushed the descending waterfall in its leap over the rock side, and her eyes could rest themselves on the green meadow land below, and the smooth water of the Debateable Ford; nay— far, far away beyond retreating ridges of wood and field—she thought she could track a silver line and, guided by it, a something that might be a city. Her heart leapt towards it, but she was recalled by Ermentrude's fretfully imperious voice.

"I was only looking forth from the window, lady," she said, returning.

"Ah! thou saw'st no travellers at the Ford?" cried Ermentrude, starting up with lively interest.

"No, lady; I was gazing at the far distance. Know you if it be indeed Ulm that we see from these windows?"

"Ulm? That is where thou comest from?" said Ermentrude languidly.

"My happy home, with my dear uncle and aunt! O, if I can but see it hence, it will be joy!"

The Dove in the Eagle's Nest

"I do not know. Let me see," said Ermentrude, rising; but at the window her pale blue eyes gazed vacantly as if she did not know what she was looking at or for.

"Ah! if the steeple of the Dome Kirk were but finished, I could not mistake it," said Christina. "How beauteous the white spire will look from hence!"

"Dome Kirk?" repeated Ermentrude; "what is that?"

Such an entire blank as the poor child's mind seemed to be was inconceivable to the maiden, who had been bred up in the busy hum of men, where the constant resort of strange merchants, the daily interests of a self-governing municipality, and the numerous festivals, both secular and religious, were an unconscious education, even without that which had been bestowed upon her by teachers, as well as by her companionship with her uncle, and participation in his studies, taste and arts.

Ermentrude von Adlerstein had, on the contrary, not only never gone beyond the Kohler's hut on the one side, and the mountain village on the other, but she never seen more of life than the festival at the wake the hermitage chapel there on Midsummer-day. The only strangers who ever came to the castle were disbanded lanzknechts who took service with her father, or now and then a captive whom he put to ransom. She knew absolutely nothing of the world, except for a general belief that Freiherren lived there to do what they chose with other people, and that the House of Adlerstein was the freest and noblest in existence. Also there was a very positive hatred to the house of Schlangenwald, and no less to that of Adlerstein Wildschloss, for no reason that Christina could discover save that, being a younger branch of the family, they had submitted to the Emperor. To destroy either the Graf von Schlangenwald, or her Wildschloss cousin, was evidently the highest gratification Ermentrude could conceive; and, for the rest, that her father and brother should make successful captures at the Debateable Ford was the more abiding, because more practicable hope. She had no further ideas, except perhaps to elude her mother's severity, and to desire her brother's success in chamois-hunting. The only mental culture she had ever received was that old Ursel had taught her the Credo, Pater Noster, and Ave, as correctly as might be expected from a long course of traditionary repetitions of an incomprehensible language. And she knew besides a few German rhymes and jingles, half Christian, half heathen, with a legend or two which, if the names were Christian, ran grossly wild from all Christian meaning or morality. As to the amenities, nay, almost the proprieties, of life, they were less known in that baronial castle than in any artisan's house at Ulm. So little had the sick girl figured them to herself, that she did not even desire any greater means of ease than she possessed. She moaned and fretted indeed, with aching limbs and blank weariness, but without the slightest formed desire for anything to remove her discomfort, except the few ameliorations she knew, such as sitting on her brother's knee, with her head on his shoulder, or tasting the mountain berries that he gathered for her. Any other desire she exerted herself to frame was for finery to be gained from the spoils of travellers.

And this was Christina's charge, whom she must look upon as the least alien spirit in this dreadful castle of banishment! The young and old lords seemed to her savage bandits, who frightened her only less than did the proud sinister expression of the old lady, for she had not even the merit of showing any tenderness towards the sickly girl, of whom she was ashamed, and evidently regarded the town-bred attendant as a contemptible interloper.

Long, long did the maiden weep and pray that night after Ermentrude had sunk to sleep. She strained her eyes with home-sick longings to detect lights where she thought Ulm might be; and, as she thought of her uncle and aunt, the poodle and the cat round the stove, the maids spinning and the prentices knitting as her uncle read aloud some grave good book, most probably the legend of the saint of the day, and contrasted it with the rude gruff sounds of revelry that found their way up the turret stairs, she could hardly restrain her sobs from awakening the young lady whose bed she was to share. She thought almost with envy of her own patroness, who was cast into the lake of Bolsena with a millstone about her neck—a better fate, thought she, than to live on in such an abode of loathsomeness and peril.

But then had not St. Christina floated up alive, bearing up her millstone with her? And had not she been put into a dungeon full of venomous reptiles who, when they approached her, had all been changed to harmless doves? Christina had once asked Father Balthazar how this could be; and had he not replied that the Church did not teach these miracles as matters of faith, but that she might there discern in figure how meek Christian holiness rose above all crushing burthens, and transformed the rudest natures. This poor maiden– dying, perhaps; and oh! how unfit to live or die!—might it be her part to do some good work by her, and infuse some Christian hope, some godly fear? Could it be for this that the saints had led her hither?

CHAPTER III: THE FLOTSAM AND JETSAM OF THE DEBATEABLE FORD

Life in Schloss Adlerstein was little less intolerable than Christina's imagination had depicted it. It was entirely devoid of all the graces of chivalry, and its squalor and coarseness, magnified into absurdity by haughtiness and violence, were almost inconceivable. Fortunately for her, the inmates of the castle resided almost wholly below stairs in the hall and kitchen, and in some dismal dens in the thickness of their walls. The height of the keep was intended for dignity and defence, rather than for habitation; and the upper chamber, with its great state-bed, where everybody of the house of Adlerstein was born and died, was not otherwise used, except when Ermentrude, unable to bear the oppressive confusion below stairs, had escaped thither for quietness' sake. No one else wished to inhabit it. The chamber above was filled with the various appliances for the defence of the castle; and no one would have ever gone up the turret stairs had not a warder been usually kept on the roof to watch the roads leading to the Ford. Otherwise the Adlersteiners had all the savage instinct of herding together in as small a space as possible.

Freiherrn Kunigunde hardly ever mounted to her daughter's chamber. All her affection was centred on the strong and manly son, of whom she was proud, while the sickly pining girl, who would hardly find a mate of her own rank, and who had not even dowry enough for a convent, was such a shame and burthen to her as to be almost a distasteful object. But perversely, as it seemed to her, the only daughter was the darling of both father and brother, who were ready to do anything to gratify the girl's sick fancies, and hailed with delight her pleasure in her new attendant. Old Ursel was at first rather envious and contemptuous of the childish, fragile stranger, but her gentleness disarmed the old woman; and, when it was plain that the young lady's sufferings were greatly lessened by tender care, dislike gave way to attachment, and there was little more murmuring at the menial services that were needed by the two maidens, even when Ermentrude's feeble fancies, or Christina's views of dainty propriety, rendered them more onerous than before. She was even heard to rejoice that some Christian care and tenderness had at last reached her poor neglected child.

It was well for Christina that she had such an ally. The poor child never crept down stairs to the dinner or supper, to fetch food for Ermentrude, or water for herself, without a trembling and shrinking of heart and nerves. Her father's authority guarded her from rude actions, but from rough tongues he neither could nor would guard her, nor understand that what to some would have been a compliment seemed to her an alarming insult; and her chief safeguard lay in her own insignificance and want of attraction, and still more in the modesty that concealed her terror at rude jests sufficiently to prevent frightening her from becoming an entertainment.

Her father, whom she looked on as a cultivated person in comparison with the rest of the world, did his best for her after his own views, and gradually brought her all the properties she had left at the Kohler's hut. Therewith she made a great difference in the aspect of the chamber, under the full sanction of the lords of the castle. Wolf, deer, and sheep skins abounded; and with these, assisted by her father and old Hatto, she tapestried the lower part of the bare grim walls, a great bear's hide covered the neighbourhood of the hearth, and cushions were made of these skins, and stuffed from Ursel's stores of feathers. All these embellishments were watched with great delight by Ermentrude, who had never been made of so much importance, and was as much surprised as relieved by such attentions. She was too young and too delicate to reject civilization, and she let Christina braid her hair, bathe her, and arrange her dress, with sensations of comfort that were almost like health. To train her into occupying herself was however, as Christina soon found, in her present state, impossible. She could spin and sew a little, but hated both; and her clumsy, listless fingers only soiled and wasted Christina's needles, silk, and lute strings, and such damage was not so easily remedied as in the streets of Ulm. She was best provided for when looking on at her attendant's busy hands, and asking to be sung to, or to hear tales of the active, busy scenes of the city life—the dresses, fairs, festivals, and guild processions.

The Dove in the Eagle's Nest

The gentle nursing and the new interests made her improve in health, so that her father was delighted, and Christina began to hope for a return home. Sometimes the two girls would take the air, either, on still days, upon the battlements, where Ermentrude watched the Debateable Ford, and Christina gazed at the Danube and at Ulm; or they would find their way to a grassy nook on the mountain-side, where Christina gathered gentians and saxifrage, trying to teach her young lady that they were worth looking at, and sighing at the thought of Master Gottfried's wreath when she met with the asphodel seed-vessels. Once the quiet mule was brought into requisition; and, with her brother walking by her, and Sorel and his daughter in attendance, Ermentrude rode towards the village of Adlerstein. It was a collection of miserable huts, on a sheltered slope towards the south, where there was earth enough to grow some wretched rye and buckwheat, subject to severe toll from the lord of the soil. Perched on a hollow rock above the slope was a rude little church, over a cave where a hermit had once lived and died in such odour of sanctity that, his day happening to coincide with that of St. John the Baptist, the Blessed Freidmund had acquired the credit of the lion's share both of the saint's honours and of the old solstitial feast of Midsummer. This wake was the one gaiety of the year, and attracted a fair which was the sole occasion of coming honestly by anything from the outer world; nor had his cell ever lacked a professional anchorite.

The Freiherr of his day had been a devout man, who had gone a pilgrimage with Kaiser Friedrich of the Red Beard, and had brought home a bit of stone from the council chamber of Nicaea, which he had presented to the little church that he had built over the cavern. He had named his son Friedmund; and there were dim memories of his days as of a golden age, before the Wildschlossen had carried off the best of the property, and when all went well.

This was Christina's first sight of a church since her arrival, except that in the chapel, which was a dismal neglected vault, where a ruinous altar and mouldering crucifix testified to its sacred purpose. The old baron had been excommunicated for twenty years, ever since he had harried the wains of the Bishop of Augsburg on his way to the Diet; and, though his household and family were not under the same sentence, "Sunday didna come abune the pass." Christina's entreaty obtained permission to enter the little building, but she had knelt there only a few moments before her father came to hurry her away, and her supplications that he would some day take her to mass there were whistled down the wind; and indeed the hermit was a layman, and the church was only served on great festivals by a monk from the convent of St. Ruprecht, on the distant side of the mountain, which was further supposed to be in the Schlangenwald interest. Her best chance lay in infusing the desire into Ermentrude, who by watching her prayers and asking a few questions had begun to acquire a few clearer ideas. And what Ermentrude wished had always hitherto been acquiesced in by the two lords.

The elder baron came little into Christina's way. He meant to be kind to her, but she was dreadfully afraid of him, and, when he came to visit his daughter, shrank out of his notice as much as possible, shuddering most of all at his attempts at civilities. His son she viewed as one of the thickwitted giants meant to be food for the heroism of good knights of romance. Except that he was fairly conversant with the use of weapons, and had occasionally ridden beyond the shadow of his own mountain, his range was quite as limited as his sister's; and he had an equal scorn for all beyond it. His unfailing kindness to his sister was however in his favour, and he always eagerly followed up any suggestion Christina made for her pleasure.

Much of his time was spent on the child, whose chief nurse and playmate he had been throughout her malady; and when she showed him the stranger's arrangements, or repeated to him, in a wondering, blundering way, with constant appeals to her attendant, the new tales she had heard, he used to listen with a pleased awkward amazement at his little Ermentrude's astonishing cleverness, joined sometimes with real interest, which was evinced by his inquiries of Christina. He certainly did not admire the little, slight, pale bower-maiden, but he seemed to look upon her like some strange, almost uncanny, wise spirit out of some other sphere, and his manner towards her had none of the offensive freedom apparent in even the old man's patronage. It was, as Ermentrude once said, laughing, almost as if he feared that she might do something to him.

Christina had expected to see a ruffian, and had found a boor; but she was to be convinced that the ruffian existed in him. Notice came up to the castle of a convoy of waggons, and all was excitement. Men-at-arms were mustered, horses led down the Eagle's Ladder, and an ambush prepared in the woods. The autumn rains were already swelling the floods, and the passage of the ford would be difficult enough to afford the assailants an easy prey.

The Dove in the Eagle's Nest

The Freiherrinn Kunigunde herself, and all the women of the castle, hurried into Ermentrude's room to enjoy the view from her window. The young lady herself was full of eager expectation, but she knew enough of her maiden to expect no sympathy from her, and loved her well enough not to bring down on her her mother's attention; so Christina crept into her turret, unable to withdraw her eyes from the sight, trembling, weeping, praying, longing for power to give a warning signal. Could they be her own townsmen stopped on the way to dear Ulm?

She could see the waggons in mid-stream, the warriors on the bank; she heard the triumphant outcries of the mother and daughter in the outer room. She saw the overthrow, the struggle, the flight of a few scattered dark figures on the farther side, the drawing out of the goods on the nearer. Oh! were those leaping waves bearing down any good men's corpses to the Danube, slain, foully slain by her own father and this gang of robbers?

She was glad that Ermentrude went down with her mother to watch the return of the victors. She crouched on the floor, sobbing, shuddering with grief and indignation, and telling her beads alike for murdered and murderers, till, after the sounds of welcome and exultation, she heard Sir Eberhard's heavy tread, as he carried his sister up stairs. Ermentrude went up at once to Christina.

"After all there was little for us!" she said. "It was only a wain of wine barrels; and now will the drunkards down stairs make good cheer. But Ebbo could only win for me this gold chain and medal which was round the old merchant's neck."

"Was he slain?" Christina asked with pale lips.

"I only know I did not kill him," returned the baron; "I had him down and got the prize, and that was enough for me. What the rest of the fellows may have done, I cannot say."

"But he has brought thee something, Stina," continued Ermentrude. "Show it to her, brother."

"My father sends you this for your care of my sister," said Eberhard, holding out a brooch that had doubtless fastened the band of the unfortunate wine-merchant's bonnet.

"Thanks, sir; but, indeed, I may not take it," said Christina, turning crimson, and drawing back.

"So!" he exclaimed, in amaze; then bethinking himself,—"They are no townsfolk of yours, but Constance cowards."

"Take it, take it, Stina, or you will anger my father," added Ermentrude.

"No, lady, I thank the barons both, but it were sin in me," said Christina, with trembling voice.

"Look you," said Eberhard; "we have the full right—'tis a seignorial right—to all the goods of every wayfarer that may be overthrown in our river—as I am a true knight!" he added earnestly.

"A true knight!" repeated Christina, pushed hard, and very indignant in all her terror. "The true knight's part is to aid, not rob, the weak." And the dark eyes flashed a vivid light.

"Christina!" exclaimed Ermentrude in the extremity of her amazement, "know you what you have said?—that Eberhard is no true knight!"

He meanwhile stood silent, utterly taken by surprise, and letting his little sister fight his battles.

"I cannot help it, Lady Ermentrude," said Christina, with trembling lips, and eyes filling with tears. "You may drive me from the castle—I only long to be away from it; but I cannot stain my soul by saying that spoil and rapine are the deeds of a true knight."

The Dove in the Eagle's Nest

"My mother will beat you," cried Ermentrude, passionately, ready to fly to the head of the stairs; but her brother laid his hand upon her.

"Tush, Trudchen; keep thy tongue still, child! What does it hurt me?"

And he turned on his heels and went down stairs. Christina crept into her turret, weeping bitterly and with many a wild thought. Would they visit her offence on her father? Would they turn them both out together? If so, would not her father hurl her down the rocks rather than return her to Ulm? Could she escape? Climb down the dizzy rocks, it might be, succour the merchant lying half dead on the meadows, protect and be protected, be once more among God-fearing Christians? And as she felt her helplessness, the selfish thoughts passed into a gush of tears for the murdered man, lying suffering there, and for his possible wife and children watching for him. Presently Ermentrude peeped in.

"Stina, Stina, don't cry; I will not tell my mother! Come out, and finish my kerchief! Come out! No one shall beat you."

"That is not what I wept for, lady," said Christina. "I do not think you would bring harm on me. But oh! I would I were at home! I grieve for the bloodshed that I must see and may not hinder, and for that poor merchant."

"Oh," said Ermentrude, "you need not fear for him! I saw his own folk return and lift him up. But what is he to thee or to us?"

"I am a burgher maid, lady," said Christina, recovering herself, and aware that it was of little use to bear testimony to such an auditor as poor little Ermentrude against the deeds of her own father and brother, which had in reality the sort of sanction Sir Eberhard had mentioned, much akin to those coast rights that were the temptation of wreckers.

Still she could not but tremble at the thought of her speech, and went down to supper in greater trepidation than usual, dreading that she should be expected to thank the Freiherr for his gift. But, fortunately, manners were too rare at Adlerstein for any such omission to be remarkable, and the whole establishment was in a state of noisy triumph and merriment over the excellence of the French wine they had captured, so that she slipped into her seat unobserved.

Every available drinking-horn and cup was full. Ermentrude was eagerly presented with draughts by both father and brother, and presently Sir Eberhard exclaimed, turning towards the shrinking Christina with a rough laugh, "Maiden, I trow thou wilt not taste?"

Christina shook her head, and framed a negative with her lips.

"What's this?" asked her father, close to whom she sat. "Is't a fast-day?"

There was a pause. Many were present who regarded a fast-day much more than the lives or goods of their neighbours. Christina again shook her head.

"No matter," said good-natured Sir Eberhard, evidently wishing to avert any ill consequence from her. "'Tis only her loss."

The mirth went on rough and loud, and Christina felt this the worst of all the miserable meals she had partaken of in fear and trembling at this place of her captivity. Ermentrude, too, was soon in such a state of excitement, that not only was Christina's womanhood bitterly ashamed and grieved for her, but there was serious danger that she might at any moment break out with some allusion to her maiden's recusancy in her reply to Sir Eberhard.

Presently however Ermentrude laid down her head and began to cry— violent headache had come on—and her brother took her in his arms to carry her up the stairs; but his potations had begun before hers, and his step was far from steady; he stumbled more than once on the steps, shook and frightened his sister, and set her down weeping petulantly. And then came a more terrible moment; his awe of Christina had passed away; he swore that she was a lovely maiden, with only too free a tongue, and that a kiss must be the seal of her pardon.

A house full of intoxicated men, no living creature who would care to protect her, scarce even her father! But extremity of terror gave her strength. She spoke resolutely—"Sir Eberhard, your sister is ill—you are in no state to be here. Go down at once, nor insult a free maiden."

Probably the low-toned softness of the voice, so utterly different from the shrill wrangling notes of all the other women he had known, took him by surprise. He was still sober enough to be subdued, almost cowed, by resistance of a description unlike all he had ever seen; his alarm at Christina's superior power returned in full force, he staggered to the stairs, Christina rushed after him, closed the heavy door with all her force, fastened it inside, and would have sunk down to weep but for Ermentrude's peevish wail of distress.

Happily Ermentrude was still a child, and, neglected as she had been, she still had had no one to make her precocious in matters of this kind. She was quite willing to take Christina's view of the case, and not resent the exclusion of her brother; indeed, she was unwell enough to dread the loudness of his voice and rudeness of his revelry.

So the door remained shut, and Christina's resolve was taken that she would so keep it while the wine lasted. And, indeed, Ermentrude had so much fever all that night and the next day that no going down could be thought of. Nobody came near the maidens but Ursel, and she described one continued orgie that made Christina shudder again with fear and disgust. Those below revelled without interval, except for sleep; and they took their sleep just where they happened to sink down, then returned again to the liquor. The old baroness repaired to the kitchen when the revelry went beyond even her bearing; but all the time the wine held out, the swine in the court were, as Ursel averred, better company than the men in the hall. Yet there might have been worse even than this; for old Ursel whispered that at the bottom of the stairs there was a trap-door. Did the maiden know what it covered? It was an oubliette. There was once a Strasburg armourer who had refused ransom, and talked of appealing to the Kaiser. He trod on that door and—Ursel pointed downwards. "But since that time," she said, "my young lord has never brought home a prisoner."

No wonder that all this time Christina cowered at the discordant sounds below, trembled, and prayed while she waited on her poor young charge, who tossed and moaned in fever and suffering. She was still far from recovered when the materials of the debauch failed, and the household began to return to its usual state. She was soon restlessly pining for her brother; and when her father came up to see her, received him with scant welcome, and entreaties for Ebbo. She knew she should be better if she might only sit on his knee, and lay her head on his shoulder. The old Freiherr offered to accommodate her; but she rejected him petulantly, and still called for Ebbo, till he went down, promising that her brother should come.

With a fluttering heart Christina awaited the noble whom she had perhaps insulted, and whose advances had more certainly insulted her. Would he visit her with his anger, or return to that more offensive familiarity? She longed to flee out of sight, when, after a long interval, his heavy tread was heard; but she could not even take refuge in her turret, for Ermentrude was leaning against her. Somehow, the step was less assured than usual; he absolutely knocked at the door; and, when he came in, he acknowledged her by a slight inclination of the head. If she only had known it, this was the first time that head had ever been bent to any being, human or Divine; but all she did perceive was that Sir Eberhard was in neither of the moods she dreaded, only desperately shy and sheepish, and extremely ashamed, not indeed of his excess, which would have been, even to a much tamer German baron, only a happy accident, but of what had passed between himself and her.

He was much grieved to perceive how much ground Ermentrude had lost, and gave himself up to fondling and comforting her; and in a few days more, in their common cares for the sister, Christina lost her newly-acquired horror of the brother, and could not but be grateful for his forbearance; while she was almost entertained by the increased awe of herself shown by this huge robber baron.

CHAPTER IV: SNOW-WREATHS WHEN 'TIS THAW

Ermentrude had by no means recovered the ground she had lost, before the winter set in; and blinding snow came drifting down day and night, rendering the whole view, above and below, one expanse of white, only broken by the peaks of rock which were too steep to sustain the snow. The waterfall lengthened its icicles daily, and the whole court was heaped with snow, up even to the top of the high steps to the hall; and thus, Christina was told, would it continue all the winter. What had previously seemed to her a strangely door- like window above the porch now became the only mode of egress, when the barons went out bear or wolf-hunting, or the younger took his crossbow and hound to provide the wild-fowl, which, under Christina's skilful hands, would tempt the feeble appetite of Ermentrude when she was utterly unable to touch the salted meats and sausages of the household.

In spite of all endeavours to guard the windows and keep up the fire, the cold withered the poor child like a fading leaf, and she needed more and more of tenderness and amusement to distract her attention from her ailments. Christina's resources were unfailing. Out of the softer pine and birch woods provided for the fire, she carved a set of draughtsmen, and made a board by ruling squares on the end of a settle, and painting the alternate ones with a compound of oil and charcoal. Even the old Baron was delighted with this contrivance, and the pleasure it gave his daughter. He remembered playing at draughts in that portion of his youth which had been a shade more polished, and he felt as if the game were making Ermentrude more hike a lady. Christina was encouraged to proceed with a set of chessmen, and the shaping of their characteristic heads under her dexterous fingers was watched by Ermentrude like something magical. Indeed, the young lady entertained the belief that there was no limit to her attendant's knowledge or capacity.

Truly there was a greater brightness and clearness beginning to dawn even upon poor little Ermentrude's own dull mind. She took more interest in everything: songs were not solely lullabies, but she cared to talk them over; tales to which she would once have been incapable of paying attention were eagerly sought after; and, above all, the spiritual vacancy that her mind had hitherto presented was beginning to be filled up. Christina had brought her own books—a library of extraordinary extent for a maiden of the fifteenth century, but which she owed to her uncle's connexion with the arts of wood-cutting and printing. A Vulgate from Dr. Faustus's own press, a mass book and breviary, Thomas a Kempis's Imitation and the Nuremburg Chronicle all in Latin, and the poetry of the gentle Minnesinger and bird lover, Walther von Vogelweide, in the vernacular: these were her stock, which Hausfrau Johanna had viewed as a foolish encumbrance, and Hugh Sorel would never have transported to the castle unless they had been so well concealed in Christina's kirtles that he had taken them for parts of her wardrobe.

Most precious were they now, when, out of the reach of all teaching save her own, she had to infuse into the sinking girl's mind the great mysteries of life and death, that so she might not leave the world without more hope or faith than her heathen forefathers. For that Ermentrude would live Christina had never hoped, since that fleeting improvement had been cut short by the fever of the wine-cup; the look, voice, and tone had become so completely the same as those of Regina Grundt's little sister who had pined and died. She knew she could not cure, but she could, she felt she could, comfort, cheer, and soften, and she no longer repined at her enforced sojourn at Adlerstein. She heartily loved her charge, and could not bear to think how desolate Ermentrude would be without her. And now the poor girl had become responsive to her care. She was infinitely softened in manner, and treated her parents with forms of respect new to them; she had learnt even to thank old Ursel, dropped her imperious tone, and struggled with her petulance; and, towards her brother, the domineering, uncouth adherence was becoming real, tender affection; while the dependent, reverent love she bestowed upon Christina was touching and endearing in the extreme.

Freiherr von Adlerstein saw the change, and congratulated himself on the effect of having a town-bred bower woman; nay, spoke of the advantage it would be to his daughter, if he could persuade himself to make the submission to the Kaiser which the late improvements decided on at the Diet were rendering more and more inevitable. NOW how happy would be the winner of his gentle Ermentrude!

Freiherrinn von Adlerstein thought the alteration the mere change from child to woman, and felt insulted by the supposition that any one might not have been proud to match with a daughter of Adlerstein, be she what she might. As to submission to the Kaiser, that was mere folly and weakness—kaisers, kings, dukes, and counts had broken their teeth against the rock of Adlerstein before now! What had come over her husband and her son to make them cravens?

For Freiherr Eberhard was more strongly convinced than was his father of the untenableness of their present position. Hugh Sorel's reports of what he heard at Ulm had shown that the league that had been discussed at Regensburg was far more formidable than anything that had ever previously threatened Schloss Adlerstein, and that if the Graf von Schlangenwald joined in the coalition, there would be private malice to direct its efforts against the Adlerstein family. Feud-letters or challenges had been made unlawful for ten years, and was not Adlerstein at feud with the world?

Nor did Eberhard look on the submission with the sullen rage and grief that his father felt in bringing himself to such a declension from the pride of his ancestors. What the young Baron heard up stairs was awakening in him a sense of the poorness and narrowness of his present life. Ermentrude never spared him what interested her; and, partly from her lips, partly through her appeals to her attendant, he had learnt that life had better things to offer than independence on these bare rocks, and that homage might open the way to higher and worthier exploits than preying upon overturned waggons.

Dietrich of Berne and his two ancestors, whose lengthy legend Christina could sing in a low, soft recitative, were revelations to him of what she meant by a true knight—the lion in war, the lamb in peace; the quaint oft-repeated portraits, and still quainter cities, of the Chronicle, with her explanations and translations, opened his mind to aspirations for intercourse with his fellows, for an honourable name, and for esteem in its degree such as was paid to Sir Parzival, to Karl the Great, or to Rodolf of Hapsburgh, once a mountain lord like himself. Nay, as Ermentrude said, stroking his cheek, and smoothing the flaxen beard, that somehow had become much less rough and tangled than it used to be, "Some day wilt thou be another Good Freiherr Eberhard, whom all the country-side loved, and who gave bread at the castle-gate to all that hungered."

Her brother believed nothing of her slow declension in strength, ascribing all the change he saw to the bitter cold, and seeing but little even of that alteration, though he spent many hours in her room, holding her in his arms, amusing her, or talking to her and to Christina. All Christina's fear of him was gone. As long as there was no liquor in the house, and he was his true self, she felt him to be a kind friend, bound to her by strong sympathy in the love and care for his sister. She could talk almost as freely before him as when alone with her young lady; and as Ermentrude's religious feelings grew stronger, and were freely expressed to him, surely his attention was not merely kindness and patience with the sufferer.

The girl's soul ripened rapidly under the new influences during her bodily decay; and, as the days lengthened, and the stern hold of winter relaxed upon the mountains, Christina looked with strange admiration upon the expression that had dawned upon the features once so vacant and dull, and listened with the more depth of reverence to the sweet words of faith, hope and love, because she felt that a higher, deeper teaching than she could give must have come to mould the spirit for the new world to which it was hastening.

"Like an army defeated,
The snow had retreated,"

out of the valley, whose rich green shone smiling round the pool into which the Debateable Ford spread. The waterfall had burst its icy bonds, and dashed down with redoubled voice, roaring rather than babbling. Blue and pink hepaticas—or, as Christina called them, liver-krauts—had pushed up their starry heads, and had even been gathered by Sir Eberhard, and laid on his sister's pillow. The dark peaks of rock came out all glistening with moisture, and the snow only retained possession of the deep hollows and crevices, into which however its retreat was far more graceful than when, in the city, it was trodden by horse and man, and soiled with smoke.

Christina dreaded indeed that the roads should be open, but she could not love the snow; it spoke to her of dreariness, savagery, and captivity, and she watched the dwindling stripes with satisfaction, and hailed the fall of the petty avalanches from one Eagle's Step to another as her forefathers might have rejoiced in the defeat of the Frost giants.

The Dove in the Eagle's Nest

But Ermentrude had a love for the white sheet that lay covering a gorge running up from the ravine. She watched its diminution day by day with a fancy that she was melting away with it; and indeed it was on the very day that a succession of drifting showers had left the sheet alone, and separated it from the masses of white above, that it first fully dawned upon the rest of the family that, for the little daughter of the house, spring was only bringing languor and sinking instead of recovery.

Then it was that Sir Eberhard first really listened to her entreaty that she might not die without a priest, and comforted her by passing his word to her that, if—he would not say when—the time drew near, he would bring her one of the priests who had only come from St. Ruprecht's cloister on great days, by a sort of sufferance, to say mass at the Blessed Friedmund's hermitage chapel.

The time was slow in coming. Easter had passed with Ermentrude far too ill for Christina to make the effort she had intended of going to the church, even if she could get no escort but old Ursel—the sheet of snow had dwindled to a mere wreath—the ford looked blue in the sunshine—the cascade tinkled merrily down its rock—mountain primroses peeped out, when, as Father Norbert came forth from saying his ill-attended Pentecostal mass, and was parting with the infirm peasant hermit, a tall figure strode up the pass, and, as the villagers fell back to make way, stood before the startled priest, and said, in a voice choked with grief, "Come with me."

"Who needs me?" began the astonished monk.

"Follow him not, father!" whispered the hermit. "It is the young Freiherr.—Oh have mercy on him, gracious sir; he has done your noble lordships no wrong."

"I mean him no ill," replied Eberhard, clearing his voice with difficulty; "I would but have him do his office. Art thou afraid, priest?"

"Who needs my office?" demanded Father Norbert. "Show me fit cause, and what should I dread? Wherefore dost thou seek me?"

"For my sister," replied Eberhard, his voice thickening again. "My little sister lies at the point of death, and I have sworn to her that a priest she shall have. Wilt thou come, or shall I drag thee down the pass?"

"I come, I come with all my heart, sir knight," was the ready response. "A few moments and I am at your bidding."

He stepped back into the hermit's cave, whence a stair led up to the chapel. The anchorite followed him, whispering—"Good father, escape! There will be full time ere he misses you. The north door leads to the Gemsbock's Pass; it is open now."

"Why should I baulk him? Why should I deny my office to the dying?" said Norbert.

"Alas! holy father, thou art new to this country, and know'st not these men of blood! It is a snare to make the convent ransom thee, if not worse. The Freiherrinn is a fiend for malice, and the Freiherr is excommunicate."

"I know it, my son," said Norbert; "but wherefore should their child perish unassoilzied?"

"Art coming, priest?" shouted Eberhard, from his stand at the mouth of the cave.

And, as Norbert at once appeared with the pyx and other appliances that he had gone to fetch, the Freiherr held out his hand with an offer to "carry his gear for him;" and, when the monk refused, with an inward shudder at entrusting a sacred charge to such unhallowed hands, replied, "You will have work enow for both hands ere the castle is reached."

The Dove in the Eagle's Nest

But Father Norbert was by birth a sturdy Switzer, and thought little of these Swabian Alps; and he climbed after his guide through the most rugged passages of Eberhard's shortest and most perpendicular cut without a moment's hesitation, and with agility worthy of a chamois. The young baron turned for a moment, when the level of the castle had been gained, perhaps to see whether he were following, but at the same time came to a sudden, speechless pause.

On the white masses of vapour that floated on the opposite side of the mountain was traced a gigantic shadowy outline of a hermit, with head bent eagerly forward, and arm outstretched.

The monk crossed himself. Eberhard stood still for a moment, and then said, hoarsely,—"The Blessed Friedmund! He is come for her;" then strode on towards the postern gate, followed by Brother Norbert, a good deal reassured both as to the genuineness of the young Baron's message and the probable condition of the object of his journey, since the patron saint of her race was evidently on the watch to speed her departing spirit.

Sir Eberhard led the way up the turret stairs to the open door, and the monk entered the death-chamber. The elder Baron sat near the fire in the large wooden chair, half turned towards his daughter, as one who must needs be present, but with his face buried in his hands, unable to endure the spectacle. Nearer was the tall form of his wife, standing near the foot of the bed, her stern, harsh features somewhat softened by the feelings of the moment. Ursel waited at hand, with tears running down her furrowed cheeks.

For such as these Father Norbert was prepared; but he little expected to meet so pure and sweet a gaze of reverential welcome as beamed on him from the soft, dark eyes of the little white-checked maiden who sat on the bed, holding the sufferer in her arms. Still less had he anticipated the serene blessedness that sat on the wasted features of the dying girl, and all the anguish of labouring breath.

She smiled a smile of joy, held up her hand, and thanked her brother. Her father scarcely lifted his head, her mother made a rigid curtsey, and with a grim look of sorrow coming over her features, laid her hand over the old Baron's shoulder. "Come away, Herr Vater," she said; "he is going to hear her confession, and make her too holy for the like of us to touch."

The old man rose up, and stepped towards his child. Ermentrude held out her arms to him, and murmured –

"Father, father, pardon me; I would have been a better daughter if I had only known—" He gathered her in his arms; he was quite past speaking; and they only heard his heavy breathing, and one more whisper from Ermentrude—"And oh! father, one day wilt thou seek to be absolved?" Whether he answered or not they knew not; he only gave her repeated kisses, and laid her down on her pillows, then rushed to the door, and the passionate sobs of the strong man's uncontrolled nature might be heard upon the stair. The parting with the others was not necessarily so complete, as they were not, like him, under censure of the Church; but Kunigunde leant down to kiss her; and, in return to her repetition of her entreaty for pardon, replied, "Thou hast it, child, if it will ease thy mind; but it is all along of these new fancies that ever an Adlerstein thought of pardon. There, there, I blame thee not, poor maid; it thou wert to die, it may be even best as it is. Now must I to thy father; he is troubled enough about this gear."

But when Eberhard moved towards his sister, she turned to the priest, and said, imploringly, "Not far, not far! Oh! let them," pointing to Eberhard and Christina, "let them not be quite out of sight!"

"Out of hearing is all that is needed, daughter," replied the priest; and Ermentrude looked content as Christina moved towards the empty north turret, where, with the door open, she was in full view, and Eberhard followed her thither. It was indeed fully out of earshot of the child's faint, gasping confession. Gravely and sadly both stood there. Christina looked up the hillside for the snow-wreath. The May sunshine had dissolved it; the green pass lay sparkling without a vestige of its white coating. Her eyes full of tears, she pointed the spot out to Eberhard. He understood; but, leaning towards her, told, under his breath, of the phantom he had seen. Her eyes expanded with awe of the supernatural. "It was the Blessed Friedmund," said Eberhard. "Never hath he so greeted one of our race since the pious Freiherrinn Hildegarde. Maiden, hast thou brought us back a blessing?"

"Ah! well may she be blessed—well may the saints stoop to greet her," murmured Christina, with strangled voice, scarcely able to control her sobs.

Father Norbert came towards them. The simple confession had been heard, and he sought the aid of Christina in performing the last rites of the Church.

"Maiden," he said to her, "thou hast done a great and blessed work, such as many a priest might envy thee."

Eberhard was not excluded during the final services by which the soul was to be dismissed from its earthly dwelling-place. True, he comprehended little of their import, and nothing of the words, but he gazed meekly, with uncovered head, and a bewildered look of sadness, while Christina made her responses and took her part with full intelligence and deep fervour, sorrowing indeed for the companion who had become so dear to her, but deeply thankful for the spiritual consolation that had come at last. Ermentrude lay calm, and, as it were, already rapt into a higher world, lighting up at the German portions of the service, and not wholly devoid of comprehension of the spirit even of the Latin, as indeed she had come to the border of the region where human tongues and languages are no more.

She was all but gone when the rite of extreme unction was completed, and they could only stand round her, Eberhard, Christina, Ursel, and the old Baroness, who had returned again, watching the last flutterings of the breath, the window thrown wide open that nothing might impede the passage of the soul to the blue vault above.

The priest spoke the beautiful commendation, "Depart, O Christian soul." There was a faint gesture in the midst for Christina to lift her in her arms—a sign to bend down and kiss her brow—but her last look was for her brother, her last murmur, "Come after me; be the Good Baron Ebbo."

CHAPTER V: THE YOUNG FREIHERR

Ermentrude von Adlerstein slept with her forefathers in the vaults of the hermitage chapel, and Christina Sorel's work was done.

Surely it was time for her to return home, though she should be more sorry to leave the mountain castle than she could ever have believed possible. She entreated her father to take her home, but she received a sharp answer that she did not know what she was talking of: the Schlangenwald Reitern were besetting all the roads; and moreover the Ulm burghers had taken the capture of the Constance wine in such dudgeon that for a retainer of Adlerstein to show himself in the streets would be an absolute asking for the wheel.

But was there any hope for her? Could he not take her to some nunnery midway, and let her write to her uncle to fetch her from thence?

He swore at woman's pertinacity, but allowed at last that if the plan, talked of by the Barons, of going to make their submission to the Emperor at Linz, with a view to which all violence at the ford had ceased, should hold good, it might be possible thus to drop her on their way.

With this Christina must needs content herself. Poor child, not only had Ermentrude's death deprived her of the sole object of her residence at Schloss Adlerstein, but it had infinitely increased the difficulties of her position. No one interfered with her possession of the upper room and its turrets; and it was only at meal times that she was obliged to mingle with the other inhabitants, who, for the most part, absolutely overlooked the little shrinking pale maiden but with one exception, and that the most perplexing of all. She had been on terms with Freiherr Eberhard that were not so easily broken off as if she had been an old woman of Ursel's age. All through his sister's decline she had been his comforter, assistant, director, living in intercourse and sympathy that ought surely to cease when she was no longer his sister's attendant, yet which must be more than ever missed in the full freshness of the stroke.

The Dove in the Eagle's Nest

Even on the earliest day of bereavement, a sudden thought of Hausfrau Johanna flashed upon Christina, and reminded her of the guard she must keep over herself if she would return to Ulm the same modest girl whom her aunt could acquit of all indiscretion. Her cheeks flamed, as she sat alone, with the very thought, and the next time she heard the well-known tread on the stair, she fled hastily into her own turret chamber, and shut the door. Her heart beat fast. She could hear Sir Eberhard moving about the room, and listened to his heavy sigh as he threw himself into the large chair. Presently he called her by name, and she felt it needful to open her door and answer, respectfully,

"What would you, my lord?"

"What would I? A little peace, and heed to her who is gone. To see my father and mother one would think that a partridge had but flown away. I have seen my father more sorrowful when his dog had fallen over the abyss."

"Mayhap there is more sorrow for a brute that cannot live again," said Christina. "Our bird has her nest by an Altar that is lovelier and brighter than even our Dome Kirk will ever be."

"Sit down, Christina," he said, dragging a chair nearer the hearth. "My heart is sore, and I cannot bear the din below. Tell me where my bird is flown."

"Ah! sir; pardon me. I must to the kitchen," said Christina, crossing her hands over her breast, to still her trembling heart, for she was very sorry for his grief, but moving resolutely.

"Must? And wherefore? Thou hast nought to do there; speak truth! Why not stay with me?" and his great light eyes opened wide.

"A burgher maid may not sit down with a noble baron."

"The devil! Has my mother been plaguing thee, child?"

"No, my lord," said Christina, "she reeks not of me; but"—steadying her voice with great difficulty—"it behoves me the more to be discreet."

"And you would not have me come here!" he said, with a wistful tone of reproach.

"I have no power to forbid you; but if you do, I must betake me to Ursel in the kitchen," said Christina, very low, trembling and half choked.

"Among the rude wenches there!" he cried, starting up. "Nay, nay, that shall not be! Rather will I go."

"But this is very cruel of thee, maiden," he added, lingering, "when I give thee my knightly word that all should be as when she whom we both loved was here," and his voice shook.

"It could not so be, my lord," returned Christina with drooping, blushing face; "it would not be maidenly in me. Oh, my lord, you are kind and generous, make it not hard for me to do what other maidens less lonely have friends to do for them!"

"Kind and generous?" said Eberhard, leaning over the back of the chair as if trying to begin a fresh score. "This from you, who told me once I was no true knight!"

"I shall call you a true knight with all my heart," cried Christina, the tears rushing into her eyes, "if you will respect my weakness and loneliness."

The Dove in the Eagle's Nest

He stood up again, as if to move away; then paused, and, twisting his gold chain, said, "And how am I ever to be what the happy one bade me, if you will not show me how?"

"My error would never show you the right," said Christina, with a strong effort at firmness, and retreating at once through the door of the staircase, whence she made her way to the kitchen, and with great difficulty found an excuse for her presence there.

It had been a hard struggle with her compassion and gratitude, and, poor little Christina felt with dismay, with something more than these. Else why was it that, even while principle and better sense summoned her back to Ulm, she experienced a deadly weariness of the city-pent air, of the grave, heavy roll of the river, nay, even of the quiet, well-regulated household? Why did such a marriage as she had thought her natural destiny, with some worthy, kind-hearted brother of the guild, become so hateful to her that she could only aspire to a convent life? This same burgomaster would be an estimable man, no doubt, and those around her were ruffians, but she felt utterly contemptuous and impatient of him. And why was the interchange of greetings, the few words at meals, worth all the rest of the day besides to her? Her own heart was the traitor, and to her own sensations the poor little thing had, in spirit at least, transgressed all Aunt Johanna's precepts against young Barons. She wept apart, and resolved, and prayed, cruelly ashamed of every start of joy or pain that the sight of Eberhard cost her. From almost the first he had sat next her at the single table that accommodated the whole household at meals, and the custom continued, though on some days he treated her with sullen silence, which she blamed herself for not rejoicing in, sometimes he spoke a few friendly words; but he observed, better than she could have dared to expect, her test of his true knighthood, and never again forced himself into her apartment, though now and then he came to the door with flowers, with mountain strawberries, and once with two young doves. "Take them, Christina," he said, "they are very like yourself;" and he always delayed so long that she was forced to be resolute, and shut the door on him at last.

Once, when there was to be a mass at the chapel, Hugh Sorel, between a smile and a growl, informed his daughter that he would take her thereto. She gladly prepared, and, bent on making herself agreeable to her father, did not once press on him the necessity of her return to Ulm. To her amazement and pleasure, the young Baron was at church, and when on the way home, he walked beside her mule, she could see no need of sending him away.

He had been in no school of the conventionalities of life, and, when he saw that Hugh Sorel's presence had obtained him this favour, he wistfully asked, "Christina, if I bring your father with me, will you not let me in?"

"Entreat me not, my lord," she answered, with fluttering breath.

She felt the more that she was right in this decision, when she encountered her father's broad grin of surprise and diversion, at seeing the young Baron help her to dismount. It was a look of receiving an idea both new, comical, and flattering, but by no means the look of a father who would resent the indignity of attentions to his daughter from a man whose rank formed an insuperable barrier to marriage.

The effect was a new, urgent, and most piteous entreaty, that he would find means of sending her home. It brought upon her the hearing put into words what her own feelings had long shrunk from confessing to herself.

"Ah! Why, what now? What, is the young Baron after thee? Ha! ha! petticoats are few enough up here, but he must have been ill off ere he took to a little ghost like thee! I saw he was moping and doleful, but I thought it was all for his sister."

"And so it is, father."

"Tell me that, when he watches every turn of that dark eye of thine— the only good thing thou took'st of mine! Thou art a witch, Stina."

"Hush, oh hush, for pity's sake, father, and let me go home!"

"What, thou likest him not? Thy mind is all for the mincing goldsmith opposite, as I ever told thee."

"My mind is—is to return to my uncle and aunt the true-hearted maiden they parted with," said Christina, with clasped hands. "And oh, father, as you were the son of a true and faithful mother, be a father to me now! Jeer not your motherless child, but protect her and help her."

Hugh Sorel was touched by this appeal, and he likewise recollected how much it was for his own interest that his brother should be satisfied with the care he took of his daughter. He became convinced that the sooner she was out of the castle the better, and at length bethought him that, among the merchants who frequented the Midsummer Fair at the Blessed Friedmund's Wake, a safe escort might be found to convey her back to Ulm.

If the truth were known, Hugh Sorel was not devoid of a certain feeling akin to contempt, both for his young master's taste, and for his forbearance in not having pushed matters further with a being so helpless, meek, and timid as Christina, more especially as such slackness had not been his wont in other cases where his fancy had been caught.

But Sorel did not understand that it was not physical beauty that here had been the attraction, though to some persons, the sweet, pensive eyes, the delicate, pure skin, the slight, tender form, might seem to exceed in loveliness the fully developed animal comeliness chiefly esteemed at Adlerstein. It was rather the strangeness of the power and purity of this timid, fragile creature, that had struck the young noble. With all their brutal manners reverence for a lofty female nature had been in the German character ever since their Velleda prophesied to them, and this reverence in Eberhard bowed at the feet of the pure gentle maiden, so strong yet so weak, so wistful and entreating even in her resolution, refined as a white flower on a heap of refuse, wise and dexterous beyond his slow and dull conception, and the first being in whom he had ever seen piety or goodness; and likewise with a tender, loving spirit of consolation such as he had both beheld and tasted by his sister's deathbed.

There was almost a fear mingled with his reverence. If he had been more familiar with the saints, he would thus have regarded the holy virgin martyrs, nay, even Our Lady herself; and he durst not push her so hard as to offend her, and excite the anger or the grief that he alike dreaded. He was wretched and forlorn without the resources he had found in his sister's room; the new and better cravings of his higher nature had been excited only to remain unsupplied and disappointed; and the affectionate heart in the freshness of its sorrow yearned for the comfort that such conversation had supplied: but the impression that had been made on him was still such, that he knew that to use rough means of pressing his wishes would no more lead to his real gratification than it would to appropriate a snow-bell by crushing it in his gauntlet.

And it was on feeble little Christina, yielding in heart, though not in will, that it depended to preserve this reverence, and return unscathed from this castle, more perilous now than ever.

CHAPTER VI: THE BLESSED FRIEDMUND'S WAKE

Midsummer-Day arrived, and the village of Adlerstein presented a most unusual spectacle. The wake was the occasion of a grand fair for all the mountain-side, and it was an understood thing that the Barons, instead of molesting the pedlars, merchants, and others who attended it, contented themselves with demanding a toll from every one who passed the Kohler's hut on the one side, or the Gemsbock's Pass on the other; and this toll, being the only coin by which they came honestly in the course of the year, was regarded as a certainty and highly valued. Moreover, it was the only time that any purchases could be made, and the flotsam of the ford did not always include all even of the few requirements of the inmates of the castle; it was the only holiday, sacred or secular, that ever gladdened the Eagle's Rock.

So all the inmates of the castle prepared to enjoy themselves, except the heads of the house. The Freiherr had never been at one of these wakes since the first after he was excommunicated, when he had stalked round to show his indifference to the sentence; and the Freiherrinn snarled out such sentences of disdain towards the concourse, that it might be supposed that she hated the sight of her kind; but Ursel had all the household purchases to make, and the kitchen underlings were to take turns to go and come, as indeed were the men-at-arms, who were set to watch the toll-bars.

Christina had packed up a small bundle, for the chance of being unable to return to the castle without missing her escort, though she hoped that the fair might last two days, and that she should thus be enabled to return and bring away the rest of her property. She was more and more resolved on going, but her heart was less and less inclined to departure. And bitter had been her weeping through all the early light hours of the long morning—weeping that she tried to think was all for Ermentrude; and all, amid prayers she could scarce trust herself to offer, that the generous, kindly nature might yet work free of these evil surroundings, and fulfil the sister's dying wish, she should never see it; but, when she should hear that the Debateable Ford was the Friendly Ford, then would she know that it was the doing of the Good Baron Ebbo. Could she venture on telling him so? Or were it not better that there were no farewell? And she wept again that he should think her ungrateful. She could not persuade herself to release the doves, but committed the charge to Ursel to let them go in case she should not return.

So tear-stained was her face, that, ashamed that it should be seen, she wrapped it closely in her hood and veil when she came down and joined her father. The whole scene swam in tears before her eyes when she saw the whole green slope from the chapel covered with tents and booths, and swarming with pedlars and mountaineers in their picturesque dresses. Women and girls were exchanging the yarn of their winter's spinning for bright handkerchiefs; men drove sheep, goats, or pigs to barter for knives, spades, or weapons; others were gazing at simple shows—a dancing bear or ape—or clustering round a Minnesinger; many even then congregating in booths for the sale of beer. Further up, on the flat space of sward above the chapel, were some lay brothers, arranging for the representation of a mystery—a kind of entertainment which Germany owed to the English who came to the Council of Constance, and which the monks of St. Ruprecht's hoped might infuse some religious notions into the wild, ignorant mountaineers.

First however Christina gladly entered the church. Crowded though it were, it was calmer than the busy scene without. Faded old tapestry was decking its walls, representing apparently some subject entirely alien to St. John or the blessed hermit; Christina rather thought it was Mars and Venus, but that was all the same to every one else. And there was a terrible figure of St. John, painted life-like, with a real hair-cloth round his loins, just opposite to her, on the step of the Altar; also poor Friedmund's bones, dressed up in a new serge amice and hood; the stone from Nicaea was in a gilded box, ready in due time to be kissed; and a preaching friar (not one of the monks of St. Ruprecht's) was in the midst of a sermon, telling how St. John presided at the Council of Nicaea till the Emperor Maximius cut off his head at the instance of Herodius—full justice being done to the dancing—and that the blood was sprinkled on this very stone, whereupon our Holy Father the Pope decreed that whoever would kiss the said stone, and repeat the Credo five times afterwards, should be capable of receiving an indulgence for 500 years: which indulgence must however be purchased at the rate of six groschen, to be bestowed in alms at Rome. And this inestimable benefit he, poor Friar Peter, had come from his brotherhood of St. Francis at Offingen solely to dispense to the poor mountaineers.

It was disapointing to find this profane mummery going on instead of the holy services to which Christina had looked forward for strength and comfort; she was far too well instructed not to be scandalized at the profane deception which was ripening fast for Luther, only thirty years later; and, when the stone was held up by the friar in one hand, the printed briefs of indulgence in the other, she shrunk back. Her father however said, "Wilt have one, child? Five hundred years is no bad bargain."

"My uncle has small trust in indulgences," she whispered.

"All lies, of course," quoth Hugh; "yet they've the Pope's seal, and I have more than half a mind to get one. Five hundred years is no joke, and I am sure of purgatory, since I bought this medal at the Holy House of Loretto."

And he went forward, and invested six groschen in one of the papers, the most religious action poor Christina had ever seen him perform. Other purchasers came forward—several, of the castle knappen, and a few peasant women who offered yarn or cheeses as equivalents for money, but were told with some insolence to go and sell their goods, and bring the coin.

The Dove in the Eagle's Nest

After a time, the friar, finding his traffic slack, thought fit to remove, with his two lay assistants, outside the chapel, and try the effects of an out-of-door sermon. Hugh Sorel, who had been hitherto rather diverted by the man's gestures and persuasions, now decided on going out into the fair in quest of an escort for his daughter, but as she saw Father Norbert and another monk ascending from the stairs leading to the hermit's cell, she begged to be allowed to remain in the church, where she was sure to be safe, instead of wandering about with him in the fair.

He was glad to be unencumbered, though he thought her taste unnatural; and, promising to return for her when he had found an escort, he left her.

Father Norbert had come for the very purpose of hearing confessions, and Christina's next hour was the most comfortable she had spent since Ermentrude's death.

After this however the priests were called away, and long, long did Christina first kneel and then sit in the little lonely church, hearing the various sounds without, and imagining that her father had forgotten her, and that he and all the rest were drinking, and then what would become of her? Why had she quitted old Ursel's protection?

Hours of waiting and nameless alarm must have passed, for the sun was waxing low, when at length she heard steps coming up the hermit's cell, and a head rose above the pavement which she recognized with a wild throb of joy, but, repressing her sense of gladness, she only exclaimed, "Oh, where is my father!"

"I have sent him to the toll at the Gemsbock's Pass," replied Sir Eberhard, who had by this time come up the stairs, followed by Brother Peter and the two lay assistants. Then, as Christina turned on him her startled, terrified eyes in dismay and reproach for such thoughtlessness, he came towards her, and, bending his head and opening his hand, he showed on his palm two gold rings. "There, little one," he said; "now shalt thou never again shut me out."

Her senses grew dizzy. "Sir," she faintly said, "this is no place to delude a poor maiden."

"I delude thee not. The brother here waits to wed us."

"Impossible! A burgher maid is not for such as you."

"None but a burgher maid will I wed," returned Sir Eberhard, with all the settled resolution of habits of command. "See, Christina, thou art sweeter and better than any lady in the land; thou canst make me what she—the blessed one who lies there—would have me. I love thee as never knight loved lady. I love thee so that I have not spoken a word to offend thee when my heart was bursting; and"—as he saw her irrepressible tears—"I think thou lovest me a little."

"Ah!" she gasped with a sob, "let me go."

"Thou canst not go home; there is none here fit to take charge of thee. Or if there were, I would slay him rather than let thee go. No, not so," he said, as he saw how little those words served his cause; "but without thee I were a mad and desperate man. Christina, I will not answer for myself if thou dost not leave this place my wedded wife."

"Oh!" implored Christina, "if you would only betroth me, and woo me like an honourable maiden from my home at Ulm!"

"Betroth thee, ay, and wed thee at once," replied Eberhard, who, all along, even while his words were most pleading, had worn a look and manner of determined authority and strength, good-natured indeed, but resolved. "I am not going to miss my opportunity, or baulk the friar."

The friar, who had meantime been making a few needful arrangements for the ceremony, advanced towards them. He was a good-humoured, easy-going man, who came prepared to do any office that came in his way on such festival days at the villages round; and peasant marriages at such times were not uncommon. But something now staggered him, and he said anxiously –

"This maiden looks convent-bred! Herr Reiter, pardon me; but if this be the breaking of a cloister, I can have none of it."

"No such thing," said Eberhard; "she is town-bred, that is all."

"You would swear to it, on the holy mass yonder, both of you?" said the friar, still suspiciously.

"Yea," replied Eberhard, "and so dost thou, Christina."

This was the time if ever to struggle against her destiny. The friar would probably have listened to her if she had made any vehement opposition to a forced marriage, and if not, a few shrieks would have brought perhaps Father Norbert, and certainly the whole population; but the horror and shame of being found in such a situation, even more than the probability that she might meet with vengeance rather than protection, withheld her. Even the friar could hardly have removed her, and this was her only chance of safety from the Baroness's fury. Had she hated and loathed Sir Eberhard, perhaps she had striven harder, but his whole demeanour constrained and quelled her, and the chief effort she made against yielding was the reply, "I am no cloister maid, holy father, but—"

The "but" was lost in the friar's jovial speech. "Oh, then, all is well! Take thy place, pretty one, there, by the door, thou know'st it should be in the porch, but—ach, I understand!" as Eberhard quietly drew the bolt within. "No, no, little one, I have no time for bride scruples and coyness; I have to train three dull-headed louts to be Shem, Ham, and Japhet before dark. Hast confessed of late?"

"This morning, but—" said Christina, and "This morning," to her great joy, said Eberhard, and, in her satisfaction thereat, her second "but" was not followed up.

The friar asked their names, and both gave the Christian name alone; then the brief and simple rite was solemnized in its shortest form. Christina had, by very force of surprise and dismay, gone through all without signs of agitation, except the quivering of her whole frame, and the icy coldness of the hand, where Eberhard had to place the ring on each finger in turn.

But each mutual vow was a strange relief to her long-tossed and divided mind, and it was rest indeed to let her affection have its will, and own him indeed as a protector to be loved instead of shunned. When all was over, and he gathered the two little cold hands into his large one, his arm supporting her trembling form, she felt for the moment, poor little thing, as if she could never be frightened again.

Parish registers were not, even had this been a parish church, but Brother Peter asked, when he had concluded, "Well, my son, which of his flock am I to report to your Pfarrer as linked together?"

"The less your tongue wags on that matter till I call on you, the better," was the stern reply. "Look you, no ill shall befall you if you are wise, but remember, against the day I call you to bear witness, that you have this day wedded Baron Eberhard von Adlerstein the younger, to Christina, the daughter of Hugh Sorel, the Esquire of Ulm."

"Thou hast played me a trick, Sir Baron!" said the friar, somewhat dismayed, but more amused, looking up at Eberhard, who, as Christina now saw, had divested himself of his gilt spurs, gold chain, silvered belt and horn, and eagle's plume, so as to have passed for a simple lanzknecht. "I would have had no such gear as this!"

"So I supposed," said Eberhard coolly.

"Young folks! young folks!" laughed the friar, changing his tone, and holding up his finger slyly; "the little bird so cunningly nestled in the church to fly out my Lady Baroness! Well, so thou hast a pretty, timid lambkin there, Sir Baron.

The Dove in the Eagle's Nest

Take care you use her mildly."

Eberhard looked into Christina's face with a smile, that to her, at least, was answer enough; and he held out half a dozen links of his gold chain to the friar, and tossed a coin to each of the lay brethren.

"Not for the poor friar himself," explained Brother Peter, on receiving this marriage fee; "it all goes to the weal of the brotherhood."

"As you please," said Eberhard. "Silence, that is all! And thy friary—?"

"The poor house of St. Francis at Offingen for the present, noble sir," said the priest. "There will you hear of me, if you find me not. And now, fare thee well, my gracious lady. I hope one day thou wilt have more words to thank the poor brother who has made thee a noble Baroness."

"Ah, good father, pardon my fright and confusion," Christina tried to murmur, but at that moment a sudden glow and glare of light broke out on the eastern rock, illuminating the fast darkening little church with a flickering glare, that made her start in terror as if the fires of heaven were threatening this stolen marriage; but the friar and Eberhard both exclaimed, "The Needfire alight already!" And she recollected how often she had seen these bonfires on Midsummer night shining red on every hill around Ulm. Loud shouts were greeting the uprising flame, and the people gathering thicker and thicker on the slope. The friar undid the door to hasten out into the throng, and Eberhard said he had left his spurs and belt in the hermit's cell, and must return thither, after which he would walk home with his bride, moving at the same time towards the stair, and thereby causing a sudden scuffle and fall. "So, master hermit," quoth Eberhard, as the old man picked himself up, looking horribly frightened; "that's your hermit's abstraction, is it? No whining, old man, I am not going to hurt thee, so thou canst hold thy tongue. Otherwise I will smoke thee out of thy hole like a wild cat! What, thou aiding me with my belt, my lovely one? Thanks; the snap goes too hard for thy little hands. Now, then, the fire will light us gaily down the mountain side."

But it soon appeared that to depart was impossible, unless by forcing a way through the busy throng in the full red glare of the firelight, and they were forced to pause at the opening of the hermit's cave, Christina leaning on her husband's arm, and a fold of his mantle drawn round her to guard her from the night-breeze of the mountain, as they waited for a quiet space in which to depart unnoticed. It was a strange, wild scene! The fire was on a bare, flat rock, which probably had been yearly so employed ever since the Kelts had brought from the East the rite that they had handed on to the Swabians—the Beltane fire, whose like was blazing everywhere in the Alps, in the Hartz, nay, even in England, Scotland, and on the granite points of Ireland. Heaped up for many previous days with faggots from the forest, then apparently inexhaustible, the fire roared and crackled, and rose high, red and smoky, into the air, paling the moon, and obscuring the stars. Round it, completely hiding the bonfire itself, were hosts of dark figures swarming to approach it—all with a purpose. All held old shoes or superannuated garments in their hands to feed the flame; for it was esteemed needful that every villager should contribute something from his house—once, no doubt, as an offering to Bel, but now as a mere unmeaning observance. And shrieks of merriment followed the contribution of each too well-known article of rubbish that had been in reserve for the Needfire! Girls and boys had nuts to throw in, in pairs, to judge by their bounces of future chances of matrimony. Then came a shouting, tittering, and falling back, as an old boor came forward like a priest with something heavy and ghastly in his arms, which was thrown on with a tremendous shout, darkened the glow for a moment, then hissed, cracked, and emitted a horrible odour.

It was a horse's head, the right owner of which had been carefully kept for the occasion, though long past work. Christina shuddered, and felt as if she had fallen upon a Pagan ceremony; as indeed was true enough, only that the Adlersteiners attached no meaning to the performance, except a vague notion of securing good luck.

With the same idea the faggots were pulled down, and arranged so as to form a sort of lane of fire. Young men rushed along it, and then bounded over the diminished pile, amid loud shouts of laughter and either admiration or derision; and, in the meantime, a variety of odd, recusant noises, grunts, squeaks, and lowings proceeding from the darkness were explained to the startled little bride by her husband to come from all the cattle of the mountain farms around, who were to have their weal secured by being driven through the Needfire.

It may well be imagined that the animals were less convinced of the necessity of this performance than their masters. Wonderful was the clatter and confusion, horrible the uproar raised behind to make the poor things proceed at all, desperate the shout when some half- frantic creature kicked or attempted a charge wild the glee when a persecuted goat or sheep took heart of grace, and flashed for one moment between the crackling, flaring, smoking walls. When one cow or sheep off a farm went, all the others were pretty sure to follow it, and the owner had then only to be on the watch at the other end to turn them back, with their flame-dazzled eyes, from going unawares down the precipice, a fate from which the passing through the fire was evidently not supposed to ensure them. The swine, those special German delights, were of course the most refractory of all. Some, by dint of being pulled away from the lane of fire, were induced to rush through it; but about half-way they generally made a bolt, either sidelong through the flaming fence or backwards among the legs of their persecutors, who were upset amid loud imprecations. One huge, old, lean, high-backed sow, with a large family, truly feminine in her want of presence of mind, actually charged into the midst of the bonfire itself, scattering it to the right and left with her snout, and emitting so horrible a smell of singed bacon, that it might almost be feared that some of her progeny were anticipating the invention of Chinese roasting-pigs. However, their proprietor, Jobst, counted them out all safe on the other side, and there only resulted some sighs and lamentations among the seniors, such as Hatto and Ursel, that it boded ill to have the Needfire trodden out by an old sow.

All the castle live-stock were undergoing the same ceremony. Eberhard concerned himself little about the vagaries of the sheep and pigs, and only laughed a little as the great black goat, who had seen several Midsummer nights, and stood on his guard, made a sudden short run and butted down old Hatto, then skipped off like a chamois into the darkness, unheeding, the old rogue, the whispers that connected his unlucky hue with the doings of the Walpurgisnacht. But when it came to the horses, Eberhard could not well endure the sight of the endeavours to force them, snorting, rearing, and struggling, through anything so abhorrent to them as the hedge of fire.

The Schneiderlein, with all the force of his powerful arm, had hold of Eberhard's own young white mare, who, with ears turned back, nostrils dilated, and wild eyes, her fore-feet firmly planted wide apart, was using her whole strength for resistance; and, when a heavy blow fell on her, only plunged backwards, and kicked without advancing. It was more than Eberhard could endure, and Christina's impulse was to murmur, "O do not let him do it;" but this he scarcely heard, as he exclaimed, "Wait for me here!" and, as he stepped forward, sent his voice before him, forbidding all blows to the mare.

The creature's extreme terror ceased at once upon hearing his voice, and there was an instant relaxation of all violence of resistance as he came up to her, took her halter from the Schneiderlein, patted her glossy neck, and spoke to her. But the tumult of warning voices around him assured him that it would be a fatal thing to spare the steed the passage through the fire, and he strove by encouragements and caresses with voice and hand to get her forward, leading her himself; but the poor beast trembled so violently, and, though making a few steps forward, stopped again in such exceeding horror of the flame, that Eberhard had not the heart to compel her, turned her head away, and assured her that she should not be further tormented.

"The gracious lordship is wrong," said public opinion, by the voice of old Bauer Ulrich, the sacrificer of the horse's head. "Heaven forfend that evil befall him and that mare in the course of the year."

And the buzz of voices concurred in telling of the recusant pigs who had never developed into sausages, the sheep who had only escaped to be eaten by wolves, the mule whose bones had been found at the bottom of an abyss.

Old Ursel was seriously concerned, and would have laid hold on her young master to remonstrate, but a fresh notion had arisen—Would the gracious Freiherr set a-rolling the wheel, which was already being lighted in the fire, and was to conclude the festivities by being propelled down the hill—figuring, only that no one present knew it, the sun's declension from his solstitial height? Eberhard made no objection; and Christina, in her shelter by the cave, felt no little dismay at being left alone there, and moreover had a strange, weird feeling at the wild, uncanny ceremony he was engaged in, not knowing indeed that it was sun-worship, but afraid that it could be no other than unholy sorcery.

The wheel, flaring or reddening in all its spokes, was raised from the bonfire, and was driven down the smoothest piece of green sward, which formed an inclined plane towards the stream. If its course was smooth, and it only became extinguished by leaping into the water, the village would flourish; and prosperity above all was expected if it should spring over the narrow channel, and attempt to run up the other side. Such things had happened in the days of the good Freiherren Ebbo and Friedel, though the wheel had never gone right since the present baron had been excommunicated; but his heir having been twice seen at mass in this last month great hopes were founded upon him.

There was a shout to clear the slope. Eberhard, in great earnest and some anxiety, accepted the gauntlet that he was offered to protect his hand, steadied the wheel therewith, and, with a vigorous impulse from hand and foot, sent it bounding down the slope, among loud cries and a general scattering of the idlers who had crowded full into the very path of the fiery circle, which flamed up brilliantly for the moment as it met the current of air. But either there was an obstacle in the way, or the young Baron's push had not been quite straight: the wheel suddenly swerved aside, its course swerved to the right, maugre all the objurgations addressed to it as if it had been a living thing, and the next moment it had disappeared, all but a smoky, smouldering spot of red, that told where it lay, charring and smoking on its side, without having fulfilled a quarter of its course.

People drew off gravely and silently, and Eberhard himself was strangely discomfited when he came back to the hermitage, and, wrapping Christina in his cloak, prepared to return, so soon as the glare of the fire should have faded from his eyesight enough to make it safe to tread so precipitous a path. He had indeed this day made a dangerous venture, and both he and Christina could not but feel disheartened by the issue of all the omens of the year, the more because she had a vague sense of wrong in consulting or trusting them. It seemed to her all one frightened, uncomprehended dream ever since her father had left her in the chapel; and, though conscious of her inability to have prevented her marriage, yet she blamed herself, felt despairing as she thought of the future, and, above all, dreaded the Baron and the Baroness and their anger. Eberhard, after his first few words, was silent, and seemed solely absorbed in leading her safely along the rocky path, sometimes lifting her when he thought her in danger of stumbling. It was one of the lightest, shortest nights of the year, and a young moon added to the brightness in open places, while in others it made the rocks and stones cast strange elvish shadows. The distance was not entirely lost; other Beltane fires could be seen, like beacons, on every hill, and the few lights in the castle shone out like red fiery eyes in its heavy dark pile of building.

Before entering, Eberhard paused, pulled off his own wedding-ring, and put it into his bosom, and taking his bride's hand in his, did the same for her, and bade her keep the ring till they could wear them openly.

"Alas! then," said Christina, "you would have this secret?"

"Unless I would have to seek thee down the oubliette, my little one," said Eberhard "or, what might even be worse, see thee burnt on the hillside for bewitching me with thine arts! No, indeed, my darling. Were it only my father, I could make him love thee; but my mother—I could not trust her where she thought the honour of our house concerned. It shall not be for long. Thou know'st we are to make peace with the Kaiser, and then will I get me employment among Kurfurst Albrecht's companies of troops, and then shalt thou prank it as my Lady Freiherrinn, and teach me the ways of cities."

"Alas! I fear me it has been a great sin!" sighed the poor little wife.

"For thee—thou couldst not help it," said Eberhard; "for me—who knows how many deadly ones it may hinder? Cheer up, little one; no one can harm thee while the secret is kept."

Poor Christina had no choice but submission; but it was a sorry bridal evening, to enter her husband's home in shrinking terror; with the threat of the oubliette before her, and with a sense of shame and deception hanging upon her, making the wonted scowl of the old baroness cut her both with remorse and dread.

She did indeed sit beside her bridegroom at the supper, but how little like a bride! even though he pushed the salt-cellar, as if by accident, below her place. She thought of her myrtle, tended in vain at home by Barbara Schmidt; she thought of Ulm courtships, and how all ought to have been; the solemn embassage to her uncle, the stately negotiations; the troth plight before the circle of ceremonious kindred and merry maidens, of whom she had often been one—the subsequent attentions of the betrothed on all festival days, the piles of linen and all plenishings accumulated since babyhood, and all reviewed and laid out for general admiration (Ah! poor Aunt Johanna still spinning away to add to the many webs in her walnut presses!)—then the grand procession to fetch home the bride, the splendid festival with the musicians, dishes, and guest-tables to the utmost limit that was allowed by the city laws, and the bride's hair so joyously covered by her matron's curch amid the merriment of her companion maidens.

Poor child! After she had crept away to her own room, glad that her father was not yet returned, she wept bitterly over the wrong that she felt she had done to the kind uncle and aunt, who must now look in vain for their little Christina, and would think her lost to them, and to all else that was good. At least she had had the Church's blessing—but that, strange to say, was regarded, in burgher life before the Reformation, as rather the ornament of a noble marriage than as essential to the civil contract; and a marriage by a priest was regarded by the citizens rather as a means of eluding the need of obtaining the parent's consent, than as a more regular and devout manner of wedding. However, Christina felt this the one drop of peace. The blessings and prayers were warm at her heart, and gave her hope. And as to drops of joy, of them there was no lack, for had not she now a right to love Eberhard with all her heart and conscience, and was not it a wonderful love on his part that had made him stoop to the little white-faced burgher maid, despised even by her own father? O better far to wear the maiden's uncovered head for him than the myrtle wreath for any one else!

CHAPTER VII: THE SCHNEIDERLEIN'S RETURN

The poor little unowned bride had more to undergo than her imagination had conceived at the first moment.

When she heard that the marriage was to be a secret, she had not understood that Eberhard was by no means disposed to observe much more caution than mere silence. A rough, though kindly man, he did not thoroughly comprehend the shame and confusion that he was bringing upon her by departing from his former demeanour. He knew that, so enormous was the distance then supposed to exist between the noble and the burgher, there was no chance of any one dreaming of the true state of the case, and that as long as Christina was not taken for his wife, there was no personal danger for her from his mother, who—so lax were the morals of the German nobility with regard to all of inferior rank—would tolerate her with complacency as his favourite toy; and he was taken by surprise at the agony of grief and shame with which she slowly comprehended his assurance that she had nothing to fear.

There was no help for it. The oubliette would probably be the portion of the low-born girl who had interfered with the sixteen quarterings of the Adlerstein shield, and poor Christina never stepped across its trap-door without a shudder lest it should open beneath her. And her father would probably have been hung from the highest tower, in spite of his shrewd care to be aware of nothing. Christina consoled herself with the hope that he knew all the time why he had been sent out of the way, for, with a broad grin that had made her blush painfully, he had said he knew she would be well taken care of, and that he hoped she was not breaking her heart for want of an escort. She tried to extort Eberhard's permission to let him at least know how it was; but Eberhard laughed, saying he believed the old fox knew just as much as he chose; and, in effect, Sorel, though now and then gratifying his daughter's scruples, by serving as a shield to her meetings with the young Baron, never allowed himself to hear a hint of the true state of affairs.

Eberhard's love and reverence were undiminished, and the time spent with him would have been perfectly happy could she ever have divested herself of anxiety and alarm; but the periods of his absence from the castle were very terrible to her, for the other women of the household, quick to perceive that she no longer repelled him, had lost that awe that had hitherto kept them at a distance from her, and treated her with a familiarity, sometimes coarse, sometimes spiteful, always hateful and degrading. Even old Ursel had become half-pitying, half-patronizing; and the old Baroness, though not molesting her, took not the slightest notice of her.

The Dove in the Eagle's Nest

This state of things lasted much longer than there had been reason to expect at the time of the marriage. The two Freiherren then intended to set out in a very short time to make their long talked-of submission to the Emperor at Ratisbon; but, partly from their German tardiness of movement, partly from the obstinate delays interposed by the proud old Freiherrinn, who was as averse as ever to the measure, partly from reports that the Court was not yet arrived at Ratisbon, the expedition was again and again deferred, and did not actually take place till September was far advanced.

Poor Christina would have given worlds to go with them, and even entreated to be sent to Ulm with an avowal of her marriage to her uncle and aunt, but of this Eberhard would not hear. He said the Ulmers would thus gain an hostage, and hamper his movements; and, if her wedding was not to be confessed—poor child!—she could better bear to remain where she was than to face Hausfrau Johanna. Eberhard was fully determined to enrol himself in some troop, either Imperial, or, if not, among the Free Companies, among whom men of rank were often found, and he would then fetch or send for his wife and avow her openly, so soon as she should be out of his mother's reach. He longed to leave her father at home, to be some protection to her, but Hugh Sorel was so much the most intelligent and skilful of the retainers as to be absolutely indispensable to the party—he was their only scribe; and moreover his new suit of buff rendered him a creditable member of a troop that had been very hard to equip. It numbered about ten men-at-arms, only three being left at home to garrison the castle—namely, Hatto, who was too old to take; Hans, who had been hopelessly lame and deformed since the old Baron had knocked him off a cliff in a passion; and Squinting Matz, a runaway servant, who had murdered his master, the mayor of Strasburg, and might be caught and put to death if any one recognized him. If needful the villagers could always be called in to defend the castle: but of this there was little or no danger—the Eagle's Steps were defence enough in themselves, and the party were not likely to be absent more than a week or ten days—a grievous length of time, poor Christina thought, as she stood straining her eyes on the top of the watch-tower, to watch them as far as possible along the plain. Her heart was very sad, and the omen of the burning wheel so continually haunted her that even in her sleep that night she saw its brief course repeated, beheld its rapid fall and extinction, and then tracked the course of the sparks that darted from it, one rising and gleaming high in air till it shone like a star, another pursuing a fitful and irregular, but still bright course amid the dry grass on the hillside, just as she had indeed watched some of the sparks on that night, minding her of the words of the Allhallow-tide legend: "Fulgebunt justi et tanquam scintillae in arundinete discurrent"—a sentence which remained with her when awake, and led her to seek it out in her Latin Bible in the morning.

Reluctantly had she gone down to the noontide meal, feeling, though her husband and father were far less of guardians than they should have been, yet that there was absolute rest, peace, and protection in their presence compared with what it was to be alone with Freiherrinn Kunigunde and her rude women without them. A few sneers on her daintiness and uselessness had led her to make an offer of assisting in the grand chopping of sausage meat and preparation of winter stores, and she had been answered with contempt that my young lord would not have her soil her delicate hands, when one of the maids who had been sent to fetch beer from the cellar came back with startled looks, and the exclamation, "There is the Schneiderlein riding up the Eagle's Ladder upon Freiherr Ebbo's white mare!"

All the women sprang up together, and rushed to the window, whence they could indeed recognize both man and horse; and presently it became plain that both were stained with blood, weary, and spent; indeed, nothing but extreme exhaustion would have induced the man-at-arms to trust the tired, stumbling horse up such a perilous path.

Loud were the exclamations, "Ah! no good could come of not leading that mare through the Johannisfeuer."

"This shameful expedition! Only harm could befall. This is thy doing, thou mincing city-girl."

"All was certain to go wrong when a pale mist widow came into the place."

The angry and dismayed cries all blended themselves in confusion in the ears of the only silent woman present; the only one that sounded distinctly on her brain was that of the last speaker, "A pale, mist widow," as, holding herself a little in the rear of the struggling, jostling little mob of women, who hardly made way even for their acknowledged lady, she followed with failing limbs the universal rush to the entrance as soon as man and horse had mounted the slope and were lost sight of.

The Dove in the Eagle's Nest

A few moments more, and the throng of expectants was at the foot of the hall steps, just as the lanzknecht reached the arched entrance. His comrade Hans took his bridle, and almost lifted him from his horse; he reeled and stumbled as, pale, battered, and bleeding, he tried to advance to Freiherinn Kunigunde, and, in answer to her hasty interrogation, faltered out, "Ill news, gracious lady. We have been set upon by the accursed Schlangenwaldern, and I am the only living man left."

Christina scarce heard even these last words; senses and powers alike failed her, and she sank back on the stone steps in a deathlike swoon.

When she came to herself she was lying on her bed, Ursel and Else, another of the women, busy over her, and Ursel's voice was saying, "Ah, she is coming round. Look up, sweet lady, and fear not. You are our gracious Lady Baroness."

"Is he here? O, has he said so? O, let me see him—Sir Eberhard," faintly cried Christina with sobbing breath.

"Ah, no, no," said the old woman; "but see here," and she lifted up Christina's powerless, bloodless hand, and showed her the ring on the finger. Her bosom had been evidently searched when her dress was loosened in her swoon, and her ring found and put in its place. "There, you can hold up your head with the best of them; he took care of that—my dear young Freiherr, the boy that I nursed," and the old woman's burst of tears brought back the truth to Christina's s reviving senses.

"Oh, tell me," she said, trying to raise herself, "was it indeed so? O say it was not as he said!"

"Ah, woe's me, woe's me, that it was even so," lamented Ursel; "but oh, be still, look not so wild, dear lady. The dear, true-hearted young lord, he spent his last breath in owning you for his true lady, and in bidding us cherish you and our young baron that is to be. And the gracious lady below—she owns you; there is no fear of her now; so vex not yourself, dearest, most gracious lady."

Christina did not break out into the wailing and weeping that the old nurse expected; she was still far too much stunned and overwhelmed, and she entreated to be told all, lying still, but gazing at Ursel with piteous bewildered eyes. Ursel and Else helping one another out, tried to tell her, but they were much confused; all they knew was that the party had been surprised at night in a village hostel by the Schlangenwaldern, and all slain, though the young Baron had lived long enough to charge the Schneiderlein with his commendation of his wife to his mother; but all particulars had been lost in the general confusion.

"Oh, let me see the Schneiderlein," implored Christina, by this time able to rise and cross the room to the large carved chair; and Ursel immediately turned to her underling, saying, "Tell the Schneiderlein that the gracious Lady Baroness desires his presence."

Else's wooden shoes clattered down stairs, but the next moment she returned. "He cannot come; he is quite spent, and he will let no one touch his arm till Ursel can come, not even to get off his doublet."

"I will go to him," said Christina, and, revived by the sense of being wanted, she moved at once to the turret, where she kept some rag and some ointment, which she had found needful in the latter stages of Ermentrude's illness—indeed, household surgery was a part of regular female education, and Christina had had plenty of practice in helping her charitable aunt, so that the superiority of her skill to that of Ursel had long been avowed in the castle. Ursel made no objection further than to look for something that could be at once converted into a widow's veil—being in the midst of her grief quite alive to the need that no matronly badge should be omitted—but nothing came to hand in time, and Christina was descending the stairs, on her way to the kitchen, where she found the fugitive man- at-arms seated on a rough settle, his head and wounded arm resting on the table, while groans of pain, weariness, and impatience were interspersed with imprecations on the stupid awkward girls who surrounded him.

Pity and the instinct of affording relief must needs take the precedence even of the desire to hear of her husband's fate; and, as the girls hastily whispered, "Here she is," and the lanzknecht hastily tried to gather himself up, and rise with tokens of respect; she bade him remain still, and let her see what she could do for him. In fact, she at once perceived that he was in no condition to give a coherent account of anything, he was so completely worn out, and in so much suffering. She bade at once that some water should be heated, and some of the broth of the dinner set on the fire; then with the shears at her girdle, and her soft, light fingers, she removed the torn strip of cloth that had been wound round the arm, and cut away the sleeve, showing the arm not broken, but gashed at the shoulder, and thence the whole length grazed and wounded by the descent of the sword down to the wrist. So tender was her touch, that he scarcely winced or moaned under her hand; and, when she proceeded, with Ursel's help, to bathe the wound with the warm water, the relief was such that the wearied man absolutely slumbered during the process, which Christina protracted on that very account. She then dressed and bandaged the arm, and proceeded to skim—as no one else in the castle would do—the basin of soup, with which she then fed her patient as he leant back in the corner of the settle, at first in the same somnolent, half-conscious state in which he had been ever since the relief from the severe pain; but after a few spoonfuls the light and life came back to his eye, and he broke out, "Thanks, thanks, gracious lady! This is the Lady Baroness for me! My young lord was the only wise man! Thanks, lady; now am I my own man again. It had been long ere the old Freiherrinn had done so much for me! I am your man, lady, for life or death!" And, before she knew what he was about, the gigantic Schneiderlein had slid down on his knees, seized her hand, and kissed it—the first act of homage to her rank, but most startling and distressing to her. "Nay," she faltered, "prithee do not; thou must rest. Only if—if thou canst only tell me if he, my own dear lord, sent me any greeting, I would wait to hear the rest till thou hast slept."

"Ah! the dog of Schlangenwald!" was the first answer; then, as he continued, "You see, lady, we had ridden merrily as far as Jacob Muller's hostel, the traitor," it became plain that he meant to begin at the beginning. She allowed Ursel to seat her on the bench opposite to his settle, and, leaning forward, heard his narrative like one in a dream. There, the Schneiderlein proceeded to say, they put up for the night, entirely unsuspicious of evil; Jacob Muller, who was known to himself, as well as to Sorel and to the others, assuring them that the way was clear to Ratisbon, and that he heard the Emperor was most favourably disposed to any noble who would tender his allegiance. Jacob's liquors were brought out, and were still in course of being enjoyed, when the house was suddenly surrounded by an overpowering number of the retainers of Schlangenwald, with their Count himself at their head. He had been evidently resolved to prevent the timely submission of the enemies of his race, and suddenly presenting himself before the elder Baron, had challenged him to instantaneous battle, claiming credit to himself for not having surprised them when asleep. The disadvantage had been scarcely less than if this had been the case, for the Adlersteinern were all half-intoxicated, and far inferior in numbers—at least, on the showing of the Schneiderlein—and a desperate fight had ended by his being flung aside in a corner, bound fast by the ankles and wrists, the only living prisoner, except his young lord, who, having several terrible wounds, the worst in his chest, was left unbound.

Both lay helpless, untended, and silent, while the revel that had been so fatal to them was renewed by their captors, who finally all sunk into a heavy sleep. The torches were not all spent, and the moonlight shone into the room, when the Schneiderlein, desperate from the agony caused by the ligature round his wounded arm, sat up and looked about him. A knife thrown aside by one of the drunkards lay near enough to be grasped by his bound hands, and he had just reached it when Sir Eberhard made a sign to him to put it into his hand, and therewith contrived to cut the rope round both hands and feet—then pointed to the door.

There was nothing to hinder an escape; the men slept the sleep of the drunken; but the Schneiderlein, with the rough fidelity of a retainer, would have lingered with a hope of saving his master. But Eberhard shook his head, and signed again to escape; then, making him bend down close to him, he used all his remaining power to whisper, as he pressed his sword into the retainer's hand, –

"Go home; tell my mother—all the world—that Christina Sorel is my wife, wedded on the Friedmund Wake by Friar Peter of Offingen, and if she should bear a child, he is my true and lawful heir. My sword for him—my love to her. And if my mother would not be haunted by me, let her take care of her."

These words were spoken with extreme difficulty, for the nature of the wound made utterance nearly impossible, and each broken sentence cost a terrible effusion of blood. The final words brought on so choking and fatal a gush that, said the

Schneiderlein, "he fell back as I tried to hold him up, and I saw that it was all at an end, and a kind and friendly master and lord gone from me. I laid him down, and put his cross on his breast that I had seen him kissing many a time that evening; and I crossed his hands, and wiped the blood from them and his face. And, lady, he had put on his ring; I trust the robber caitiff's may have left it to him in his grave. And so I came forth, walking soft, and opening the door in no small dread, not of the snoring swine, but of the dogs without. But happily they were still, and even by the door I saw all our poor fellows stark and stiff."

"My father?" asked Christina.

"Ay! with his head cleft open by the Graf himself. He died like a true soldier, lady, and we have lost the best head among us in him. Well, the knave that should have watched the horses was as drunken as the rest of them, and I made a shift to put the bridle on the white mare and ride off."

Such was the narrative of the Schneiderlein, and all that was left to Christina was the picture of her husband's dying effort to guard her, and the haunting fancy of those long hours of speechless agony on the floor of the hostel, and how direful must have been his fears for her. Sad and overcome, yet not sinking entirely while any work of comfort remained, her heart yearned over her companion in misfortune, the mother who had lost both husband and son; and all her fears of the dread Freiherrinn could not prevent her from bending her steps, trembling and palpitating as she was, towards the hall, to try whether the daughter-in-law's right might be vouchsafed to her, of weeping with the elder sufferer.

The Freiherrinn sat by the chimney, rocking herself to and fro, and holding consultation with Hatto. She started as she saw Christina approaching, and made a gesture of repulsion; but, with the feeling of being past all terror in this desolate moment, Christina stepped nearer, knelt, and, clasping her hands, said, "Your pardon, lady."

"Pardon!" returned the harsh voice, even harsher for very grief, "thou hast naught to fear, girl. As things stand, thou canst not have thy deserts. Dost hear?"

"Ah, lady, it was not such pardon that I meant. If you would let me be a daughter to you."

"A daughter! A wood-carver's girl to be a daughter of Adlerstein!" half laughed the grim Baroness. "Come here, wench," and Christina underwent a series of sharp searching questions on the evidences of her marriage.

"So," ended the old lady, "since better may not be, we must own thee for the nonce. Hark ye all, this is the Frau Freiherrinn, Freiherr Eberhard's widow, to be honoured as such," she added, raising her voice. "There, girl, thou hast what thou didst strive for. Is not that enough?"

"Alas! lady," said Christina, her eyes swimming in tears, "I would fain have striven to be a comforter, or to weep together."

"What! to bewitch me as thou didst my poor son and daughter, and well-nigh my lord himself! Girl! Girl! Thou know'st I cannot burn thee now; but away with thee; try not my patience too far."

And, more desolate than ever, the crushed and broken-hearted Christina, a widow before she had been owned a wife, returned to the room that was now so full of memories as to be even more home than Master Gottfried's gallery at Ulm.

CHAPTER VIII: PASSING THE OUBLIETTE

Who can describe the dreariness of being snowed-up all the winter with such a mother-in-law as Freiherrinn Kunigunde?

The Dove in the Eagle's Nest

Yet it was well that the snow came early, for it was the best defence of the lonely castle from any attack on the part of the Schlangenwaldern, the Swabian League, or the next heir, Freiherr Kasimir von Adlerstein Wildschloss. The elder Baroness had, at least, the merit of a stout heart, and, even with her sadly-reduced garrison, feared none of them. She had been brought up in the faith that Adlerstein was impregnable, and so she still believed; and, if the disaster that had cut off her husband and son was to happen at all, she was glad that it had befallen before the homage had been paid. Probably the Schlangenwald Count knew how tough a morsel the castle was like to prove, and Wildschloss was serving at a distance, for nothing was heard of either during the short interval while the roads were still open. During this time an attempt had been made through Father Norbert to ascertain what had become of the corpses of the two Barons and their followers, and it had appeared that the Count had carried them all off from the inn, no doubt to adorn his castle with their limbs, or to present them to the Emperor in evidence of his zeal for order. The old Baron could not indeed have been buried in consecrated ground, nor have masses said for him; but for the weal of her son's soul Dame Kunigunde gave some of her few ornaments, and Christina added her gold earrings, and all her scanty purse, that both her husband and father might be joined in the prayers of the Church—trying with all her might to put confidence in Hugh Sorel's Loretto relic, and the Indulgence he had bought, and trusting with more consolatory thoughts to the ever stronger dawnings of good she had watched in her own Eberhard.

She had some consoling intercourse with the priest while all this was pending; but throughout the winter she was entirely cut off from every creature save the inmates of the castle, where, as far as the old lady was concerned, she only existed on sufferance, and all her meekness and gentleness could not win for her more than the barest toleration.

That Eberhard had for a few hours survived his father, and that thus the Freiherrinn Christina was as much the Dowager Baroness as Kunigunde herself, was often insisted on in the kitchen by Ursel, Hatto, and the Schneiderlein, whom Christina had unconsciously rendered her most devoted servant, not only by her daily care of his wound, but by her kind courteous words, and by her giving him his proper name of Heinz, dropping the absurd nom de guerre of the Schneiderlein, or little tailor, which had been originally conferred on him in allusion to the valiant Tailorling who boasted of having killed seven flies at a blow, and had been carried on chiefly because of the contradiction between such a title and his huge brawny strength and fierce courage. Poor Eberhard, with his undaunted bravery and free reckless good-nature, a ruffian far more by education than by nature, had been much loved by his followers. His widow would have reaped the benefit of that affection even if her exceeding sweetness had not gained it on her own account; and this giant was completely gained over to her, when, amid all her sorrow and feebleness, she never failed to minister to his sufferings to the utmost, while her questions about his original home, and revival of the name of his childhood, softened him, and awoke in him better feelings. He would have died to serve her, and she might have headed an opposition party in the castle, had she not been quite indifferent to all save her grief; and, except by sitting above the salt at the empty table, she laid no claim to any honours or authority, and was more seldom than ever seen beyond what was now called her own room.

At last, when for the second time she was seeing the snow wreaths dwindle, and the drops shine forth in moisture again, while the mountain paths were set free by the might of the springtide sun, she spoke almost for the first time with authority, as she desired Heinz to saddle her mule, and escort her to join in the Easter mass at the Blessed Friedmund's Chapel. Ursel heaped up objections; but so urgent was Christina for confession and for mass, that the old woman had not the heart to stop her by a warning to the elder Baroness, and took the alternative of accompanying her. It was a glorious sparkling Easter Day, lovely blue sky above, herbage and flowers glistening below, snow dazzling in the hollows, peasants assembling in holiday garb, and all rejoicing. Even the lonely widow, in her heavy veil and black mufflings, took hope back to her heart, and smiled when at the church door a little child came timidly up to her with a madder-tinted Easter egg—a gift once again like the happy home customs of Ulm. She gave the child a kiss—she had nothing else to give, but the sweet face sent it away strangely glad.

The festival mass in all its exultation was not fully over, when anxious faces began to be seen at the door, and whisperings went round and many passed out. Nobody at Adlerstein was particular about silence in church, and, when the service was not in progress, voices were not even lowered, and, after many attempts on the part of the Schneiderlein to attract the attention of his mistress, his voice immediately succeeded the Ite missa est, "Gracious lady, we must begone. Your mule is ready. There is a party at the Debateable Ford, whether Schlangenwald or Wildschloss we know not yet, but either way you must be the first thing placed in safety."

Christina turned deadly pale. She had long been ready to welcome death as a peaceful friend; but, sheltered as her girlhood had been in the quiet city, she had never been brought in contact with warfare, and her nervous, timid temperament made the thought most appalling and frightful to her, certain as she was that the old Baroness would resist to the uttermost. Father Norbert saw her extreme terror, and, with the thought that he might comfort and support her, perhaps mediate between the contending parties, plead that it was holy-tide, and proclaim the peace of the church, or at the worst protect the lady herself, he offered his company; but, though she thanked him, it was as if she scarcely understood his kindness, and a shudder passed over her whenever the serfs, hastily summoned to augment the garrison, came hurrying down the path, or turned aside into the more rugged and shorter descents. It was strange, the good father thought, that so timorous and fragile a being should have her lot cast amid these rugged places and scenes of violence, with no one to give her the care and cherishing she so much required.

Even when she crept up the castle stairs, she was met with an angry rebuke, not so much for the peril she had incurred as for having taken away the Schneiderlein, by far the most availing among the scanty remnant of the retainers of Adlerstein. Attempting no answer, and not even daring to ask from what quarter came the alarm, Christina made her way out of the turmoil to that chamber of her own, the scene of so much fear and sorrow, and yet of some share of peace and happiness. But from the window, near the fast subsiding waters of the Debateable Ford, could plainly be seen the small troop of warriors, of whom Jobst the Kohler had brought immediate intelligence. The sun glistened on their armour, and a banner floated gaily on the wind; but they were a fearful sight to the inmates of the lonely castle.

A stout heart was however Kunigunde's best endowment; and, with the steadiness and precision of a general, her commands rang out, as she arranged and armed her garrison, perfectly resolved against any submission, and confident in the strength of her castle; nay, not without a hope of revenge either against Schlangenwald or Wildschloss, whom, as a degenerate Adlerstein, she hated only less than the slayer of her husband and son.

The afternoon of Easter Day however passed away without any movement on the part of the enemy, and it was not till the following day that they could be seen struggling through the ford, and preparing to ascend the mountain. Attacks had sometimes been disconcerted by posting men in the most dangerous passes; but, in the lack of numbers, and of trustworthy commanders, the Freiherrinn had judged it wiser to trust entirely to her walls, and keep her whole force within them.

The new comers could hardly have had any hostile intentions, for, though well armed and accoutred, their numbers did not exceed twenty- five. The banner borne at their head was an azure one, with a white eagle, and their leader could be observed looking with amazement at the top of the watch-tower, where the same eagle had that morning been hoisted for the first time since the fall of the two Freiherren.

So soon as the ascent had been made, the leader wound his horn, and, before the echoes had died away among the hills, Hatto, acting as seneschal, was demanding his purpose.

"I am Kasimir von Adlerstein Wildschloss," was the reply. "I have hitherto been hindered by stress of weather from coming to take possession of my inheritance. Admit me, that I may arrange with the widowed Frau Freiherrinn as to her dower and residence."

"The widowed Frau Freiherrinn, born of Adlerstein," returned Hatto, "thanks the Freiherr von Adlerstein Wildschloss; but she holds the castle as guardian to the present head of the family, the Freiherr von Adlerstein."

"It is false, old man," exclaimed the Wildschloss; "the Freiherr had no other son."

"No," said Hatto, "but Freiherr Eberhard hath left us twin heirs, our young lords, for whom we hold this castle."

The Dove in the Eagle's Nest

"This trifling will not serve!" sternly spoke the knight. "Eberhard von Adlerstein died unmarried."

"Not so," returned Hatto, "our gracious Frau Freiherrinn, the younger, was wedded to him at the last Friedmund Wake, by the special blessing of our good patron, who would not see our house extinct."

"I must see thy lady, old man," said Sir Kasimir, impatiently, not in the least crediting the story, and believing his cousin Kunigunde quite capable of any measure that could preserve to her the rule in Schloss Adlerstein, even to erecting some passing love affair of her son's into a marriage. And he hardly did her injustice, for she had never made any inquiry beyond the castle into the validity of Christina's espousals, nor sought after the friar who had performed the ceremony. She consented to an interview with the claimant of the inheritance, and descended to the gateway for the purpose. The court was at its cleanest, the thawing snow having newly washed away its impurities, and her proud figure, under her black hood and veil, made an imposing appearance as she stood tall and defiant in the archway.

Sir Kasimir was a handsome man of about thirty, of partly Polish descent, and endowed with Slavonic grace and courtesy, and he had likewise been employed in negotiations with Burgundy, and had acquired much polish and knowledge of the world.

"Lady," he said, "I regret to disturb and intrude on a mourning family, but I am much amazed at the tidings I have heard; and I must pray of you to confirm them."

"I thought they would confound you," composedly replied Kunigunde.

"And pardon me, lady, but the Diet is very nice in requiring full proofs. I would be glad to learn what lady was chosen by my deceased cousin Eberhard."

"The lady is Christina, daughter of his esquire, Hugh Sorel, of an honourable family at Ulm."

"Ha! I know who and what Sorel was!" exclaimed Wildschloss. "Lady cousin, thou wouldst not stain the shield of Adlerstein with owning aught that cannot bear the examination of the Diet!"

"Sir Kasimir," said Kunigunde proudly, "had I known the truth ere my son's death, I had strangled the girl with mine own hands! But I learnt it only by his dying confession; and, had she been a beggar's child, she was his wedded wife, and her babes are his lawful heirs."

"Knowest thou time—place—witnesses?" inquired Sir Kasimir.

"The time, the Friedmund Wake; the place, the Friedmund Chapel," replied the Baroness. "Come hither, Schneiderlein. Tell the knight thy young lord's confession."

He bore emphatic testimony to poor Eberhard's last words; but as to the point of who had performed the ceremony, he knew not,—his mind had not retained the name.

"I must see the Frau herself," said Wildschloss, feeling certain that such a being as he expected in a daughter of the dissolute lanzknecht Sorel would soon, by dexterous questioning, be made to expose the futility of her pretensions so flagrantly that even Kunigunde could not attempt to maintain them.

For one moment Kunigunde hesitated, but suddenly a look of malignant satisfaction crossed her face. She spoke a few words to Squinting Matz, and then replied that Sir Kasimir should be allowed to satisfy himself, but that she could admit no one else into the castle; hers was a widow's household, the twins were only a few hours old, and she could not open her gates to admit any person besides himself.

The Dove in the Eagle's Nest

So resolved on judging for himself was Adlerstein Wildschloss that all this did not stagger him; for, even if he had believed more than he did of the old lady's story, there would have been no sense of intrusion or impropriety in such a visit to the mother. Indeed, had Christina been living in the civilized world, her chamber would have been hung with black cloth, black velvet would have enveloped her up to the eyes, and the blackest of cradles would have stood ready for her fatherless babe; two steps, in honour of her baronial rank, would have led to her bed, and a beaufet with the due baronial amount of gold and silver plate would have held the comfits and caudle to be dispensed to all visitors. As it was, the two steps built into the floor of the room, and the black hood that Ursel tied over her young mistress's head, were the only traces that such etiquette had ever been heard of.

But when Baron Kasimir had clanked up the turret stairs, each step bringing to her many a memory of him who should have been there, and when he had been led to the bedside, he was completely taken by surprise.

Instead of the great, flat-faced, coarse comeliness of a German wench, treated as a lady in order to deceive him, he saw a delicate, lily-like face, white as ivory, and the soft, sweet brown eyes under their drooping lashes, so full of innocence and sad though thankful content, that he felt as if the inquiries he came to make were almost sacrilege.

He had seen enough of the world to know that no agent in a clumsy imposition would look like this pure white creature, with her arm encircling the two little swaddled babes, whose red faces and bald heads alone were allowed to appear above their mummy-like wrappings; and he could only make an obeisance lower and infinitely more respectful than that with which he had favoured the Baroness nee von Adlerstein, with a few words of inquiry and apology.

But Christina had her sons' rights to defend now, and she had far more spirit to do so than ever she had had in securing her own position, and a delicate rose tint came into her cheek as she said in her soft voice, "The Baroness tells me, that you, noble sir, would learn who wedded me to my dear and blessed lord, Sir Eberhard. It was Friar Peter of the Franciscan brotherhood of Offingen, an agent for selling indulgences. Two of his lay brethren were present. My dear lord gave his own name and mine in full after the holy rite; the friar promising his testimony if it were needed. He is to be found, or at least heard of, at his own cloister; and the hermit at the chapel likewise beheld a part of the ceremony."

"Enough, enough, lady," replied Sir Kasimir; "forgive me for having forced the question upon you."

"Nay," replied Christina, with her blush deepening, "it is but just and due to us all;" and her soft eyes had a gleam of exultation, as she looked at the two little mummies that made up the US—"I would have all inquiries made in full."

"They shall be made, lady, as will be needful for the establishment of your son's right as a free Baron of the empire, but not with any doubt on my part, or desire to controvert that right. I am fully convinced, and only wish to serve you and my little cousins. Which of them is the head of our family?" he added, looking at the two absolutely undistinguishable little chrysalises, so exactly alike that Christina herself was obliged to look for the black ribbon, on which a medal had been hung, round the neck of the elder. Sir Kasimir put one knee to the ground as he kissed the red cheek of the infant and the white hand of the mother.

"Lady cousin," he said to Kunigunde, who had stood by all this time with an anxious, uneasy, scowling expression on her face, "I am satisfied. I own this babe as the true Freiherr von Adlerstein, and far be it from me to trouble his heritage. Rather point out the way in which I may serve you and him. Shall I represent all to the Emperor, and obtain his wardship, so as to be able to protect you from any attacks by the enemies of the house?"

"Thanks, sir," returned the elder lady, severely, seeing Christina's gratified, imploring face. "The right line of Adlerstein can take care of itself without greedy guardians appointed by usurpers. Our submission has never been made, and the Emperor cannot dispose of our wardship."

And Kunigunde looked defiant, regarding herself and her grandson as quite as good as the Emperor, and ready to blast her daughter-in-law with her eyes for murmuring gratefully and wistfully, "Thanks, noble sir, thanks!"

The Dove in the Eagle's Nest

"Let me at least win a friendly right in my young cousins," said Sir Kasimir, the more drawn by pitying admiration towards their mother, as he perceived more of the grandmother's haughty repulsiveness and want of comprehension of the dangers of her position. "They are not baptized? Let me become their godfather."

Christina's face was all joy and gratitude, and even the grandmother made no objection; in fact, it was the babes' only chance of a noble sponsor; and Father Norbert, who had already been making ready for the baptism, was sent for from the hall. Kunigunde, meantime, moved about restlessly, went half-way down the stairs, and held council with some one there; Ursel likewise, bustled about, and Sir Kasimir remained seated on the chair that had been placed for him near Christina's bed.

She was able again to thank him, and add, "It may be that you will have more cause than the lady grandmother thinks to remember your offer of protection to my poor orphans. Their father and grandfather were, in very deed, on their way to make submission."

"That is well known to me," said Sir Kasimir. "Lady, I will do all in my power for you. The Emperor shall hear the state of things; and, while no violence is offered to travellers," he added, lowering his tone, "I doubt not he will wait for full submission till this young Baron be of age to tender it."

"We are scarce in force to offer violence," said Christina sighing. "I have no power to withstand the Lady Baroness. I am like a stranger here; but, oh! sir, if the Emperor and Diet will be patient and forbearing with this desolate house, my babes, if they live, shall strive to requite their mercy by loyalty. And the blessing of the widow and fatherless will fall on you, most generous knight," she added, fervently, holding out her hand.

"I would I could do more for you," said the knight. "Ask, and all I can do is at your service."

"Ah, sir," cried Christina, her eyes brightening, "there is one most inestimable service you could render me—to let my uncle, Master Gottfried, the wood-carver of Ulm, know where I am, and of my state, and of my children."

Sir Kasimir repeated the name.

"Yes," she said. "There was my home, there was I brought up by my dear uncle and aunt, till my father bore me away to attend on the young lady here. It is eighteen months since they had any tidings from her who was as a daughter to them."

"I will see them myself," said Kasimir; "I know the name. Carved not Master Gottfried the stall-work at Augsburg?"

"Yes, indeed! In chestnut leaves! And the Misereres all with fairy tales!" exclaimed Christina. "Oh, sir, thanks indeed! Bear to the dear, dear uncle and aunt their child's duteous greetings, and tell them she loves them with all her heart, and prays them to forgive her, and to pray for her and her little ones! And," she added, "my uncle may not have learnt how his brother, my father, died by his lord's side. Oh! pray him, if ever he loved his little Christina, to have masses sung for my father and my own dear lord."

As she promised, Ursel came to make the babes ready for their baptism, and Sir Kasimir moved away towards the window. Ursel was looking uneasy and dismayed, and, as she bent over her mistress, she whispered, "Lady, the Schneiderlein sends you word that Matz has called him to help in removing the props of the door you wot of when HE yonder steps across it. He would know if it be your will?"

"The oubliette!" This was Frau Kunigunde's usage of the relative who was doing his best for the welfare of her grandsons! Christina's whole countenance looked so frozen with horror, that Ursel felt as if she had killed her on the spot; but the next moment a flash of relief came over the pale features, and the trembling lip commanded itself to say, "My best thanks to good Heinz. Say to him that I forbid it. If he loves the life of his master's children, he will abstain! Tell him so. My blessings on him if this knight leave the castle safe, Ursel." And her terrified earnest eyes impelled Ursel to hasten to do her bidding; but whether it had been executed, there was no knowing, for almost immediately the Freiherrinn and Father Norbert entered, and Ursel returned with them. Nay, the message given, who could tell if Heinz would be able to act upon it? In the ordinary condition of the castle, he was indeed its most efficient inmate; Matz did not approach him in strength, Hans was a cripple, Hatto would be on the right side; but Jobst the Kohler, and the other serfs who had been called in for the defence, were more likely to hold with the elder than the younger lady. And Frau Kunigunde herself, knowing well that the five-and-twenty men outside would be incompetent to avenge their master, confident in her narrow-minded, ignorant pride that no one could take Schloss Adlerstein, and incapable of understanding the changes in society that were rendering her isolated condition untenable, was certain to scout any representation of the dire consequences that the crime would entail. Kasimir had no near kindred, and private revenge was the only justice the Baroness believed in; she only saw in her crime the satisfaction of an old feud, and the union of the Wildschloss property with the parent stem.

Seldom could such a christening have taken place as that of which Christina's bed-room was the scene—the mother scarcely able even to think of the holy sacrament for the horror of knowing that the one sponsor was already exulting in the speedy destruction of the other; and, poor little feeble thing, rallying the last remnants of her severely-tried powers to prevent the crime at the most terrible of risks.

The elder babe received from his grandmother the hereditary name of Eberhard, but Sir Kasimir looked at the mother inquiringly, ere he gave the other to the priest. Christina had well-nigh said, "Oubliette," but, recalling herself in time, she feebly uttered the name she had longed after from the moment she had known that two sons had been her Easter gift, "Gottfried," after her beloved uncle. But Kunigunde caught the sound, and exclaimed, "No son of Adlerstein shall bear abase craftsman's name. Call him Racher (the avenger);" and in the word there already rang a note of victory and revenge that made Christina's blood run cold. Sir Kasimir marked her trouble. "The lady mother loves not the sound," he said, kindly. "Lady, have you any other wish? Then will I call him Friedmund."

Christina had almost smiled. To her the omen was of the best. Baron Friedmund had been the last common ancestor of the two branches of the family, the patron saint was so called, his wake was her wedding- day, the sound of the word imported peace, and the good Barons Ebbo and Friedel had ever been linked together lovingly by popular memory. And so the second little Baron received the name of Friedmund, and then the knight of Wildschloss, perceiving, with consideration rare in a warrior, that the mother looked worn out and feverish, at once prepared to kiss her hand and take leave.

"One more favour, Sir Knight," she said, lifting up her head, while a burning spot rose on either cheek. "I beg of you to take my two babes down—yes, both, both, in your own arms, and show them to your men, owning them as your kinsmen and godsons."

Sir Kasimir looked exceedingly amazed, as if he thought the lady's senses taking leave of her, and Dame Kunigunde broke out into declarations that it was absurd, and she did not know what she was talking of; but she repeated almost with passion, "Take them, take them, you know not how much depends on it." Ursel, with unusual readiness of wit, signed and whispered that the young mother must be humoured, for fear of consequences; till the knight, in a good- natured, confused way, submitted to receive the two little bundles in his arms, while he gave place to Kunigunde, who hastily stepped before him in a manner that made Christina trust that her precaution would be effectual.

The room was reeling round with her. The agony of those few minutes was beyond all things unspeakable. What had seemed just before like a certain way of saving the guest without real danger to her children, now appeared instead the most certain destruction to all, and herself the unnatural mother who had doomed her new-born babes for a stranger's sake. She could not even pray; she would have shrieked to have them brought back, but her voice was dead within her, her tongue clave to the roof of her mouth, ringings in her ears hindered her even from listening to the descending steps. She lay as one dead, when ten minutes afterwards the cry of one of her babes struck on her ear, and the next moment Ursel stood beside her, laying them down close to her, and saying exultingly, "Safe! safe out at the gate, and down the hillside, and my old lady ready to gnaw off her hands for spite!"

CHAPTER IX: THE EAGLETS

Christina's mental and bodily constitution had much similarity— apparently most delicate, tender, and timid, yet capable of a vigour, health, and endurance that withstood shocks that might have been fatal to many apparently stronger persons. The events of that frightful Easter Monday morning did indeed almost kill her; but the effects, though severe, were not lasting; and by the time the last of Ermentrude's snow-wreath had vanished, she was sunning her babes at the window, happier than she had ever thought to be—above all, in the possession of both the children. A nurse had been captured for the little Baron from the village on the hillside; but the woman had fretted, the child had pined, and had been given back to his mother to save his life; and ever since both had thriven perfectly under her sole care, so that there was very nearly joy in that room.

Outside it, there was more bitterness than ever. The grandmother had softened for a few moments at the birth of the children, with satisfaction at obtaining twice as much as she had hoped; but the frustration of her vengeance upon Kasimir of Adlerstein Wildschloss had renewed all her hatred, and she had no scruple in abusing "the burgher-woman" to the whole household for her artful desire to captivate another nobleman. She, no doubt, expected that degenerate fool of a Wildschlosser to come wooing after her; "if he did he should meet his deserts." It was the favourite reproach whenever she chose to vent her fury on the mute, blushing, weeping young widow, whose glance at her babies was her only appeal against the cruel accusation.

On Midsummer eve, Heinz the Schneiderlein, who had all day been taking toll from the various attendants at the Friedmund Wake, came up and knocked at the door. He had a bundle over his shoulder and a bag in his hand, which last he offered to her.

"The toll! It is for the Lady Baroness."

"You are my Lady Baroness. I levy toll for this my young lord."

"Take it to her, good Heinz, she must have the charge, and needless strife I will not breed."

The angry notes of Dame Kunigunde came up: "How now, knave Schneiderlein! Come down with the toll instantly. It shall not be tampered with! Down, I say, thou thief of a tailor."

"Go; prithee go, vex her not," entreated Christina.

"Coming, lady!" shouted Heinz, and, disregarding all further objurgations from beneath, he proceeded to deposit his bundle, and explain that it had been entrusted to him by a pedlar from Ulm, who would likewise take charge of anything she might have to send in return, and he then ran down just in time to prevent a domiciliary visit from the old lady.

From Ulm! The very sound was joy; and Christina with trembling hands unfastened the cords and stitches that secured the canvas covering, within which lay folds on folds of linen, and in the midst a rich silver goblet, long ago brought by her father from Italy, a few of her own possessions, and a letter from her uncle secured with black floss silk, with a black seal.

She kissed it with transport, but the contents were somewhat chilling by their grave formality. The opening address to the "honour-worthy Lady Baroness and love-worthy niece," conveyed to her a doubt on good Master Gottfried's part whether she were still truly worthy of love or honour. The slaughter at Jacob Muller's had been already known to him, and he expressed himself as relieved, but greatly amazed, at the information he had received from the Baron of Adlerstein Wildschloss, who had visited him at Ulm, after having verified what had been alleged at Schloss Adlerstein by application to the friar at Offingen.

Freiherr von Adlerstein Wildschloss had further requested him to make known that, feud-briefs having regularly passed between Schlangenwald and Adlerstein, and the two Barons not having been within the peace of the empire, no justice could be exacted for their deaths; yet, in consideration of the tender age of the present heirs, the question of forfeiture or submission should be waived till they could act for themselves, and Schlangenwald should be withheld from injuring them so long as no molestation was offered to travellers. It was plain that Sir Kasimir had well and generously done his best to protect the helpless twins, and he sent respectful but cordial greetings to their mother. These however were far less heeded by her than the coldness of her uncle's letter. She had drifted beyond the reckoning of her kindred, and they were sending her her property and bridal linen, as if they had done with her, and had lost their child in the robber-baron's wife. Yet at the end there was a touch of old times in offering a blessing, should she still value it, and the hopes that heaven and the saints would comfort her; "for surely, thou poor child, thou must have suffered much, and, if thou wiliest still to write to thy city kin, thine aunt would rejoice to hear that thou and thy babes were in good health."

Precise grammarian and scribe as was Uncle Gottfried, the lapse from the formal Sie to the familiar Du went to his niece's heart. Whenever her little ones left her any leisure, she spent this her first wedding-day in writing so earnest and loving a letter as, in spite of mediaeval formality, must assure the good burgomaster that, except in having suffered much and loved much, his little Christina was not changed since she had left him.

No answer could be looked for till another wake-day; but, when it came, it was full and loving, and therewith were sent a few more of her favourite books, a girdle, and a richly-scented pair of gloves, together with two ivory boxes of comfits, and two little purple silk, gold-edged, straight, narrow garments and tight round brimless lace caps, for the two little Barons. Nor did henceforth a wake-day pass by without bringing some such token, not only delightful as gratifying Christina's affection by the kindness that suggested them, but supplying absolute wants in the dire stress of poverty at Schloss Adlerstein.

Christina durst not tell her mother-in-law of the terms on which they were unmolested, trusting to the scantiness of the retinue, and to her own influence with the Schneiderlein to hinder any serious violence. Indeed, while the Count of Schlangenwald was in the neighbourhood, his followers took care to secure all that could be captured at the Debateable Ford, and the broken forces of Adlerstein would have been insane had they attempted to contend with such superior numbers. That the castle remained unattacked was attributed by the elder Baroness to its own merits; nor did Christina undeceive her. They had no intercourse with the outer world, except that once a pursuivant arrived with a formal intimation from their kinsman, the Baron of Adlerstein Wildschloss, of his marriage with the noble Fraulein, Countess Valeska von Trautbach, and a present of a gay dagger for each of his godsons. Frau Kunigunde triumphed a good deal over the notion of Christina's supposed disappointment; but the tidings were most welcome to the younger lady, who trusted they would put an end to all future taunts about Wildschloss. Alas! the handle for abuse was too valuable to be relinquished.

The last silver cup the castle had possessed had to be given as a reward to the pursuivant, and mayhap Frau Kunigunde reckoned this as another offence of her daughter-in-law, since, had Sir Kasimir been safe in the oubliette, the twins might have shared his broad lands on the Danube, instead of contributing to the fees of his pursuivant. The cup could indeed be ill spared. The cattle and swine, the dues of the serfs, and the yearly toll at the wake were the sole resources of the household; and though there was no lack of meat, milk, and black bread, sufficient garments could scarce be come by, with all the spinning of the household, woven by the village webster, of whose time the baronial household, by prescriptive right, owned the lion's share.

These matters little troubled the two beings in whom Christina's heart was wrapped up. Though running about barefooted and bareheaded, they were healthy, handsome, straight-limbed, noble-looking creatures, so exactly alike, and so inseparable, that no one except herself could tell one from the other save by the medal of Our Lady worn by the elder, and the little cross carved by the mother for the younger; indeed, at one time, the urchins themselves would feel for cross or medal, ere naming themselves "Ebbo," or "Friedel." They were tall for their age, but with the slender make of their foreign ancestry; and, though their fair rosy complexions were brightened by mountain mists and winds, their rapidly darkening hair, and large liquid brown eyes, told of their Italian blood. Their grandmother looked on their colouring as a taint, and Christina herself had hoped to see their father's simple, kindly blue eyes revive in his boys; but she could hardly have desired anything different from the dancing, kindling, or earnest glances that used to flash from under their long black lashes when they were nestling in her lap, or playing by her knee, making music with their prattle, or listening to her answers with faces alive with intelligence. They scarcely left her time for sorrow or regret.

They were never quarrelsome. Either from the influence of her gentleness, or from their absolute union, they could do and enjoy nothing apart, and would as soon have thought of their right and left hands falling out as of Ebbo and Friedel disputing. Ebbo however was always the right hand. THE Freiherr, as he had been called from the first, had, from the time he could sit at the table at all, been put into the baronial chair with the eagle carved at the back; every member of the household, from his grandmother downwards, placed him foremost, and Friedel followed their example, at the less loss to himself, as his hand was always in Ebbo's, and all their doings were in common. Sometimes however the mother doubted whether there would have been this perfect absence of all contest had the medal of the firstborn chanced to hang round Friedmund's neck instead of Eberhard's. At first they were entirely left to her. Their grandmother heeded them little as long as they were healthy, and evidently regarded them more as heirs of Adlerstein than as grandchildren; but, as they grew older, she showed anxiety lest their mother should interfere with the fierce, lawless spirit proper to their line.

One winter day, when they were nearly six years old, Christina, spinning at her window, had been watching them snowballing in the castle court, smiling and applauding every large handful held up to her, every laughing combat, every well-aimed hit, as the hardy little fellows scattered the snow in showers round them, raising their merry fur-capped faces to the bright eyes that "rained influence and judged the prize."

By and by they stood still; Ebbo—she knew him by the tossed head and commanding air—was proposing what Friedel seemed to disapprove; but, after a short discussion, Ebbo flung away from him, and went towards a shed where was kept a wolf-cub, recently presented to the young Barons by old Ulrich's son. The whelp was so young as to be quite harmless, but it was far from amiable; Friedel never willingly approached it, and the snarling and whining replies to all advances had begun to weary and irritate Ebbo. He dragged it out by its chain, and, tethering it to a post, made it a mark for his snowballs, which, kneaded hard, and delivered with hearty good-will by his sturdy arms, made the poor little beast yelp with pain and terror, till the more tender-hearted Friedel threw himself on his brother to withhold him, while Matz stood by laughing and applauding the Baron. Seeing Ebbo shake Friedel off with unusual petulance, and pitying the tormented animal, Christina flung a cloak round her head and hastened down stairs, entering the court just as the terrified whelp had made a snap at the boy, which was returned by angry, vindictive pelting, not merely with snow, but with stones. Friedel sprang to her crying, and her call to Ebbo made him turn, though with fury in his face, shouting, "He would bite me! the evil beast!"

"Come with me, Ebbo," she said.

"He shall suffer for it, the spiteful, ungrateful brute! Let me alone, mother!" cried Ebbo, stamping on the snow, but still from habit yielding to her hand on his shoulder.

"What now?" demanded the old Baroness, appearing on the scene. "Who is thwarting the Baron?"

"She; she will not let me deal with yonder savage whelp," cried the boy.

"She! Take thy way, child," said the old lady. "Visit him well for his malice. None shall withstand thee here. At thy peril!" she added, turning on Christina. "What, art not content to have brought base mechanical blood into a noble house? Wouldst make slaves and cowards of its sons?"

"I would teach them true courage, not cruelty," she tried to say.

"What should such as thou know of courage? Look here, girl: another word to daunt the spirit of my grandsons, and I'll have thee scourged down the mountain-side! On! At him, Ebbo! That's my gallant young knight! Out of the way, girl, with thy whining looks! What, Friedel, be a man, and aid thy brother! Has she made thee a puling woman already?" And

The Dove in the Eagle's Nest

Kunigunde laid an ungentle grasp upon Friedmund, who was clinging to his mother, hiding his face in her gown. He struggled against the clutch, and would not look up or be detached.

"Fie, poor little coward!" taunted the old lady; "never heed him, Ebbo, my brave Baron!"

Cut to the heart, Christina took refuge in her room, and gathered her Friedel to her bosom, as he sobbed out, "Oh, mother, the poor little wolf! Oh, mother, are you weeping too? The grandmother should not so speak to the sweetest, dearest motherling," he added, throwing his arms round her neck.

"Alas, Friedel, that Ebbo should learn that it is brave to hurt the weak!"

"It is not like Walther of Vogelwiede," said Friedel, whose mind had been much impressed by the Minnesinger's bequest to the birds.

"Nor like any true Christian knight. Alas, my poor boys, must you be taught foul cruelty and I too weak and cowardly to save you?"

"That never will be," said Friedel, lifting his head from her shoulder. "Hark! what a howl was that!"

"Listen not, dear child; it does but pain thee."

"But Ebbo is not shouting. Oh, mother, he is vexed—he is hurt!" cried Friedel, springing from her lap; but, ere either could reach the window, Ebbo had vanished from the scene. They only saw the young wolf stretched dead on the snow, and the same moment in burst Ebbo, and flung himself on the floor in a passion of weeping. Stimulated by the applause of his grandmother and of Matz, he had furiously pelted the poor animal with all missiles that came to hand, till a blow, either from him or Matz, had produced such a howl and struggle of agony, and then such terrible stillness, as had gone to the young Baron's very heart, a heart as soft as that of his father had been by nature. Indeed, his sobs were so piteous that his mother was relieved to hear only, "The wolf! the poor wolf!" and to find that he himself was unhurt; and she was scarcely satisfied of this when Dame Kunigunde came up also alarmed, and thus turned his grief to wrath. "As if I would cry in that way for a bite!" he said. "Go, grandame; you made me do it, the poor beast!" with a fresh sob.

"Ulrich shall get thee another cub, my child."

"No, no; I never will have another cub! Why did you let me kill it?"

"For shame, Ebbo! Weep for a spiteful brute! That's no better than thy mother or Friedel."

"I love my mother! I love Friedel! They would have withheld me. Go, go; I hate you!"

"Peace, peace, Ebbo," exclaimed his mother; "you know not what you say. Ask your grandmother's pardon."

"Peace, thou fool!" screamed the old lady. "The Baron speaks as he will in his own castle. He is not to be checked here, and thwarted there, and taught to mince his words like a cap-in-hand pedlar. Pardon! When did an Adlerstein seek pardon? Come with me, my Baron; I have still some honey-cakes."

"Not I," replied Ebbo; "honey-cakes will not cure the wolf whelp. Go: I want my mother and Friedel."

Alone with them his pride and passion were gone; but alas! what augury for the future of her boys was left with the mother!

The Dove in the Eagle's Nest

CHAPTER X: THE EAGLE'S PREY

"It fell about the Lammas tide,
When moor men win their hay,"

That all the serfs of Adlerstein were collected to collect their lady's hay to be stored for the winter's fodder of the goats, and of poor Sir Eberhard's old white mare, the only steed as yet ridden by the young Barons.

The boys were fourteen years old. So monotonous was their mother's life that it was chiefly their growth that marked the length of her residence in the castle. Otherwise there had been no change, except that the elder Baroness was more feeble in her limbs, and still more irritable and excitable in temper. There were no events, save a few hunting adventures of the boys, or the yearly correspondence with Ulm; and the same life continued, of shrinking in dread from the old lady's tyrannous dislike, and of the constant endeavour to infuse better principles into the boys, without the open opposition for which there was neither power nor strength.

The boys' love was entirely given to their mother. Far from diminishing with their dependence on her, it increased with the sense of protection; and, now that they were taller than herself, she seemed to be cherished by them more than ever. Moreover, she was their oracle. Quick-witted and active-minded, loving books the more because their grandmother thought signing a feud-letter the utmost literary effort becoming to a noble, they never rested till they had acquired all that their mother could teach them; or, rather, they then became more restless than ever. Long ago had her whole store of tales and ballads become so familiar, by repetition, that the boys could correct her in the smallest variation; reading and writing were mastered as for pleasure; and the Nuremberg Chronicle, with its wonderful woodcuts, excited such a passion of curiosity that they must needs conquer its Latin and read it for themselves. This World History, with Alexander and the Nine Worthies, the cities and landscapes, and the oft-repeated portraits, was Eberhard's study; but Friedmund continued—constant to Walther of Vogelweide. Eberhard cared for no character in the Vulgate so much as for Judas the Maccabee; but Friedmund's heart was all for King David; and to both lads, shut up from companionship as they were, every acquaintance in their books was a living being whose like they fancied might be met beyond their mountain. And, when they should go forth, like Dietrich of Berne, in search of adventures, doughty deeds were chiefly to fall to the lot of Ebbo's lance; while Friedel was to be their Minnesinger; and indeed certain verses, that he had murmured in his brother's ear, had left no doubt in Ebbo's mind that the exploits would be worthily sung.

The soft dreamy eye was becoming Friedel's characteristic, as fire and keenness distinguished his brother's glance. When at rest, the twins could be known apart by their expression, though in all other respects they were as alike as ever; and let Ebbo look thoughtful or Friedel eager and they were again undistinguishable; and indeed they were constantly changing looks. Had not Friedel been beside him, Ebbo would have been deemed a wondrous student for his years; had not Ebbo been the standard of comparison, Friedel would have been in high repute for spirit and enterprise and skill as a cragsman, with the crossbow, and in all feats of arms that the Schneiderlein could impart. They shared all occupations; and it was by the merest shade that Ebbo excelled with the weapon, and Friedel with the book or tool. For the artist nature was in them, not intentionally excited by their mother, but far too strong to be easily discouraged. They had long daily gazed at Ulm in the distance, hoping to behold the spire completed; and the illustrations in their mother's books excited a strong desire to imitate them. The floor had often been covered with charcoal outlines even before Christina was persuaded to impart the rules she had learnt from her uncle; and her carving-tools were soon seized upon. At first they were used only upon knobs of sticks; but one day when the boys, roaming on the mountain, had lost their way, and coming to the convent had been there hospitably welcomed by Father Norbert, they came home wild to make carvings like what they had seen in the chapel. Jobst the Kohler was continually importuned for soft wood; the fair was ransacked for knives; and even the old Baroness could not find great fault with the occupation, base and mechanical though it were, which disposed of the two restless spirits during the many hours when winter storms confined them to the castle. Rude as was their work, the constant observation and choice of subjects were an unsuspected training and softening. It was not in vain that they lived in the glorious mountain fastness, and saw the sun descend in his majesty, dyeing the masses of rock with purple and crimson; not in vain that they beheld peak and ravine clothed in purest snow, flushed with rosy light at morn and eve, or contrasted with the purple blue of the sky; or that they stood marvelling at ice caverns with gigantic crystal pendants shining with the most magical pure depths of sapphire and emerald, "as if," said Friedel, "winter kept in his service all the jewel-forging dwarfs of the motherling's tales." And, when the snow melted and the buds returned, the ivy spray, the smiling saxifrage, the purple gentian bell, the feathery rowan leaf, the symmetrical lady's mantle, were hailed and loved first as models, then for themselves.

One regret their mother had, almost amounting to shame. Every virtuous person believed in the efficacy of the rod, and, maugre her own docility, she had been chastised with it almost as a religious duty; but her sons had never felt the weight of a blow, except once when their grandmother caught them carving a border of eagles and doves round the hall table, and then Ebbo had returned the blow with all his might. As to herself, if she ever worked herself up to attempt chastisement, the Baroness was sure to fall upon her for insulting the noble birth of her sons, and thus gave them a triumph far worse for them than impunity. In truth, the boys had their own way, or rather the Baron had his way, and his way was Baron Friedmund's. Poor, bare, and scanty as were all the surroundings of their life, everything was done to feed their arrogance, with only one influence to counteract their education in pride and violence—a mother's influence, indeed, but her authority was studiously taken from her, and her position set at naught, with no power save what she might derive from their love and involuntary honour, and the sight of the pain caused her by their wrong-doings.

And so the summer's hay-harvest was come. Peasants clambered into the green nooks between the rocks to cut down with hook or knife the flowery grass, for there was no space for the sweep of a scythe. The best crop was on the bank of the Braunwasser, by the Debateable Ford, but this was cut and carried on the backs of the serfs, much earlier than the mountain grass, and never without much vigilance against the Schlangenwaldern; but this year the Count was absent at his Styrian castle, and little had been seen or heard of his people.

The full muster of serfs appeared, for Frau Kunigunde admitted of no excuses, and the sole absentee was a widow who lived on the ledge of the mountain next above that on which the castle stood. Her son reported her to be very ill, and with tears in his eyes entreated Baron Friedel to obtain leave for him to return to her, since she was quite alone in her solitary hut, with no one even to give her a drink of water. Friedel rushed with the entreaty to his grandmother, but she laughed it to scorn. Lazy Koppel only wanted an excuse, or, if not, the woman was old and useless, and men could not be spared.

"Ah! good grandame," said Friedel, "his father died with ours."

"The more honour for him! The more he is bound to work for us. Off, junker, make no loiterers."

Grieved and discomfited, Friedel betook himself to his mother and brother.

"Foolish lad not to have come to me!" said the young Baron. "Where is he? I'll send him at once."

But Christina interposed an offer to go and take Koppel's place beside his mother, and her skill was so much prized over all the mountain-side, that the alternative was gratefully accepted, and she was escorted up the steep path by her two boys to the hovel, where she spent the day in attendance on the sick woman.

Evening came on, the patient was better, but Koppel did not return, nor did the young Barons come to fetch their mother home. The last sunbeams were dying off the mountain-tops, and, beginning to suspect something amiss, she at length set off, and half way down met Koppel, who replied to her question, "Ah, then, the gracious lady has not heard of our luck. Excellent booty, and two prisoners! The young Baron has been a hero indeed, and has won himself a knightly steed." And, on her further interrogation, he added, that an unusually rich but small company had been reported by Jobst the Kohler to be on the way to the ford, where he had skilfully prepared a stumbling-block. The gracious Baroness had caused Hatto to jodel all the hay-makers together, and they had fallen on the travellers by the straight path down the crag. "Ach! did not the young Baron spring like a young gemsbock? And in midstream down came their pack-horses and their wares! Some of them took to flight, but, pfui, there were enough for my young lord to show his mettle upon. Such a prize the saints have not sent since the old Baron's time."

The Dove in the Eagle's Nest

Christina pursued her walk in dismay at this new beginning of freebooting in its worst form, overthrowing all her hopes. The best thing that could happen would be the immediate interference of the Swabian League, while her sons were too young to be personally held guilty. Yet this might involve ruin and confiscation; and, apart from all consequences, she bitterly grieved that the stain of robbery should have fallen on her hitherto innocent sons.

Every peasant she met greeted her with praises of their young lord, and, when she mounted the hall-steps, she found the floor strewn with bales of goods.

"Mother," cried Ebbo, flying up to her, "have you heard? I have a horse! a spirited bay, a knightly charger, and Friedel is to ride him by turns with me. Where is Friedel? And, mother, Heinz said I struck as good a stroke as any of them, and I have a sword for Friedel now. Why does he not come? And, motherling, this is for you, a gown of velvet, a real black velvet, that will make you fairer than our Lady at the Convent. Come to the window and see it, mother dear."

The boy was so joyously excited that she could hardly withstand his delight, but she did not move.

"Don't you like the velvet?" he continued. "We always said that, the first prize we won, the motherling should wear velvet. Do but look at it."

"Woe is me, my Ebbo!" she sighed, bending to kiss his brow.

He understood her at once, coloured, and spoke hastily and in defiance. "It was in the river, mother, the horses fell; it is our right."

"Fairly, Ebbo?" she asked in a low voice.

"Nay, mother, if Jobst DID hide a branch in midstream, it was no doing of mine; and the horses fell. The Schlangenwaldern don't even wait to let them fall. We cannot live, if we are to be so nice and dainty."

"Ah! my son, I thought not to hear you call mercy and honesty mere niceness."

"What do I hear?" exclaimed Frau Kunigunde, entering from the storeroom, where she had been disposing of some spices, a much esteemed commodity. "Are you chiding and daunting this boy, as you have done with the other?"

"My mother may speak to me!" cried Ebbo, hotly, turning round.

"And quench thy spirit with whining fooleries! Take the Baron's bounty, woman, and vex him not after his first knightly exploit."

"Heaven knows, and Ebbo knows," said the trembling Christina, "that, were it a knightly exploit, I were the first to exult."

"Thou! thou craftsman's girl! dost presume to call in question the knightly deeds of a noble house! There!" cried the furious Baroness, striking her face. Now! dare to be insolent again." Her hand was uplifted for another blow, when it was grasped by Eberhard, and, the next moment, he likewise held the other hand, with youthful strength far exceeding hers. She had often struck his mother before, but not in his presence, and the greatness of the shock seemed to make him cool and absolutely dignified.

"Be still, grandame," he said. "No, mother, I am not hurting her," and indeed the surprise seemed to have taken away her rage and volubility, and unresistingly she allowed him to seat her in a chair. Still holding her arm, he made his clear boyish voice resound through the hall, saying, "Retainers all, know that, as I am your lord and master, so is my honoured mother lady of the castle, and she is never to be gainsay'ed, let her say or do what she will."

The Dove in the Eagle's Nest

"You are right, Herr Freiherr," said Heinz. "The Frau Christina is our gracious and beloved dame. Long live the Freiherrinn Christina!" And the voices of almost all the serfs present mingled in the cry.

"And hear you all," continued Eberhard, "she shall rule all, and never be trampled on more. Grandame, you understand?"

The old woman seemed confounded, and cowered in her chair without speaking. Christina, almost dismayed by this silence, would have suggested to Ebbo to say something kind or consoling; but at that moment she was struck with alarm by his renewed inquiry for his brother.

"Friedel! Was not he with thee?"

"No; I never saw him!"

Ebbo flew up the stairs, and shouted for his brother; then, coming down, gave orders for the men to go out on the mountain-side, and search and jodel. He was hurrying with them, but his mother caught his arm. "O Ebbo, how can I let you go? It is dark, and the crags are so perilous!"

"Mother, I cannot stay!" and the boy flung his arms round her neck, and whispered in her ear, "Friedel said it would be a treacherous attack, and I called him a craven. Oh, mother, we never parted thus before! He went up the hillside. Oh, where is he?"

Infected by the boy's despairing voice, yet relieved that Friedel at least had withstood the temptation, Christina still held Ebbo's hand, and descended the steps with him. The clear blue sky was fast showing the stars, and into the evening stillness echoed the loud wide jodeln, cast back from the other side of the ravine. Ebbo tried to raise his voice, but broke down in the shout, and, choked with agitation, said, "Let me go, mother. None know his haunts as I do!"

"Hark!" she said, only grasping him tighter.

Thinner, shriller, clearer came a far-away cry from the heights, and Ebbo thrilled from head to foot, then sent up another pealing mountain shout, responded to by a jodel so pitched as to be plainly not an echo. "Towards the Red Eyrie," said Hans.

"He will have been to the Ptarmigan's Pool," said Ebbo, sending up his voice again, in hopes that the answer would sound less distant; but, instead of this, its intonations conveyed, to these adepts in mountain language, that Friedel stood in need of help.

"Depend upon it," said the startled Ebbo, "that he has got up amongst those rocks where the dead chamois rolled down last summer; then, as Christina uttered a faint cry of terror, Heinz added, "Fear not, lady, those are not the jodeln of one who has met with a hurt. Baron Friedel has the sense to be patient rather than risk his bones if he cannot move safely in the dark."

"Up after him!" said Ebbo, emitting a variety of shouts intimating speedy aid, and receiving a halloo in reply that reassured even his mother. Equipped with a rope and sundry torches of pinewood, Heinz and two of the serfs were speedily ready, and Christina implored her son to let her come so far as where she should not impede the others. He gave her his arm, and Heinz held his torch so as to guide her up a winding path, not in itself very steep, but which she could never have climbed had daylight shown her what it overhung. Guided by the constant exchange of jodeln, they reached a height where the wind blew cold and wild, and Ebbo pointed to an intensely black shadow overhung by a peak rising like the gable of a house into the sky. "Yonder lies the tarn," he said. "Don't stir. This way lies the cliff. Fried-mund!" exchanging the jodel for the name.

The Dove in the Eagle's Nest

"Here!—this way! Under the Red Eyrie," called back the wanderer; and steering their course round the rocks above the pool, the rescuers made their way towards the base of the peak, which was in fact the summit of the mountain, the top of the Eagle's Ladder, the highest step of which they had attained. The peak towered over them, and beneath, the castle lights seemed as if it would be easy to let a stone fall straight down on them.

Friedel's cry seemed to come from under their feet. "I am here! I am safe; only it grew so dark that I durst not climb up or down."

The Schneiderlein explained that he would lower down a rope, which, when fastened round Friedel's waist, would enable him to climb safely up; and, after a breathless space, the torchlight shone upon the longed-for face, and Friedel springing on the path, cried, "The mother!—and here!" –

"Oh, Friedel, where have you been? What is this in your arms?"

He showed them the innocent face of a little white kid.

"Whence is it, Friedel?"

He pointed to the peak, saying, "I was lying on my back by the tarn, when my lady eagle came sailing overhead, so low that I could see this poor little thing, and hear it bleat."

"Thou hast been to the Eyrie—the inaccessible Eyrie!" exclaimed Ebbo, in amazement.

"That's a mistake. It is not hard after the first" said Friedel. "I only waited to watch the old birds out again."

"Robbed the eagles! And the young ones?"

"Well," said Friedmund, as if half ashamed, "they were twin eaglets, and their mother had left them, and I felt as though I could not harm them; so I only bore off their provisions, and stuck some feathers in my cap. But by that time the sun was down, and soon I could not see my footing; and, when I found that I had missed the path, I thought I had best nestle in the nook where I was, and wait for day. I grieved for my mother's fear; but oh, to see her here!"

"Ah, Friedel! didst do it to prove my words false?" interposed Ebbo, eagerly.

"What words?"

"Thou knowest. Make me not speak them again."

"Oh, those!" said Friedel, only now recalling them. "No, verily; they were but a moment's anger. I wanted to save the kid. I think it is old mother Rika's white kid. But oh, motherling! I grieve to have thus frightened you."

Not a single word passed between them upon Ebbo's exploits. Whether Friedel had seen all from the heights, or whether he intuitively perceived that his brother preferred silence, he held his peace, and both were solely occupied in assisting their mother down the pass, the difficulties of which were far more felt now than in the excitement of the ascent; only when they were near home, and the boys were walking in the darkness with arms round one another's necks, Christina heard Friedel say low and rather sadly, "I think I shall be a priest, Ebbo."

To which Ebbo only answered, "Pfui!"

Christina understood that Friedel meant that robbery must be a severance between the brothers. Alas! had the moment come when their paths must diverge? Could Ebbo's step not be redeemed?

Ursel reported that Dame Kunigunde had scarcely spoken again, but had retired, like one stunned, into her bed. Friedel was half asleep after the exertions of the day; but Ebbo did not speak, and both soon betook themselves to their little turret chamber within their mother's.

Christina prayed long that night, her heart full of dread of the consequence of this transgression. Rumours of freebooting castles destroyed by the Swabian League had reached her every wake day, and, if this outrage were once known, the sufferance that left Adlerstein unmolested must be over. There was hope indeed in the weakness and uncertainty of the Government; but present safety would in reality be the ruin of Ebbo, since he would be encouraged to persist in the career of violence now unhappily begun. She knew not what to ask, save that her sons might be shielded from evil, and might fulfil that promise of her dream, the star in heaven, the light on earth. And for the present!—the good God guide her and her sons through the difficult morrow, and turn the heart of the unhappy old woman below!

When, exhausted with weeping and watching, she rose from her knees, she stole softly into her sons' turret for a last look at them. Generally they were so much alike in their sleep that even she was at fault between them; but that night there was no doubt. Friedel, pale after the day's hunger and fatigue, slept with relaxed features in the most complete calm; but though Ebbo's eyes were closed, there was no repose in his face—his hair was tossed, his colour flushed, his brow contracted, the arm flung across his brother had none of the ease of sleep. She doubted whether he were not awake; but, knowing that he would not brook any endeavour to force confidence he did not offer, she merely hung over them both, murmured a prayer and blessing, and left them.

CHAPTER XI: THE CHOICE IN LIFE

"Friedel, wake!"

"Is it day?" said Friedel, slowly wakening, and crossing himself as he opened his eyes. "Surely the sun is not up—?"

"We must be before the sun!" said Ebbo, who was on his feet, beginning to dress himself. "Hush, and come! Do not wake the mother. It must be ere she or aught else be astir! Thy prayers—I tell thee this is a work as good as prayer."

Half awake, and entirely bewildered, Friedel dipped his finger in the pearl mussel shell of holy water over their bed, and crossed his own brow and his brother's; then, carrying their shoes, they crossed their mother's chamber, and crept down stairs. Ebbo muttered to his brother, "Stand thou still there, and pray the saints to keep her asleep;" and then, with bare feet, moved noiselessly behind the wooden partition that shut off his grandmother's box–bedstead from the rest of the hall. She lay asleep with open mouth, snoring loudly, and on her pillow lay the bunch of castle keys, that was always carried to her at night. It was a moment of peril when Ebbo touched it; but he had nerved himself to be both steady and dexterous, and he secured it without a jingle, and then, without entering the hall, descended into a passage lit by a rough opening cut in the rock. Friedel, who began to comprehend, followed him close and joyfully, and at the first door he fitted in, and with some difficulty turned, a key, and pushed open the door of a vault, where morning light, streaming through the grated window, showed two captives, who had started to their feet, and now stood regarding the pair in the doorway as if they thought their dreams were multiplying the young Baron who had led the attack.

"Signori—" began the principal of the two; but Ebbo spoke.

"Sir, you have been brought here by a mistake in the absence of my mother, the lady of the castle. If you will follow me, I will restore all that is within my reach, and put you on your way."

The merchant's knowledge of German was small, but the purport of the words was plain, and he gladly left the damp, chilly vault. Ebbo pointed to the bales that strewed the hall. "Take all that can be carried," he said. "Here is your sword, and your purse," he said, for these had been given to him in the moment of victory. "I will bring out your horse and lead you to the pass."

The Dove in the Eagle's Nest

"Give him food," whispered Friedel; but the merchant was too anxious to have any appetite. Only he faltered in broken German a proposal to pay his respects to the Signora Castellana, to whom he owed so much.

"No! Dormit in lecto," said Ebbo, with a sudden inspiration caught from the Latinized sound of some of the Italian words, but colouring desperately as he spoke.

The Latin proved most serviceable, and the merchant understood that his property was restored, and made all speed to gather it together, and transport it to the stable. One or two of his beasts of burden had been lost in the fray, and there were more packages than could well be carried by the merchant, his servant, and his horse. Ebbo gave the aid of the old white mare—now very white indeed—and in truth the boys pitied the merchant's fine young bay for being put to base trading uses, and were rather shocked to hear that it had been taken in payment for a knight's branched velvet gown, and would be sold again at Ulm.

"What a poor coxcomb of a knight!" said they to one another, as they patted the creature's neck with such fervent admiration that the merchant longed to present it to them, when he saw that the old white mare was the sole steed they possessed, and watched their tender guidance both of her and of the bay up the rocky path so familiar to them.

"But ah, signorini miei, I am an infelice infelicissimo, ever persecuted by le Fate."

"By whom? A count like Schlangenwald?" asked Ebbo.

"Das Schicksal," whispered Friedel.

"Three long miserable years did I spend as a captive among the Moors, having lost all, my ships and all I had, and being forced to row their galleys, gli scomunicati."

"Galleys!" exclaimed Ebbo; "there are some pictured in our World History before Carthage. Would that I could see one!"

"The signorino would soon have seen his fill, were he between the decks, chained to the bench for weeks together, without ceasing to row for twenty-four hours together, with a renegade standing over to lash us, or to put a morsel into our mouths if we were fainting."

"The dogs! Do they thus use Christian men?" cried Friedel.

"Si, si—ja wohl. There were a good fourscore of us, and among them a Tedesco, a good man and true, from whom I learnt la lingua loro."

"Our tongue!—from whom?" asked one twin of the other.

"A Tedesco, a fellow-countryman of sue eccellenze."

"Deutscher!" cried both boys, turning in horror, "our Germans so treated by the pagan villains?"

"Yea, truly, signorini miei. This fellow-captive of mine was a cavaliere in his own land, but he had been betrayed and sold by his enemies, and he mourned piteously for la sposa sua—his bride, as they say here. A goodly man and a tall, piteously cramped in the narrow deck, I grieved to leave him there when the good confraternita at Genoa paid my ransom. Having learnt to speak il Tedesco, and being no longer able to fit out a vessel, I made my venture beyond the Alps; but, alas! till this moment fortune has still been adverse. My mules died of the toil of crossing the mountains; and, when with reduced baggage I came to the river beneath there—when my horses fell and my servants fled, and the peasants came down with their hayforks—I thought myself in hands no better than those of the Moors themselves."

The Dove in the Eagle's Nest

"It was wrongly done," said Ebbo, in an honest, open tone, though blushing. "I have indeed a right to what may be stranded on the bank, but never more shall foul means be employed for the overthrow."

The boys had by this time led the traveller through the Gemsbock's Pass, within sight of the convent. "There," said Ebbo, "will they give you harbourage, food, a guide, and a beast to carry the rest of your goods. We are now upon convent land, and none will dare to touch your bales; so I will unload old Schimmel."

"Ah, signorino, if I might offer any token of gratitude—"

"Nay," said Ebbo, with boyish lordliness, "make me not a spoiler."

"If the signorini should ever come to Genoa," continued the trader, "and would honour Gian Battista dei Battiste with a call, his whole house would be at their feet."

"Thanks; I would that we could see strange lands!" said Ebbo. "But come, Friedel, the sun is high, and I locked them all into the castle to make matters safe."

"May the liberated captive know the name of his deliverers, that he may commend it to the saints?" asked the merchant.

"I am Eberhard, Freiherr von Adlerstein, and this is Freiherr Friedmund, my brother. Farewell, sir."

"Strange," muttered the merchant, as he watched the two boys turn down the pass, "strange how like one barbarous name is to another. Eberardo! That was what we called il Tedesco, and, when he once told me his family name, it ended in stino; but all these foreign names sound alike. Let us speed on, lest these accursed peasants should wake, and be beyond the control of the signorino."

"Ah!" sighed Ebbo, as soon as he had hurried out of reach of the temptation, "small use in being a baron if one is to be no better mounted!"

"Thou art glad to have let that fair creature go free, though," said Friedel.

"Nay, my mother's eyes would let me have no rest in keeping him. Otherwise—Talk not to me of gladness, Friedel! Thou shouldst know better. How is one to be a knight with nothing to ride but a beast old enough to be his grandmother?"

"Knighthood of the heart may be content to go afoot," said Friedel. "Oh, Ebbo, what a brother thou art! How happy the mother will be!"

"Pfui, Friedel; what boots heart without spur? I am sick of being mewed up here within these walls of rock! No sport, not even with falling on a traveller. I am worse off than ever were my forefathers!"

"But how is it? I cannot understand," asked Friedel. "What has changed thy mind?"

"Thou, and the mother, and, more than all, the grandame. Listen, Friedel: when thou camest up, in all the whirl of eagerness and glad preparation, with thy grave face and murmur that Jobst had put forked stakes in the stream, it was past man's endurance to be baulked of the fray. Thou hast forgotten what I said to thee then, good Friedel?"

"Long since. No doubt I thrust in vexatiously."

"Not so," said Ebbo; "and I saw thou hadst reason, for the stakes were most maliciously planted, with long branches hid by the current; but the fellows were showing fight, and I could not stay to think then, or I should have seemed to fear them! I can tell you we made them run! But I never meant the grandmother to put yon poor fellow in the dungeon, and use him worse than a dog. I wot that he was my captive, and none of hers. And then came the mother; and oh, Friedel, she looked as if I were slaying her when she saw the spoil; and, ere I had made her see right and reason, the old lady came swooping down in full malice and spite, and actually came to blows. She struck the motherling—struck her on the face, Friedel!"

"I fear me it has so been before," said Friedel, sadly.

"Never will it be so again," said Ebbo, standing still. "I took the old hag by the hands, and told her she had ruled long enough! My father's wife is as good a lady of the castle as my grandfather's, and I myself am lord thereof; and, since my Lady Kunigunde chooses to cross me and beat my mother about this capture, why she has seen the last of it, and may learn who is master, and who is mistress!"

"Oh, Ebbo! I would I had seen it! But was not she outrageous? Was not the mother shrinking and ready to give back all her claims at once?"

"Perhaps she would have been, but just then she found thou wast not with me, and I found thou wast not with her, and we thought of nought else. But thou must stand by me, Friedel, and help to keep the grandmother in her place, and the mother in hers."

"If the mother WILL be kept," said Friedel. "I fear me she will only plead to be left to the grandame's treatment, as before."

"Never, Friedel! I will never see her so used again. I released this man solely to show that she is to rule here.—Yes, I know all about freebooting being a deadly sin, and moreover that it will bring the League about our ears; and it was a cowardly trick of Jobst to put those branches in the stream. Did I not go over it last night till my brain was dizzy? But still, it is but living and dying like our fathers, and I hate tameness or dullness, and it is like a fool to go back from what one has once begun."

"No; it is like a brave man, when one has begun wrong," said Friedel.

"But then I thought of the grandame triumphing over the gentle mother—and I know the mother wept over her beads half the night. She SHALL find she has had her own way for once this morning."

Friedel was silent for a few moments, then said, "Let me tell thee what I saw yesterday, Ebbo."

"So," answered the other brother.

"I liked not to vex my mother by my tidings, so I climbed up to the tarn. There is something always healing in that spot, is it not so, Ebbo? When the grandmother has been raving" (hitherto Friedel's worst grievance) "it is like getting up nearer the quiet sky in the stillness there, when the sky seems to have come down into the deep blue water, and all is so still, so wondrous still and calm. I wonder if, when we see the great Dome Kirk itself, it will give one's spirit wings, as does the gazing up from the Ptarmigan's Pool."

"Thou minnesinger, was it the blue sky thou hadst to tell me of?"

"No, brother, it was ere I reached it that I saw this sight. I had scaled the peak where grows the stunted rowan, and I sat down to look down on the other side of the gorge. It was clear where I sat, but the ravine was filled with clouds, and upon them—"

"The shape of the blessed Friedmund, thy patron?"

The Dove in the Eagle's Nest

"OUR patron," said Friedel; "I saw him, a giant form in gown and hood, traced in grey shadow upon the dazzling white cloud; and oh, Ebbo! he was struggling with a thinner, darker, wilder shape bearing a club. He strove to withhold it; his gestures threatened and warned! I watched like one spell-bound, for it was to me as the guardian spirit of our race striving for thee with the enemy."

"How did it end?"

"The cloud darkened, and swallowed them; nor should I have known the issue, if suddenly, on the very cloud where the strife had been, there had not beamed forth a rainbow—not a common rainbow, Ebbo, but a perfect ring, a soft-glancing, many-tinted crown of victory. Then I knew the saint had won, and that thou wouldst win."

"I! What, not thyself—his own namesake?"

"I thought, Ebbo, if the fight went very hard—nay, if for a time the grandame led thee her way—that belike I might serve thee best by giving up all, and praying for thee in the hermit's cave, or as a monk."

"Thou!—thou, my other self! Aid me by burrowing in a hole like a rat! What foolery wilt say next? No, no, Friedel, strike by my side, and I will strike with thee; pray by my side, and I will pray with thee; but if thou takest none of the strokes, then will I none of the prayers!"

"Ebbo, thou knowest not what thou sayest."

"No one knows better! See, Friedel, wouldst thou have me all that the old Adlersteinen were, and worse too? then wilt thou leave me and hide thine head in some priestly cowl. Maybe thou thinkest to pray my soul into safety at the last moment as a favour to thine own abundant sanctity; but I tell thee, Friedel, that's no manly way to salvation. If thou follow'st that track, I'll take care to get past the border-line within which prayer can help."

Friedel crossed himself, and uttered an imploring exclamation of horror at these wild words.

"Stay," said Ebbo; "I said not I meant any such thing—so long as thou wilt be with me. My purpose is to be a good man and true, a guard to the weak, a defence against the Turk, a good lord to my vassals, and, if it may not be otherwise, I will take my oath to the Kaiser, and keep it. Is that enough for thee, Friedel, or wouldst thou see me a monk at once?"

"Oh, Ebbo, this is what we ever planned. I only dreamed of the other when—when thou didst seem to be on the other track."

"Well, what can I do more than turn back? I'll get absolution on Sunday, and tell Father Norbert that I will do any penance he pleases; and warn Jobst that, if he sets any more traps in the river, I will drown him there next! Only get this priestly fancy away, Friedel, once and for ever!"

"Never, never could I think of what would sever us," cried Friedel, "save—when—" he added, hesitating, unwilling to harp on the former string. Ebbo broke in imperiously,

"Friedmund von Adlerstein, give me thy solemn word that I never again hear of this freak of turning priest or hermit. What! art slow to speak? Thinkest me too bad for thee?"

"No, Ebbo. Heaven knows thou art stronger, more resolute than I. I am more likely to be too bad for thee. But so long as we can be true, faithful God-fearing Junkern together, Heaven forbid that we should part!"

"It is our bond!" said Ebbo; "nought shall part us."

The Dove in the Eagle's Nest

"Nought but death," said Friedmund, solemnly.

"For my part," said Ebbo, with perfect seriousness, "I do not believe that one of us can live or die without the other. But, hark! there's an outcry at the castle! They have found out that they are locked in! Ha! ho! hilloa, Hatto, how like you playing prisoner?"

Ebbo would have amused himself with the dismay of his garrison a little longer, had not Friedel reminded him that their mother might be suffering for their delay, and this suggestion made him march in hastily. He found her standing drooping under the pitiless storm which Frau Kunigunde was pouring out at the highest pitch of her cracked, trembling voice, one hand uplifted and clenched, the other grasping the back of a chair, while her whole frame shook with rage too mighty for her strength.

"Grandame," said Ebbo, striding up to the scene of action, "cease. Remember my words yestereve."

"She has stolen the keys! She has tampered with the servants! She has released the prisoner—thy prisoner, Ebbo! She has cheated us as she did with Wildschloss! False burgherinn! I trow she wanted another suitor! Bane—pest of Adlerstein!"

Friedmund threw a supporting arm round his mother, but Ebbo confronted the old lady. "Grandmother," he said, "I freed the captive. I stole the keys—I and Friedel! No one else knew my purpose. He was my captive, and I released him because he was foully taken. I have chosen my lot in life," he added; and, standing in the middle of the hall, he took off his cap, and spoke gravely:– "I will not be a treacherous robber–outlaw, but, so help me God, a faithful, loyal, godly nobleman."

His mother and Friedel breathed an "Amen" with all their hearts; and he continued,

"And thou, grandame, peace! Such reverence shalt thou have as befits my father's mother; but henceforth mine own lady–mother is the mistress of this castle, and whoever speaks a rude word to her offends the Freiherr von Adlerstein."

That last day's work had made a great step in Ebbo's life, and there he stood, grave and firm, ready for the assault; for, in effect, he and all besides expected that the old lady would fly at him or at his mother like a wild cat, as she would assuredly have done in a like case a year earlier; but she took them all by surprise by collapsing into her chair and sobbing piteously. Ebbo, much distressed, tried to make her understand that she was to have all care and honour; but she muttered something about ingratitude, and continued to exhaust herself with weeping, spurning away all who approached her; and thenceforth she lived in a gloomy, sullen acquiescence in her deposition.

Christina inclined to the opinion that she must have had some slight stroke in the night, for she was never the same woman again; her vigour had passed away, and she would sit spinning, or rocking herself in her chair, scarcely alive to what passed, or scolding and fretting like a shadow of her old violence. Nothing pleased her but the attentions of her grandsons, and happily she soon ceased to know them apart, and gave Ebbo credit for all that was done for her by Friedel, whose separate existence she seemed to have forgotten.

As long as her old spirit remained she would not suffer the approach of her daughter–in–law, and Christina could only make suggestions for her comfort to be acted on by Ursel; and though the reins of government fast dropped from the aged hands, they were but gradually and cautiously assumed by the younger Baroness.

Only Elsie remained of the rude, demoralized girls whom she had found in the castle, and their successors, though dull and uncouth, were meek and manageable; the men of the castle had all, except Matz, been always devoted to the Frau Christina; and Matz, to her great relief, ran away so soon as he found that decency and honesty were to be the rule. Old Hatto, humpbacked Hans, and Heinz the Schneiderlein, were the whole male establishment, and had at least the merit of attachment to herself and her sons; and in time there was a shade of greater civilization about the castle, though impeded both by dire poverty and the doggedness of the old retainers. At least the court was cleared of the swine, and, within doors, the table was spread with dainty linen out of the parcels from Ulm, and the meals served with orderliness that annoyed the boys at first, but soon became a subject of pride and pleasure.

Frau Kunigunde lingered long, with increasing infirmities. After the winter day, when, running down at a sudden noise, Friedel picked her up from the hearthstone, scorched, bruised, almost senseless, she accepted Christina's care with nothing worse than a snarl, and gradually seemed to forget the identity of her nurse with the interloping burgher girl. Thanks or courtesy had been no part of her nature, least of all towards her own sex, and she did little but grumble, fret, and revile her attendant; but she soon depended so much on Christina's care, that it was hardly possible to leave her. At her best and strongest, her talk was maundering abuse of her son's low-born wife; but at times her wanderings showed black gulfs of iniquity and coarseness of soul that would make the gentle listener tremble, and be thankful that her sons were out of hearing. And thus did Christina von Adlerstein requite fifteen years of persecution.

The old lady's first failure had been in the summer of 1488; it was the Advent season of 1489, when the snow was at the deepest, and the frost at the hardest, that the two hardy mountaineer grandsons fetched over the pass Father Norbert, and a still sturdier, stronger monk, to the dying woman.

"Are we in time, mother?" asked Ebbo, from the door of the upper chamber, where the Adlersteins began and ended life, shaking the snow from his mufflings. Ruddy with exertion in the sharp wind, what a contrast he was to all within the room!

"Who is that?" said a thin, feeble voice.

"It is Ebbo. It is the Baron," said Christina. "Come in, Ebbo. She is somewhat revived."

"Will she be able to speak to the priest?" asked Ebbo.

"Priest!" feebly screamed the old woman. "No priest for me! My lord died unshriven, unassoilzied. Where he is, there will I be. Let a priest approach me at his peril!"

Stony insensibility ensued; nor did she speak again, though life lasted many hours longer. The priests did their office; for, impenitent as the life and frantic as the words had been, the opinions of the time deemed that their rites might yet give the departing soul a chance, though the body was unconscious.

When all was over, snow was again falling, shifting and drifting, so that it was impossible to leave the castle, and the two monks were kept there for a full fortnight, during which Christmas solemnities were observed in the chapel, for the first time since the days of Friedmund the Good. The corpse of Kunigunde, preserved—we must say the word—salted, was placed in a coffin, and laid in that chapel to await the melting of the snows, when the vault at the Hermitage could be opened. And this could not be effected till Easter had nearly come round again, and it was within a week of their sixteenth birthday that the two young Barons stood together at the coffin's head, serious indeed, but more with the thought of life than of death.

CHAPTER XII: BACK TO THE DOVECOTE

For the first time in her residence at Adlerstein, now full half her life, the Freiherrinn Christina ventured to send a messenger to Ulm, namely, a lay brother of the convent of St. Ruprecht, who undertook to convey to Master Gottfried Sorel her letter, informing him of the death of her mother-in-law, and requesting him to send the same tidings to the Freiherr von Adlerstein Wildschloss, the kinsman and godfather of her sons.

She was used to wait fifty-two weeks for answers to her letters, and was amazed when, at the end of three, two stout serving-men were guided by Jobst up the pass; but her heart warmed to their flat caps and round jerkins, they looked so like home. They bore a letter of invitation to her and her sons to come at once to her uncle's house. The King of the

The Dove in the Eagle's Nest

Romans, and perhaps the Emperor, were to come to the city early in the summer, and there could be no better opportunity of presenting the young Barons to their sovereign. Sir Kasimir of Adlerstein Wildschloss would meet them there for the purpose, and would obtain their admission to the League, in which all Swabian nobles had bound themselves to put down robbery and oppression, and outside which there was nothing but outlawry and danger.

"So must it be?" said Ebbo, between his teeth, as he leant moodily against the wall, while his mother was gone to attend to the fare to be set before the messengers.

"What! art not glad to take wing at last?" exclaimed Friedel, cut short in an exclamation of delight.

"Take wing, forsooth! To be guest of a greasy burgher, and call cousin with him! Fear not, Friedel; I'll not vex the motherling. Heaven knows she has had pain, grief, and subjection enough in her lifetime, and I would not hinder her visit to her home; but I would she could go alone, nor make us show our poverty to the swollen city folk, and listen to their endearments. I charge thee, Friedel, do as I do; be not too familiar with them. Could we but sprain an ankle over the crag—"

"Nay, she would stay to nurse us," said Friedel, laughing; "besides, thou art needed for the matter of homage."

"Look, Friedel," said Ebbo, sinking his voice, "I shall not lightly yield my freedom to king or Kaiser. Maybe, there is no help for it; but it irks me to think that I should be the last Lord of Adlerstein to whom the title of Freiherr is not a mockery. Why dost bend thy brow, brother? What art thinking of?"

"Only a saying in my mother's book, that well-ordered service is true freedom," said Friedel. "And methinks there will be freedom in rushing at last into the great far-off!"—the boy's eye expanded and glistened with eagerness. "Here are we prisoners—to ourselves, if you like—but prisoners still, pent up in the rocks, seeing no one, hearing scarce an echo from the knightly or the poet world, nor from all the wonders that pass. And the world has a history going on still, like the Chronicle. Oh, Ebbo, think of being in the midst of life, with lance and sword, and seeing the Kaiser—the Kaiser of the holy Roman Empire!"

"With lance and sword, well and good; but would it were not at the cost of liberty!"

However Ebbo forbore to damp his mother's joy, save by the one warning—"Understand, mother, that I will not be pledged to anything. I will not bend to the yoke ere I have seen and judged for myself."

The manly sound of the words gave a sweet sense of exultation to the mother, even while she dreaded the proud spirit, and whispered, "God direct thee, my son."

Certainly Ebbo, hitherto the most impetuous and least thoughtful of the two lads, had a gravity and seriousness about him, that, but for his naturally sweet temper, would have seemed sullen. His aspirations for adventure had hitherto been more vehement than Friedel's; but, when the time seemed at hand, his regrets at what he might have to yield overpowered his hopes of the future. The fierce haughtiness of the old Adlersteins could not brook the descent from the crag, even while the keen, clear burgher wit that Ebbo inherited from the other side of the house taught him that the position was untenable, and that his isolated glory was but a poor mean thing after all. And the struggle made him sad and moody.

Friedel, less proud, and with nothing to yield, was open to blithe anticipations of what his fancy pictured as the home of all the beauty, sacred or romantic, that he had glimpsed at through his mother. Religion, poetry, learning, art, refinement, had all come to him through her; and though he had a soul that dreamt and soared in the lonely grandeur of the mountain heights, it craved further aliment for its yearnings for completeness and perfection. Long ago had Friedel come to the verge of such attainments as he could work out of his present materials, and keen had been his ardour for the means of progress, though only the mountain tarn had ever been witness to the full outpouring of the longings with which he gazed upon the dim, distant city like a land of enchantment.

The Dove in the Eagle's Nest

The journey was to be at once, so as to profit by the escort of Master Sorel's men. Means of transport were scanty, but Ebbo did not choose that the messengers should report the need, and bring back a bevy of animals at the burgher's expense; so the mother was mounted on the old white mare, and her sons and Heinz trusted to their feet. By setting out early on a May morning, the journey could be performed ere night, and the twilight would find them in the domains of the free city, where their small numbers would be of no importance. As to their appearance, the mother wore a black woollen gown and mantle, and a black silk hood tied under her chin, and sitting loosely round the stiff frame of her white cap—a nun-like garb, save for the soft brown hair, parted over her brow, and more visible than she sometimes thought correct, but her sons would not let her wear it out of sight.

The brothers had piece by piece surveyed the solitary suit of armour remaining in the castle; but, though it might serve for defence, it could not be made fit for display, and they must needs be contented with blue cloth, spun, woven, dyed, fashioned, and sewn at home, chiefly by their mother, and by her embroidered on the breast with the white eagle of Adlerstein. Short blue cloaks and caps of the same, with an eagle plume in each, and leggings neatly fashioned of deerskin, completed their equipments. Ebbo wore his father's sword, Friedel had merely a dagger and crossbow. There was not a gold chain, not a brooch, not an approach to an ornament among the three, except the medal that had always distinguished Ebbo, and the coral rosary at Christina's girdle. Her own trinkets had gone in masses for the souls of her father and husband; and though a few costly jewels had been found in Frau Kunigunde's hoards, the mode of their acquisition was so doubtful, that it had seemed fittest to bestow them in alms and masses for the good of her soul.

"What ornament, what glory could any one desire better than two such sons?" thought Christina, as for the first time for eighteen years she crossed the wild ravine where her father had led her, a trembling little captive, longing for wings like a dove's to flutter home again. Who would then have predicted that she should descend after so long and weary a time, and with a gallant boy on either side of her, eager to aid her every step, and reassure her at each giddy pass, all joy and hope before her and them? Yet she was not without some dread and misgiving, as she watched her elder son, always attentive to her, but unwontedly silent, with a stern gravity on his young brow, a proud sadness on his lip. And when he had come to the Debateable Ford, and was about to pass the boundaries of his own lands, he turned and gazed back on the castle and mountain with a silent but passionate ardour, as though he felt himself doing them a wrong by perilling their independence.

The sun had lately set, and the moon was silvering the Danube, when the travellers came full in view of the imperial free city, girt in with mighty walls and towers—the vine-clad hill dominated by its crowning church; the irregular outlines of the unfinished spire of the cathedral traced in mysterious dark lacework against the pearly sky; the lofty steeple-like gate-tower majestically guarding the bridge. Christina clasped her hands in thankfulness, as at the familiar face of a friend; Friedel glowed like a minstrel introduced to his fair dame, long wooed at a distance; Ebbo could not but exclaim, "Yea, truly, a great city is a solemn and a glorious sight!"

The gates were closed, and the serving-men had to parley at the barbican ere the heavy door was opened to admit the party to the bridge, between deep battlemented stone walls, with here and there loopholes, showing the shimmering of the river beneath. The slow, tired tread of the old mare sounded hollow; the river rushed below with the full swell of evening loudness; a deep-toned convent-bell tolled gravely through the stillness, while, between its reverberations, clear, distinct notes of joyous music were borne on the summer wind, and a nightingale sung in one of the gardens that bordered the banks.

"Mother, it is all that I dreamt!" breathlessly murmured Friedel, as they halted under the dark arch of the great gateway tower.

Not however in Friedel's dreams had been the hearty voice that proceeded from the lighted guard-room in the thickness of the gateway. "Freiherrinn von Adlerstein! Is it she? Then must I greet my old playmate!" And the captain of the watch appeared among upraised lanterns and torches that showed a broad, smooth, plump face beneath a plain steel helmet.

"Welcome, gracious lady, welcome to your old city. What! do you not remember Lippus Grundt, your poor Valentine?"

The Dove in the Eagle's Nest

"Master Philip Grundt!" exclaimed Christina, amazed at the breadth of visage and person; "and how fares it with my good Regina?"

"Excellent well, good lady. She manages her trade and house as well as the good man Bartolaus Fleischer himself. Blithe will she be to show you her goodly ten, as I shall my eight," he continued, walking by her side; "and Barbara—you remember Barbara Schmidt, lady—"

"My dear Barbara?—That do I indeed! Is she your wife?"

"Ay, truly, lady," he answered, in an odd sort of apologetic tone; "you see, you returned not, and the housefathers, they would have it so—and Barbara is a good housewife."

"Truly do I rejoice!" said Christina, wishing she could convey to him how welcome he had been to marry any one he liked, as far as she was concerned—he, in whom her fears of mincing goldsmiths had always taken form—then signing with her hand, "I have my sons likewise to show her."

"Ah, on foot!" muttered Grundt, as a not well-conceived apology for not having saluted the young gentlemen. "I greet you well, sirs," with a bow, most haughtily returned by Ebbo, who was heartily wishing himself on his mountain. "Two lusty, well-grown Junkern indeed, to whom my Martin will be proud to show the humours of Ulm. A fair good night, lady! You will find the old folks right cheery."

Well did Christina know the turn down the street, darkened by the overhanging brows of the tall houses, but each lower window laughing with the glow of light within that threw out the heavy mullions and the circles and diamonds of the latticework, and here and there the brilliant tints of stained glass sparkled like jewels in the upper panes, pictured with Scripture scene, patron saint, or trade emblem. The familiar porch was reached, the familiar knock resounded on the iron-studded door. Friedel lifted his mother from her horse, and felt that she was quivering from head to foot, and at the same moment the light streamed from the open door on the white horse, and the two young faces, one eager, the other with knit brows and uneasy eyes. A kind of echo pervaded the house, "She is come! she is come!" and as one in a dream Christina entered, crossed the well-known hall, looked up to her uncle and aunt on the stairs, perceived little change on their countenances, and sank upon her knees, with bowed head and clasped hands.

"My child! my dear child!" exclaimed her uncle, raising her with one hand, and crossing her brow in benediction with the other. "Art thou indeed returned?" and he embraced her tenderly.

"Welcome, fair niece!" said Hausfrau Johanna, more formally. "I am right glad to greet you here."

"Dear, dear mother!" cried Christina, courting her fond embrace by gestures of the most eager affection, "how have I longed for this moment! and, above all, to show you my boys! Herr Uncle, let me present my sons—my Eberhard, my Friedmund. O Housemother, are not my twins well-grown lads?" And she stood with a hand on each, proud that their heads were so far above her own, and looking still so slight and girlish in figure that she might better have been their sister than their mother. The cloud that the sudden light had revealed on Ebbo's brow had cleared away, and he made an inclination neither awkward nor ungracious in its free mountain dignity and grace, but not devoid of mountain rusticity and shy pride, and far less cordial than was Friedel's manner. Both were infinitely relieved to detect nothing of the greasy burgher, and were greatly struck with the fine venerable head before them; indeed, Friedel would, like his mother, have knelt to ask a blessing, had he not been under command not to outrun his brother's advances towards her kindred.

"Welcome, fair Junkern!" said Master Gottfried; "welcome both for your mother's sake and your own! These thy sons, my little one?" he added, smiling. "Art sure I neither dream nor see double! Come to the gallery, and let me see thee better."

And, ceremoniously giving his hand, he proceeded to lead his niece up the stairs, while Ebbo, labouring under ignorance of city forms and uncertainty of what befitted his dignity, presented his hand to his aunt with an air that half-amused, half-offended the shrewd dame.

"All is as if I had left you but yesterday!" exclaimed Christina. "Uncle, have you pardoned me? You bade me return when my work was done."

"I should have known better, child. Such return is not to be sought on this side the grave. Thy work has been more than I then thought of."

"Ah! and now will you deem it begun—not done!" softly said Christina, though with too much heartfelt exultation greatly to doubt that all the world must be satisfied with two such boys, if only Ebbo would be his true self.

The luxury of the house, the wainscoted and tapestried walls, the polished furniture, the lamps and candles, the damask linen, the rich array of silver, pewter, and brightly-coloured glass, were a great contrast to the bare walls and scant necessaries of Schloss Adlerstein; but Ebbo was resolved not to expose himself by admiration, and did his best to stifle Friedel's exclamations of surprise and delight. Were not these citizens to suppose that everything was tenfold more costly at the baronial castle? And truly the boy deserved credit for the consideration for his mother, which made him merely reserved, while he felt like a wild eagle in a poultry-yard. It was no small proof of his affection to forbear more interference with his mother's happiness than was the inevitable effect of that intuition which made her aware that he was chafing and ill at ease. For his sake, she allowed herself to be placed in the seat of honour, though she longed, as of old, to nestle at her uncle's feet, and be again his child; but, even while she felt each acceptance of a token of respect as almost an injury to them, every look and tone was showing how much the same Christina she had returned.

In truth, though her life had been mournful and oppressed, it had not been such as to age her early. It had been all submission, without wear and tear of mind, and too simple in its trials for care and moiling; so the fresh, lily-like sweetness of her maiden bloom was almost intact, and, much as she had undergone, her once frail health had been so braced by the mountain breezes, that, though delicacy remained, sickliness was gone from her appearance. There was still the exquisite purity and tender modesty of expression, but with greater sweetness in the pensive brown eyes.

"Ah, little one!" said her uncle, after duly contemplating her; "the change is all for the better! Thou art grown a wondrously fair dame. There will scarce be a lovelier in the Kaiserly train."

Ebbo almost pardoned his great-uncle for being his great-uncle.

"When she is arrayed as becomes the Frau Freiherrinn," said the housewife aunt, looking with concern at the coarse texture of her black sleeve. "I long to see our own lady ruffle it in her new gear. I am glad that the lofty pointed cap has passed out; the coif becomes my child far better, and I see our tastes still accord as to fashion."

"Fashion scarce came above the Debateable Ford," said Christina, smiling. "I fear my boys look as if they came out of the Weltgeschichte, for I could only shape their garments after my remembrance of the gallants of eighteen years ago."

"Their garments are your own shaping!" exclaimed the aunt, now in an accent of real, not conventional respect.

"Spinning and weaving, shaping and sewing," said Friedel, coming near to let the housewife examine the texture.

"Close woven, even threaded, smooth tinted! Ah, Stina, thou didst learn something! Thou wert not quite spoilt by the housefather's books and carvings."

"I cannot tell whose teachings have served me best, or been the most precious to me," said Christina, with clasped hands, looking from one to another with earnest love.

The Dove in the Eagle's Nest

"Thou art a good child. Ah! little one, forgive me; you look so like our child that I cannot bear in mind that you are the Frau Freiherrinn."

"Nay, I should deem myself in disgrace with you, did you keep me at a distance, and not THOU me, as your little Stina," she fondly answered, half regretting her fond eager movement, as Ebbo seemed to shrink together with a gesture perceived by her uncle.

"It is my young lord there who would not forgive the freedom," he said, good-humouredly, though gravely.

"Not so," Ebbo forced himself to say; "not so, if it makes my mother happy."

He held up his head rather as if he thought it a fool's paradise, but Master Gottfried answered: "The noble Freiherr is, from all I have heard, too good a son to grudge his mother's duteous love even to burgher kindred."

There was something in the old man's frank, dignified tone of grave reproof that at once impressed Ebbo with a sense of the true superiority of that wise and venerable old age to his own petulant baronial self-assertion. He had both head and heart to feel the burgher's victory, and with a deep blush, though not without dignity, he answered, "Truly, sir, my mother has ever taught us to look up to you as her kindest and best—"

He was going to say "friend," but a look into the grand benignity of the countenance completed the conquest, and he turned it into "father." Friedel at the same instant bent his knee, exclaiming, "It is true what Ebbo says! We have both longed for this day. Bless us, honoured uncle, as you have blessed my mother."

For in truth there was in the soul of the boy, who had never had any but women to look up to, a strange yearning towards reverence, which was called into action with inexpressible force by the very aspect and tone of such a sage elder and counsellor as Master Gottfried Sorel, and he took advantage of the first opening permitted by his brother. And the sympathy always so strong between the two quickened the like feeling in Ebbo, so that the same movement drew him on his knee beside Friedel in oblivion or renunciation of all lordly pride towards a kinsman such as he had here encountered.

"Truly and heartily, my fair youths," said Master Gottfried, with the same kind dignity, "do I pray the good God to bless you, and render you faithful and loving sons, not only to your mother, but to your fatherland."

He was unable to distinguish between the two exactly similar forms that knelt before him, yet there was something in the quivering of Friedel's head, which made him press it with a shade more of tenderness than the other. And in truth tears were welling into the eyes veiled by the fingers that Friedel clasped over his face, for such a blessing was strange and sweet to him.

Their mother was ready to weep for joy. There was now no drawback to her bliss, since her son and her uncle had accepted one another; and she repaired to her own beloved old chamber a happier being than she had been since she had left its wainscoted walls.

Nay, as she gazed out at the familiar outlines of roof and tower, and felt herself truly at home, then knelt by the little undisturbed altar of her devotions, with the cross above and her own patron saint below in carved wood, and the flowers which the good aunt had ever kept as a freshly renewed offering, she felt that she was happier, more fully thankful and blissful than even in the girlish calm of her untroubled life. Her prayer that she might come again in peace had been more than fulfilled; nay, when she had seen her boys kneel meekly to receive her uncle's blessing, it was in some sort to her as if the work was done, as if the millstone had been borne up for her, and had borne her and her dear ones with it.

But there was much to come. She knew full well that, even though her sons' first step had been in the right direction, it was in a path beset with difficulties; and how would her proud Ebbo meet them?

CHAPTER XIII: THE EAGLETS IN THE CITY

After having once accepted Master Gottfried, Ebbo froze towards him and Dame Johanna no more, save that a naturally imperious temper now and then led to fitful stiffnesses and momentary haughtiness, which were easily excused in one so new to the world and afraid of compromising his rank. In general he could afford to enjoy himself with a zest as hearty as that of the simpler-minded Friedel.

They were early afoot, but not before the heads of the household were coming forth for the morning devotions at the cathedral; and the streets were stirring into activity, and becoming so peopled that the boys supposed that it was a great fair day. They had never seen so many people together even at the Friedmund Wake, and it was several days before they ceased to exclaim at every passenger as a new curiosity.

The Dome Kirk awed and hushed them. They had looked to it so long that perhaps no sublunary thing could have realized their expectations, and Friedel avowed that he did not know what he thought of it. It was not such as he had dreamt, and, like a German as he was, he added that he could not think, he could only feel, that there was something ineffable in it; yet he was almost disappointed to find his visions unfulfilled, and the hues of the painted glass less pure and translucent than those of the ice crystals on the mountains. However after his eye had become trained, the deep influence of its dim solemn majesty, and of the echoes of its organ tones, and chants of high praise or earnest prayer, began to enchain his spirit; and, if ever he were missing, he was sure to be found among the mysteries of the cathedral aisles, generally with Ebbo, who felt the spell of the same grave fascination, since whatever was true of the one brother was generally true of the other. They were essentially alike, though some phases of character and taste were more developed in the one or the other.

Master Gottfried was much edified by their perfect knowledge of the names and numbers of his books. They instantly, almost resentfully, missed the Cicero's Offices that he had parted with, and joyfully hailed his new acquisitions, often sitting with heads together over the same book, reading like active-minded youths who were used to out-of-door life and exercise in superabundant measure, and to study as a valued recreation, with only food enough for the intellect to awaken instead of satisfying it.

They were delighted to obtain instruction from a travelling student, then attending the schools of Ulm—a meek, timid lad who, for love of learning and desire of the priesthood, had endured frightful tyranny from the Bacchanten or elder scholars, and, having at length attained that rank, had so little heart to retaliate on the juniors that his contemporaries despised him, and led him a cruel life until he obtained food and shelter from Master Gottfried at the pleasant cost of lessons to the young Barons. Poor Bastien! this land of quiet, civility, and books was a foretaste of Paradise to him after the hard living, barbarity, and coarse vices of his comrades, of whom he now and then disclosed traits that made his present pupils long to give battle to the big shaggy youths who used to send out the lesser lads to beg and steal for them, and cruelly maltreated such as failed in the quest.

Lessons in music and singing were gladly accepted by both lads, and from their uncle's carving they could not keep their hands. Ebbo had begun by enjoining Friedel to remember that the work that had been sport in the mountains would be basely mechanical in the city, and Friedel as usual yielded his private tastes; but on the second day Ebbo himself was discovered in the workshop, watching the magic touch of the deft workman, and he was soon so enticed by the perfect appliances as to take tool in hand and prove himself not unadroit in the craft. Friedel however excelled in delicacy of touch and grace and originality of conception, and produced such workmanship that Master Gottfried could not help stroking his hair and telling him it was a pity he was not born to belong to the guild.

"I cannot spare him, sir," cried Ebbo; "priest, scholar, minstrel, artist—all want him."

"What, Hans of all streets, Ebbo?" interrupted Friedel.

"And guildmaster of none," said Ebbo, "save as a warrior; the rest only enough for a gentleman! For what I am thou must

The Dove in the Eagle's Nest

be!"

But Ebbo did not find fault with the skill Friedel was bestowing on his work—a carving in wood of a dove brooding over two young eagles— –the device that both were resolved to assume. When their mother asked what their lady-loves would say to this, Ebbo looked up, and with the fullest conviction in his lustrous eyes declared that no love should ever rival his motherling in his heart. For truly her tender sweetness had given her sons' affection a touch of romance, for which Master Gottfried liked them the better, though his wife thought their familiarity with her hardly accordant with the patriarchal discipline of the citizens.

The youths held aloof from these burghers, for Master Gottfried wisely desired to give them time to be tamed before running risk of offence, either to, or by, their wild shy pride; and their mother contrived to time her meetings with her old companions when her sons were otherwise occupied. Master Gottfried made it known that the marriage portion he had designed for his niece had been intrusted to a merchant trading in peltry to Muscovy, and the sum thus realized was larger than any bride had yet brought to Adlerstein. Master Gottfried would have liked to continue the same profitable speculations with it; but this would have been beyond the young Baron's endurance, and his eyes sparkled when his mother spoke of repairing the castle, refitting the chapel, having a resident chaplain, cultivating more land, increasing the scanty stock of cattle, and attempting the improvements hitherto prevented by lack of means. He fervently declared that the motherling was more than equal to the wise spinning Queen Bertha of legend and lay; and the first pleasant sense of wealth came in the acquisition of horses, weapons, and braveries. In his original mood, Ebbo would rather have stood before the Diet in his home-spun blue than have figured in cloth of gold at a burgher's expense; but he had learned to love his uncle, he regarded the marriage portion as family property, and moreover he sorely longed to feel himself and his brother well mounted, and scarcely less to see his mother in a velvet gown.

Here was his chief point of sympathy with the housemother, who, herself precluded from wearing miniver, velvet, or pearls, longed to deck her niece therewith, in time to receive Sir Kasimir of Adlerstein Wildschloss, as he had promised to meet his godsons at Ulm. The knight's marriage had lasted only a few years, and had left him no surviving children except one little daughter, whom he had placed in a nunnery at Ulm, under the care of her mother's sister. His lands lay higher up the Danube, and he was expected at Ulm shortly before the Emperor's arrival. He had been chiefly in Flanders with the King of the Romans, and had only returned to Germany when the Netherlanders had refused the regency of Maximilian, and driven him out of their country, depriving him of the custody of his children.

Pfingsttag, or Pentecost-day, was the occasion of Christina's first full toilet, and never was bride more solicitously or exultingly arrayed than she, while one boy held the mirror and the other criticized and admired as the aunt adjusted the pearl-bordered coif, and long white veil floating over the long-desired black velvet dress. How the two lads admired and gazed, caring far less for their own new and noble attire! Friedel was indeed somewhat concerned that the sword by his side was so much handsomer than that which Ebbo wore, and which, for all its dinted scabbard and battered hilt, he was resolved never to discard.

It was a festival of brilliant joy. Wreaths of flowers hung from the windows; rich tapestries decked the Dome Kirk, and the relics were displayed in shrines of wonderful costliness of material and beauty of workmanship; little birds, with thin cakes fastened to their feet, were let loose to fly about the church, in strange allusion to the event of the day; the clergy wore their most gorgeous robes; and the exulting music of the mass echoed from the vaults of the long-drawn aisles, and brought a rapt look of deep calm ecstasy over Friedel's sensitive features. The beggars evidently considered a festival as a harvest-day, and crowded round the doors of the cathedral. As the Lady of Adlerstein came out leaning on Ebbo's arm, with Friedel on her other side, they evidently attracted the notice of a woman whose thin brown face looked the darker for the striped red and yellow silk kerchief that bound the dark locks round her brow, as, holding out a beringed hand, she fastened her glittering jet black eyes on them, and exclaimed, "Alms! if the fair dame and knightly Junkern would hear what fate has in store for them."

"We meddle not with the future, I thank thee," said Christina, seeing that her sons, to whom gipsies were an amazing novelty, were in extreme surprise at the fortune-telling proposal.

"Yet could I tell much, lady," said the woman, still standing in the way. "What would some here present give to know that the locks that were shrouded by the widow's veil ere ever they wore the matron's coif shall yet return to the coif once more?"

Ebbo gave a sudden start of dismay and passion; his mother held him fast. "Push on, Ebbo, mine; heed her not; she is a mere Bohemian."

"But how knew she your history, mother?" asked Friedel, eagerly.

"That might be easily learnt at our Wake," began Christina; but her steps were checked by a call from Master Gottfried just behind. "Frau Freiherrinn, Junkern, not so fast. Here is your noble kinsman."

A tall, fine-looking person, in the long rich robe worn on peaceful occasions, stood forth, doffing his eagle-plumed bonnet, and, as the lady turned and curtsied low, he put his knee to the ground and kissed her hand, saying, "Well met, noble dame; I felt certain that I knew you when I beheld you in the Dome."

"He was gazing at her all the time," whispered Ebbo to his brother; while their mother, blushing, replied, "You do me too much honour, Herr Freiherr."

"Once seen, never to be forgotten," was the courteous answer: "and truly, but for the stately height of these my godsons I would not believe how long since our meeting was."

Thereupon, in true German fashion, Sir Kasimir embraced each youth in the open street, and then, removing his long, embroidered Spanish glove, he offered his hand, or rather the tips of his fingers, to lead the Frau Christina home.

Master Sorel had invited him to become his guest at a very elaborate ornamental festival meal in honour of the great holiday, at which were to be present several wealthy citizens with their wives and families, old connections of the Sorel family. Ebbo had resolved upon treating them with courteous reserve and distance; but he was surprised to find his cousin of Wildschloss comporting himself among the burgomasters and their dames as freely as though they had been his equals, and to see that they took such demeanour as perfectly natural. Quick to perceive, the boy gathered that the gulf between noble and burgher was so great that no intimacy could bridge it over, no reserve widen it, and that his own bashful hauteur was almost a sign that he knew that the gulf had been passed by his own parents; but shame and consciousness did not enable him to alter his manner but rather added to its stiffness.

"The Junker is like an Englishman," said Sir Kasimir, who had met many of the exiles of the Roses at the court of Mary of Burgundy; and then he turned to discuss with the guildmasters the interruption to trade caused by Flemish jealousies.

After the lengthy meal, the tables were removed, the long gallery was occupied by musicians, and Master Gottfried crossed the hall to tell his eldest grandnephew that to him he should depute the opening of the dance with the handsome bride of the Rathsherr, Ulrich Burger. Ebbo blushed up to the eyes, and muttered that he prayed his uncle to excuse him.

"So!" said the old citizen, really displeased; "thy kinsman might have proved to thee that it is no derogation of thy lordly dignity. I have been patient with thee, but thy pride passes—"

"Sir," interposed Friedel hastily, raising his sweet candid face with a look between shame and merriment, "it is not that; but you forget what poor mountaineers we are. Never did we tread a measure save now and then with our mother on a winter evening, and we know no more than a chamois of your intricate measures."

Master Gottfried looked perplexed, for these dances were matters of great punctilio. It was but seven years since the Lord of Praunstein had defied the whole city of Frankfort because a damsel of that place had refused to dance with one of his Cousins; and, though "Fistright" and letters of challenge had been made illegal, yet the whole city of Ulm would have resented the affront put on it by the young lord of Adlerstein. Happily the Freiherr of Adlerstein Wildschloss was at hand. "Herr Burgomaster," he said, "let me commence the dance with your fair lady niece. By your testimony," he added, smiling to the youths, "she can tread a measure. And, after marking us, you may try your success with the Rathsherrinn."

Christina would gladly have transferred her noble partner to the Rathsherrinn, but she feared to mortify her good uncle and aunt further, and consented to figure alone with Sir Kasimir in one of the majestic, graceful dances performed by a single couple before a gazing assembly. So she let him lead her to her place, and they bowed and bent, swept past one another, and moved in interlacing lines and curves, with a grand slow movement that displayed her quiet grace and his stately port and courtly air.

"Is it not beautiful to see the motherling?" said Friedel to his brother; "she sails like a white cloud in a soft wind. And he stands grand as a stag at gaze."

"Like a malapert peacock, say I," returned Ebbo; "didst not see, Friedel, how he kept his eyes on her in church? My uncle says the Bohemians are mere deceivers. Depend on it the woman had spied his insolent looks when she made her ribald prediction."

"See," said Friedel, who had been watching the steps rather than attending, "it will be easy to dance it now. It is a figure my mother once tried to teach us. I remember it now."

"Then go and do it, since better may not be."

"Nay, but it should be thou."

"Who will know which of us it is? I hated his presumption too much to mark his antics."

Friedel came forward, and the substitution was undetected by all save their mother and uncle; by the latter only because, addressing Ebbo, he received a reply in a tone such as Friedel never used.

Natural grace, quickness of ear and eye, and a skilful partner, rendered Friedel's so fair a performance that he ventured on sending his brother to attend the councilloress with wine and comfits; while he in his own person performed another dance with the city dame next in pretension, and their mother was amused by Sir Kasimir's remark, that her second son danced better than the elder, but both must learn.

The remark displeased Ebbo. In his isolated castle he knew no superior, and his nature might yield willingly, but rebelled at being put down. His brother was his perfect equal in all mental and bodily attributes, but it was the absence of all self-assertion that made Ebbo so often give him the preference; it was his mother's tender meekness in which lay her power with him; and if he yielded to Gottfried Sorel's wisdom and experience, it was with the inward consciousness of voluntary deference to one of lower rank. But here was Wildschloss, of the same noble blood with himself, his elder, his sponsor, his protector, with every right to direct him, so that there was no choice between grateful docility and headstrong folly. If the fellow had been old, weak, or in any way inferior, it would have been more bearable; but he was a tried warrior, a sage counsellor, in the prime vigour of manhood, and with a kindly reasonable authority to which only a fool could fail to attend, and which for that very reason chafed Ebbo excessively.

Moreover there was the gipsy prophecy ever rankling in the lad's heart, and embittering to him the sight of every civility from his kinsman to his mother. Sir Kasimir lodged at a neighbouring hostel; but he spent much time with his cousins, and tried to make them friends with his squire, Count Rudiger. A great offence to Ebbo was however the criticisms of both knight and squire on the bearing of the young Barons in military exercises. Truly, with no instructor but the rough lanzknecht Heinz, they must, as Friedel said, have been born paladins to have equalled youths whose life had been spent in chivalrous training.

The Dove in the Eagle's Nest

"See us in a downright fight," said Ebbo; "we could strike as hard as any courtly minion."

"As hard, but scarce as dexterously," said Friedel, "and be called for our pains the wild mountaineers. I heard the men-at-arms saying I sat my horse as though it were always going up or down a precipice; and Master Schmidt went into his shop the other day shrugging his shoulders, and saying we hailed one another across the market-place as if we thought Ulm was a mountain full of gemsbocks."

"Thou heardst! and didst not cast his insolence in his teeth?" cried Ebbo.

"How could I," laughed Friedel, "when the echo was casting back in my teeth my own shout to thee? I could only laugh with Rudiger."

"The chief delight I could have, next to getting home, would be to lay that fellow Rudiger on his back in the tilt-yard," said Ebbo.

But, as Rudiger was by four years his senior, and very expert, the upshot of these encounters was quite otherwise, and the young gentlemen were disabused of the notion that fighting came by nature, and found that, if they desired success in a serious conflict, they must practise diligently in the city tilt-yard, where young men were trained to arms. The crossbow was the only weapon with which they excelled; and, as shooting was a favourite exercise of the burghers, their proficiency was not as exclusive as had seemed to Ebbo a baronial privilege. Harquebuses were novelties to them, and they despised them as burgher weapons, in spite of Sir Kasimir's assurance that firearms were a great subject of study and interest to the King of the Romans. The name of this personage was, it may be feared, highly distasteful to the Freiherr von Adlerstein, both as Wildschloss's model of knightly perfection, and as one who claimed submission from his haughty spirit. When Sir Kasimir spoke to him on the subject of giving his allegiance, he stiffly replied, "Sir, that is a question for ripe consideration."

"It is the question," said Wildschloss, rather more lightly than agreed with the Baron's dignity, "whether you like to have your castle pulled down about your ears."

"That has never happened yet to Adlerstein!" said Ebbo, proudly.

"No, because since the days of the Hohenstaufen there has been neither rule nor union in the empire. But times are changing fast, my Junker, and within the last ten years forty castles such as yours have been consumed by the Swabian League, as though they were so many walnuts."

"The shell of Adlerstein was too hard for them, though. They never tried."

"And wherefore, friend Eberhard? It was because I represented to the Kaiser and the Graf von Wurtemberg that little profit and no glory would accrue from attacking a crag full of women and babes, and that I, having the honour to be your next heir, should prefer having the castle untouched, and under the peace of the empire, so long as that peace was kept. When you should come to years of discretion, then it would be for you to carry out the intention wherewith your father and grandfather left home."

"Then we have been protected by the peace of the empire all this time?" said Friedel, while Ebbo looked as if the notion were hard of digestion.

"Even so; and, had you not freely and nobly released your Genoese merchant, it had gone hard with Adlerstein."

"Could Adlerstein be taken?" demanded Ebbo triumphantly.

The Dove in the Eagle's Nest

"Your grandmother thought not," said Sir Kasimir, with a shade of irony in his tone. "It would be a troublesome siege; but the League numbers 1,500 horse, and 9,000 foot, and, with Schlangenwald's concurrence, you would be assuredly starved out."

Ebbo was so much the more stimulated to take his chance, and do nothing on compulsion; but Friedel put in the question to what the oaths would bind them.

"Only to aid the Emperor with sword and counsel in field or Diet, and thereby win fame and honour such as can scarce be gained by carrying prey to yon eagle roost."

"One may preserve one's independence without robbery," said Ebbo coldly.

"Nay, lad: did you ever hear of a wolf that could live without marauding? Or if he tried, would he get credit for so doing?"

"After all," said Friedel, "does not the present agreement hold till we are of age? I suppose the Swabian League would attempt nothing against minors, unless we break the peace?"

"Probably not; I will do my utmost to give the Freiherr there time to grow beyond his grandmother's maxims," said Wildschloss. "If Schlangenwald do not meddle in the matter, he may have the next five years to decide whether Adlerstein can hold out against all Germany."

"Freiherr Kasimir von Adlerstein Wildschloss," said Eberhard, turning solemnly on him, "I do you to wit once for all that threats will not serve with me. If I submit, it will be because I am convinced it is right. Otherwise we had rather both be buried in the ruins of our castle, as its last free lords."

"So!" said the provoking kinsman; "such burials look grim when the time comes, but happily it is not coming yet!"

Meantime, as Ebbo said to Friedel, how much might happen—a disruption of the empire, a crusade against the Turks, a war in Italy, some grand means of making the Diet value the sword of a free baron, without chaining him down to gratify the greed of hungry Austria. If only Wildschloss could be shaken off! But he only became constantly more friendly and intrusive, almost paternal. No wonder, when the mother and her uncle made him so welcome, and were so intolerably grateful for his impertinent interference, while even Friedel confessed the reasonableness of his counsels, as if that were not the very sting of them.

He even asked leave to bring his little daughter Thekla from her convent to see the Lady of Adlerstein. She was a pretty, flaxen-haired maiden of five years old, in a round cap, and long narrow frock, with a little cross at the neck. She had never seen any one beyond the walls of the nunnery; and, when her father took her from the lay sister's arms, and carried her to the gallery, where sat Hausfrau Johanna, in dark green, slashed with cherry colour, Master Gottfried, in sober crimson, with gold medal and chain, Freiherrinn Christina, in silver-broidered black, and the two Junkern stood near in the shining mail in which they were going to the tilt yard, she turned her head in terror, struggled with her scarce known father, and shrieked for Sister Grethel.

"It was all too sheen," she sobbed, in the lay sister's arms; "she did not want to be in Paradise yet, among the saints! O! take her back! The two bright, holy Michaels would let her go, for indeed she had made but one mistake in her Ave."

Vain was the attempt to make her lift her face from the black serge shoulder where she had hidden it. Sister Grethel coaxed and scolded, Sir Kasimir reproved, the housemother offered comfits, and Christina's soft voice was worst of all, for the child, probably taking her for Our Lady herself, began to gasp forth a general confession. "I will never do so again! Yes, it was a fib, but Mother Hildegard gave me a bit of marchpane not to tell—" Here the lay sister took strong measures for closing the little mouth, and Christina drew back, recommending that the child should be left gradually to discover their terrestrial nature. Ebbo had looked on with extreme disgust, trying to hurry Friedel, who had delayed to trace some lines for his mother on her broidery pattern. In passing the step where Grethel sat with Thekla on her lap, the clank of their armour caused the uplifting of the little flaxen head, and two wide blue eyes looked over Grethel's shoulder, and met Friedel's sunny glance. He smiled; she laughed back again. He held out his arms, and, though his hands were gauntleted, she let him lift her up, and curiously smoothed and patted his cheek, as if he had been a strange animal.

"You have no wings," she said. "Are you St. George, or St. Michael?"

"Neither the one nor the other, pretty one. Only your poor cousin Friedel von Adlerstein, and here is Ebbo, my brother."

It was not in Ebbo's nature not to smile encouragement at the fair little face, with its wistful look. He drew off his glove to caress her silken hair, and for a few minutes she was played with by the two brothers like a newly-invented toy, receiving their attentions with pretty half-frightened graciousness, until Count Rudiger hastened in to summon them, and Friedel placed her on his mother's knee, where she speedily became perfectly happy, and at ease.

Her extreme delight, when towards evening the Junkern returned, was flattering even to Ebbo; and, when it was time for her to be taken home, she made strong resistance, clinging fast to Christina, with screams and struggles. To the lady's promise of coming to see her she replied, "Friedel and Ebbo, too," and, receiving no response to this request, she burst out, "Then I won't come! I am the Freiherrinn Thekla, the heiress of Adlerstein Wildschloss and Felsenbach. I won't be a nun. I'll be married! You shall be my husband," and she made a dart at the nearest youth, who happened to be Ebbo.

"Ay, ay, you shall have him. He will come for you, sweetest Fraulein," said the perplexed Grethel, "so only you will come home! Nobody will come for you if you are naughty."

"Will you come if I am good?" said the spoilt cloister pet, clinging tight to Ebbo.

"Yes," said her father, as she still resisted, "come back, my child, and one day shall you see Ebbo, and have him for a brother."

Thereat Ebbo shook off the little grasping fingers, almost as if they had belonged to a noxious insect.

"The matron's coif should succeed the widow's veil." He might talk with scholarly contempt of the new race of Bohemian impostors; but there was no forgetting that sentence. And in like manner, though his grandmother's allegation that his mother had been bent on captivating Sir Kasimir in that single interview at Adlerstein, had always seemed to him the most preposterous of all Kunigunde's forms of outrage, the recollection would recur to him; and he could have found it in his heart to wish that his mother had never heard of the old lady's designs as to the oubliette. He did most sincerely wish Master Gottfried had never let Wildschloss know of the mode in which his life had been saved. Yet, while it would have seemed him profane to breathe even to Friedel the true secret of his repugnance to this meddlesome kinsman, it was absolutely impossible to avoid his most distasteful authority and patronage.

And the mother herself was gently, thankfully happy and unsuspicious, basking in the tender home affection of which she had so long been deprived, proud of her sons, and, though anxious as to Ebbo's decision, with a quiet trust in his foundation of principle, and above all trusting to prayer.

CHAPTER XIV: THE DOUBLE-HEADED EAGLE

One summer evening, when shooting at a bird on a pole was in full exercise in the tilt-yard, the sports were interrupted by a message from the Provost that a harbinger had brought tidings that the Imperial court was within a day's journey.

All was preparation. Fresh sand had to be strewn on the arena. New tapestry hangings were to deck the galleries, the houses and balconies to be brave with drapery, the fountain in the market-place was to play Rhine wine, all Ulm was astir to do honour to itself and to the Kaisar, and Ebbo stood amid all the bustle, drawing lines in the sand with the stock of his arblast, subject to all that oppressive self-magnification so frequent in early youth, and which made it seem to him as if the Kaisar and the King of the Romans were coming to Ulm with the mere purpose of destroying his independence, and as if the eyes of all Germany were watching for his humiliation.

"See! see!" suddenly exclaimed Friedel; "look! there is something among the tracery of the Dome Kirk Tower. Is it man or bird?"

"Bird, folly! Thou couldst see no bird less than an eagle from hence," said Ebbo. "No doubt they are about to hoist a banner."

"That is not their wont," returned Sir Kasimir.

"I see him," interrupted Ebbo. "Nay, but he is a bold climber! We went up to that stage, close to the balcony, but there's no footing beyond but crockets and canopies."

"And a bit of rotten scaffold," added Friedel. "Perhaps he is a builder going to examine it! Up higher, higher!"

"A builder!" said Ebbo; "a man with a head and foot like that should be a chamois hunter! Shouldst thou deem it worse than the Red Eyrie, Friedel?"

"Yea, truly! The depth beneath is plainer! There would be no climbing there without—"

"Without what, cousin?" asked Wildschloss.

"Without great cause," said Friedel. "It is fearful! He is like a fly against the sky."

"Beaten again!" muttered Ebbo; "I did think that none of these town-bred fellows could surpass us when it came to a giddy height! Who can he be?"

"Look! look!" burst out Friedel. "The saints protect him! He is on that narrowest topmost ledge—measuring; his heel is over the parapet—half his foot!"

"Holding on by the rotten scaffold pole! St. Barbara be his speed; but he is a brave man!" shouted Ebbo. "Oh! the pole has broken."

"Heaven forefend!" cried Wildschloss, with despair on his face unseen by the boys, for Friedel had hidden his eyes, and Ebbo was straining his with the intense gaze of horror. He had carried his glance downwards, following the 380 feet fall that must be the lot of the adventurer. Then looking up again he shouted, "I see him! I see him! Praise to St. Barbara! He is safe! He has caught by the upright stone work."

"Where? where? Show me!" cried Wildschloss, grasping Ebbo's arm.

"There! clinging to that upright bit of tracery, stretching his foot out to yonder crocket."

"I cannot see. Mine eyes swim and dazzle," said Wildschloss. "Merciful heavens! is this another tempting of Providence? How is it with him now, Ebbo?"

"Swarming down another slender bit of the stone network. It must be easy now to one who could keep head and hand steady in such a shock."

"There!" added Friedel, after a breathless space, "he is on the lower parapet, whence begins the stair. Do you know him, sir? Who is he?"

"Either a Venetian mountebank," said Wildschloss, "or else there is only one man I know of either so foolhardy or so steady of head."

"Be he who he may," said Ebbo, "he is the bravest man that ever I beheld. Who is he, Sir Kasimir?"

"An eagle of higher flight than ours, no doubt," said Wildschloss. "But come; we shall reach the Dome Kirk by the time the climber has wound his way down the turret stairs, and we shall see what like he is."

Their coming was well timed, for a small door at the foot of the tower was just opening to give exit to a very tall knight, in one of those short Spanish cloaks the collar of which could be raised so as to conceal the face. He looked to the right and left, and had one hand raised to put up the collar when he recognized Sir Kasimir, and, holding out both hands, exclaimed, "Ha, Adlerstein! well met! I looked to see thee here. No unbonneting; I am not come yet. I am at Strasburg, with the Kaisar and the Archduke, and am not here till we ride in, in purple and in pall by the time the good folk have hung out their arras, and donned their gold chains, and conned their speeches, and mounted their mules."

"Well that their speeches are not over the lykewake of his kingly kaisarly highness," gravely returned Sir Kasimir.

"Ha! Thou sawest? I came out here to avoid the gaping throng, who don't know what a hunter can do. I have been in worse case in the Tyrol. Snowdrifts are worse footing than stone vine leaves."

"Where abides your highness?" asked Wildschloss.

"I ride back again to the halting-place for the night, and meet my father in time to do my part in the pageant. I was sick of the addresses, and, moreover, the purse-proud Flemings have made such a stiff little fop of my poor boy that I am ashamed to look at him, or hear his French accent. So I rode off to get a view of this notable Dom in peace, ere it be bedizened in holiday garb; and one can't stir without all the Chapter waddling after one."

"Your highness has found means of distancing them."

"Why, truly, the Prior would scarce delight in the view from yonder parapet," laughed his highness. "Ha! Adlerstein, where didst get such a perfect pair of pages? I would I could match my hounds as well."

"They are no pages of mine, so please you," said the knight; "rather this is the head of my name. Let me present to your kingly highness the Freiherr von Adlerstein."

"Thou dost not thyself distinguish between them!" said Maximilian, as Friedmund stepped back, putting forward Eberhard, whose bright, lively smile of interest and admiration had been the cause of his cousin's mistake. They would have doffed their caps and bent the knee, but were hastily checked by Maximilian. "No, no, Junkern, I shall owe you no thanks for bringing all the street on me!—that's enough. Reserve the rest for Kaisar Fritz." Then, familiarly taking Sir Kasimir's arm, he walked on, saying, "I remember now. Thou wentest after an inheritance from the old Mouser of the Debateable Ford, and wert ousted by a couple of lusty boys sprung of a peasant wedlock."

"Nay, my lord, of a burgher lady, fair as she is wise and virtuous; who, spite of all hindrances, has bred up these youths in all good and noble nurture."

"Is this so?" said the king, turning sharp round on the twins. "Are ye minded to quit freebooting, and come a crusading against the Turks with me?"

The Dove in the Eagle's Nest

"Everywhere with such a leader!" enthusiastically exclaimed Ebbo.

"'What? up there?" said Maximilian, smiling. "Thou hast the tread of a chamois-hunter."

"Friedel has been on the Red Eyrie," exclaimed Ebbo; then, thinking he had spoken foolishly, he coloured.

"Which is the Red Eyrie?" good-humouredly asked the king.

"It is the crag above our castle," said Friedel, modestly.

"None other has been there," added Ebbo, perceiving his auditor's interest; "but he saw the eagle flying away with a poor widow's kid, and the sight must have given him wings, for we never could find the same path; but here is one of the feathers he brought down"—taking off his cap so as to show a feather rather the worse for wear, and sheltered behind a fresher one.

"Nay," said Friedel, "thou shouldst say that I came to a ledge where I had like to have stayed all night, but that ye all came out with men and ropes."

"We know what such a case is!" said the king. "It has chanced to us to hang between heaven and earth; I've even had the Holy Sacrament held up for my last pious gaze by those who gave me up for lost on the mountain-side. Adlerstein? The peak above the Braunwasser? Some day shall ye show me this eyrie of yours, and we will see whether we can amaze our cousins the eagles. We see you at our father's court to-morrow?" he graciously added, and Ebbo gave a ready bow of acquiescence.

"There," said the king, as after their dismissal he walked on with Sir Kasimir, "never blame me for rashness and imprudence. Here has this height of the steeple proved the height of policy. It has made a loyal subject of a Mouser on the spot."

"Pray Heaven it may have won a heart, true though proud!" said Wildschloss; "but mousing was cured before by the wise training of the mother. Your highness will have taken out the sting of submission, and you will scarce find more faithful subjects."

"How old are the Junkern?"

"Some sixteen years, your highness."

"That is what living among mountains does for a lad. Why could not those thrice-accursed Flemish towns let me breed up my boy to be good for something in the mountains, instead of getting duck-footed and muddy-witted in the fens?"

In the meantime Ebbo and Friedel were returning home in that sort of passion of enthusiasm that ingenuous boyhood feels when first brought into contact with greatness or brilliant qualities.

And brilliance was the striking point in Maximilian. The Last of the Knights, in spite of his many defects, was, by personal qualities, and the hereditary influence of long-descended rank, verily a king of men in aspect and demeanour, even when most careless and simple. He was at this time a year or two past thirty, unusually tall, and with a form at once majestic and full of vigour and activity; a noble, fair, though sunburnt countenance; eyes of dark gray, almost black; long fair hair, a keen aquiline nose, a lip only beginning to lengthen to the characteristic Austrian feature, an expression always lofty, sometimes dreamy, and yet at the same time full of acuteness and humour. His abilities were of the highest order, his purposes, especially at this period of his life, most noble and becoming in the first prince of Christendom; and, if his life were a failure, and his reputation unworthy of his endowments, the cause seems to have been in great measure the bewilderment and confusion that unusual gifts sometimes cause to their possessor, whose sight their conflicting illumination dazzles so as to impair his steadiness of aim, while their contending gleams light him into various directions, so that one object is deserted for another ere its completion. Thus Maximilian cuts a figure in history far inferior to that made by his grandson, Charles V., whom he nevertheless excelled in every personal quality, except the most needful of all, force of character; and, in like manner, his remote descendant, the narrow-minded Ferdinand of Styria, gained his ends, though the able and brilliant Joseph II. was to die broken-hearted, calling his reign a failure and mistake. However, such terms as these could not be applied to Maximilian with regard to home affairs. He has had hard measure from those who have only regarded his vacillating foreign policy, especially with respect to Italy—ever the temptation and the bane of Austria; but even here much of his uncertain conduct was owing to the unfulfilled promises of what he himself called his "realm of kings," and a sovereign can only justly be estimated by his domestic policy. The contrast of the empire before his time with the subsequent Germany is that of chaos with order. Since the death of Friedrich II. the Imperial title had been a mockery, making the prince who chanced to bear it a mere mark for the spite of his rivals; there was no centre of justice, no appeal; everybody might make war on everybody, with the sole preliminary of exchanging a challenge; "fist-right" was the acknowledged law of the land; and, except in the free cities, and under such a happy accident as a right-minded prince here and there, the state of Germany seems to have been rather worse than that of Scotland from Bruce to the union of the Crowns. Under Maximilian, the Diet became an effective council, fist-right was abolished, independent robber-lords put down, civilization began to effect an entrance, the system of circles was arranged, and the empire again became a leading power in Europe, instead of a mere vortex of disorder and misrule. Never would Charles V. have held the position he occupied had he come after an ordinary man, instead of after an able and sagacious reformer like that Maximilian who is popularly regarded as a fantastic caricature of a knight-errant, marred by avarice and weakness of purpose.

At the juncture of which we are writing, none of Maximilian's less worthy qualities had appeared; he had not been rendered shifty and unscrupulous by difficulties and disappointments in money matters, and had not found it impossible to keep many of the promises he had given in all good faith. He stood forth as the hope of Germany, in salient contrast to the feeble and avaricious father, who was felt to be the only obstacle in the way of his noble designs of establishing peace and good discipline in the empire, and conducting a general crusade against the Turks, whose progress was the most threatening peril of Christendom. His fame was, of course, frequently discussed among the citizens, with whom he was very popular, not only from his ease and freedom of manner, but because his graceful tastes, his love of painting, sculpture, architecture, and the mechanical turn which made him an improver of fire-arms and a patron of painting and engraving, rendered their society more agreeable to him than that of his dull, barbarous nobility. Ebbo had heard so much of the perfections of the King of the Romans as to be prepared to hate him; but the boy, as we have seen, was of a generous, sensitive nature, peculiarly prone to enthusiastic impressions of veneration; and Maximilian's high-spirited manhood, personal fascination, and individual kindness had so entirely taken him by surprise, that he talked of him all the evening in a more fervid manner than did even Friedel, though both could scarcely rest for their anticipations of seeing him on the morrow in the full state of his entry.

Richly clad, and mounted on cream-coloured steeds, nearly as much alike as themselves, the twins were a pleasant sight for a proud mother's eyes, as they rode out to take their place in the procession that was to welcome the royal guests. Master Sorel, in ample gown, richly furred, with medal and chain of office, likewise went forth as Guildmaster; and Christina, with smiling lips and liquid eyes, recollected the days when to see him in such array was her keenest pleasure, and the utmost splendour her fancy could depict.

Arrayed, as her sons loved to see her, in black velvet, and with pearl-bordered cap, Christina sat by her aunt in the tapestried balcony, and between them stood or sat little Thekla von Adlerstein Wildschloss, whose father had entrusted her to their care, to see the procession pass by. A rich Eastern carpet, of gorgeous colouring, covered the upper balustrade, over which they leant, in somewhat close quarters with the scarlet-bodiced dames of the opposite house, but with ample space for sight up and down the rows of smiling expectants at each balcony, or window, equally gay with hangings, while the bells of all the churches clashed forth their gayest chimes, and fitful bursts of music were borne upon the breeze. Little Thekla danced in the narrow space for very glee, and wondered why any one should live in a cloister when the world was so wide and so fair. And Dame Johanna tried to say something pious of worldly temptations, and the cloister shelter; but Thekla interrupted her, and, clinging to Christina, exclaimed, "Nay, but I am always naughty with Mother Ludmilla in the convent, and I know I should never be naughty out here with you and the barons; I should be so happy."

"Hush! hush! little one; here they come!"

On they came—stout lanzknechts first, the city guard with steel helmets unadorned, buff suits, and bearing either harquebuses, halberts, or those handsome but terrible weapons, morning stars. Then followed guild after guild, each preceded by the banner bearing its homely emblem—the cauldron of the smiths, the hose of the clothiers, the helmet of the armourers, the bason of the barbers, the boot of the sutors; even the sausage of the cooks, and the shoe of the shoeblacks, were re-presented, as by men who gloried in the calling in which they did life's duty and task.

First in each of these bands marched the prentices, stout, broad, flat-faced lads, from twenty to fourteen years of age, with hair like tow hanging from under their blue caps, staves in their hands, and knives at their girdles. Behind them came the journeymen, in leathern jerkins and steel caps, and armed with halberts or cross- bows; men of all ages, from sixty to one or two and twenty, and many of the younger ones with foreign countenances and garb betokening that they were strangers spending part of their wandering years in studying the Ulm fashions of their craft. Each trade showed a large array of these juniors; but the masters who came behind were comparatively few, mostly elderly, long-gowned, gold-chained personages, with a weight of solid dignity on their wise brows—men who respected themselves, made others respect them, and kept their city a peaceful, well-ordered haven, while storms raged in the realm beyond—men too who had raised to the glory of their God a temple, not indeed fulfilling the original design, but a noble effort, and grand monument of burgher devotion.

Then came the ragged regiment of scholars, wild lads from every part of Germany and Switzerland, some wan and pinched with hardship and privation, others sturdy, selfish rogues, evidently well able to take care of themselves. There were many rude, tyrannical-looking lads among the older lads; and, though here and there a studious, earnest face might be remarked, the prospect of Germany's future priests and teachers was not encouraging. And what a searching ordeal was awaiting those careless lads when the voice of one, as yet still a student, should ring through Germany!

Contrasting with these ill-kempt pupils marched the grave professors and teachers, in square ecclesiastic caps and long gowns, whose colours marked their degrees and the Universities that had conferred them—some thin, some portly, some jocund, others dreamy; some observing all the humours around, others still intent on Aristotelian ethics; all men of high fame, with doctor at the beginning of their names, and "or" or "us" at the close of them. After them rode the magistracy, a burgomaster from each guild, and the Herr Provost himself—as great a potentate within his own walls as the Doge of Venice or of Genoa, or perhaps greater, because less jealously hampered. In this dignified group was Uncle Gottfried, by complacent nod and smile acknowledging his good wife and niece, who indeed had received many a previous glance and bow from friends passing beneath. But Master Sorel was no new spectacle in a civic procession, and the sight of him was only a pleasant fillip to the excitement of his ladies.

Here was jingling of spurs and trampling of horses; heraldic achievements showed upon the banners, round which rode the mail-clad retainers of country nobles who had mustered to meet their lords. Then, with still more of clank and tramp, rode a bright-faced troop of lads, with feathered caps and gay mantles. Young Count Rudiger looked up with courteous salutation; and just behind him, with smiling lips and upraised faces, were the pair whose dark eyes, dark hair, and slender forms rendered them conspicuous among the fair Teutonic youth. Each cap was taken off and waved, and each pair of lustrous eyes glanced up pleasure and exultation at the sight of the lovely "Mutterlein." And she? The pageant was well-nigh over to her, save for heartily agreeing with Aunt Johanna that there was not a young noble of them all to compare with the twin Barons of Adlerstein! However, she knew she should be called to account if she did not look well at "the Romish King;" besides, Thekla was shrieking with delight at the sight of her father, tall and splendid on his mighty black charger, with a smile for his child, and for the lady a bow so low and deferential that it was evidently remarked by those at whose approach every lady in the balconies was rising, every head in the street was bared.

A tall, thin, shrivelled, but exceedingly stately old man on a gray horse was in the centre. Clad in a purple velvet mantle, and bowing as he went, he looked truly the Kaisar, to whom stately courtesy was second nature. On one side, in black and gold, with the jewel of the Golden Fleece on his breast, rode Maximilian, responding gracefully to the salutations of the people, but his keen gray eye roving in search of the object of Sir Kasimir's salute, and lighting on Christina with such a rapid, amused glance of discovery that, in her confusion, she missed what excited Dame Johanna's rapturous admiration—the handsome boy on the Emperor's other side, a fair, plump lad, the young sovereign of the Low Countries, beautiful in feature and complexion, but lacking the fire and the loftiness that characterized his father's countenance. The train was closed by the Reitern of the Emperor's guard—steel-clad mercenaries who were looked on with no friendly eyes by the few gazers in the street who had been left behind in the general rush to keep up with the attractive part of the show.

Pageants of elaborate mythological character impeded the imperial progress at every stage, and it was full two hours ere the two youths returned, heartily weary of the lengthened ceremonial, and laughing at having actually seen the King of the Romans enduring to be conducted from shrine to shrine in the cathedral by a large proportion of its dignitaries. Ebbo was sure he had caught an archly disconsolate wink!

Ebbo had to dress for the banquet spread in the town-hall. Space was wanting for the concourse of guests, and Master Sorel had decided that the younger Baron should not be included in the invitation. Friedel pardoned him more easily than did Ebbo, who not only resented any slight to his double, but in his fits of shy pride needed the aid of his readier and brighter other self. But it might not be, and Sir Kasimir and Master Gottfried alone accompanied him, hoping that he would not look as wild as a hawk, and would do nothing to diminish the favourable impression he had made on the King of the Romans.

Late, according to mediaeval hours, was the return, and Ebbo spoke in a tone of elation. "The Kaisar was most gracious, and the king knew me," he said, "and asked for thee, Friedel, saying one of us was nought without the other. But thou wilt go to-morrow, for we are to receive knighthood."

"Already!" exclaimed Friedel, a bright glow rushing to his cheek.

"Yea," said Ebbo. "The Romish king said somewhat about waiting to win our spurs; but the Kaisar said I was in a position to take rank as a knight, and I thanked him, so thou shouldst share the honour."

"The Kaisar," said Wildschloss, "is not the man to let a knight's fee slip between his fingers. The king would have kept off their grip, and reserved you for knighthood from his own sword under the banner of the empire; but there is no help for it now, and you must make your vassals send in their dues."

"My vassals?" said Ebbo; "what could they send?"

"The aid customary on the knighthood of the heir."

"But there is—there is nothing!" said Friedel. "They can scarce pay meal and poultry enough for our daily fare; and if we were to flay them alive, we should not get sixty groschen from the whole."

"True enough! Knighthood must wait till we win it," said Ebbo, gloomily.

"Nay, it is accepted," said Wildschloss. "The Kaisar loves his iron chest too well to let you go back. You must be ready with your round sum to the chancellor, and your spur-money and your fee to the heralds, and largess to the crowd."

"Mother, the dowry," said Ebbo.

"At your service, my son," said Christina, anxious to chase the cloud from his brow.

But it was a deep haul, for the avaricious Friedrich IV. made exorbitant charges for the knighting his young nobles; and Ebbo soon saw that the improvements at home must suffer for the honours that would have been so much better won than bought.

"If your vassals cannot aid, yet may not your kinsman—?" began Wildschloss.

"No!" interrupted Ebbo, lashed up to hot indignation. "No, sir! Rather will my mother, brother, and I ride back this very night to unfettered liberty on our mountain, without obligation to any living man."

"Less hotly, Sir Baron," said Master Gottfried, gravely. "You broke in on your noble godfather, and you had not heard me speak. You and your brother are the old man's only heirs, nor do ye incur any obligation that need fret you by forestalling what would be your just right. I will see my nephews as well equipped as any young baron of them."

The mother looked anxiously at Ebbo. He bent his head with rising colour, and said, "Thanks, kind uncle. From YOU I have learnt to look on goodness as fatherly."

"Only," added Friedel, "if the Baron's station renders knighthood fitting for him, surely I might remain his esquire."

"Never, Friedel!" cried his brother. "Without thee, nothing."

"Well said, Freiherr," said Master Sorel; "what becomes the one becomes the other. I would not have thee left out, my Friedel, since I cannot leave thee the mysteries of my craft."

"To-morrow!" said Friedel, gravely. "Then must the vigil be kept to-night."

"The boy thinks these are the days of Roland and Karl the Great," said Wildschloss. "He would fain watch his arms in the moonlight in the Dome Kirk! Alas! no, my Friedel! Knighthood in these days smacks more of bezants than of deeds of prowess."

"Unbearable fellow!" cried Ebbo, when he had latched the door of the room he shared with his brother. "First, holding up my inexperience to scorn! As though the Kaisar knew not better than he what befits me! Then trying to buy my silence and my mother's gratitude with his hateful advance of gold. As if I did not loathe him enough without! If I pay my homage, and sign the League to-morrow, it will be purely that he may not plume himself on our holding our own by sufferance, in deference to him."

"You will sign it—you will do homage!" exclaimed Friedel. "How rejoiced the mother will be."

"I had rather depend at once—if depend I must—on yonder dignified Kaisar and that noble king than on our meddling kinsman," said Ebbo. "I shall be his equal now! Ay, and no more classed with the court Junkern I was with to-day. The dullards! No one reasonable thing know they but the chase. One had been at Florence; and when I asked him of the Baptistery and rare Giotto of whom my uncle told us, he asked if he were a knight of the Medici. All he knew was that there were ortolans at Ser Lorenzo's table; and he and the rest of them talked over wines as many and as hard to call as the roll of AEneas's comrades; and when each one must drink to her he loved best, and I said I loved none like my sweet mother, they gibed me for a simple dutiful mountaineer. Yea, and when the servants brought a bowl, I thought it was a wholesome draught of spring water after all their hot wines and fripperies. Pah!"

"The rose-water, Ebbo! No wonder they laughed! Why, the bowls for our fingers came round at the banquet here."

"Ah! thou hast eyes for their finikin manners! Yet what know they of what we used to long for in polished life! Not one but vowed he abhorred books, and cursed Dr. Faustus for multiplying them. I may not know the taste of a stew, nor the fit of a glove, as they do, but I trust I bear a less empty brain. And the young Netherlanders that came with the Archduke were worst of all. They got together and gabbled French, and treated the German Junkern with the very same sauce with which they had served me. The Archduke laughed with them, and when the Provost addressed him, made as if he understood not, till his father heard, and thundered out, 'How now, Philip! Deaf on thy German ear? I tell thee, Herr Probst, he knows his own tongue as well as thou or I, and thou shalt hear him speak as becomes the son of an Austrian hunter.' That Romish king is a knight of knights, Friedel. I could follow him to the world's end. I wonder whether he will ever come to climb the Red Eyrie."

"It does not seem the world's end when one is there," said Friedel, with strange yearnings in his breast.

"Even the Dom steeple never rose to its full height," he added, standing in the window, and gazing pensively into the summer sky. "Oh, Ebbo! this knighthood has come very suddenly after our many dreams; and, even though its outward tokens be lowered, it is still a holy, awful thing."

Nurtured in mountain solitude, on romance transmitted through the pure medium of his mother's mind, and his spirit untainted by contact with the world, Friedmund von Adlerstein looked on chivalry with the temper of a Percival or Galahad, and regarded it with a sacred awe. Eberhard, though treating it more as a matter of business, was like enough to his brother to enter into the force of the vows they were about to make; and if the young Barons of Adlerstein did not perform the night-watch over their armour, yet they kept a vigil that impressed their own minds as deeply, and in early morn they went to confession and mass ere the gay parts of the city were astir.

"Sweet niece," said Master Sorel, as he saw the brothers' grave, earnest looks, "thou hast done well by these youths; yet I doubt me at times whether they be not too much lifted out of this veritable world of ours."

"Ah, fair uncle, were they not above it, how could they face its temptations?"

"True, my child; but how will it be when they find how lightly others treat what to them is so solemn?"

"There must be temptations for them, above all for Ebbo," said Christina, "but still, when I remember how my heart sank when their grandmother tried to bring them up to love crime as sport and glory, I cannot but trust that the good work will be wrought out, and my dream fulfilled, that they may be lights on earth and stars in heaven. Even this matter of homage, that seemed so hard to my Ebbo, has now been made easy to him by his veneration for the Emperor."

It was even so. If the sense that he was the last veritable FREE lord of Adlerstein rushed over Ebbo, he was, on the other hand, overmastered by the kingliness of Friedrich and Maximilian, and was aware that this submission, while depriving him of little or no actual power, brought him into relations with the civilized world, and opened to him paths of true honour. So the ceremonies were gone through, his oath of allegiance was made, investiture was granted to him by the delivery of a sword, and both he and Friedel were dubbed knights. Then they shared another banquet, where, as away from the Junkern and among elder men, Ebbo was happier than the day before. Some of the knights seemed to him as rude and ignorant as the Schneiderlein, but no one talked to him nor observed his manners, and he could listen to conversation on war and policy such as interested him far more than the subjects affected by youths a little older than himself. Their lonely life and training had rendered the minds of the brothers as much in advance of their fellows as they were behind them in knowledge of the world.

The crass obtuseness of most of the nobility made it a relief to return to the usual habits of the Sorel household when the court had left Ulm. Friedmund, anxious to prove that his new honours were not to alter his home demeanour, was drawing on a block of wood from a tinted pen-and-ink sketch; Ebbo was deeply engaged with a newly- acquired copy of Virgil; and their mother was embroidering some draperies for the long-neglected castle chapel,—all sitting, as Master Gottfried loved to have them, in his studio, whence he had a few moments before been called away, when, as the door slowly opened, a voice was heard that made both lads start and rise.

"Yea, truly, Herr Guildmaster, I would see these masterpieces. Ha! What have you here for masterpieces? Our two new double-ganger knights?" And Maximilian entered in a simple riding-dress, attended by Master Gottfried, and by Sir Kasimir of Adlerstein Wildschloss.

The Dove in the Eagle's Nest

Christina would fain have slipped out unperceived, but the king was already removing his cap from his fair curling locks, and bending his head as he said, "The Frau Freiherrinn von Adlerstein? Fair lady, I greet you well, and thank you in the Kaisar's name and mine for having bred up for us two true and loyal subjects."

"May they so prove themselves, my liege!" said Christina, bending low.

"And not only loyal-hearted," added Maximilian, smiling, "but ready- brained, which is less frequent among our youth. What is thy book, young knight? Virgilius Maro? Dost thou read the Latin?" he added, in that tongue.

"Not as well as we wish, your kingly highness," readily answered Ebbo, in Latin, "having learnt solely of our mother till we came hither."

"Never fear for that, my young blade," laughed the king. "Knowst not that the wiseacres thought me too dull for teaching till I was past ten years? And what is thy double about? Drawing on wood? How now! An able draughtsman, my young knight?"

"My nephew Sir Friedmund is good to the old man," said Gottfried, himself almost regretting the lad's avocation. "My eyes are failing me, and he is aiding me with the graving of this border. He has the knack that no teaching will impart to any of my present journeymen."

"Born, not made," quoth Maximilian. "Nay," as Friedel coloured deeper at the sense that Ebbo was ashamed of him, "no blushes, my boy; it is a rare gift. I can make a hundred knights any day, but the Almighty alone can make a genius. It was this very matter of graving that led me hither."

For Maximilian had a passion for composition, and chiefly for autobiography, and his head was full of that curious performance, Der Weisse Konig, which occupied many of the leisure moments of his life, being dictated to his former writing-master, Marcus Sauerwein. He had already designed the portrayal of his father as the old white king, and himself as the young white king, in a series of woodcuts illustrating the narrative which culminated in the one romance of his life, his brief happy marriage with Mary of Burgundy; and he continued eagerly to talk to Master Gottfried about the mystery of graving, and the various scenes in which he wished to depict himself learning languages from native speakers—Czech from a peasant with a basket of eggs, English from the exiles at the Burgundian court, who had also taught him the use of the longbow, building from architects and masons, painting from artists, and, more imaginatively, astrology from a wonderful flaming sphere in the sky, and the black art from a witch inspired by a long-tailed demon perched on her shoulder. No doubt "the young white king" made an exceedingly prominent figure in the discourse, but it was so quaint and so brilliant that it did not need the charm of royal condescension to entrance the young knights, who stood silent auditors. Ebbo at least was convinced that no species of knowledge or skill was viewed by his kaisarly kingship as beneath his dignity; but still he feared Friedel's being seized upon to be as prime illustrator to the royal autobiography—a lot to which, with all his devotion to Maximilian, he could hardly have consigned his brother, in the certainty that the jeers of the ruder nobles would pursue the craftsman baron.

However, for the present, Maximilian was keen enough to see that the boy's mechanical skill was not as yet equal to his genius; so he only encouraged him to practise, adding that he heard there was a rare lad, one Durer, at Nuremburg, whose productions were already wonderful. "And what is this?" he asked; "what is the daintily- carved group I see yonder?"

"Your highness means, 'The Dove in the Eagle's Nest,'" said Kasimir. "It is the work of my young kinsmen, and their appropriate device."

"As well chosen as carved," said Maximilian, examining it. "Well is it that a city dove should now and then find her way to the eyrie. Some of my nobles would cut my throat for the heresy, but I am safe here, eh, Sir Kasimir? Fare ye well, ye dove-trained eaglets. We will know one another better when we bear the cross against the infidel."

The brothers kissed his hand, and he descended the steps from the hall door. Ere he had gone far, he turned round upon Sir Kasimir with a merry smile

"A very white and tender dove indeed, and one who might easily nestle in another eyrie, methinks."

"Deems your kingly highness that consent could be won?" asked Wildschloss

"From the Kaisar? Pfui, man, thou knowst as well as I do the golden key to his consent. So thou wouldst risk thy luck again! Thou hast no male heir."

"And I would fain give my child a mother who would deal well with her. Nay, to say sooth, that gentle, innocent face has dwelt with me for many years. But for my pre-contract, I had striven long ago to win her, and had been a happier man, mayhap. And, now I have seen what she has made of her sons, I feel I could scarce find her match among our nobility."

"Nor elsewhere," said the king; "and I honour thee for not being so besotted in our German haughtiness as not to see that it is our free cities that make refined and discreet dames. I give you good speed, Adlerstein; but, if I read aright the brow of one at least of these young fellows, thou wilt scarce have a willing or obedient stepson.'

CHAPTER XV: THE RIVAL EYRIE

Ebbo trusted that his kinsman of Wildschloss was safe gone with the Court, and his temper smoothed and his spirits rose in proportion while preparations for a return to Adlerstein were being completed— preparations by which the burgher lady might hope to render the castle far more habitable, not to say baronial, than it had ever been.

The lady herself felt thankful that her stay at Ulm had turned out well beyond all anticipations in the excellent understanding between her uncle and her sons, and still more in Ebbo's full submission and personal loyalty towards the imperial family. The die was cast, and the first step had been taken towards rendering the Adlerstein family the peaceful, honourable nobles she had always longed to see them.

She was one afternoon assisting her aunt in some of the duties of her wirthschaft, when Master Gottfried entered the apartment with an air of such extreme complacency that both turned round amazed; the one exclaiming, "Surely funds have come in for finishing the spire!" the other, "Have they appointed thee Provost for next year, house- father?"

"Neither the one nor the other," was the reply. "But heard you not the horse's feet? Here has the Lord of Adlerstein Wildschloss been with me in full state, to make formal proposals for the hand of our child, Christina."

"For Christina!" cried Hausfrau Johanna with delight; "truly that is well. Truly our maiden has done honour to her breeding. A second nobleman demanding her—and one who should be able richly to endow her!"

"And who will do so," said Master Gottfried. "For morning gift he promises the farms and lands of Grunau—rich both in forest and corn glebe. Likewise, her dower shall be upon Wildschloss—where the soil is of the richest pasture, and there are no less than three mills, whence the lord obtains large rights of multure. Moreover, the Castle was added to and furnished on his marriage with the late baroness, and might serve a Kurfurst; and though the jewels of Freiherrinn Valeska must be inherited by her daughter, yet there are many of higher price which have descended from his own ancestresses, and which will all be hers."

"And what a wedding we will have!" exclaimed Johanna; "it shall be truly baronial. I will take my hood and go at once to neighbour Sophie Lemsberg, who was wife to the Markgraf's Under Keller-Meister. She will tell me point device the ceremonies befitting the espousals of a baron's widow."

The Dove in the Eagle's Nest

Poor Christina had sat all this time with drooping head and clasped hands, a tear stealing down as the formal terms of the treaty sent her spirit back to the urgent, pleading, imperious voice that had said, "Now, little one, thou wilt not shut me out;" and as she glanced at the ring that had lain on that broad palm, she felt as if her sixteen cheerful years had been an injury to her husband in his nameless bloody grave. But protection was so needful in those rude ages, and second marriages so frequent, that reluctance was counted as weakness. She knew her uncle and aunt would never believe that aught but compulsion had bound her to the rude outlaw, and her habit of submission was so strong that, only when her aunt was actually rising to go and consult her gossip, she found breath to falter,

"Hold, dear aunt—my sons—"

"Nay, child, it is the best thing thou couldst do for them. Wonders hast thou wrought, yet are they too old to be without fatherly authority. I speak not of Friedel; the lad is gentle and pious, though spirited, but for the baron. The very eye and temper of my poor brother Hugh—thy father, Stine—are alive again in him. Yea, I love the lad the better for it, while I fear. He minds me precisely of Hugh ere he was 'prenticed to the weapon–smith, and all became bitterness."

"Ah, truly," said Christina, raising her eyes "all would become bitterness with my Ebbo were I to give a father's power to one whom he would not love."

"Then were he sullen and unruly, indeed!" said the old burgomaster with displeasure; "none have shown him more kindness, none could better aid him in court and empire. The lad has never had restraint enough. I blame thee not, child, but he needs it sorely, by thine own showing."

"Alas, uncle! mine be the blame, but it is over late. My boy will rule himself for the love of God and of his mother, but he will brook no hand over him—least of all now he is a knight and thinks himself a man. Uncle, I should be deprived of both my sons, for Friedel's very soul is bound up with his brother's. I pray thee enjoin not this thing on me," she implored.

"Child!" exclaimed Master Gottfried, "thou thinkst not that such a contract as this can be declined for the sake of a wayward Junker!"

"Stay, house–father, the little one will doubtless hear reason and submit," put in the aunt. "Her sons were goodly and delightsome to her in their upgrowth, but they are well–nigh men. They will be away to court and camp, to love and marriage; and how will it be with her then, young and fair as she still is? Well will it be for her to have a stately lord of her own, and a new home of love and honour springing round her."

"True," continued Sorel; "and though she be too pious and wise to reck greatly of such trifles, yet it may please her dreamy brain to hear that Sir Kasimir loves her even like a paladin, and the love of a tried man of six–and–forty is better worth than a mere kindling of youthful fancy."

"Mine Eberhard loved me!" murmured Christina, almost to herself, but her aunt caught the word.

"And what was such love worth? To force thee into a stolen match, and leave thee alone and unowned to the consequences!"

"Peace!" exclaimed Christina, with crimson cheek and uplifted head. "Peace! My own dear lord loved me with true and generous love! None but myself knows how much. Not a word will I hear against that tender heart."

"Yes, peace," returned Gottfried in a conciliatory tone,—"peace to the brave Sir Eberhard. Thine aunt meant no ill of him. He truly would rejoice that the wisdom of his choice should receive such testimony, and that his sons should be thus well handled. Nay, little as I heed such toys, it will doubtless please the lads that the baron will obtain of the Emperor letters of nobility for this house, which verily sprang of a good Walloon family, and so their shield will have no blank. The Romish king promises to give thee rank with any baroness, and hath fully owned what a pearl thou art, mine own sweet dove!

Nay, Sir Kasimir is coming to-morrow in the trust to make the first betrothal with Graf von Kaulwitz as a witness, and I thought of asking the Provost on the other hand."

"To-morrow!" exclaimed Johanna; "and how is she to be meetly clad? Look at this widow-garb; and how is time to be found for procuring other raiment? House-father, a substantial man like you should better understand! The meal too! I must to gossip Sophie!"

"Verily, dear mother and father," said Christina, who had rallied a little, "have patience with me. I may not lightly or suddenly betroth myself; I know not that I can do so at all, assuredly not unless my sons were heartily willing. Have I your leave to retire?"

"Granted, my child, for meditation will show thee that this is too fair a lot for any but thee. Much had I longed to see thee wedded ere thy sons outgrew thy care, but I shunned proposing even one of our worthy guildmasters, lest my young Freiherr should take offence; but this knight, of his own blood, true and wise as a burgher, and faithful and God-fearing withal, is a better match than I durst hope, and is no doubt a special reward from thy patron saint."

"Let me entreat one favour more," implored Christina. "Speak of this to no one ere I have seen my sons."

She made her way to her own chamber, there to weep and flutter. Marriage was a matter of such high contract between families that the parties themselves had usually no voice in the matter, and only the widowed had any chance of a personal choice; nor was this always accorded in the case of females, who remained at the disposal of their relatives. Good substantial wedded affection was not lacking, but romantic love was thought an unnecessary preliminary, and found a vent in extravagant adoration, not always in reputable quarters. Obedience first to the father, then to the husband, was the first requisite; love might shift for itself; and the fair widow of Adlerstein, telling her beads in sheer perplexity, knew not whether her strong repugnance to this marriage and warm sympathy with her son Ebbo were not an act of rebellion. Yet each moment did her husband rise before her mind more vividly, with his rugged looks, his warm, tender heart, his dawnings of comprehension, his generous forbearance and reverential love—the love of her youth—to be equalled by no other. The accomplished courtier and polished man of the world might be his superior, but she loathed the superiority, since it was to her husband. Might not his one chosen dove keep heart-whole for him to the last? She recollected that coarsest, cruellest reproach of all that her mother-in-law had been wont to fling at her,—that she, the recent widow, the new-made mother of Eberhard's babes, in her grief, her terror, and her weakness had sought to captivate this suitor by her blandishments. The taunt seemed justified, and her cheeks burned with absolute shame "My husband! my loving Eberhard! left with none but me to love thee, unknown to thine own sons! I cannot, I will not give my heart away from thee! Thy little bride shall be faithful to thee, whatever betide. When we meet beyond the grave I will have been thine only, nor have set any before thy sons. Heaven forgive me if I be undutiful to my uncle; but thou must be preferred before even him! Hark!" and she started as if at Eberhard's foot-step; then smiled, recollecting that Ebbo had his father's tread. But her husband had been too much in awe of her to enter with that hasty agitated step and exclamation, "Mother, mother, what insolence is this!"

"Hush, Ebbo! I prayed mine uncle to let me speak to thee."

"It is true, then," said Ebbo, dashing his cap on the ground; "I had soundly beaten that grinning 'prentice for telling Heinz."

"Truly the house rings with the rumour, mother," said Friedel, "but we had not believed it."

"I believed Wildschloss assured enough for aught," said Ebbo, "but I thought he knew where to begin. Does he not know who is head of the house of Adlerstein, since he must tamper with a mechanical craftsman, cap in hand to any sprig of nobility! I would have soon silenced his overtures!"

The Dove in the Eagle's Nest

"Is it in sooth as we heard?" asked Friedel, blushing to the ears, for the boy was shy as a maiden. "Mother, we know what you would say," he added, throwing himself on his knees beside her, his arm round her waist, his cheek on her lap, and his eyes raised to hers.

She bent down to kiss him. "Thou knewst it, Friedel, and now must thou aid me to remain thy father's true widow, and to keep Ebbo from being violent."

Ebbo checked his hasty march to put his hand on her chair and kiss her brow. "Motherling, I will restrain myself, so you will give me your word not to desert us."

"Nay, Ebbo," said Friedel, "the motherling is too true and loving for us to bind her."

"Children," she answered, "hear me patiently. I have been communing with myself, and deeply do I feel that none other can I love save him who is to you a mere name, but to me a living presence. Nor would I put any between you and me. Fear me not, Ebbo. I think the mothers and sons of this wider, fuller world do not prize one another as we do. But, my son, this is no matter for rage or ingratitude. Remember it is no small condescension in a noble to stoop to thy citizen mother."

"He knew what painted puppets noble ladies are," growled Ebbo.

"Moreover," continued Christina, "thine uncle is highly gratified, and cannot believe that I can refuse. He understands not my love for thy father, and sees many advantages for us all. I doubt me if he believes I have power to resist his will, and for thee, he would not count thine opposition valid. And the more angry and vehement thou art, the more will he deem himself doing thee a service by overruling thee."

"Come home, mother. Let Heinz lead our horses to the door in the dawn, and when we are back in free Adlerstein it will be plain who is master."

"Such a flitting would scarce prove our wisdom," said Christina, "to run away with thy mother like a lover in a ballad. Nay, let me first deal gently with thine uncle, and speak myself with Sir Kasimir, so that I may show him the vanity of his suit. Then will we back to Adlerstein without leaving wounds to requite kindness."

Ebbo was wrought on to promise not to attack the burgomaster on the subject, but he was moody and silent, and Master Gottfried let him alone, considering his gloom as another proof of his need of fatherly authority, and as a peace-lover forbearing to provoke his fiery spirit.

But when Sir Kasimir's visit was imminent, and Christina had refused to make the change in her dress by which a young widow was considered to lay herself open to another courtship, Master Gottfried called the twins apart.

"My young lords," he said, "I fear me ye are vexing your gentle mother by needless strife at what must take place."

"Pardon me, good uncle," said Ebbo, "I utterly decline the honour of Sir Kasimir's suit to my mother."

Master Gottfried smiled. "Sons are not wont to be the judges in such cases, Sir Eberhard."

"Perhaps not," he answered; "but my mother's will is to the nayward, nor shall she be coerced."

"It is merely because of you and your pride," said Master Gottfried.

"I think not so," rejoined the calmer Friedel; "my mother's love for my father is still fresh."

The Dove in the Eagle's Nest

"Young knights," said Master Gottfried, "it would scarce become me to say, nor you to hear, how much matter of fancy such love must have been towards one whom she knew but for a few short months, though her pure sweet dreams, through these long years, have moulded him into a hero. Boys, I verily believe ye love her truly. Would it be well for her still to mourn and cherish a dream while yet in her fresh age, capable of new happiness, fuller than she has ever enjoyed?"

"She is happy with us," rejoined Ebbo.

"And ye are good lads and loving sons, though less duteous in manner than I could wish. But look you, you may not ever be with her, and when ye are absent in camp or court, or contracting a wedlock of your own, would you leave her to her lonesome life in your solitary castle?"

Friedel's unselfishness might have been startled, but Ebbo boldly answered, "All mine is hers. No joy to me but shall be a joy to her. We can make her happier than could any stranger. Is it not so, Friedel?"

"It is," said Friedel, thoughtfully.

"Ah, rash bloods, promising beyond what ye can keep. Nature will be too strong for you. Love your mother as ye may, what will she be to you when a bride comes in your way? Fling not away in wrath, Sir Baron; it was so with your parents both before you; and what said the law of the good God at the first marriage? How can you withstand the nature He has given?"

"Belike I may wed," said Ebbo, bluntly; "but if it be not for my mother's happiness, call me man−sworn knight."

"Not so," good−humouredly answered Gottfried, "but boy−sworn paladin, who talks of he knows not what. Speak knightly truth, Sir Baron, and own that this opposition is in verity from distaste to a stepfather's rule."

"I own that I will not brook such rule," said Ebbo; "nor do I know what we have done to deserve that it should be thrust on us. You have never blamed Friedel, at least; and verily, uncle, my mother's eye will lead me where a stranger's hand shall never drive me. Did I even think she had for this man a quarter of the love she bears to my dead father, I would strive for endurance; but in good sooth we found her in tears, praying us to guard her from him. I may be a boy, but I am man enough to prevent her from being coerced."

"Was this so, Friedel?" asked Master Gottfried, moved more than by all that had gone before. "Ach, I thought ye all wiser. And spake she not of Sir Kasimir's offers?—Interest with the Romish king?— Yea, and a grant of nobility and arms to this house, so as to fill the blank in your scutcheon?"

"My father never asked if she were noble," said Ebbo. "Nor will I barter her for a cantle of a shield."

"There spake a manly spirit," said his uncle, delighted. "Her worth hath taught thee how little to prize these gewgaws! Yet, if you look to mingling with your own proud kind, ye may fall among greater slights than ye can brook. It may matter less to you, Sir Baron, but Friedel here, ay, and your sons, will be ineligible to the choicest orders of knighthood, and the canonries and chapters that are honourable endowments."

Friedel looked as if he could bear it, and Eberhard said, "The order of the Dove of Adlerstein is enough for us."

"Headstrong all, headstrong all," sighed Master Gottfried. "One romantic marriage has turned all your heads."

The Baron of Adlerstein Wildschloss, unprepared for the opposition that awaited him, was riding down the street equipped point device, and with a goodly train of followers, in brilliant suits. Private wooing did not enter into the honest ideas of the burghers, and the suitor was ushered into the full family assembly, where Christina rose and came forward a few steps to meet him, curtseying as low as he bowed, as he said, "Lady, I have preferred my suit to you through your honour-worthy uncle, who is good enough to stand my friend."

"You are over good, sir. I feel the honour, but a second wedlock may not be mine."

"Now," murmured Ebbo to his brother, as the knight and lady seated themselves in full view, "now will the smooth-tongued fellow talk her out of her senses. Alack! that gipsy prophecy!"

Wildschloss did not talk like a young wooer; such days were over for both; but he spoke as a grave and honourable man, deeply penetrated with true esteem and affection. He said that at their first meeting he had been struck with her sweetness and discretion, and would soon after have endeavoured to release her from her durance, but that he was bound by the contract already made with the Trautbachs, who were dangerous neighbours to Wildschloss. He had delayed his distasteful marriage as long as possible, and it had caused him nothing but trouble and strife; his children would not live, and Thekla, the only survivor, was, as his sole heiress, a mark for the cupidity of her uncle, the Count of Trautbach, and his almost savage son Lassla; while the right to the Wildschloss barony would become so doubtful between her and Ebbo, as heir of the male line, that strife and bloodshed would be well-nigh inevitable. These causes made it almost imperative that he should re-marry, and his own strong preference and regard for little Thekla directed his wishes towards the Freiherrinn von Adlerstein. He backed his suit with courtly compliments, as well as with representations of his child's need of a mother's training, and the twins' equal want of fatherly guidance, dilating on the benefits he could confer on them.

Christina felt his kindness, and had full trust in his intentions. "No" was a difficult syllable to her, but she had that within her which could not accept him; and she firmly told him that she was too much bound to both her Eberhards. But there was no daunting him, nor preventing her uncle and aunt from encouraging him. He professed that he would wait, and give her time to consider; and though she reiterated that consideration would not change her mind, Master Gottfried came forward to thank him, and express his confidence of bringing her to reason.

"While I, sir," said Ebbo, with flashing eyes, and low but resentful voice, "beg to decline the honour in the name of the elder house of Adlerstein."

He held himself upright as a dart, but was infinitely annoyed by the little mocking bow and smile that he received in return, as Sir Kasimir, with his long mantle, swept out of the apartment, attended by Master Gottfried.

"Burgomaster Sorel," said the boy, standing in the middle of the floor as his uncle returned, "let me hear whether I am a person of any consideration in this family or not?"

"Nephew baron," quietly replied Master Gottfried, "it is not the use of us Germans to be dictated to by youths not yet arrived at years of discretion."

"Then, mother," said Ebbo, "we leave this place to-morrow morn." And at her nod of assent the house-father looked deeply grieved, the house-mother began to clamour about ingratitude. "Not so," answered Ebbo, fiercely. "We quit the house as poor as we came, in homespun and with the old mare."

"Peace, Ebbo!" said his mother, rising; "peace, I entreat, house- mother! pardon, uncle, I pray thee. O, why will not all who love me let me follow that which I believe to be best!"

"Child," said her uncle, "I cannot see thee domineered over by a youth whose whole conduct shows his need of restraint."

"Nor am I," said Christina. "It is I who am utterly averse to this offer. My sons and I are one in that; and, uncle, if I pray of you to consent to let us return to our castle, it is that I would not see the visit that has made us so happy stained with strife and dissension! Sure, sure, you cannot be angered with my son for his love for me."

"For the self-seeking of his love," said Master Gottfried. "It is to gratify his own pride that he first would prevent thee from being enriched and ennobled, and now would bear thee away to the scant— Nay, Freiherr, I will not seem to insult you, but resentment would make you cruel to your mother."

"Not cruel!" said Friedel, hastily. "My mother is willing. And verily, good uncle, methinks that we all were best at home. We have benefited much and greatly by our stay; we have learnt to love and reverence you; but we are wild mountaineers at the best; and, while our hearts are fretted by the fear of losing our sweet mother, we can scarce be as patient or submissive as if we had been bred up by a stern father. We have ever judged and acted for ourselves, and it is hard to us not to do so still, when our minds are chafed."

"Friedel," said Ebbo, sternly, "I will have no pardon asked for maintaining my mother's cause. Do not thou learn to be smooth-tongued."

"O thou wrong-headed boy!" half groaned Master Gottfried. "Why did not all this fall out ten years sooner, when thou wouldst have been amenable? Yet, after all, I do not know that any noble training has produced a more high-minded loving youth," he added, half relenting as he looked at the gallant, earnest face, full of defiance indeed, but with a certain wistful appealing glance at "the motherling," softening the liquid lustrous dark eye. "Get thee gone, boy, I would not quarrel with you; and it may be, as Friedel says, that we are best out of one another's way. You are used to lord it, and I can scarce make excuses for you."

"Then," said Ebbo, scarce appeased, "I take home my mother, and you, sir, cease to favour Kasimir's suit."

"No, Sir Baron. I cease not to think that nothing would be so much for your good. It is because I believe that a return to your own old castle will best convince you all that I will not vex your mother by further opposing your departure. When you perceive your error may it only not be too late! Such a protector is not to be found every day."

"My mother shall never need any protector save myself," said Ebbo; "but, sir, she loves you, and owes all to you. Therefore I will not be at strife with you, and there is my hand."

He said it as if he had been the Emperor reconciling himself to all the Hanse towns in one. Master Gottfried could scarce refrain from shrugging his shoulders, and Hausfrau Johanna was exceedingly angry with the petulant pride and insolence of the young noble; but, in effect, all were too much relieved to avoid an absolute quarrel with the fiery lad to take exception at minor matters. The old burgher was forbearing; Christina, who knew how much her son must have swallowed to bring him to this concession for love of her, thought him a hero worthy of all sacrifices; and peace-making Friedel, by his aunt's side, soon softened even her, by some of the persuasive arguments that old dames love from gracious, graceful, great-nephews.

And when, by and by, Master Gottfried went out to call on Sir Kasimir, and explain how he had thought it best to yield to the hot-tempered lad, and let the family learn how to be thankful for the goods they had rejected, he found affairs in a state that made him doubly anxious that the young barons should be safe on their mountain without knowing of them. The Trautbach family had heard of Wildschloss's designs, and they had set abroad such injurious reports respecting the Lady of Adlerstein, that Sir Kasimir was in the act of inditing a cartel to be sent by Count Kaulwitz, to demand an explanation—not merely as the lady's suitor, but as the only Adlerstein of full age. Now, if Ebbo had heard of the rumour, he would certainly have given the lie direct, and taken the whole defence on himself; and it may be feared that, just as his cause might have been, Master Gottfried's faith did not stretch to believing that it would make his sixteen-year-old arm equal to the brutal might of Lassla of Trautbach. So he heartily thanked the Baron of Wildschloss, agreed with him that the young knights were not as yet equal to the maintenance of the cause, and went home again to watch carefully that no report reached either of his nephews. Nor did he breathe freely till he had seen the little party ride safe off in the early morning, in much more lordly guise than when they had entered the city.

As to Wildschloss and his nephew of Trautbach, in spite of their relationship they had a sharp combat on the borders of their own estates, in which both were severely wounded; but Sir Kasimir, with the misericorde in his grasp, forced Lassla to retract whatever he had said in dispraise of the Lady of Adlerstein. Wily old Gottfried took care that the tidings should be sent in a form that might at once move Christina with pity and gratitude towards her champion, and convince her sons that the adversary was too much hurt for them to attempt a fresh challenge.

CHAPTER XVI: THE EAGLE AND THE SNAKE

The reconciliation made Ebbo retract his hasty resolution of relinquishing all the benefits resulting from his connection with the Sorel family, and his mother's fortune made it possible to carry out many changes that rendered the castle and its inmates far more prosperous in appearance than had ever been the case before. Christina had once again the appliances of a wirthschaft, such as she felt to be the suitable and becoming appurtenance of a right-minded Frau, gentle or simple, and she felt so much the happier and more respectable.

A chaplain had also been secured. The youths had insisted on his being capable of assisting their studies, and, a good man had been found who was fearfully learned, having studied at all possible universities, but then failing as a teacher, because he was so dreamy and absent as to be incapable of keeping the unruly students in order. Jobst Schon was his proper name, but he was translated into Jodocus Pulcher. The chapel was duly adorned, the hall and other chambers were fitted up with some degree of comfort; the castle court was cleansed, the cattle sheds removed to the rear, and the serfs were presented with seed, and offered payment in coin if they would give their labour in fencing and clearing the cornfield and vineyard which the barons were bent on forming on the sunny slope of the ravine. Poverty was over, thanks to the marriage portion, and yet Ebbo looked less happy than in the days when there was but a bare subsistence; and he seemed to miss the full tide of city life more than did his brother, who, though he had enjoyed Ulm more heartily at the time, seemed to have returned to all his mountain delights with greater zest than ever. At his favourite tarn, he revelled in the vast stillness with the greater awe for having heard the hum of men, and his minstrel dreams had derived fresh vigour from contact with the active world. But, as usual, he was his brother's chief stay in the vexations of a reformer. The serfs had much rather their lord had turned out a freebooter than an improver. Why should they sow new seeds, when the old had sufficed their fathers? Work, beyond the regulated days when they scratched up the soil of his old enclosure, was abhorrent to them. As to his offered coin, they needed nothing it would buy, and had rather bask in the sun or sleep in the smoke. A vineyard had never been heard of on Adlerstein mountain: it was clean contrary to his forefathers' habits; and all came of the bad drop of restless burgher blood, that could not let honest folk rest.

Ebbo stormed, not merely with words, but blows, became ashamed of his violence, tried to atone for it by gifts and kind words, and in return was sulkily told that he would bring more good to the village by rolling the fiery wheel straight down hill at the wake, than by all his new-fangled ways. Had not Koppel and a few younger men been more open to influence, his agricultural schemes could hardly have begun; but Friedel's persuasions were not absolutely without success, and every rood that was dug was achieved by his patience and perseverance.

Next came home the Graf von Schlangenwald. He had of late inhabited his castle in Styria, but in a fierce quarrel with some of his neighbours he had lost his eldest son, and the pacification enforced by the King of the Romans had so galled and infuriated him that he had deserted that part of the country and returned to Swabia more fierce and bitter than ever. Thenceforth began a petty border warfare such as had existed when Christina first knew Adlerstein, but had of late died out. The shepherd lad came home weeping with wrath. Three mounted Schlangenwaldern had driven off his four best sheep, and beaten himself with their halberds, though he was safe on Adlerstein ground. Then a light thrown by a Schlangenwald reiter consumed all Jobst's pile of wood. The swine did not come home, and were found with spears sticking in them; the great broad-horned bull that Ebbo had brought from the pastures of Ulm vanished from the Alp below the Gemsbock's Pass, and was known to be salted for winter use at Schlangenwald.

Still Christina tried to persuade her sons that this might be only the retainers' violence, and induced Ebbo to write a letter, complaining of the outrages, but not blaming the Count, only begging that his followers might be better restrained. The letter was conveyed by a lay brother—no other messenger being safe. Ebbo had protested from the first that it would be of no use, but he waited anxiously for the answer.

Thus it stood, when conveyed to him by a tenant of the Ruprecht cloister

"Wot you, Eberhard, Freiherr von Adlerstein, that your house have injured me by thought, word, and deed. Your great-grandfather usurped my lands at the ford. Your grandfather stole my cattle and burnt my mills. Then, in the war, he slew my brother Johann and lamed for life my cousin Matthias. Your father slew eight of my retainers and spoiled my crops. You yourself claim my land at the ford, and secure the spoil which is justly mine. Therefore do I declare war and feud against you. Therefore to you and all yours, to your helpers and helpers' helpers, am I a foe. And thereby shall I have maintained my honour against you and yours.

WOLFGANG, Graf von Schlangenwald. HIEROM, Graf von Schlangenwald—his cousin."

And a long list of names, all connected with Schlangenwald, followed; and a large seal, bearing the snake of Schlangenwald, was appended thereto.

"The old miscreant!" burst out Ebbo; "it is a feud brief."

"A feud brief!" exclaimed Friedel; "they are no longer according to the law."

"Law?—what cares he for law or mercy either? Is this the way men act by the League? Did we not swear to send no more feud letters, nor have recourse to fist-right?"

"We must appeal to the Markgraf of Wurtemburg," said Friedel.

It was the only measure in their power, though Ebbo winced at it; but his oaths were recent, and his conscience would not allow him to transgress them by doing himself justice. Besides, neither party could take the castle of the other, and the only reprisals in his power would have been on the defenceless peasants of Schlangenwald. He must therefore lay the whole matter before the Markgraf, who was the head of the Swabian League, and bound to redress his wrongs. He made his arrangements without faltering, selecting the escort who were to accompany him, and insisting on leaving Friedel to guard his mother and the castle. He would not for the world have admitted the suggestion that the counsel and introduction of Adlerstein Wildschloss would have been exceedingly useful to him.

Poor Christina! It was a great deal too like that former departure, and her heart was heavy within her! Friedel was equally unhappy at letting his brother go without him, but it was quite necessary that he and the few armed men who remained should show themselves at all points open to the enemy in the course of the day, lest the Freiherr's absence should be remarked. He did his best to cheer his mother, by reminding her that Ebbo was not likely to be taken at unawares as their father had been; and he shared the prayers and chapel services, in which she poured out her anxiety.

The blue banner came safe up the Pass again, but Wurtemburg had been formally civil to the young Freiherr; but he had laughed at the fend letter as a mere old-fashioned habit of Schangenwald's that it was better not to notice, and he evidently regarded the stealing of a bull or the misusing of a serf as far too petty a matter for his attention. It was as if a judge had been called by a crying child to settle a nursery quarrel. He told Ebbo that, being a free Baron of the empire, he must keep his bounds respected; he was free to take and hang any spoiler he could catch, but his bulls were his own affair: the League was not for such gear.

And a knight who had ridden out of Stuttgard with Ebbo had told him that it was no wonder that this had been his reception, for not only was Schlangenwald an old intimate of the Markgraf, but Swabia was claimed as a fief of Wurtemburg, so that Ebbo's direct homage to the Emperor, without the interposition of the Markgraf, had made him no object of favour.

The Dove in the Eagle's Nest

"What could be done?" asked Ebbo.

"Fire some Schlangenwald hamlet, and teach him to respect yours," said the knight.

"The poor serfs are guiltless."

"Ha! ha! as if they would not rob any of yours. Give and take, that's the way the empire wags, Sir Baron. Send him a feud letter in return, with a goodly file of names at its foot, and teach him to respect you."

"But I have sworn to abstain from fist–right."

"Much you gain by so abstaining. If the League will not take the trouble to right you, right yourself."

"I shall appeal to the Emperor, and tell him how his League is administered."

"Young sir, if the Emperor were to guard every cow in his domains he would have enough to do. You will never prosper with him without some one to back your cause better than that free tongue of yours. Hast no sister that thou couldst give in marriage to a stout baron that could aid you with strong arm and prudent head?"

"I have only one twin brother."

"Ah! the twins of Adlerstein! I remember me. Was not the other Adlerstein seeking an alliance with your lady mother? Sure no better aid could be found. He is hand and glove with young King Max."

"That may never be," said Ebbo, haughtily. And, sure that he should receive the same advice, he decided against turning aside to consult his uncle at Ulm, and returned home in a mood that rejoiced Heinz and Hatto with hopes of the old days, while it filled his mother with dreary dismay and apprehension.

"Schlangenwald should suffer next time he transgressed," said Ebbo. "It should not again be said that he himself was a coward who appealed to the law because his hand could not keep his head."

The "next time" was when the first winter cold was setting in. A party of reitern came to harry an outlying field, where Ulrich had raised a scanty crop of rye. Tidings reached the castle in such good time that the two brothers, with Heinz, the two Ulm grooms, Koppel, and a troop of serfs, fell on the marauders before they had effected much damage, and while some remained to trample out the fire, the rest pursued the enemy even to the village of Schlangenwald.

"Burn it, Herr Freiherr," cried Heinz, hot with victory. "Let them learn how to make havoc of our corn."

But a host of half–naked beings rushed out shrieking about sick children, bed–ridden grandmothers, and crippled fathers, and falling on their knees, with their hands stretched out to the young barons. Ebbo turned away his head with hot tears in his eyes. "Friedel, what can we do?"

"Not barbarous murder," said Friedel.

"But they brand us for cowards!"

"The cowardice were in striking here," and Friedel sprang to withhold Koppel, who had lighted a bundle of dried fern ready to thrust into the thatch.

"Peasants!" said Ebbo, with the same impulse, "I spare you. You did not this wrong. But bear word to your lord, that if he will meet me with lance and sword, he will learn the valour of Adlerstein."

The Dove in the Eagle's Nest

The serfs flung themselves before him in transports of gratitude, but he turned hastily away and strode up the mountain, his cheek glowing as he remembered, too late, that his defiance would be scoffed at, as a boy's vaunt. By and by he arrived at the hamlet, where he found a prisoner, a scowling, abject fellow, already well beaten, and now held by two serfs.

"The halter is ready, Herr Freiherr," said old Ulrich, "and yon rowan stump is still as stout as when your Herr grandsire hung three lanzknechts on it in one day. We only waited your bidding."

"Quick then, and let me hear no more," said Ebbo, about to descend the pass, as if hastening from the execution of a wolf taken in a gin.

"Has he seen the priest?" asked Friedel.

The peasants looked as if this were one of Sir Friedel's unaccountable fancies. Ebbo paused, frowned, and muttered, but seeing a move as if to drag the wretch towards the stunted bush overhanging an abyss, he shouted, "Hold, Ulrich! Little Hans, do thou run down to the castle, and bring Father Jodocus to do his office!"

The serfs were much disgusted. "It never was so seen before, Herr Freiherr," remonstrated Heinz; "fang and hang was ever the word."

"What shrift had my lord's father, or mine?" added Koppel.

"Look you!" said Ebbo, turning sharply. "If Schlangenwald be a godless ruffian, pitiless alike to soul and body, is that a cause that I should stain myself too?"

"It were true vengeance," growled Koppel.

"And now," grumbled Ulrich, "will my lady hear, and there will be feeble pleadings for the vermin's life."

Like mutterings ensued, the purport of which was caught by Friedel, and made him say to Ebbo, who would again have escaped the disagreeableness of the scene, "We had better tarry at hand. Unless we hold the folk in some check there will be no right execution. They will torture him to death ere the priest comes."

Ebbo yielded, and began to pace the scanty area of the flat rock where the need–fire was wont to blaze. After a time he exclaimed: "Friedel, how couldst ask me? Knowst not that it sickens me to see a mountain cat killed, save in full chase. And thou—why, thou art white as the snow crags!"

"Better conquer the folly than that he there should be put to needless pain," said Friedel, but with labouring breath that showed how terrible was the prospect to his imaginative soul not inured to death-scenes like those of his fellows.

Just then a mocking laugh broke forth. "Ha!" cried Ebbo, looking keenly down, "what do ye there? Fang and hang may be fair; fang and torment is base! What was it, Lieschen?"

"Only, Herr Freiherr, the caitiff craved drink, and the fleischerinn gave him a cup from the stream behind the slaughter-house, where we killed the swine. Fit for the like of him!"

"By heavens, when I forbade torture!" cried Ebbo, leaping from the rock in time to see the disgusting draught held to the lips of the captive, whose hands were twisted back and bound with cruel tightness; for the German boor, once roused from his lazy good– nature, was doubly savage from stolidity.

The Dove in the Eagle's Nest

"Wretches!" cried Ebbo, striking right and left with the back of his sword, among the serfs, and then cutting the thong that was eating into the prisoner's flesh, while Friedel caught up a wooden bowl, filled it with pure water, and offered it to the captive, who drank deeply.

"Now," said Ebbo, "hast ought to say for thyself?"

A low curse against things in general was the only answer.

"What brought thee here?" continued Ebbo, in hopes of extracting some excuse for pardon; but the prisoner only hung his head as one stupefied, brutally indifferent and hardened against the mere trouble of answering. Not another word could be extracted, and Ebbo's position was very uncomfortable, keeping guard over his condemned felon, with the sulky peasants herding round, in fear of being balked of their prey; and the reluctance growing on him every moment to taking life in cold blood. Right of life and death was a heavy burden to a youth under seventeen, unless he had been thoughtless and reckless, and from this Ebbo had been prevented by his peculiar life. The lion cub had never tasted blood.

The situation was prolonged beyond expectation.

Many a time had the brothers paced their platform of rock, the criminal had fallen into a dose, and women and boys were murmuring that they must call home their kine and goats, and it was a shame to debar them of the sight of the hanging, long before Hans came back between crying and stammering, to say that Father Jodocus had fallen into so deep a study over his book, that he only muttered "Coming," then went into another musing fit, whence no one could rouse him to do more than say "Coming! Let him wait."

"I must go and bring him, if the thing is to be done," said Friedel.

"And let it last all night!" was the answer. "No, if the man were to die, it should be at once, not by inches. Hark thee, rogue!" stirring him with his foot.

"Well, sir," said the man, "is the hanging ready yet? You've been long enough about it for us to have twisted the necks of every Adlerstein of you all."

"Look thee, caitiff!" said Ebbo; "thou meritest the rope as well as any wolf on the mountain, but we have kept thee so long in suspense, that if thou canst say a word for thy life, or pledge thyself to meddle no more with my lands, I'll consider of thy doom."

"You have had plenty of time to consider it," growled the fellow.

A murmur, followed by a wrathful shout, rose among the villagers. "Letting off the villain! No! No! Out upon him! He dares not!"

"Dare!" thundered Ebbo, with flashing eyes. "Rascals as ye are, think ye to hinder me from daring? Your will to be mine? There, fellow; away with thee! Up to the Gemsbock's Pass! And whoso would follow him, let him do so at his peril!"

The prisoner was prompt to gather himself up and rush like a hunted animal to the path, at the entrance of which stood both twins, with drawn swords, to defend the escape. Of course no one ventured to follow; and surly discontented murmurs were the sole result as the peasants dispersed. Ebbo, sheathing his sword, and putting his arm into his brother's, said: "What, Friedel, turned stony-hearted? Hadst never a word for the poor caitiff?"

"I knew thou wouldst never do the deed," said Friedel, smiling.

"It was such wretched prey," said Ebbo. "Yet shall I be despised for this! Would that thou hadst let me string him up shriftless, as any other man had done, and there would have been an end of it!"

And even his mother's satisfaction did not greatly comfort Ebbo, for he was of the age to feel more ashamed of a solecism than a crime. Christina perceived that this was one of his most critical periods of life, baited as he was by the enemy of his race, and feeling all the disadvantages which heart and conscience gave him in dealing with a man who had neither, at a time when public opinion was always with the most masterful. The necessity of arming his retainers and having fighting men as a guard were additional temptations to hereditary habits of violence; and that so proud and fiery a nature as his should never become involved in them was almost beyond hope. Even present danger seemed more around than ever before. The estate was almost in a state of siege, and Christina never saw her sons quit the castle without thinking of their father's fate, and passing into the chapel to entreat for their return unscathed in body or soul. The snow, which she had so often hailed as a friend, was never more welcome than this winter; not merely as shutting the enemy out, and her sons in, but as cutting off all danger of a visit from her suitor, who would now come armed with his late sufferings in her behalf; and, moreover, with all the urgent need of a wise and respected head and protector for her sons. Yet the more evident the expediency became, the greater grew her distaste.

Still the lonely life weighed heavily on Ebbo. Light-hearted Friedel was ever busy and happy, were he chasing the grim winter game—the bear and wolf—with his brother, fencing in the hall, learning Greek with the chaplain, reading or singing to his mother, or carving graceful angel forms to adorn the chapel. Or he could at all times soar into a minstrel dream of pure chivalrous semi-allegorical romance, sometimes told over the glowing embers to his mother and brother. All that came to Friedel was joy, from battling with the bear on a frozen rock, to persuading rude little Hans to come to the Frau Freiherrinn to learn his Paternoster. But the elder twin might hunt, might fence, might smile or kindle at his brother's lay, but ever with a restless gloom on him, a doubt of the future which made him impatient of the present, and led to a sharpness and hastiness of manner that broke forth in anger at slight offences.

"The matron's coif succeeding the widow's veil," Friedel heard him muttering even in sleep, and more than once listened to it as Ebbo leant over the battlements—as he looked over the white world to the gray mist above the city of Ulm.

"Thou, who mockest my forebodings and fancies, to dwell on that gipsy augury!" argued Friedel. "As thou saidst at the time, Wildschloss's looks gave shrewd cause for it."

"The answer is in mine own heart," answered Ebbo. "Since our stay at Ulm, I have ever felt as though the sweet motherling were less my own! And the same with my house and lands. Rule as I will, a mocking laugh comes back to me, saying: 'Thou art but a boy, Sir Baron, thou dost but play at lords and knights.' If I had hung yon rogue of a reiter, I wonder if I had felt my grasp more real?"

"Nay," said Friedel, glancing from the sparkling white slopes to the pure blue above, "our whole life is but a play at lords and knights, with the blessed saints as witnesses of our sport in the tilt-yard."

"Were it merely that," said Ebbo, impatiently, "I were not so galled. Something hangs over us, Friedel! I long that these snows would melt, that I might at least know what it is!"

CHAPTER XVII: BRIDGING THE FORD

The snow melted, the torrent became a flood, then contracted itself, but was still a broad stream, when one spring afternoon Ebbo showed his brother some wains making for the ford, adding, "It cannot be rightly passable. They will come to loss. I shall get the men together to aid them."

He blew a blast on his horn, and added, "The knaves will be alert enough if they hope to meddle with honest men's luggage."

The Dove in the Eagle's Nest

"See," and Friedel pointed to the thicket to the westward of the meadow around the stream, where the beech trees were budding, but not yet forming a full mass of verdure, "is not the Snake in the wood? Methinks I spy the glitter of his scales."

"By heavens, the villains are lying in wait for the travellers at our landing-place," cried Ebbo, and again raising the bugle to his lips, he sent forth three notes well known as a call to arms. Their echoes came back from the rocks, followed instantly by lusty jodels, and the brothers rushed into the hall to take down their light head-pieces and corslets, answering in haste their mother's startled questions, by telling of the endangered travellers, and the Schlangenwald ambush. She looked white and trembled, but said no word to hinder them; only as she clasped Friedel's corslet, she entreated them to take fuller armour.

"We must speed the short way down the rock," said Ebbo, "and cannot be cumbered with heavy harness. Sweet motherling, fear not; but let a meal be spread for our rescued captives. Ho, Heinz, 'tis against the Schlangenwald rascals. Art too stiff to go down the rock path?"

"No; nor down the abyss, could I strike a good stroke against Schlangenwald at the bottom of it," quoth Heinz.

"Nor see vermin set free by the Freiherr," growled Koppel; but the words were lost in Ebbo's loud commands to the men, as Friedel and Hatto handed down the weapons to them.

The convoy had by this time halted, evidently to try the ford. A horseman crossed, and found it practicable, for a waggon proceeded to make the attempt.

"Now is our time," said Ebbo, who was standing on the narrow ledge between the castle and the precipitous path leading to the meadow. "One waggon may get over, but the second or third will stick in the ruts that it leaves. Now we will drop from our crag, and if the Snake falls on them, why, then for a pounce of the Eagle."

The two young knights, so goodly in their bright steel, knelt for their mother's blessing, and then sprang like chamois down the ivy- twined steep, followed by their men, and were lost to sight among the bushes and rocks. Yet even while her frame quivered with fear, her heart swelled at the thought what a gulf there was between these days and those when she had hidden her face in despair, while Ermentrude watched the Debateable Ford.

She watched now in suspense, indeed, but with exultation instead of shame, as two waggons safely crossed; but the third stuck fast, and presently turned over in the stream, impelled sideways by the efforts of the struggling horses. Then, amid endeavours to disentangle the animals and succour the driver, the travellers were attacked by a party of armed men, who dashed out of the beechwood, and fell on the main body of the waggons, which were waiting on the bit of bare shingly soil that lay between the new and old channels. A wild melee was all that Christina could see—weapons raised, horses starting, men rushing from the river, while the clang and the shout rose even to the castle.

Hark! Out rings the clear call, "The Eagle to the rescue!" There they speed over the meadow, the two slender forms with glancing helms! O overrun not the followers, rush not into needless danger! There is Koppel almost up with them with his big axe—Heinz's broad shoulders near. Heaven strike with them! Visit not their forefathers' sin on those pure spirits. Some are flying. Some one has fallen! O heavens! on which side? Ah! it is into the Schlangenwald woods that the fugitives direct their flight. Three— four—the whole troop pursued! Go not too far! Run not into needless risk! Your work is done, and gallantly. Well done, young knights of Adlerstein! Which of you is it that stands pointing out safe standing-ground for the men that are raising the waggon? Which of you is it who stands in converse with a burgher form? Thanks and blessings! the lads are safe, and full knightly hath been their first emprise.

A quarter of an hour later, a gay step mounted the ascent, and Friedel's bright face laughed from his helmet: "There, mother, will you crown your knights? Could you see Ebbo bear down the chief squire? for the old Snake was not there himself. And whom do you think we rescued, besides a whole band of Venetian traders to whom he had joined himself?

The Dove in the Eagle's Nest

Why, my uncle's friend, the architect, of whom he used to speak—Master Moritz Schleiermacher."

"Moritz Schleiermacher! I knew him as a boy."

"He had been laying out a Lustgarten for the Romish king at Innspruck, and he is a stout man of his hands, and attempted defence; but he had such a shrewd blow before we came up, that he lay like one dead; and when he was lifted up, he gazed at us like one moon-struck, and said, 'Are my eyes dazed, or are these the twins of Adlerstein, that are as like as face to mirror? Lads, lads, your uncle looked not to hear of you acting in this sort.' But soon we and his people let him know how it was, and that eagles do not have the manner of snakes."

"Poor Master Moritz! Is he much hurt? Is Ebbo bringing him up hither?"

"No, mother, he is but giddied and stunned, and now must you send down store of sausage, sourkraut, meat, wine, and beer; for the wains cannot all cross till daylight, and we must keep ward all night lest the Schlangenwalden should fall on them again. Plenty of good cheer, mother, to make a right merry watch."

"Take heed, Friedel mine; a merry watch is scarce a safe one."

"Even so, sweet motherling, and therefore must Ebbo and I share it. You must mete out your liquor wisely, you see, enough for the credit of Adlerstein, and enough to keep out the marsh fog, yet not enough to make us snore too soundly. I am going to take my lute; it would be using it ill not to let it enjoy such a chance as a midnight watch."

So away went the light-hearted boy, and by and by Christina saw the red watch-fire as she gazed from her turret window. She would have been pleased to see how, marshalled by a merchant who had crossed the desert from Egypt to Palestine, the waggons were ranged in a circle, and the watches told off, while the food and drink were carefully portioned out.

Freiherr Ebbo, on his own ground, as champion and host, was far more at ease than in the city, and became very friendly with the merchants and architect as they sat round the bright fire, conversing, or at times challenging the mountain echoes by songs to the sound of Friedel's lute. When the stars grew bright, most lay down to sleep in the waggons, while others watched, pacing up and down till Karl's waggon should be over the mountain, and the vigil was relieved.

No disturbance took place, and at sunrise a hasty meal was partaken of, and the work of crossing the river was set in hand.

"Pity," said Moritz, the architect, "that this ford were not spanned by a bridge, to the avoiding of danger and spoil."

"Who could build such a bridge?" asked Ebbo.

"Yourself, Herr Freiherr, in union with us burghers of Ulm. It were well worth your while to give land and stone, and ours to give labour and skill, provided we fixed a toll on the passage, which would be willingly paid to save peril and delay."

The brothers caught at the idea, and the merchants agreed that such a bridge would be an inestimable boon to all traffickers between Constance, Ulm, and Augsburg, and would attract many travellers who were scared away by the evil fame of the Debateable Ford. Master Moritz looked at the stone of the mountain, pronounced it excellent material, and already sketched the span of the arches with a view to winter torrents. As to the site, the best was on the firm ground above the ford; but here only one side was Adlerstein, while on the other Ebbo claimed both banks, and it was probable that an equally sound foundation could be obtained, only with more cost and delay.

After this survey, the travellers took leave of the barons, promising to write when their fellow-citizens should have been sounded as to the bridge; and Ebbo remained in high spirits, with such brilliant purposes that he had quite forgotten his gloomy forebodings. "Peace instead of war at home," he said; "with the revenue it will bring, I will build a mill, and set our lads to work, so that they may become less dull and doltish than their parents. Then will we follow the Emperor with a train that none need despise! No one will talk now of Adlerstein not being able to take care of himself!"

Letters came from Ulm, saying that the guilds of mercers and wine merchants were delighted with the project, and invited the Baron of Adlerstein to a council at the Rathhaus. Master Sorel begged the mother to come with her sons to be his guest; but fearing the neighbourhood of Sir Kasimir, she remained at home, with Heinz for her seneschal while her sons rode to the city. There Ebbo found that his late exploit and his future plan had made him a person of much greater consideration than on his last visit, and he demeaned himself with far more ease and affability in consequence. He had affairs on his hands too, and felt more than one year older.

The two guilds agreed to build the bridge, and share the toll with the Baron in return for the ground and materials; but they preferred the plan that placed one pier on the Schlangenwald bank, and proposed to write to the Count an offer to include him in the scheme, awarding him a share of the profits in proportion to his contribution. However vexed at the turn affairs had taken, Ebbo could offer no valid objection, and was obliged to affix his signature to the letter in company with the guildmasters.

It was despatched by the city pursuivants –

The only men who safe might ride;

Their errands on the border side and a meeting was appointed in the Rathhaus for the day of their expected return. The higher burghers sat on their carved chairs in the grand old hall, the lesser magnates on benches, and Ebbo, in an elbowed seat far too spacious for his slender proportions, met a glance from Friedel that told him his merry brother was thinking of the frog and the ox. The pursuivants entered—hardy, shrewd-looking men, with the city arms decking them wherever there was room for them.

"Honour-worthy sirs," they said, "no letter did the Graf von Schlangenwald return."

"Sent he no message?" demanded Moritz Schleiermacher.

"Yea, worthy sir, but scarce befitting this reverend assembly." On being pressed, however, it was repeated: "The Lord Count was pleased to swear at what he termed the insolence of the city in sending him heralds, 'as if,' said he, 'the dogs,' your worships, 'were his equals.' Then having cursed your worships, he reviled the crooked writing of Herr Clerk Diedrichson, and called his chaplain to read it to him. Herr Priest could scarce read three lines for his foul language about the ford. 'Never,' said he, 'would he consent to raising a bridge—a mean trick,' so said he, 'for defrauding him of his rights to what the flood sent him.'"

"But," asked Ebbo, "took he no note of our explanation, that if he give not the upper bank, we will build lower, where both sides are my own?"

"He passed it not entirely over," replied the messenger.

"What said he—the very words?" demanded Ebbo, with the paling cheek and low voice that made his passion often seem like patience.

"He said—(the Herr Freiherr will pardon me for repeating the words)– –he said, 'Tell the misproud mongrel of Adlerstein that he had best sit firm in his own saddle ere meddling with his betters, and if he touch one pebble of the Braunwasser, he will rue it. And before your city-folk take up with him or his, they had best learn whether he have any right at all in the case.'"

"His right is plain," said Master Gottfried; "full proofs were given in, and his investiture by the Kaisar forms a title in itself. It is mere bravado, and an endeavour to make mischief between the Baron and the city."

"Even so did I explain, Herr Guildmaster," said the pursuivant; "but, pardon me, the Count laughed me to scorn, and quoth he, 'asked the Kaisar for proof of his father's death!'"

"Mere mischief-making, as before," said Master Gottfried, while his nephews started with amaze. "His father's death was proved by an eye-witness, whom you still have in your train, have you not, Herr Freiherr?"

"Yea," replied Ebbo, "he is at Adlerstein now, Heinrich Bauermann, called the Schneiderlein, a lanzknecht, who alone escaped the slaughter, and from whom we have often heard how my father died, choked in his own blood, from a deep breast-wound, immediately after he had sent home his last greetings to my lady mother."

"Was the corpse restored?" asked the able Rathsherr Ulrich.

"No," said Ebbo. "Almost all our retainers had perished, and when a friar was sent to the hostel to bring home the remains, it appeared that the treacherous foe had borne them off—nay, my grandfather's head was sent to the Diet!"

The whole assembly agreed that the Count could only mean to make the absence of direct evidence about a murder committed eighteen years ago tell in sowing distrust between the allies. The suggestion was not worth a thought, and it was plain that no site would be available except the Debateable Strand. To this, however, Ebbo's title was assailable, both on account of his minority, as well as his father's unproved death, and of the disputed claim to the ground. The Rathsherr, Master Gottfried, and others, therefore recommended deferring the work till the Baron should be of age, when, on again tendering his allegiance, he might obtain a distinct recognition of his marches. But this policy did not consort with the quick spirit of Moritz Schleiermacher, nor with the convenience of the mercers and wine-merchants, who were constant sufferers by the want of a bridge, and afraid of waiting four years, in which a lad like the Baron might return to the nominal instincts of his class, or the Braunwasser might take back the land it had given; whilst Ebbo himself was urgent, with all the defiant fire of youth, to begin building at once in spite of all gainsayers.

"Strife and blood will it cost," said Master Sorel, gravely.

"What can be had worth the having save at cost of strife and blood?" said Ebbo, with a glance of fire.

"Youth speaks of counting the cost. Little knows it what it saith," sighed Master Gottfried.

"Nay," returned the Rathsherr, "were it otherwise, who would have the heart for enterprise?"

So the young knights mounted, and had ridden about half the way in silence, when Ebbo exclaimed, "Friedel"—and as his brother started, "What art musing on?"

"What thou art thinking of," said Friedel, turning on him an eye that had not only something of the brightness but of the penetration of a sunbeam.

"I do not think thereon at all," said Ebbo, gloomily. "It is a figment of the old serpent to hinder us from snatching his prey from him."

"Nevertheless," said Friedel, "I cannot but remember that the Genoese merchant of old told us of a German noble sold by his foes to the Moors."

"Folly! That tale was too recent to concern my father."

"I did not think it did," said Friedel; "but mayhap that noble's family rest equally certain of his death."

"Pfui!" said Ebbo, hotly; "hast not heard fifty times how he died even in speaking, and how Heinz crossed his hands on his breast? What wouldst have more?"

"Hardly even that," said Friedel, slightly smiling.

"Tush!" hastily returned his brother, "I meant only by way of proof. Would an honest old fellow like Heinz be a deceiver?"

"Not wittingly. Yet I would fain ride to that hostel and make inquiries!"

"The traitor host met his deserts, and was broken on the wheel for murdering a pedlar a year ago," said Ebbo. "I would I knew where my father was buried, for then would I bring his corpse honourably back; but as to his being a living man, I will not have it spoken of to trouble my mother."

"To trouble her?" exclaimed Friedel.

"To trouble her," repeated Ebbo. "Long since hath passed the pang of his loss, and there is reason in what old Sorel says, that he must have been a rugged, untaught savage, with little in common with the gentle one, and that tender memory hath decked him out as he never could have been. Nay, Friedel, it is but sense. What could a man have been under the granddame's breeding?"

"It becomes not thee to say so!" returned Friedel. "Nay, he could learn to love our mother."

"One sign of grace, but doubtless she loved him the better for their having been so little together. Her heart is at peace, believing him in his grave; but let her imagine him in Schlangenwald's dungeon, or some Moorish galley, if thou likest it better, and how will her mild spirit be rent!"

"It might be so," said Friedel, thoughtfully. "It may be best to keep this secret from her till we have fuller certainty."

"Agreed then," said Ebbo, "unless the Wildschloss fellow should again molest us, when his answer is ready."

"Is this just towards my mother?" said Friedel.

"Just! What mean'st thou? Is it not our office and our dearest right to shield our mother from care? And is not her chief wish to be rid of the Wildschloss suit?"

Nevertheless Ebbo was moody all the way home, but when there he devoted himself in his most eager and winning way to his mother, telling her of Master Gottfried's woodcuts, and Hausfrau Johanna's rheumatism, and of all the news of the country, in especial that the Kaisar was at Lintz, very ill with a gangrene in his leg, said to have been caused by his habit of always kicking doors open, and that his doctors thought of amputation, a horrible idea in the fifteenth century. The young baron was evidently bent on proving that no one could make his mother so happy as he could; and he was not far wrong there.

Friedel, however, could not rest till he had followed Heinz to the stable, and speaking over the back of the old white mare, the only other survivor of the massacre, had asked him once more for the particulars, a tale he was never loth to tell; but when Friedel further demanded whether he was certain of having seen the death of his younger lord, he replied, as if hurt: "What, think you I would have quitted him while life was yet in him?"

"No, certainly, good Heinz; yet I would fain know by what tokens thou knewest his death."

"Ah! Sir Friedel; when you have seen a stricken field or two, you will not ask how I know death from life."

"Is a swoon so utterly unlike death?"

"I say not but that an inexperienced youth might be mistaken," said Heinz; "but for one who had learned the bloody trade, it were impossible. Why ask, sir?"

"Because," said Friedel, low and mysteriously—"my brother would not have my mother know it, but—Count Schlangenwald demanded whether we could prove my father's death."

"Prove! He could not choose but die with three such wounds, as the old ruffian knows. I shall bless the day, Sir Friedmund, when I see you or your brother give back those strokes! A heavy reckoning be his."

"We all deem that line only meant to cross our designs," said Friedel. "Yet, Heinz, I would I knew how to find out what passed when thou wast gone. Is there no servant at the inn—no retainer of Schlangenwald that aught could be learnt from?"

"By St. Gertrude," roughly answered the Schneiderlein, "if you cannot be satisfied with the oath of a man like me, who would have given his life to save your father, I know not what will please you."

Friedel, with his wonted good-nature, set himself to pacify the warrior with assurances of his trust; yet while Ebbo plunged more eagerly into plans for the bridge-building, Friedel drew more and more into his old world of musings; and many a summer afternoon was spent by him at the Ptarmigan's Mere, in deep communings with himself, as one revolving a purpose.

Christina could not but observe, with a strange sense of foreboding, that, while one son was more than ever in the lonely mountain heights, the other was far more at the base. Master Moritz Schleiermacher was a constant guest at the castle, and Ebbo was much taken up with his companionship. He was a strong, shrewd man, still young, but with much experience, and he knew how to adapt himself to intercourse with the proud nobility, preserving an independent bearing, while avoiding all that haughtiness could take umbrage at; and thus he was acquiring a greater influence over Ebbo than was perceived by any save the watchful mother, who began to fear lest her son was acquiring an infusion of worldly wisdom and eagerness for gain that would indeed be a severance between him and his brother.

If she had known the real difference that unconsciously kept her sons apart, her heart would have ached yet more.

CHAPTER XVIII: FRIEDMUND IN THE CLOUDS

The stone was quarried high on the mountain, and a direct road was made for bringing it down to the water-side. The castle profited by the road in accessibility, but its impregnability was so far lessened. However, as Ebbo said, it was to be a friendly harbour, instead of a robber crag, and in case of need the communication could easily be destroyed. The blocks of stone were brought down, and wooden sheds were erected for the workmen in the meadow.

In August, however, came tidings that, after two amputations of his diseased limb, the Kaisar Friedrich III. had died—it was said from over free use of melons in the fever consequent on the operation. His death was not likely to make much change in the government, which had of late been left to his son. At this time the King of the Romans (for the title of Kaisar was conferred only by coronation by the Pope, and this Maximilian never received) was at Innspruck collecting troops for the deliverance of Styria and Carinthia from a horde of invading Turks. The Markgraf of Wurtemburg sent an intimation to all the Swabian League that the new sovereign would be best pleased if their homage were paid to him in his camp at the head of their armed retainers.

Here was the way of enterprise and honour open at last, and the young barons of Adlerstein eagerly prepared for it, equipping their vassals and sending to Ulm to take three or four men-at-arms into their pay, so as to make up twenty

The Dove in the Eagle's Nest

lances as the contingent of Adlerstein. It was decided that Christina should spend the time of their absence at Ulm, whither her sons would escort her on their way to the camp. The last busy day was over, and in the summer evening Christina was sitting on the castle steps listening to Ebbo's eager talk of his plans of interesting his hero, the King of the Romans, in his bridge, and obtaining full recognition of his claim to the Debateable Strand, where the busy workmen could be seen far below.

Presently Ebbo, as usual when left to himself, grew restless for want of Friedel, and exclaiming, "The musing fit is on him!—he will stay all night at the tarn if I fetch him not," he set off in quest of him, passing through the hamlet to look for him in the chapel on his way.

Not finding Friedel there, he was, however, some way up towards the tarn, when he met his brother wearing the beamy yet awestruck look that he often brought from the mountain height, yet with a steadfast expression of resolute purpose on his face.

"Ah, dreamer!" said Ebbo, "I knew where to seek thee! Ever in the clouds!"

"Yes, I have been to the tarn," said Friedel, throwing his arm round his brother's neck in their boyish fashion. "It has been very dear to me, and I longed to see its gray depths once more."

"Once! Yea manifold times shalt thou see them," said Ebbo. "Schleiermacher tells me that these are no Janissaries, but a mere miscreant horde, even by whom glory can scarce be gained, and no peril at all."

"I know not," said Friedel, "but it is to me as if I were taking my leave of all these purple hollows and heaven–lighted peaks cleaving the sky. All the more, Ebbo, since I have made up my mind to a resolution."

"Nay, none of the old monkish fancies," cried Ebbo, "against them thou art sworn, so long as I am true knight."

"No, it is not the monkish fancy, but I am convinced that it is my duty to strive to ascertain my father's fate. Hold, I say not that it is thine. Thou hast thy charge here—"

"Looking for a dead man," growled Ebbo; "a proper quest!"

"Not so," returned Friedel. "At the camp it will surely be possible to learn, through either Schlangenwald or his men, how it went with my father. Men say that his surviving son, the Teutonic knight, is of very different mould. He might bring something to light. Were it proved to be as the Schneiderlein avers, then would our conscience be at rest; but, if he were in Schlangenwald's dungeon—"

"Folly! Impossible!"

"Yet men have pined eighteen years in dark vaults," said Friedel; "and, when I think that so may he have wasted for the whole of our lives that have been so free and joyous on his own mountain, it irks me to bound on the heather or gaze at the stars."

"If the serpent hath dared," cried Ebbo, "though it is mere folly to think of it, we would summon the League and have his castle about his ears! Not that I believe it."

"Scarce do I," said Friedel; "but there haunts me evermore the description of the kindly German chained between the decks of the Corsair's galley. Once and again have I dreamt thereof. And, Ebbo, recollect the prediction that so fretted thee. Might not yon dark–cheeked woman have had some knowledge of the East and its captives?"

The Dove in the Eagle's Nest

Ebbo started, but resumed his former tone. "So thou wouldst begin thine errantry like Sir Hildebert and Sir Hildebrand in the 'Rose garden'? Have a care. Such quests end in mortal conflict between the unknown father and son."

"I should know him," said Friedel, enthusiastically, "or, at least, he would know my mother's son in me; and, could I no otherwise ransom him, I would ply the oar in his stead."

"A fine exchange for my mother and me," gloomily laughed Ebbo, "to lose thee, my sublimated self, for a rude, savage lord, who would straightway undo all our work, and rate and misuse our sweet mother for being more civilized than himself."

"Shame, Ebbo!" cried Friedel, "or art thou but in jest?"

"So far in jest that thou wilt never go, puissant Sir Hildebert," returned Ebbo, drawing him closer. "Thou wilt learn—as I also trust to do—in what nameless hole the serpent hid his remains. Then shall they be duly coffined and blazoned. All the monks in the cloisters for twenty miles round shall sing requiems, and thou and I will walk bareheaded, with candles in our hands, by the bier, till we rest him in the Blessed Friedmund's chapel; and there Lucas Handlein shall carve his tomb, and thou shalt sit for the likeness."

"So may it end," said Friedel, "but either I will know him dead, or endeavour somewhat in his behalf. And that the need is real, as well as the purpose blessed, I have become the more certain, for, Ebbo, as I rose to descend the hill, I saw on the cloud our patron's very form—I saw myself kneel before him and receive his blessing."

Ebbo burst out laughing. "Now know I that it is indeed as saith Schleiermacher," he said, "and that these phantoms of the Blessed Friedmund are but shadows cast by the sun on the vapours of the ravine. See, Friedel, I had gone to seek thee at the chapel, and meeting Father Norbert, I bent my knee, that I might take his farewell blessing. I had the substance, thou the shadow, thou dreamer!"

Friedel was as much mortified for the moment as his gentle nature could be. Then he resumed his sweet smile, saying, "Be it so! I have oft read that men are too prone to take visions and special providences to themselves, and now I have proved the truth of the saying."

"And," said Ebbo, "thou seest thy purpose is as baseless as thy vision?"

"No, Ebbo. It grieves me to differ from thee, but my resolve is older than the fancy, and may not be shaken because I was vain enough to believe that the Blessed Friedmund could stoop to bless me."

"Ha!" shouted Ebbo, glad to see an object on which to vent his secret annoyance. "Who goes there, skulking round the rocks? Here, rogue, what art after here?"

"No harm," sullenly replied a half-clad boy.

"Whence art thou? From Schlangenwald, to spy what more we can be robbed of? The lash—"

"Hold," interposed Friedel. "Perchance the poor lad had no evil purposes. Didst lose thy way?"

"No, sir, my mother sent me."

"I thought so," cried Ebbo. "This comes of sparing the nest of thankless adders!"

"Nay," said Friedel, "mayhap it is because they are not thankless that the poor fellow is here."

The Dove in the Eagle's Nest

"Sir," said the boy, coming nearer, "I will tell YOU—YOU I will tell—not him who threatens. Mother said you spared our huts, and the lady gave us bread when we came to the castle gate in winter, and she would not see the reiters lay waste your folk's doings down there without warning you."

"My good lad! What saidst thou?" cried Ebbo, but the boy seemed dumb before him, and Friedel repeated the question ere he answered: "All the lanzknechts and reiters are at the castle, and the Herr Graf has taken all my father's young sheep for them, a plague upon him. And our folk are warned to be at the muster rock to-morrow morn, each with a bundle of straw and a pine brand; and Black Berend heard the body squire say the Herr Graf had sworn not to go to the wars till every stick at the ford be burnt, every stone drowned, every workman hung."

Ebbo, in a transport of indignation and gratitude, thrust his hand into his pouch, and threw the boy a handful of groschen, while Friedel gave warm thanks, in the utmost haste, ere both brothers sprang with headlong speed down the wild path, to take advantage of the timely intelligence.

The little council of war was speedily assembled, consisting of the barons, their mother, Master Moritz Schleiermacher, Heinz, and Hatto. To bring up to the castle the workmen, their families, and the more valuable implements, was at once decided; and Christina asked whether there would be anything left worth defending, and whether the Schlangenwalden might not expend their fury on the scaffold, which could be newly supplied from the forest, the huts, which could be quickly restored, and the stones, which could hardly be damaged. The enemy must proceed to the camp in a day or two, and the building would be less assailable by their return; and, besides, it was scarcely lawful to enter on a private war when the imperial banner was in the field.

"Craving your pardon, gracious lady," said the architect, "that blame rests with him who provokes the war. See, lord baron, there is time to send to Ulm, where the two guilds, our allies, will at once equip their trained bands and despatch them. We meanwhile will hold the knaves in check, and, by the time our burghers come up, the snake brood will have had such a lesson as they will not soon forget. Said I well, Herr Freiherr?"

"Right bravely," said Ebbo. "It consorts not with our honour or rights, with my pledges to Ulm, or the fame of my house, to shut ourselves up and see the rogues work their will scatheless. My own score of men, besides the stouter masons, carpenters, and serfs, will be fully enough to make the old serpent of the wood rue the day, even without the aid of the burghers. Not a word against it, dearest mother. None is so wise as thou in matters of peace, but honour is here concerned."

"My question is," persevered the mother, "whether honour be not better served by obeying the summons of the king against the infidel, with the men thou hast called together at his behest? Let the count do his worst; he gives thee legal ground of complaint to lay before the king and the League, and all may there be more firmly established."

"That were admirable counsel, lady," said Schleiermacher, "well suited to the honour-worthy guildmaster Sorel, and to our justice- loving city; but, in matters of baronial rights and aggressions, king and League are wont to help those that help themselves, and those that are over nice as to law and justice come by the worst."

"Not the worst in the long run," said Friedel.

"Thine unearthly code will not serve us here, Friedel mine," returned his brother. "Did I not defend the work I have begun, I should be branded as a weak fool. Nor will I see the foes of my house insult me without striking a fair stroke. Hap what hap, the Debateable Ford shall be debated! Call in the serfs, Hatto, and arm them. Mother, order a good supper for them. Master Moritz, let us summon thy masons and carpenters, and see who is a good man with his hands among them."

Christina saw that remonstrance was vain. The days of peril and violence were coming back again; and all she could take comfort in was, that, if not wholly right, her son was far from wholly wrong, and that with a free heart she could pray for a blessing on him and on his arms.

CHAPTER XIX: THE FIGHT AT THE FORD

By the early September sunrise the thicket beneath the pass was sheltering the twenty well-appointed reiters of Adlerstein, each standing, holding his horse by the bridle, ready to mount at the instant. In their rear were the serfs and artisans, some with axes, scythes, or ploughshares, a few with cross-bows, and Jobst and his sons with the long blackened poles used for stirring their charcoal fires. In advance were Master Moritz and the two barons, the former in a stout plain steel helmet, cuirass, and gauntlets, a sword, and those new-fashioned weapons, pistols; the latter in full knightly armour, exactly alike, from the gilt-spurred heel to the eagle-crested helm, and often moving restlessly forward to watch for the enemy, though taking care not to be betrayed by the glitter of their mail. So long did they wait that there was even a doubt whether it might not have been a false alarm; the boy was vituperated, and it was proposed to despatch a spy to see whether anything were doing at Schlangenwald.

At length a rustling and rushing were heard; then a clank of armour. Ebbo vaulted into the saddle, and gave the word to mount; Schleiermacher, who always fought on foot, stepped up to him. "Keep back your men, Herr Freiherr. Let his design be manifest. We must not be said to have fallen on him on his way to the muster."

"It would be but as he served my father!" muttered Ebbo, forced, however, to restrain himself, though with boiling blood, as the tramp of horses shook the ground, and bright armour became visible on the further side of the stream.

For the first time, the brothers beheld the foe of their line. He was seated on a clumsy black horse, and sheathed in full armour, and was apparently a large heavy man, whose powerful proportions were becoming unwieldy as he advanced in life. The dragon on his crest and shield would have made him known to the twins, even without the deadly curse that passed the Schneiderlein's lips at the sight. As the armed troop, out-numbering the Adlersteiners by about a dozen, and followed by a rabble with straw and pine brands, came forth on the meadow, the count halted and appeared to be giving orders.

"The ruffian! He is calling them on! Now—" began Ebbo.

"Nay, there is no sign yet that he is not peacefully on his journey to the camp," responded Moritz; and, chafing with impatient fury, the knight waited while Schlangenwald rode towards the old channel of the Braunwasser, and there, drawing his rein, and sitting like a statue in his stirrups, he could hear him shout: "The lazy dogs are not astir yet. We will give them a reveille. Forward with your brands!"

"Now!" and Ebbo's cream-coloured horse leapt forth, as the whole band flashed into the sunshine from the greenwood covert.

"Who troubles the workmen on my land?" shouted Ebbo.

"Who you may be I care not," replied the count, "but when I find strangers unlicensed on my lands, I burn down their huts. On, fellows!"

"Back, fellows!" called Ebbo. "Whoso touches a stick on Adlerstein ground shall suffer."

"So!" said the count, "this is the burgher-bred, burgher-fed varlet, that calls himself of Adlerstein! Boy, thou had best be warned. Wert thou true-blooded, it were worth my while to maintain my rights against thee. Craven as thou art, not even with spirit to accept my feud, I would fain not have the trouble of sweeping thee from my path."

"Herr Graf, as true Freiherr and belted knight, I defy thee! I proclaim my right to this ground, and whoso damages those I place there must do battle with me."

The Dove in the Eagle's Nest

"Thou wilt have it then," said the count, taking his heavy lance from his squire, closing his visor, and wheeling back his horse, so as to give space for his career.

Ebbo did the like, while Friedel on one side, and Hierom von Schlangenwald on the other, kept their men in array, awaiting the issue of the strife between their leaders—the fire of seventeen against the force of fifty-six.

They closed in full shock, with shivered lances and rearing, pawing horses, but without damage to either. Each drew his sword, and they were pressing together, when Heinz, seeing a Schlangenwalder aiming with his cross-bow, rode at him furiously, and the melee became general; shots were fired, not only from cross-bows, but from arquebuses, and in the throng Friedel lost sight of the main combat between his brother and the count.

Suddenly however there was a crash, as of falling men and horses, with a shout of victory strangely mingled with a cry of agony, and both sides became aware that their leaders had fallen. Each party rushed to its fallen head. Friedel beheld Ebbo under his struggling horse, and an enemy dashing at his throat, and, flying to the rescue, he rode down the assailant, striking him with his sword; and, with the instinct of driving the foe as far as possible from his brother, he struck with a sort of frenzy, shouting fiercely to his men, and leaping over the dry bed of the river, rushing onward with an intoxication of ardour that would have seemed foreign to his gentle nature, but for the impetuous desire to protect his brother. Their leaders down, the enemy had no one to rally them, and, in spite of their superiority in number, gave way in confusion before the furious onset of Adlerstein. So soon, however, as Friedel perceived that he had forced the enemy far back from the scene of conflict, his anxiety for his brother returned, and, leaving the retainers to continue the pursuit, he turned his horse. There, on the green meadow, lay on the one hand Ebbo's cream-coloured charger, with his master under him, on the other the large figure of the count; and several other prostrate forms likewise struggled on the sand and pebbles of the strand, or on the turf.

"Ay," said the architect, who had turned with Friedel, "'twas a gallant feat, Sir Friedel, and I trust there is no great harm done. Were it the mere dint of the count's sword, your brother will be little the worse."

"Ebbo! Ebbo mine, look up!" cried Friedel, leaping from his horse, and unclasping his brother's helmet.

"Friedel!" groaned a half-suffocated voice. "O take away the horse."

One or two of the artisans were at hand, and with their help the dying steed was disengaged from the rider, who could not restrain his moans, though Friedel held him in his arms, and endeavoured to move him as gently as possible. It was then seen that the deep gash from the count's sword in the chest was not the most serious injury, but that an arquebus ball had pierced his thigh, before burying itself in the body of his horse; and that the limb had been further crushed and wrenched by the animal's struggles. He was nearly unconscious, and gasped with anguish, but, after Moritz had bathed his face and moistened his lips, as he lay in his brother's arms, he looked up with clearer eyes, and said: "Have I slain him? It was the shot, not he, that sent me down. Lives he? See—thou, Friedel—thou. Make him yield."

Transferring Ebbo to the arms of Schleiermacher, Friedel obeyed, and stepped towards the fallen foe. The wrongs of Adlerstein were indeed avenged, for the blood was welling fast from a deep thrust above the collar-bone, and the failing, feeble hand was wandering uncertainly among the clasps of the gorget.

"Let me aid," said Friedel, kneeling down, and in his pity for the dying man omitting the summons to yield, he threw back the helmet, and beheld a grizzled head and stern hard features, so embrowned by weather and inflamed by intemperance, that even approaching death failed to blanch them. A scowl of malignant hate was in the eyes, and there was a thrill of angry wonder as they fell on the lad's face. "Thou again,—thou whelp! I thought at least I had made an end of thee," he muttered, unheard by Friedel, who, intent on the thought that had recurred to him with greater vividness than ever, was again filling Ebbo's helmet with water. He refreshed the dying man's face with it, held it to his lips, and said: "Herr Graf, variance and strife are ended now. For heaven's sake, say where I may find my father!"

The Dove in the Eagle's Nest

"So! Wouldst find him?" replied Schlangenwald, fixing his look on the eager countenance of the youth, while his hand, with a dying man's nervous agitation, was fumbling at his belt.

"I would bless you for ever, could I but free him."

"Know then," said the count, speaking very slowly, and still holding the young knight's gaze with a sort of intent fascination, by the stony glare of his light gray eyes, "know that thy villain father is a Turkish slave, unless he be—as I hope—where his mongrel son may find him."

Therewith came a flash, a report; Friedel leaped back, staggered, fell; Ebbo started to a sitting posture, with horrified eyes, and a loud shriek, calling on his brother; Moritz sprang to his feet, shouting, "Shame! treason!"

"I call you to witness that I had not yielded," said the count. "There's an end of the brood!" and with a grim smile, he straightened his limbs, and closed his eyes as a dead man, ere the indignant artisans fell on him in savage vengeance.

All this had passed like a flash of lightning, and Friedel had almost at the instant of his fall flung himself towards his brother, and raising himself on one hand, with the other clasped Ebbo's, saying, "Fear not; it is nothing," and he was bending to take Ebbo's head again on his knee, when a gush of dark blood, from his left side, caused Moritz to exclaim, "Ah! Sir Friedel, the traitor did his work! That is no slight hurt."

"Where? How? The ruffian!" cried Ebbo, supporting himself on his elbow, so as to see his brother, who rather dreamily put his hand to his side, and, looking at the fresh blood that immediately dyed it, said, "I do not feel it. This is more numb dulness than pain."

"A bad sign that," said Moritz, apart to one of the workmen, with whom he held counsel how to carry back to the castle the two young knights, who remained on the bank, Ebbo partly extended on the ground, partly supported on the knee and arm of Friedel, who sat with his head drooping over him, their looks fixed on one another, as if conscious of nothing else on earth.

"Herr Freiherr," said Moritz, presently, "have you breath to wind your bugle to call the men back from the pursuit?"

Ebbo essayed, but was too faint, and Friedel, rousing himself from the stupor, took the horn from him, and made the mountain echoes ring again, but at the expense of a great effusion of blood.

By this time, however, Heinz was riding back, and a moment his exultation changed to rage and despair, when he saw the condition of his young lords. Master Schleiermacher proposed to lay them on some of the planks prepared for the building, and carry them up the new road.

"Methinks," said Friedel, "that I could ride if I were lifted on horseback, and thus would our mother be less shocked."

"Well thought," said Ebbo. "Go on and cheer her. Show her thou canst keep the saddle, however it may be with me," he added, with a groan of anguish.

Friedel made the sign of the cross over him. "The holy cross keep us and her, Ebbo," he said, as he bent to assist in laying his brother on the boards, where a mantle had been spread; then kissed his brow, saying, "We shall be together again soon."

Ebbo was lifted on the shoulders of his bearers, and Friedel strove to rise, with the aid of Heinz, but sank back, unable to use his limbs; and Schleiermacher was the more concerned. "It goes so with the backbone," he said. "Sir Friedmund, you had best be carried."

The Dove in the Eagle's Nest

"Nay, for my mother's sake! And I would fain be on my good steed's back once again!" he entreated. And when with much difficulty he had been lifted to the back of his cream-colour, who stood as gently and patiently as if he understood the exigency of the moment, he sat upright, and waved his hand as he passed the litter, while Ebbo, on his side, signed to him to speed on and prepare their mother. Long, however, before the castle was reached, dizzy confusion and leaden helplessness, when no longer stimulated by his brother's presence, so grew on him that it was with much ado that Heinz could keep him in his saddle; but, when he saw his mother in the castle gateway, he again collected his forces, bade Heinz withdraw his supporting arm, and, straightening himself, waved a greeting to her, as he called cheerily; "Victory, dear mother. Ebbo has overthrown the count, and you must not be grieved if it be at some cost of blood."

"Alas, my son!" was all Christina could say, for his effort at gaiety formed a ghastly contrast with the gray, livid hue that overspread his fair young face, his bloody armour, and damp disordered hair, and even his stiff unearthly smile.

"Nay, motherling," he added, as she came so near that he could put his arm round her neck, "sorrow not, for Ebbo will need thee much. And, mother," as his face lighted up, "there is joy coming to you. Only I would that I could have brought him. Mother, he died not under the Schlangenwald swords."

"Who? Not Ebbo?" cried the bewildered mother.

"Your own Eberhard, our father," said Friedel, raising her face to him with his hand, and adding, as he met a startled look, "The cruel count owned it with his last breath. He is a Turkish slave, and surely heaven will give him back to comfort you, even though we may not work his freedom! O mother, I had so longed for it, but God be thanked that at least certainty was bought by my life." The last words were uttered almost unconsciously, and he had nearly fallen, as the excitement faded; but, as they were lifting him down, he bent once more and kissed the glossy neck of his horse. "Ah! poor fellow, thou too wilt be lonely. May Ebbo yet ride thee!"

The mother had no time for grief. Alas! She might have full time for that by and by! The one wish of the twins was to be together, and presently both were laid on the great bed in the upper chamber, Ebbo in a swoon from the pain of the transport, and Friedel lying so as to meet the first look of recovery. And, after Ebbo's eyes had re-opened, they watched one another in silence for a short space, till Ebbo said: "Is that the hue of death on thy face, brother?"

"I well believe so," said Friedel.

"Ever together," said Ebbo, holding his hand. "But alas! My mother! Would I had never sent thee to the traitor."

"Ah! So comes her comfort," said Friedel. "Heard you not? He owned that my father was among the Turks."

"And I," cried Ebbo. "I have withheld thee! O Friedel, had I listened to thee, thou hadst not been in this fatal broil!"

"Nay, ever together," repeated Friedel. "Through Ulm merchants will my mother be able to ransom him. I know she will, so oft have I dreamt of his return. Then, mother, you will give him our duteous greetings;" and he smiled again.

Like one in a dream Christina returned his smile, because she saw he wished it, just as the moment before she had been trying to staunch his wound.

It was plain that the injuries, except Ebbo's sword-cut, were far beyond her skill, and she could only endeavour to check the bleeding till better aid could be obtained from Ulm. Thither Moritz Schleiermacher had already sent, and he assured her that he was far from despairing of the elder baron, but she derived little hope from his words, for gunshot wounds were then so ill understood as generally to prove fatal.

Moreover, there was an undefined impression that the two lives must end in the same hour, even as they had begun. Indeed, Ebbo was suffering so terribly, and was so much spent with pain and loss of blood, that he seemed sinking much faster than Friedel, whose wound bled less freely, and who only seemed benumbed and torpid, except when he roused himself to speak, or was distressed by the writhings and moans which, however, for his sake, Ebbo restrained as much as he could.

To be together seemed an all-sufficient consolation, and, when the chaplain came sorrowfully to give them the last rites of the Church, Ebbo implored him to pray that he might not be left behind long in purgatory.

"Friedel," he said, clasping his brother's hand, "is even like the holy Sebastian or Maurice; but I—I was never such as he. O father, will it be my penance to be left alone when he is in paradise?"

"What is that?" said Friedel, partially roused by the sound of his name, and the involuntary pressure of his hand. "Nay, Ebbo; one repentance, one cross, one hope," and he relapsed into a doze, while Ebbo murmured over a broken, brief confession—exhausting by its vehemence of self-accusation for his proud spirit, his wilful neglect of his lost father, his hot contempt of prudent counsel.

Then, when the priest came round to Friedel's side, and the boy was wakened to make his shrift, the words were contrite and humble, but calm and full of trust. They were like two of their own mountain streams, the waters almost equally undefiled by external stain—yet one struggling, agitated, whirling giddily round; the other still, transparent, and the light of heaven smiling in its clearness.

The farewell greetings of the Church on earth breathed soft and sweet in their loftiness, and Friedel, though lying motionless, and with closed eyes, never failed in the murmured response, whether fully conscious or not, while his brother only attended by fits and starts, and was evidently often in too much pain to know what was passing.

Help was nearer than had been hoped. The summons despatched the night before had been responded to by the vintners and mercers; their train bands had set forth, and their captain, a cautious man, never rode into the way of blows without his surgeon at hand. And so it came to pass that, before the sun was low on that long and grievous day, Doctor Johannes Butteman was led into the upper chamber, where the mother looked up to him with a kind of hopeless gratitude on her face, which was nearly as white as those of her sons. The doctor soon saw that Friedel was past human aid; but, when he declared that there was fair hope for the other youth, Friedel, whose torpor had been dispelled by the examination, looked up with his beaming smile, saying, "There, motherling."

The doctor then declared that he could not deal with the Baron's wound unless he were the sole occupant of the bed, and this sentence brought the first cloud of grief or dread to Friedel's brow, but only for a moment. He looked at his brother, who had again fainted at the first touch of his wounded limb, and said, "It is well. Tell the dear Ebbo that I cannot help it if after all I go to the praying, and leave him the fighting. Dear, dear Ebbo! One day together again and for ever! I leave thee for thine own sake." With much effort he signed the cross again on his brother's brow, and kissed it long and fervently. Then, as all stood round, reluctant to effect this severance, or disturb one on whom death was visibly fast approaching, he struggled up on his elbow, and held out the other hand, saying, "Take me now, Heinz, ere Ebbo revive to be grieved. The last sacrifice," he further whispered, whilst almost giving himself to Heinz and Moritz to be carried to his own bed in the turret chamber.

There, even as they laid him down, began what seemed to be the mortal agony, and, though he was scarcely sensible, his mother felt that her prime call was to him, while his brother was in other hands. Perhaps it was well for her. Surgical practice was rough, and wounds made by fire-arms were thought to have imbibed a poison that made treatment be supposed efficacious in proportion to the pain inflicted. When Ebbo was recalled by the torture to see no white reflection of his own face on the pillow beside him, and to feel in vain for the grasp of the cold damp hand, a delirious frenzy seized him, and his struggles were frustrating the doctor's attempts, when a low soft sweet song stole through the open door.

"Friedel!" he murmured, and held his breath to listen. All through the declining day did the gentle sound continue; now of grand chants or hymns caught from the cathedral choir, now of songs of chivalry or saintly legend so often sung over the evening fire; the one flowing into the other in the wandering of failing powers, but never failing in the tender sweetness that had distinguished Friedel through life. And, whenever that voice was heard, let them do to him what they would, Ebbo was still absorbed in intense listening so as not to lose a note, and lulled almost out of sense of suffering by that swan-like music. If his attendants made such noise as to break in on it, or if it ceased for a moment, the anguish returned, but was charmed away by the weakest, faintest resumption of the song. Probably Friedel knew not, with any earthly sense, what he was doing, but to the very last he was serving his twin brother as none other could have aided him in his need.

The September sun had set, twilight was coming on, the doctor had worked his stern will, and Ebbo, quivering in every fibre, lay spent on his pillow, when his mother glided in, and took her seat near him, though where she hoped he would not notice her presence. But he raised his eyelids, and said, "He is not singing now."

"Singing indeed, but where we cannot hear him," she answered. "'Whiter than the snow, clearer than the ice-cave, more solemn than the choir. They will come at last.' That was what he said, even as he entered there." And the low dove-like tone and tender calm face continued upon Ebbo the spell that the chant had left. He dozed as though still lulled by its echo.

CHAPTER XX: THE WOUNDED EAGLE

The star and the spark in the stubble! Often did the presage of her dream occur to Christina, and assist in sustaining her hopes during the days that Ebbo's life hung in the balance, and he himself had hardly consciousness to realize either his brother's death or his own state, save as much as was shown by the words, "Let him not be taken away, mother; let him wait for me."

Friedmund did wait, in his coffin before the altar in the castle chapel, covered with a pall of blue velvet, and great white cross, mournfully sent by Hausfrau Johanna; his sword, shield, helmet, and spurs laid on it, and wax tapers burning at the head and feet. And, when Christina could leave the one son on his couch of suffering, it was to kneel beside the other son on his narrow bed of rest, and recall, like a breath of solace, the heavenly loveliness and peace that rested on his features when she had taken her last long look at them.

Moritz Schleiermacher assisted at Sir Friedmund's first solemn requiem, and then made a journey to Ulm, whence he returned to find the Baron's danger so much abated that he ventured on begging for an interview with the lady, in which he explained his purpose of repairing at once to the imperial camp, taking with him a letter from the guilds concerned in the bridge, and using his personal influence with Maximilian to obtain not only pardon for the combat, but authoritative sanction to the erection. Dankwart of Schlangenwald, the Teutonic knight, and only heir of old Wolfgang, was supposed to be with the Emperor, and it might be possible to come to terms with him, since his breeding in the Prussian commanderies had kept him aloof from the feuds of his father and brother. This mournful fight had to a certain extent equalized the injuries on either side, since the man whom Friedel had cut down was Hierom, one of the few remaining scions of Schlangenwald, and there was thus no dishonour in trying to close the deadly feud, and coming to an amicable arrangement about the Debateable Strand, the cause of so much bloodshed. What was now wanted was Freiherr Eberhard's signature to the letter to the Emperor, and his authority for making terms with the new count; and haste was needed, lest the Markgraf of Wurtemburg should represent the affray in the light of an outrage against a member of the League.

Christina saw the necessity, and undertook if possible to obtain her son's signature, but, at the first mention of Master Moritz and the bridge, Ebbo turned away his head, groaned, and begged to hear no more of either. He thought of his bold declaration that the bridge must be built, even at the cost of blood! Little did he then guess of whose blood! And in his bitterness of spirit he felt a jealousy of that influence of Schleiermacher, which had of late come between him and his brother. He hated the very name, he said, and hid his face with a shudder. He hoped the torrent would sweep away every fragment of the bridge.

The Dove in the Eagle's Nest

"Nay, Ebbo mine, wherefore wish ill to a good work that our blessed one loved? Listen, and let me tell you my dream for making yonder strand a peaceful memorial of our peaceful boy."

"To honour Friedel?" and he gazed on her with something like interest in his eyes.

"Yes, Ebbo, and as he would best brook honour. Let us seek for ever to end the rival claims to yon piece of meadow by praying this knight of a religious order, the new count, to unite with us in building there—or as near as may be safe—a church of holy peace, and a cell for a priest, who may watch over the bridge ward, and offer the holy sacrifice for the departed of either house. There will we place our gentle Friedel to be the first to guard the peace of the ford, and there will we sleep ourselves when our time shall come, and so may the cruel feud of many generations be slaked for ever."

"In his blood!" sighed Ebbo. "Ah! would that it had been mine, mother. It is well, as well as anything can be again. So shall the spot where he fell be made sacred, and fenced from rude feet, and we shall see his fair effigy keeping his armed watch there."

And Christina was thankful to see his look of gratification, sad though it was. She sat down near his bed, and began to write a letter in their joint names to Graf Dankwart von Schlangenwald, proposing that thus, after the even balance of the wrongs of the two houses, their mutual hostility might be laid to rest for ever by the consecration of the cause of their long contention. It was a stiff and formal letter, full of the set pious formularies of the age, scarcely revealing the deep heart-feeling within; but it was to the purpose, and Ebbo, after hearing it read, heartily approved, and consented to sign both it and those that Schleiermacher had brought. Christina held the scroll, and placed the pen in the fingers that had lately so easily wielded the heavy sword, but now felt it a far greater effort to guide the slender quill.

Moritz Schleiermacher went his way in search of the King of the Romans, far off in Carinthia. A full reply could not be expected till the campaign was over, and all that was known for some time was through a messenger sent back to Ulm by Schleiermacher with the intelligence that Maximilian would examine into the matter after his return, and that Count Dankwart would reply when he should come to perform his father's obsequies after the army was dispersed. There was also a letter of kind though courtly condolence from Kasimir of Wildschloss, much grieving for gallant young Sir Friedmund, proffering all the advocacy he could give the cause of Adlerstein, and covertly proffering the protection that she and her remaining son might now be more disposed to accept. Christina suppressed this letter, knowing it would only pain and irritate Ebbo, and that she had her answer ready. Indeed, in her grief for one son, and her anxiety for the other, perhaps it was this letter that first made her fully realize the drift of those earnest words of Friedel's respecting his father.

Meantime the mother and son were alone together, with much of suffering and of sorrow, yet with a certain tender comfort in the being all in all to one another, with none to intermeddle with their mutual love and grief. It was to Christina as if something of Friedel's sweetness had passed to his brother in his patient helplessness, and that, while thus fully engrossed with him, she had both her sons in one. Nay, in spite of all the pain, grief, and weariness, these were times when both dreaded any change, and the full recovery, when not only would the loss of Friedel be every moment freshly brought home to his brother, but when Ebbo would go in quest of his father.

For on this the young Baron had fixed his mind as a sacred duty, from the moment he had seen that life was to be his lot. He looked on his neglect of indications of the possibility of his father's life in the light of a sin that had led to all his disasters, and not only regarded the intended search as a token of repentance, but as a charge bequeathed to him by his less selfish brother. He seldom spoke of his intention, but his mother was perfectly aware of it, and never thought of it without such an agony of foreboding dread as eclipsed all the hope that lay beyond. She could only turn away her mind from the thought, and be thankful for what was still her own from day to day.

"Art weary, my son?" asked Christina one October afternoon, as Ebbo lay on his bed, languidly turning the pages of a noble folio of the Legends of the Saints that Master Gottfried had sent for his amusement. It was such a book as fixed the ardour a few years later of the wounded Navarrese knight, Inigo de Loyola, but Ebbo handled it as if each page were lead.

"Only thinking how Friedel would have glowed towards these as his own kinsmen," said Ebbo. "Then should I have cared to read of them!" and he gave a long sigh.

"Let me take away the book," she said. "Thou hast read long, and it is dark."

"So dark that there must surely be a snow-cloud."

"Snow is falling in the large flakes that our Friedel used to call winter-butterflies."

"Butterflies that will swarm and shut us in from the weary world," said Ebbo. "And alack! when they go, what a turmoil it will be! Councils in the Rathhaus, appeals to the League, wranglings with the Markgraf, wise saws, overweening speeches, all alike dull and dead."

"It will scarce be so when strength and spirit have returned, mine Ebbo."

"Never can life be more to me than the way to him," said the lonely boy; "and I—never like him—shall miss the road without him."

While he thus spoke in the listless dejection of sorrow and weakness, Hatto's aged step was on the stair. "Gracious lady," he said, "here is a huntsman bewildered in the hills, who has been asking shelter from the storm that is drifting up."

"See to his entertainment, then, Hatto," said the lady.

"My lady—Sir Baron," added Hatto, "I had not come up but that this guest seems scarce gear for us below. He is none of the foresters of our tract. His hair is perfumed, his shirt is fine holland, his buff suit is of softest skin, his baldric has a jewelled clasp, and his arblast! It would do my lord baron's heart good only to cast eyes on the perfect make of that arblast! He has a lordly tread, and a stately presence, and, though he has a free tongue, and made friends with us as he dried his garments, he asked after my lord like his equal."

"O mother, must you play the chatelaine?" asked Ebbo. "Who can the fellow be? Why did none ever so come when they would have been more welcome?"

"Welcomed must he be," said Christina, rising, "and thy state shall be my excuse for not tarrying longer with him than may be needful."

Yet, though shrinking from a stranger's face, she was not without hope that the variety might wholesomely rouse her son from his depression, and in effect Ebbo, when left with Hatto, minutely questioned him on the appearance of the stranger, and watched, with much curiosity, for his mother's return.

"Ebbo mine," she said, entering, after a long interval, "the knight asks to see thee either after supper, or to-morrow morn."

"Then a knight he is?"

"Yea, truly, a knight truly in every look and gesture, bearing his head like the leading stag of the herd, and yet right gracious."

"Gracious to you, mother, in your own hall?" cried Ebbo, almost fiercely.

"Ah! jealous champion, thou couldst not take offence! It was the manner of one free and courteous to every one, and yet with an inherent loftiness that pervades all."

The Dove in the Eagle's Nest

"Gives he no name?" said Ebbo.

"He calls himself Ritter Theurdank, of the suite of the late Kaisar, but I should deem him wont rather to lead than to follow."

"Theurdank," repeated Eberhard, "I know no such name! So, motherling, are you going to sup? I shall not sleep till I have seen him!"

"Hold, dear son." She leant over him and spoke low. "See him thou must, but let me first station Heinz and Koppel at the door with halberts, not within earshot, but thou art so entirely defenceless."

She had the pleasure of seeing him laugh. "Less defenceless than when the kinsman of Wildschloss here visited us, mother? I see for whom thou takest him, but let it be so; a spiritual knight would scarce wreak his vengeance on a wounded man in his bed. I will not have him insulted with precautions. If he has freely risked himself in my hands, I will as freely risk myself in his. Moreover, I thought he had won thy heart."

"Reigned over it, rather," said Christina. "It is but the disguise that I suspect and mistrust. Bid me not leave thee alone with him, my son."

"Nay, dear mother," said Ebbo, "the matters on which he is like to speak will brook no presence save our own, and even that will be hard enough to bear. So prop me more upright! So! And comb out these locks somewhat smoother. Thanks, mother. Now can he see whether he will choose Eberhard of Adlerstein for friend or foe."

By the time supper was ended, the only light in the upper room came from the flickering flames of the fire of pine knots on the hearth. It glanced on the pale features and dark sad eyes of the young Baron, sad in spite of the eager look of scrutiny that he turned on the figure that entered at the door, and approached so quickly that the partial light only served to show the gloss of long fair hair, the glint of a jewelled belt, and the outline of a tall, well-knit, agile frame.

"Welcome, Herr Ritter," he said; "I am sorry we have been unable to give you a fitter reception."

"No host could be more fully excused than you," said the stranger, and Ebbo started at his voice. "I fear you have suffered much, and still have much to suffer."

"My sword wound is healing fast," said Ebbo; "it is the shot in my broken thigh that is so tedious and painful."

"And I dare be sworn the leeches made it worse. I have hated all leeches ever since they kept me three days a prisoner in a 'pothecary's shop stinking with drugs. Why, I have cured myself with one pitcher of water of a raging fever, in their very despite! How did they serve thee, my poor boy?"

"They poured hot oil into the wound to remove the venom of the lead," said Ebbo.

"Had it been my case the lead should have been in their own brains first, though that were scarce needed, the heavy-witted Hans Sausages. Why should there be more poison in lead than in steel? I have asked all my surgeons that question, nor ever had a reasonable answer. Greater havoc of warriors do they make than ever with the arquebus—ay, even when every lanzknecht bears one."

"Alack!" Ebbo could not help exclaiming, "where will be room for chivalry?"

"Talk not old world nonsense," said Theurdank; "chivalry is in the heart, not in the weapon. A youth beforehand enough with the world to be building bridges should know that, when all our troops are provided with such an arm, then will their platoons in serried ranks be as a solid wall breathing fire, and as impregnable as the lines of English archers with long bows, or the phalanx of Macedon. And, when each man bears a pistol instead of the misericorde, his life will be far more his own."

Ebbo's face was in full light, and his visitor marked his contracted brow and trembling lip. "Ah!" he said, "thou hast had foul experience of these weapons."

"Not mine own hurt," said Ebbo; "that was but fair chance of war."

"I understand," said the knight; "it was the shot that severed the goodly bond that was so fair to see. Young man, none has grieved more truly than King Max."

"And well he may," said Ebbo. "He has not lost merely one of his best servants, but all the better half of another."

"There is still stuff enough left to make that ONE well worth having," said Theurdank, kindly grasping his hand, "though I would it were more substantial! How didst get old Wolfgang down, boy? He must have been a tough morsel for slight bones like these, even when better covered than now. Come, tell me all. I promised the Markgraf of Wurtemburg to look into the matter when I came to be guest at St. Ruprecht's cloister, and I have some small interest too with King Max."

His kindliness and sympathy were more effectual with Ebbo than the desire to represent his case favourably, for he was still too wretched to care for policy; but he answered Theurdank's questions readily, and explained how the idea of the bridge had originated in the vigil beside the broken waggons.

"I hope," said Theurdank, "the merchants made up thy share? These overthrown goods are a seignorial right of one or other of you lords of the bank."

"True, Herr Ritter; but we deemed it unknightly to snatch at what travellers lost by misfortune."

"Freiherr Eberhard, take my word for it, while thou thus holdest, all the arquebuses yet to be cut out of the Black Forest will not mar thy chivalry. Where didst get these ways of thinking?"

"My brother was a very St. Sebastian! My mother—"

"Ah! her sweet wise face would have shown it, even had not poor Kasimir of Adlerstein raved of her. Ah! lad, thou hast crossed a case of true love there! Canst not brook even such a gallant stepfather?"

"I may not," said Ebbo, with spirit; "for with his last breath Schlangenwald owned that my own father died not at the hostel, but may now be alive as a Turkish slave."

"The devil!" burst out Theurdank. "Well! that might have been a pretty mess! A Turkish slave, saidst thou! What year chanced all this matter—thy grandfather's murder and all the rest?"

"The year before my birth," said Ebbo. "It was in the September of 1475."

"Ha!" muttered Theurdank, musing to himself; "that was the year the dotard Schenk got his overthrow at the fight of Rain on Sare from the Moslem. Some composition was made by them, and old Wolfgang was not unlikely to have been the go–between. So! Say on, young knight," he added, "let us to the matter in hand. How rose the strife that kept back two troops from our—from the banner of the empire?"

Ebbo proceeded with the narration, and concluded it just as the bell now belonging to the chapel began to toll for compline, and Theurdank prepared to obey its summons, first, however, asking if he should send any one to the patient. Ebbo thanked him, but said he needed no one till his mother should come after prayers.

"Nay, I told thee I had some leechcraft. Thou art weary, and must rest more entirely;"—and, giving him little choice, Theurdank supported him with one arm while removing the pillows that propped him, then laid him tenderly down, saying, "Good night, and the saints bless thee, brave young knight. Sleep well, and recover in spite of the leeches. I cannot afford to lose both of you."

Ebbo strove to follow mentally the services that were being performed in the chapel, and whose "Amens" and louder notes pealed up to him, devoid of the clear young tones that had sung their last here below, but swelled by grand bass notes that as much distracted Ebbo's attention as the memory of his guest's conversation; and he impatiently awaited his mother's arrival.

At length, lamp in hand, she appeared with tears shining in her eyes, and bending over him said,

"He hath done honour to our blessed one, my Ebbo; he knelt by him, and crossed him with holy water, and when he led me from the chapel he told me any mother in Germany might envy me my two sons even now. Thou must love him now, Ebbo."

"Love him as one loves one's loftiest model," said Ebbo—"value the old castle the more for sheltering him."

"Hath he made himself known to thee?"

"Not openly, but there is only one that he can be."

Christina smiled, thankful that the work of pardon and reconciliation had been thus softened by the personal qualities of the enemy, whose conduct in the chapel had deeply moved her.

"Then all will be well, blessedly well," she said.

"So I trust," said Ebbo, "but the bell broke our converse, and he laid me down as tenderly as—O mother, if a father's kindness be like his, I have truly somewhat to regain."

"Knew he aught of the fell bargain?" whispered Christina.

"Not he, of course, save that it was a year of Turkish inroads. He will speak more perchance to-morrow. Mother, not a word to any one, nor let us betray our recognition unless it be his pleasure to make himself known."

"Certainly not," said Christina, remembering the danger that the household might revenge Friedel's death if they knew the foe to be in their power. Knowing as she did that Ebbo's admiration was apt to be enthusiastic, and might now be rendered the more fervent by fever and solitude, she was still at a loss to understand his dazzled, fascinated state.

When Heinz entered, bringing the castle key, which was always laid under the Baron's pillow, Ebbo made a movement with his hand that surprised them both, as if to send it elsewhere—then muttered, "No, no, not till he reveals himself," and asked, "Where sleeps the guest?"

"In the grandmother's room, which we fitted for a guest-chamber, little thinking who our first would be," said his mother.

"Never fear, lady; we will have a care to him," said Heinz, somewhat grimly.

"Yes, have a care," said Ebbo, wearily; "and take care all due honour is shown to him! Good night, Heinz."

"Gracious lady," said Heinz, when by a sign he had intimated to her his desire of speaking with her unobserved by the Baron, "never fear; I know who the fellow is as well as you do. I shall be at the foot of the stairs, and woe to whoever tries to step up them past me."

"There is no reason to apprehend treason, Heinz, yet to be on our guard can do no harm."

"Nay, lady, I could look to the gear for the oubliette if you would speak the word."

"For heaven's sake, no, Heinz. This man has come hither trusting to our honour, and you could not do your lord a greater wrong, nor one that he could less pardon, than by any attempt on our guest."

"Would that he had never eaten our bread!" muttered Heinz. "Vipers be they all, and who knows what may come next?"

"Watch, watch, Heinz; that is all," implored Christina, "and, above all, not a word to any one else."

And Christina dismissed the man-at-arms gruff and sullen, and herself retired ill at ease between fears of, and for, the unwelcome guest whose strange powers of fascination had rendered her, in his absence, doubly distrustful.

CHAPTER XXI: RITTER THEURDANK

The snow fell all night without ceasing, and was still falling on the morrow, when the guest explained his desire of paying a short visit to the young Baron, and then taking his departure. Christina would gladly have been quit of him, but she felt bound to remonstrate, for their mountain was absolutely impassable during a fall of snow, above all when accompanied by wind, since the drifts concealed fearful abysses, and the shifting masses insured destruction to the unwary wayfarer; nay, natives themselves had perished between the hamlet and the castle.

"Not the hardiest cragsman, not my son himself," she said, "could venture on such a morning to guide you to—"

"Whither, gracious dame?" asked Theurdank, half smiling.

"Nay, sir, I would not utter what you would not make known."

"You know me then?"

"Surely, sir, for our noble foe, whose generous trust in our honour must win my son's heart."

"So!" he said, with a peculiar smile, "Theurdank—Dankwart—I see! May I ask if your son likewise smelt out the Schlangenwald?"

"Verily, Sir Count, my Ebbo is not easily deceived. He said our guest could be but one man in all the empire."

Theurdank smiled again, saying, "Then, lady, you shudder not at a man whose kin and yours have shed so much of one another's blood?"

"Nay, ghostly knight, I regard you as no more stained therewith than are my sons by the deeds of their grandfather."

"If there were more like you, lady," returned Theurdank, "deadly feuds would soon be starved out. May I to your son? I have more to say to him, and I would fain hear his views of the storm."

Christina could not be quite at ease with Theurdank in her son's room, but she had no choice, and she knew that Heinz was watching on the turret stair, out of hearing indeed, but as ready to spring as a cat who sees her young ones in the hand of a child that she only half trusts.

The Dove in the Eagle's Nest

Ebbo lay eagerly watching for his visitor, who greeted him with the same almost paternal kindness he had evinced the night before, but consulted him upon the way from the castle. Ebbo confirmed his mother's opinion that the path was impracticable so long as the snow fell, and the wind tossed it in wild drifts.

"We have been caught in snow," he said, "and hard work have we had to get home! Once indeed, after a bear hunt, we fully thought the castle stood before us, and lo! it was all a cruel snow mist in that mocking shape. I was even about to climb our last Eagle's Step, as I thought, when behold, it proved to be the very brink of the abyss."

"Ah! these ravines are well−nigh as bad as those of the Inn. I've known what it was to be caught on the ledge of a precipice by a sharp wind, changing its course, mark'st thou, so swiftly that it verily tore my hold from the rock, and had well−nigh swept me into a chasm of mighty depth. There was nothing for it but to make the best spring I might towards the crag on the other side, and grip for my life at my alpenstock, which by Our Lady's grace was firmly planted, and I held on till I got breath again, and felt for my footing on the ice−glazed rock."

"Ah!" said Eberhard with a long breath, after having listened with a hunter's keen interest to this hair's−breadth escape, "it sounds like a gust of my mountain air thus let in on me."

"Truly it is dismal work for a lusty hunter to lie here," said Theurdank, "but soon shalt thou take thy crags again in full vigour, I hope. How call'st thou the deep gray lonely pool under a steep frowning crag sharpened well−nigh to a spear point, that I passed yester afternoon?"

"The Ptarmigan's Mere, the Red Eyrie," murmured Ebbo, scarcely able to utter the words as he thought of Friedel's delight in the pool, his exploit at the eyrie, and the gay bargain made in the streets of Ulm, that he should show the scaler of the Dom steeple the way to the eagle's nest.

"I remember," said his guest gravely, coming to his side. "Ah, boy! thy brother's flight has been higher yet. Weep freely; fear me not. Do I not know what it is, when those who were over−good for earth have found their eagle's wings, and left us here?"

Ebbo gazed up through his tears into the noble, mournful face that was bent kindly over him. "I will not seek to comfort thee by counselling thee to forget," said Theurdank. "I was scarce thine elder when my life was thus rent asunder, and to hoar hairs, nay, to the grave itself, will she be my glory and my sorrow. Never owned I brother, but I trow ye two were one in no common sort."

"Such brothers as we saw at Ulm were little like us," returned Ebbo, from the bottom of his heart. "We were knit together so that all will begin with me as if it were the left hand remaining alone to do it! I am glad that my old life may not even in shadow be renewed till after I have gone in quest of my father."

"Be not over hasty in that quest," said the guest, "or the infidels may chance to gain two Freiherren instead of one. Hast any designs?"

Ebbo explained that he thought of making his way to Genoa to consult the merchant Gian Battista dei Battiste, whose description of the captive German noble had so strongly impressed Friedel. Ebbo knew the difference between Turks and Moors, but Friedel's impulse guided him, and he further thought that at Genoa he should learn the way to deal with either variety of infidel. Theurdank thought this a prudent course, since the Genoese had dealings both at Tripoli and Constantinople; and, moreover, the transfer was not impossible, since the two different hordes of Moslems trafficked among themselves when either had made an unusually successful razzia.

"Shame," he broke out, "that these Eastern locusts, these ravening hounds, should prey unmolested on the fairest lands of the earth, and our German nobles lie here like swine, grunting and squealing over the plunder they grub up from one another, deaf to any summons from heaven or earth! Did not Heaven's own voice speak in thunder this last year, even in

The Dove in the Eagle's Nest

November, hurling the mighty thunderbolt of Alsace, an ell long, weighing two hundred and fifteen pounds? Did I not cause it to be hung up in the church of Encisheim, as a witness and warning of the plagues that hang over us? But no, nothing will quicken them from their sloth and drunkenness till the foe are at their doors; and, if a man arise of different mould, with some heart for the knightly, the good, and the true, then they kill him for me! But thou, Adlerstein, this pious quest over, thou wilt return to me. Thou hast head to think and heart to feel for the shame and woe of this misguided land."

"I trust so, my lord," said Ebbo. "Truly, I have suffered bitterly for pursuing my own quarrel rather than the crusade."

"I meant not thee," said Theurdank, kindly. "Thy bridge is a benefit to me, as much as, or more than, ever it can be to thee. Dost know Italian? There is something of Italy in thine eye."

"My mother's mother was Italian, my lord; but she died so early that her language has not descended to my mother or myself."

"Thou shouldst learn it. It will be pastime while thou art bed-fast, and serve thee well in dealing with the Moslem. Moreover, I may have work for thee in Welschland. Books? I will send thee books. There is the whole chronicle of Karl the Great, and all his Palsgrafen, by Pulci and Boiardo, a brave Count and gentleman himself, governor of Reggio, and worthy to sing of deeds of arms; so choice, too, as to the names of his heroes, that they say he caused his church bells to be rung when he had found one for Rodomonte, his infidel Hector. He has shown up Roland as a love-sick knight, though, which is out of all accord with Archbishop Turpin. Wilt have him?"

"When we were together, we used to love tales of chivalry."

"Ah! Or wilt have the stern old Ghibelline Florentine, who explored the three realms of the departed? Deep lore, and well-nigh unsearchable, is his; but I love him for the sake of his Beatrice, who guided him. May we find such guides in our day!"

"I have heard of him," said Ebbo. "If he will tell me where my Friedel walks in light, then, my lord, I would read him with all my heart."

"Or wouldst thou have rare Franciscus Petrarca? I wot thou art too young as yet for the yearnings of his sonnets, but their voice is sweet to the bereft heart."

And he murmured over, in their melodious Italian flow, the lines on Laura's death

"Not pallid, but yet whiter than the snow
By wind unstirred that on a hillside lies;
Rest seemed as on a weary frame to grow,
A gentle slumber pressed her lovely eyes."

"Ah!" he added aloud to himself, "it is ever to me as though the poet had watched in that chamber at Ghent."

Such were the discourses of that morning, now on poetry and book lore; now admiration of the carvings that decked the room; now talk on grand architectural designs, or improvements in fire-arms, or the discussion of hunting adventures. There seemed nothing in art, life, or learning in which the versatile mind of Theurdank was not at home, or that did not end in some strange personal reminiscence of his own. All was so kind, so gracious, and brilliant, that at first the interview was full of wondering delight to Ebbo, but latterly it became very fatiguing from the strain of attention, above all towards a guest who evidently knew that he was known, while not permitting such recognition to be avowed. Ebbo began to long for an interruption, but, though he could see by the lightened sky that the weather had cleared up, it would have been impossible to have suggested to any guest that the way might now probably be open, and more especially to such a guest as this. Considerate as his visitor had been the night before, the pleasure of talk seemed to have done away with the remembrance of his host's weakness, till Ebbo so flagged that at last he was scarcely alive to more than the continued sound of the voice, and all the pain that for a while had been in abeyance seemed to have mastered him; but his guest, half reading his books, half discoursing, seemed too much immersed in his own plans, theories, and adventures, to mark the condition of his auditor.

Interruption came at last, however. There was a sudden knock at the door at noon, and with scant ceremony Heinz entered, followed by three other of the men−at−arms, fully equipped.

"Ha! what means this?" demanded Ebbo.

"Peace, Sir Baron," said Heinz, advancing so as to place his large person between Ebbo's bed and the strange hunter. "You know nothing of it. We are not going to lose you as well as your brother, and we mean to see how this knight likes to serve as a hostage instead of opening the gates as a traitor spy. On him, Koppel! it is thy right."

"Hands off! at your peril, villains!" exclaimed Ebbo, sitting up, and speaking in the steady resolute voice that had so early rendered him thoroughly their master, but much perplexed and dismayed, and entirely unassisted by Theurdank, who stood looking on with almost a smile, as if diverted by his predicament.

"By your leave, Herr Freiherr," said Heinz, putting his hand on his shoulder, "this is no concern of yours. While you cannot guard yourself or my lady, it is our part to do so. I tell you his minions are on their way to surprise the castle."

Even as Heinz spoke, Christina came panting into the room, and, hurrying to her son's side, said, "Sir Count, is this just, is this honourable, thus to return my son's welcome, in his helpless condition?"

"Mother, are you likewise distracted?" exclaimed Ebbo. "What is all this madness?"

"Alas, my son, it is no frenzy! There are armed men coming up the Eagle's Stairs on the one hand and by the Gemsbock's Pass on the other!"

"But not a hair of your head shall they hurt, lady," said Heinz. "This fellow's limbs shall be thrown to them over the battlements. On, Koppel!"

"Off, Koppel!" thundered Ebbo. "Would you brand me with shame for ever? Were he all the Schlangenwalds in one, he should go as freely as he came; but he is no more Schlangenwald than I am."

"He has deceived you, my lord," said Heinz. "My lady's own letter to Schlangenwald was in his chamber. 'Tis a treacherous disguise."

"Fool that thou art!" said Ebbo. "I know this gentleman well. I knew him at Ulm. Those who meet him here mean me no ill. Open the gates and receive them honourably! Mother, mother, trust me, all is well. I know what I am saying."

The men looked one upon another. Christina wrung her hands, uncertain whether her son were not under some strange fatal deception.

"My lord has his fancies," growled Koppel. "I'll not be balked of my right of vengeance for his scruples! Will he swear that this fellow is what he calls himself?"

"I swear," said Ebbo, slowly, "that he is a true loyal knight, well known to me."

"Swear it distinctly, Sir Baron," said Heinz. "We have all too deep a debt of vengeance to let off any one who comes here lurking in the interest of our foe. Swear that this is Theurdank, or we send his head to greet his friends."

Drops stood on Ebbo's brow, and his breath laboured as he felt his senses reeling, and his powers of defence for his guest failing him. Even should the stranger confess his name, the people of the castle might not believe him; and here he stood like one indifferent, evidently measuring how far his young host would go in his cause.

"I cannot swear that his real name is Theurdank," said Ebbo, rallying his forces, "but this I swear, that he is neither friend nor fosterer of Schlangenwald, that I know him, and I had rather die than that the slightest indignity were offered him." Here, and with a great effort that terribly wrenched his wounded leg, he reached past Heinz, and grasped his guest's hand, pulling him as near as he could.

"Sir," he said, "if they try to lay hands on you, strike my death– blow!"

A bugle–horn was wound outside. The men stood daunted—Christina in extreme terror for her son, who lay gasping, breathless, but still clutching the stranger's hand, and with eyes of fire glaring on the mutinous warriors. Another bugle–blast! Heinz was almost in the act of grappling with the silent foe, and Koppel cried as he raised his halbert, "Now or never!" but paused.

"Never, so please you," said the strange guest. "What if your young lord could not forswear himself that my name is Theurdank! Are you foes to all the world save Theurdank?"

"No masking," said Heinz, sternly. "Tell your true name as an honest man, and we will judge whether you be friend or foe."

"My name is a mouthful, as your master knows," said the guest, slowly, looking with strangely amused eyes on the confused lanzknechts, who were trying to devour their rage. "I was baptized Maximilianus; Archduke of Austria, by birth; by choice of the Germans, King of the Romans."

"The Kaisar!"

Christina dropped on her knee; the men–at–arms tumbled backwards; Ebbo pressed the hand he held to his lips, and fainted away. The bugle sounded for the third time.

CHAPTER XXII: PEACE

Slowly and painfully did Ebbo recover from his swoon, feeling as if the means of revival were rending him away from his brother. He was so completely spent that he was satisfied with a mere assurance that nothing was amiss, and presently dropped into a profound slumber, whence he awoke to find it still broad daylight, and his mother sitting by the side of his bed, all looking so much as it had done for the last six weeks, that his first inquiry was if all that had happened had been but a strange dream. His mother would scarcely answer till she had satisfied herself that his eye was clear, his voice steady, his hand cool, and that, as she said, "That Kaisar had done him no harm."

"Ah, then it was true! Where is he? Gone?" cried Ebbo, eagerly.

"No, in the hall below, busy with letters they have brought him. Lie still, my boy; he has done thee quite enough damage for one day."

"But, mother, what are you saying! Something disloyal, was it not?"

"Well, Ebbo, I was very angry that he should have half killed you when he could so easily have spoken one word. Heaven forgive me if I did wrong, but I could not help it."

"Did HE forgive you, mother?" said Ebbo, anxiously.

"He—oh yes. To do him justice he was greatly concerned; devised ways of restoring thee, and now has promised not to come near thee again without my leave," said the mother, quite as persuaded of her own rightful sway in her son's sick chamber as ever Kunigunde had been of her dominion over the castle.

"And is he displeased with me? Those cowardly vindictive rascals, to fall on him, and set me at nought! Before him, too!" exclaimed Ebbo, bitterly.

"Nay, Ebbo, he thought thy part most gallant. I heard him say so, not only to me, but below stairs—both wise and true. Thou didst know him then?"

"From the first glance of his princely eye—the first of his keen smiles. I had seen him disguised before. I thought you knew him too, mother; I never guessed that your mind was running on Schlangenwald when we talked at cross purposes last night."

"Would that I had; but though I breathed no word openly, I encouraged Heinz's precautions. My boy, I could not help it; my heart would tremble for my only one, and I saw he could not be what he seemed."

"And what doth he here? Who were the men who were advancing?"

"They were the followers he had left at St. Ruprecht's, and likewise Master Schleiermacher and Sir Kasimir of Wildschloss."

"Ha!"

"What—he had not told thee?"

"No. He knew that I knew him, was at no pains to disguise himself, yet evidently meant me to treat him as a private knight. But what brought Wildschloss here?"

"It seems," said Christina, "that, on the return from Carinthia, the Kaisar expressed his intention of slipping away from his army in his own strange fashion, and himself inquiring into the matter of the Ford. So he took with him his own personal followers, the new Graf von Schlangenwald, Herr Kasimir, and Master Schleiermacher. The others he sent to Schlangenwald; he himself lodged at St. Ruprecht's, appointing that Sir Kasimir should meet him there this morning. From the convent he started on a chamois hunt, and made his way hither; but, when the snow came on, and he returned not, his followers became uneasy, and came in search of him."

"Ah!" said Ebbo, "he meant to intercede for Wildschloss—it might be he would have tried his power. No, for that he is too generous. How looked Wildschloss, mother?"

"How could I tell how any one looked save thee, my poor wan boy? Thou art paler than ever! I cannot have any king or kaisar of them all come to trouble thee."

"Nay, motherling, there is much more trouble and unrest to me in not knowing how my king will treat us after such a requital! Prithee let him know that I am at his service."

And, after having fed and refreshed her patient, the gentle potentate of his chamber consented to intimate her consent to admit the invader. But not till after delay enough to fret the impatient nerves of illness did Maximilian appear, handing her in, and saying, in the cheery voice that was one of his chief fascinations,

"Yea, truly, fair dame, I know thou wouldst sooner trust Schlangenwald himself than me alone with thy charge. How goes it, my true knight?"

"Well, right well, my liege," said Ebbo, "save for my shame and grief."

"Thou art the last to be ashamed for that," said the good−natured prince. "Have I never seen my faithful vassals more bent on their own feuds than on my word?—I who reign over a set of kings, who brook no will but their own."

"And may we ask your pardon," said Ebbo, "not only for ourselves, but for the misguided men−at−arms?"

"What! the grewsome giant that was prepared with the axe, and the honest lad that wanted to do his duty by his father? I honour that lad, Freiherr; I would enrol him in my guard, but that probably he is better off here than with Massimiliano pochi danari, as the Italians call me. But what I came hither to say was this," and he spoke gravely: "thou art sincere in desiring reconciliation with the house of Schlangenwald?"

"With all my heart," said Ebbo, "do I loathe the miserable debt of blood for blood!"

"And," said Maximilian, "Graf Dankwart is of like mind. Bred from pagedom in his Prussian commandery, he has never been exposed to the irritations that have fed the spirit of strife, and he will be thankful to lay it aside. The question next is how to solemnize this reconciliation, ere your retainers on one side or the other do something to set you by the ears together again, which, judging by this morning's work, is not improbable."

"Alas! no," said Ebbo, "while I am laid by."

"Had you both been in our camp, you should have sworn friendship in my chapel. Now must Dankwart come hither to thee, as I trow he had best do, while I am here to keep the peace. See, friend Ebbo, we will have him here to−morrow; thy chaplain shall deck the altar here, the Father Abbot shall say mass, and ye shall swear peace and brotherhood before me. And," he added, taking Ebbo's hand, "I shall know how to trust thine oaths as of one who sets the fear of God above that of his king."

This was truly the only chance of impressing on the wild vassals of the two houses an obligation that perhaps might override their ancient hatred; and the Baron and his mother gladly submitted to the arrangement. Maximilian withdrew to give directions for summoning the persons required and Christina was soon obliged to leave her son, while she provided for her influx of guests.

Ebbo was alone till nearly the end of the supper below stairs. He had been dozing, when a cautious tread came up the turret steps, and he started, and called out, "Who goes there? I am not asleep."

"It is your kinsman, Freiherr," said a well−known voice; "I come by your mother's leave."

"Welcome, Sir Cousin," said Ebbo, holding out his hand. "You come to find everything changed."

"I have knelt in the chapel," said Wildschloss, gravely.

"And he loved you better than I!" said Ebbo.

The Dove in the Eagle's Nest

"Your jealousy of me was a providential thing, for which all may be thankful," said Wildschloss gravely; "yet it is no small thing to lose the hope of so many years! However, young Baron, I have grave matter for your consideration. Know you the service on which I am to be sent? The Kaisar deems that the Armenians or some of the Christian nations on the skirts of the Ottoman empire might be made our allies, and attack the Turk in his rear. I am chosen as his envoy, and shall sail so soon as I can make my way to Venice. I only knew of the appointment since I came hither, he having been led thereto by letters brought him this day; and mayhap by the downfall of my hopes. He was peremptory, as his mood is, and seemed to think it no small favour," added Wildschloss, with some annoyance. "And meantime, what of my poor child? There she is in the cloister at Ulm, but an inheritance is a very mill-stone round the neck of an orphan maid. That insolent fellow, Lassla von Trautbach, hath already demanded to espouse the poor babe; he—a blood-stained, dicing, drunken rover, with whom I would not trust a dog that I loved! Yet my death would place her at the disposal of his father, who would give her at once to him. Nay, even his aunt, the abbess, will believe nothing against him, and hath even striven with me to have her betrothed at once. On the barest rumour of my death will they wed the poor little thing, and then woe to her, and woe to my vassals!"

"The King," suggested Ebbo. "Surely she might be made his ward."

"Young man," said Sir Kasimir, bending over him, and speaking in an undertone, "he may well have won your heart. As friend, when one is at his side, none can be so winning, or so sincere as he; but with all his brilliant gifts, he says truly of himself that he is a mere reckless huntsman. To-day, while I am with him, he would give me half Austria, or fight single-handed in my cause or Thekla's. Next month, when I am out of sight, comes Trautbach, just when his head is full of keeping the French out of Italy, or reforming the Church, or beating the Turk, or parcelling the empire into circles, or, maybe, of a new touch-hole for a cannon—nay, of a flower-garden, or of walking into a lion's den. He just says, 'Yea, well,' to be rid of the importunity, and all is over with my poor little maiden. Hare-brained and bewildered with schemes has he been as Romish King—how will it be with him as Kaisar? It is but of his wonted madness that he is here at all, when his Austrian states must be all astray for want of him. No, no; I would rather make a weathercock guardian to my daughter. You yourself are the only guard to whom I can safely intrust her."

"My sword as knight and kinsman—" began Ebbo.

"No, no; 'tis no matter of errant knight or distressed damsel. That is King Max's own line!" said Wildschloss, with a little of the irony that used to nettle Ebbo. "There is only one way in which you can save her, and that is as her husband."

Ebbo started, as well he might, but Sir Kasimir laid his hand on him with a gesture that bade him listen ere he spoke. "My first wish for my child," he said, "was to see her brought up by that peerless lady below stairs. The saints—in pity to one so like themselves—spared her the distress our union would have brought her. Now, it would be vain to place my little Thekla in her care, for Trautbach would easily feign my death, and claim his niece, nor are you of age to be made her guardian as head of our house. But, if this marriage rite were solemnized, then would her person and lands alike be yours, and I could leave her with an easy heart."

"But," said the confused, surprised Ebbo, "what can I do? They say I shall not walk for many weeks to come. And, even if I could, I am so young—I have so blundered in my dealings with my own mountaineers, and with this fatal bridge—how should I manage such estates as yours? Some better—"

"Look you, Ebbo," said Wildschloss; "you have erred—you have been hasty; but tell me where to find another youth, whose strongest purpose was as wise as your errors, or who cared for others' good more than for his own violence and vainglory? Brief as your time has been, one knows when one is on your bounds by the aspect of your serfs, the soundness of their dwellings, the prosperity of their crops and cattle above all, by their face and tone if one asks for their lord."

"Ah! it was Friedel they loved. They scarce knew me from Friedel."

The Dove in the Eagle's Nest

"Such as you are, with all the blunders you have made and will make, you are the only youth I know to whom I could intrust my child or my lands. The old Wildschloss castle is a male fief, and would return to you, but there are domains since granted that will cause intolerable trouble and strife, unless you and my poor little heiress are united. As for age, you are—?"

"Eighteen next Easter."

"Then there are scarce eleven years between you. You will find the little one a blooming bride when your first deeds in arms have been fought out."

"And, if my mother trains her up," said Ebbo, thoughtfully, "she will be all the better daughter to her. But, Sir Cousin, you know I too must be going. So soon as I can brook the saddle, I must seek out and ransom my father."

"That is like to be a far shorter and safer journey than mine. The Genoese and Venetians understand traffic with the infidels for their captives, and only by your own fault could you get into danger. Even at the worst, should mishap befall you, you could so order matters as to leave your girl-widow in your mother's charge."

"Then," added Ebbo, "she would still have one left to love and cherish her. Sir Kasimir, it is well; though, if you knew me without my Friedel, you would repent of your bargain."

"Thanks from my heart," said Wildschloss, "but you need not be concerned. You have never been over-friendly with me even with Friedel at your side. But to business, my son. You will endure that title from me now? My time is short."

"What would you have me do? Shall I send the little one a betrothal ring, and ride to Ulm to wed and fetch her home in spring?"

"That may hardly serve. These kinsmen would have seized on her and the castle long ere that time. The only safety is the making wedlock as fast as it can be made with a child of such tender years. Mine is the only power that can make the abbess give her up, and therefore will I ride this moonlight night to Ulm, bring the little one back with me by the time the reconciliation be concluded, and then shall ye be wed by the Abbot of St. Ruprecht's, with the Kaisar for a witness, and thus will the knot be too strong for the Trautbachs to untie."

Ebbo looked disconcerted, and gasped, as if this were over-quick work.—"To-morrow!" he said. "Knows my mother?"

"I go to speak with her at once. The Kaisar's consent I have, as he says, 'If we have one vassal who has common sense and honesty, let us make the most of him.' Ah! my son, I shall return to see you his counsellor and friend."

Those days had no delicacies as to the lady's side taking the initiative: and, in effect, the wealth and power of Wildschloss so much exceeded those of the elder branch that it would have been presumptuous on Eberhard's part to have made the proposal. It was more a treaty than an affair of hearts, and Sir Kasimir had not even gone through the form of inquiring if Ebbo were fancy-free. It was true, indeed, that he was still a boy, with no passion for any one but his mother; but had he even formed a dream of a ladye love, it would scarcely have been deemed a rational objection. The days of romance were no days of romance in marriage.

Yet Christina, wedded herself for pure love, felt this obstacle strongly. The scheme was propounded to her over the hall fire by no less a person than Maximilian himself, and he, whose perceptions were extremely keen when he was not too much engrossed to use them, observed her reluctance through all her timid deference, and probed her reasons so successfully that she owned at last that, though it might sound like folly, she could scarce endure to see her son so bind himself that the romance of his life could hardly be innocent.

"Nay, lady," was the answer, in a tone of deep feeling. "Neither lands nor honours can weigh down the up-springing of true love;" and he bowed his head between his hands.

Verily, all the Low Countries had not impeded the true-hearted affection of Maximilian and Mary; and, though since her death his want of self-restraint had marred his personal character and morals, and though he was now on the point of concluding a most loveless political marriage, yet still Mary was—as he shows her as the Beatrice of both his strange autobiographical allegories—the guiding star of his fitful life; and in heart his fidelity was so unbroken that, when after a long pause he again looked up to Christina, he spoke as well understanding her feelings.

"I know what you would say, lady; your son hardly knows as yet how much is asked of him, and the little maid, to whom he vows his heart, is over-young to secure it. But, lady, I have often observed that men, whose family affections are as deep and fervent as your son's are for you and his brother, seldom have wandering passions, but that their love flows deep and steady in the channels prepared for it. Let your young Freiherr regard this damsel as his own, and you will see he will love her as such."

"I trust so, my liege."

"Moreover, if she turn out like the spiteful Trautbach folk," said Maximilian, rather wickedly, "plenty of holes can be picked in a baby-wedding. No fear of its over-firmness. I never saw one come to good; only he must keep firm hold on the lands."

This was not easy to answer, coming from a prince who had no small experience in premature bridals coming to nothing, and Christina felt that the matter was taken out of her hands, and that she had no more to do but to enjoy the warm-hearted Kaisar's praises of her son.

In fact, the general run of nobles were then so boorish and violent compared with the citizens, that a nobleman who possessed intellect, loyalty, and conscience was so valuable to the sovereign that Maximilian was rejoiced to do all that either could bind him to his service or increase his power. The true history of this expedition on the Emperor's part was this—that he had consulted Kasimir upon the question of the Debateable Ford and the feud of Adlerstein and Schlangenwald, asking further how his friend had sped in the wooing of the fair widow, to which he remembered having given his consent at Ulm.

Wildschloss replied that, though backed up by her kindred at Ulm, he had made no progress in consequence of the determined opposition of her two sons, and he had therefore resolved to wait a while, and let her and the young Baron feel their inability to extricate themselves from the difficulties that were sure to beset them, without his authority, influence, and experience—fully believing that some predicament might arise that would bring the mother to terms, if not the sons.

This disaster did seem to have fallen out, and he had meant at once to offer himself to the lady as her supporter and advocate, able to bring about all her son could desire; though he owned that his hopes would have been higher if the survivor had been the gentle, friendly Friedmund, rather than the hot and imperious Eberhard, who he knew must be brought very low ere his objections would be withdrawn.

The touch of romance had quite fascinated Maximilian. He would see the lady and her son. He would make all things easy by the personal influence that he so well knew how to exert, backed by his imperial authority; and both should see cause to be thankful to purchase consent to the bridge-building, and pardon for the fray, by the marriage between the widow and Sir Kasimir.

But the Last of the Knights was a gentleman, and the meek dignity of his hostess had hindered him from pressing on her any distasteful subject until her son's explanation of the uncertainty of her husband's death had precluded all mention of this intention. Besides, Maximilian was himself greatly charmed by Ebbo's own qualities—partly perhaps as an intelligent auditor, but also by his good sense, high spirit, and, above all, by the ready and delicate tact that had both penetrated and respected the disguise. Moreover, Maximilian, though a faulty, was a devout man, and could appreciate the youth's unswerving truth, under circumstances that did, in effect, imperil him more really than his guest. In this mood, Maximilian felt disposed to be rid to the very utmost of poor Sir Kasimir's unlucky attachment to a wedded lady; and receiving letters suggestive of the Eastern mission, instantly decided that it would only be doing as he would be done by instantly to order the disappointed suitor off to the utmost parts of the earth, where he would much have liked to go himself, save for the unlucky clog of all the realm of Germany. That Sir Kasimir had any tie to home he had for the moment entirely forgotten; and, had he remembered it, the knight was so eminently fitted to fulfil his purpose, that it could hardly have been regarded. But, when Wildschloss himself devised his little heiress's union with the head of the direct line, it was a most acceptable proposal to the Emperor, who set himself to forward it at once, out of policy, and as compensation to all parties.

And so Christina's gentle remonstrance was passed by. Yet, with all her sense of the venture, it was thankworthy to look back on the trembling anxiety with which she had watched her boy's childhood, and all his temptations and perils, and compare her fears with his present position: his alliance courted, his wisdom honoured, the child of the proud, contemned outlaw received as the favourite of the Emperor, and the valued ally of her own honoured burgher world. Yet he was still a mere lad. How would it be for the future?

Would he be unspoiled? Yes, even as she already viewed one of her twins as the star on high—nay, when kneeling in the chapel, her dazzling tears made stars of the glint of the light reflected in his bright helmet—might she not trust that the other would yet run his course to and fro, as the spark in the stubble?

CHAPTER XXIII: THE ALTAR OF PEACE

No one could bear to waken the young Baron till the sun had risen high enough to fall on his face and unclose his eyes.

"Mother" (ever his first word), "you have let me sleep too long."

"Thou didst wake too long, I fear me."

"I hoped you knew it not. Yes, my wound throbbed sore, and the wonders of the day whirled round my brain like the wild huntsman's chase."

"And, cruel boy, thou didst not call to me."

"What, with such a yesterday, and such a morrow for you? while, chance what may, I can but lie still. I thought I must call, if I were still so wretched, when the last moonbeam faded; but, behold, sleep came, and therewith my Friedel sat by me, and has sung songs of peace ever since."

"And hath lulled thee to content, dear son?"

"Content as the echo of his voice and the fulfilment of his hope can make me," said Ebbo.

And so Christina made her son ready for the day's solemnities, arraying him in a fine holland shirt with exquisite broidery of her own on the collar and sleeves, and carefully disposing his long glossy, dark brown hair so as to fall on his shoulders as he lay propped up by cushions. She would have thrown his crimson mantle round him, but he repelled it indignantly. "Gay braveries for me, while my Friedel is not yet in his resting-place? Here—the black velvet cloak."

"Alas, Ebbo! it makes thee look more of a corpse than a bridegroom. Thou wilt scare thy poor little spouse. Ah! it was not thus I had fancied myself decking thee for thy wedding."

The Dove in the Eagle's Nest

"Poor little one!" said Ebbo. "If, as your uncle says, mourning is the seed of joy, this bridal should prove a gladsome one! But let her prove a loving child to you, and honour my Friedel's memory, then shall I love her well. Do not fear, motherling; with the roots of hatred and jealousy taken out of the heart, even sorrow is such peace that it is almost joy."

It was over early for pain and sorrow to have taught that lesson, thought the mother, as with tender tears she gave place to the priest, who was to begin the solemnities of the day by shriving the young Baron. It was Father Norbert, who had in this very chamber baptized the brothers, while their grandmother was plotting the destruction of their godfather, even while he gave Friedmund his name of peace,—Father Norbert, who had from the very first encouraged the drooping, heart-stricken, solitary Christina not to be overcome of evil, but to overcome evil with good.

A temporary altar was erected between the windows, and hung with the silk and embroidery belonging to that in the chapel: a crucifix was placed on it, with the shrine of the stone of Nicaea, one or two other relics brought on St. Ruprecht's cloister, and a beautiful mother-of-pearl and gold pyx also from the abbey, containing the host. These were arranged by the chaplain, Father Norbert, and three of his brethren from the abbey. And then the Father Abbot, a kindly, dignified old man, who had long been on friendly terms with the young Baron, entered; and after a few kind though serious words to him, assumed a gorgeous cope stiff with gold embroidery, and, standing by the altar, awaited the arrival of the other assistants at the ceremony.

The slender, youthful-looking, pensive lady of the castle, in her wonted mourning dress, was courteously handed to her son's bedside by the Emperor. He was in his plain buff leathern hunting garb, unornamented, save by the rich clasp of his sword-belt and his gold chain, and his head was only covered by the long silken locks of fair hair that hung round his shoulders; but, now that his large keen dark blue eyes were gravely restrained, and his eager face composed, his countenance was so majestic, his bearing so lofty, that not all his crowns could have better marked his dignity.

Behind him came a sunburnt, hardy man, wearing the white mantle and black fleur-de-lis-pointed cross of the Teutonic Order. A thrill passed through Ebbo's veins as he beheld the man who to him represented the murderer of his brother and both his grandfathers, the cruel oppressor of his father, and the perpetrator of many a more remote, but equally unforgotten, injury. And in like manner Sir Dankwart beheld the actual slayer of his father, and the heir of a long score of deadly retribution. No wonder then that, while the Emperor spoke a few words of salutation and inquiry, gracious though not familiar, the two foes scanned one another with a shiver of mutual repulsing, and a sense that they would fain have fought it out as in the good old times.

However, Ebbo only beheld a somewhat dull, heavy, honest-looking visage of about thirty years old, good-nature written in all its flat German features, and a sort of puzzled wonder in the wide light eyes that stared fixedly at him, no doubt in amazement that the mighty huge-limbed Wolfgang could have been actually slain by the delicately-framed youth, now more colourless than ever in consequence of the morning's fast. Schleiermacher was also present, and the chief followers on either hand had come into the lower part of the room—Hatto, Heinz, and Koppel, looking far from contented; some of the Emperor's suite; and a few attendants of Schlangenwald, like himself connected with the Teutonic Order.

The Emperor spoke: "We have brought you together, Herr Graff von Schlangenwald, and Herr Freiherr von Adlerstein, because ye have given us reason to believe you willing to lay aside the remembrance of the foul and deadly strifes of your forefathers, and to live as good Christians in friendship and brotherhood."

"Sire, it is true," said Schlangenwald; and "It is true," said Ebbo.

"That is well," replied Maximilian. "Nor can our reign better begin than by the closing of a breach that has cost the land some of its bravest sons. Dankwart von Schlangenwald, art thou willing to pardon the heir of Adlerstein for having slain thy father in free and honourable combat, as well as, doubtless, for other deeds of his ancestors, more than I know or can specify?"

"Yea, truly; I pardon him, my liege, as befits my vow."

The Dove in the Eagle's Nest

"And thou, Eberhard von Adlerstein, dost thou put from thee vengeance for thy twin brother's death, and all the other wrongs that thine house has suffered?"

"I put revenge from me for ever."

"Ye agree, further, then, instead of striving as to your rights to the piece of meadow called the Debateable Strand, and to the wrecks of burthens there cast up by the stream, ye will unite with the citizens of Ulm in building a bridge over the Braunwasser, where, your mutual portions thereof being decided by the Swabian League, toll may be taken from all vehicles and beasts passing there over?"

"We agree," said both knights.

"And I, also, on behalf of the two guilds of Ulm," added Moritz Schleiermacher.

"Likewise," continued the Emperor, "for avoidance of debate, and to consecrate the spot that has caused so much contention, ye will jointly erect a church, where may be buried both the relatives who fell in the late unhappy skirmish, and where ye will endow a perpetual mass for their souls, and those of others of your two races."

"Thereto I willingly agree," said the Teutonic knight. But to Ebbo it was a shock that the pure, gentle Friedmund should thus be classed with his treacherous assassin; and he had almost declared that it would be sacrilege, when he received from the Emperor a look of stern, surprised command, which reminded him that concession must not be all on one side, and that he could not do Friedel a greater wrong than to make him a cause of strife. So, though they half choked him, he contrived to utter the words, "I consent."

"And in token of amity I here tear up and burn all the feuds of Adlerstein," said Schlangenwald, producing from his pouch a collection of hostile literature, beginning from a crumpled strip of yellow parchment and ending with a coarse paper missive in the clerkly hand of burgher–bred Hugh Sorel, and bearing the crooked signatures of the last two Eberhards of Adlerstein—all with great seals of the eagle shield appended to them. A similar collection— which, with one or two other family defiances, and the letters of investiture recently obtained at Ulm, formed the whole archives of Adlerstein—had been prepared within Ebbo's reach; and each of the two, taking up a dagger, made extensive gashes in these documents, and then—with no mercy to the future antiquaries, who would have gloated over them—the whole were hurled into the flames on the hearth, where the odour they emitted, if not grateful to the physical sense, should have been highly agreeable to the moral.

"Then, holy Father Abbot," said Maximilian, "let us ratify this happy and Christian reconciliation by the blessed sacrifice of peace, over which these two faithful knights shall unite in swearing good–will and brotherhood."

Such solemn reconciliations were frequent, but, alas were too often a mockery. Here, however, both parties were men who felt the awe of the promise made before the Pardon–winner of all mankind. Ebbo, bred up by his mother in the true life of the Church, and comparatively apart from practical superstitions, felt the import to the depths of his inmost soul, with a force heightened by his bodily state of nervous impressibility; and his wan, wasted features and dark shining eyes had a strange spiritual beam, "half passion and half awe," as he followed the words of universal forgiveness and lofty praise that he had heard last in his anguished trance, when his brother lay dying beside him, and leaving him behind. He knew now that it was for this.

His deep repressed ardour and excitement were no small contrast to the sober, matter–of–fact demeanour of the Teutonic knight, who comported himself with the mechanical decorum of an ecclesiastic, but quite as one who meant to keep his word. Maximilian served the mass in his royal character as sub–deacon. He was fond of so doing, either from humility, or love of incongruity, or both. No one, however, communicated except the clergy and the parties concerned— Dankwart first, as being monk as well as knight, then Eberhard and his mother; and then followed, interposed into the rite, the oath of pardon, friendship, and brotherhood administered by the abbot, and followed by the solemn kiss of peace. There was now no recoil; Eberhard raised himself to meet the lips of his foe, and his heart went with the embrace. Nay, his inward ear dwelt on Friedmund's song mingling with the concluding chants of praise.

The service ended, it was part of the pledge of amity that the reconciled enemies should break their fast together, and a collation of white bread and wine was provided for the purpose. The Emperor tried to promote free and friendly talk between the two adversaries, but not with great success; for Dankwart, though honest and sincere, seemed extremely dull. He appeared to have few ideas beyond his Prussian commandery and its routine discipline, and to be lost in a castle where all was at his sole will and disposal, and he caught eagerly at all proposals made to him as if they were new lights. As, for instance, that some impartial arbitrator should be demanded from the Swabian League to define the boundary; and that next Rogation- tide the two knights should ride or climb it in company, while meantime the serfs should be strictly charged not to trespass, and any transgressor should be immediately escorted to his own lord.

"But," quoth Sir Dankwart, in a most serious tone, "I am told that a she-bear wons in a den on yonder crag, between the pass you call the Gemsbock's and the Schlangenwald valley. They told me the right in it had never been decided, and I have not been up myself. To say truth, I have lived so long in the sand plains as to have lost my mountain legs, and I hesitated to see if a hunter could mount thither for fear of fresh offence; but, if she bide there till Rogation-tide, it will be ill for the lambs."

"Is that all?" cried Maximilian. "Then will I, a neutral, kill your bear for you, gentlemen, so that neither need transgress this new crag of debate. I'll go down and look at your bear spears, friend Ebbo, and be ready so soon as Kasimir has done with his bridal."

"That crag!" cried Ebbo. "Little good will it do either of us. Sire, it is a mere wall of sloping rock, slippery as ice, and with only a stone or matting of ivy here and there to serve as foothold."

"Where bear can go, man can go," replied the Kaisar.

"Oh, yes! We have been there, craving your pardon, Herr Graf," said Ebbo, "after a dead chamois that rolled into a cleft, but it is the worst crag on all the hill, and the frost will make it slippery. Sire, if you do venture it, I conjure you to take Koppel, and climb by the rocks from the left, not the right, which looks easiest. The yellow rock, with a face like a man's, is the safer; but ach, it is fearful for one who knows not the rocks."

"If I know not the rocks, all true German rocks know me," smiled Maximilian, to whom the danger seemed to be such a stimulus that he began to propose the bear-hunt immediately, as an interlude while waiting for the bride.

However, at that moment, half-a-dozen horsemen were seen coming up from the ford, by the nearer path, and a forerunner arrived with the tidings that the Baron of Adlerstein Wildschloss was close behind with the little Baroness Thekla.

Half the moonlight night had Sir Kasimir and his escort ridden; and, after a brief sleep at the nearest inn outside Ulm, he had entered in early morning, demanded admittance at the convent, made short work with the Abbess Ludmilla's arguments, claimed his daughter, and placing her on a cushion before him on his saddle, had borne her away, telling her of freedom, of the kind lady, and the young knight who had dazzled her childish fancy.

Christina went down to receive her. There was no time to lose, for the huntsman Kaisar was bent on the slaughter of his bear before dark, and, if he were to be witness of the wedding, it must be immediate. He was in a state of much impatience, which he beguiled by teasing his friend Wildschloss by reminding him how often he himself had been betrothed, and had managed to slip his neck out of the noose. "And, if my Margot be not soon back on my hands, I shall give the French credit," he said, tossing his bear-spear in the air, and catching it again. "Why, this bride is as long of busking her as if she were a beauty of seventeen! I must be off to my Lady Bearess."

The Dove in the Eagle's Nest

Thus nothing could be done to prepare the little maiden but to divest her of her mufflings, and comb out her flaxen hair, crowning it with a wreath which Christina had already woven from the myrtle of her own girlhood, scarcely waiting to answer the bewildered queries and entreaties save by caresses and admonitions to her to be very good.

Poor little thing! She was tired, frightened, and confused; and, when she had been brought upstairs, she answered the half smiling, half shy greeting of her bridegroom with a shudder of alarm, and the exclamation, "Where is the beautiful young knight? That's a lady going to take the veil lying under the pall."

"You look rather like a little nun yourself," said Ebbo, for she wore a little conventual dress, "but we must take each other for such as we are;" and, as she hid her face and clung to his mother, he added in a more cheerful, coaxing tone, "You once said you would be my wife."

"Ah, but then there were two of you, and you were all shining bright."

Before she could be answered, the impatient Emperor returned, and brought with him the abbot, who proceeded to find the place in his book, and to ask the bridegroom for the rings. Ebbo looked at Sir Kasimir, who owned that he should have brought them from Ulm, but that he had forgotten.

"Jewels are not plenty with us," said Ebbo, with a glow of amusement and confusion dawning on his cheek, such as reassured the little maid that she beheld one of the two beautiful young knights. "Must we borrow?"

Christina looked at the ring she had first seen lying on her own Eberhard's palm, and felt as if to let it be used would sever the renewed hope she scarcely yet durst entertain; and at the same moment Maximilian glanced at his own fingers, and muttered, "None but this! Unlucky!" For it was the very diamond which Mary of Burgundy had sent to assure him of her faith, and summon him to her aid after her father's death. Sir Kasimir had not retained the pledge of his own ill-omened wedlock; but, in the midst of the dilemma, the Emperor, producing his dagger, began to detach some of the massive gold links of the chain that supported his hunting-horn. "There," said he, "the little elf of a bride can get her finger into this lesser one and you—verily this largest will fit, and the goldsmith can beat it out when needed. So on with you in St. Hubert's name, Father Abbot!"

Slender-boned and thin as was Ebbo's hand, it was a very tight fit, but the purpose was served. The service commenced; and fortunately, thanks to Thekla's conventual education, she was awed into silence and decorum by the sound of Latin and the sight of an abbot. It was a strange marriage, if only in the contrast between the pale, expressive face and sad, dark eyes of the prostrate youth, and the frightened, bewildered little girl, standing upon a stool to reach up to him, with her blue eyes stretched with wonder, and her cheeks flushed and pouting with unshed tears, her rosy plump hand enclosed in the long white wasted one that was thus for ever united to it by the broken fragments of Kaisar Max's chain.

The rite over, two attestations of the marriage of Eberhard, Freiherr von Adlerstein, and Thekla, Freiherrinn von Adlerstein Wildschloss and Felsenbach, were drawn up and signed by the abbot, the Emperor, Count Dankwart, and the father and mother of the two contracting parties; one to be committed to the care of the abbot, the other to be preserved by the house of Adlerstein.

Then the Emperor, as the concluding grace of the ceremonial, bent to kiss the bride; but, tired, terrified, and cross, Thekla, as if quite relieved to have some object for her resentment, returned his attempt with a vehement buffet, struck with all the force of her small arm, crying out, "Go away with you! I know I've never married YOU!"

"The better for my eyes!" said the good-natured Emperor, laughing heartily. "My Lady Bearess is like to prove the more courteous bride! Fare thee well, Sir Bridegroom," he added, stooping over Ebbo, and kissing his brow; "Heaven give thee joy of this day's work, and of thy faithful little fury. I'll send her the bearskin as her meetest wedding-gift."

And the next that was heard from the Kaisar was the arrival of a parcel of Italian books for the Freiherr Eberhard, and for the little Freiherrinn a large bundle, which proved to contain a softly-dressed bearskin, with the head on, the eyes being made of rubies, a gold muzzle and chain on the nose, and the claws tipped with gold. The Emperor had made a point that it should be conveyed to the castle, snow or no snow, for a yule gift.

CHAPTER XXIV: OLD IRON AND NEW STEEL

The clear sunshine of early summer was becoming low on the hillsides. Sparkling and dimpling, the clear amber-coloured stream of the Braunwasser rippled along its stony bed, winding in and out among the rocks so humbly that it seemed to be mocked by the wide span of the arch that crossed it in all the might of massive bulwarks, and dignified masonry of huge stones.

Some way above, a clearing of the wood below the mountain showed huts, and labourers apparently constructing a mill so as to take advantage of the leap of the water from the height above; and, on the left bank, an enclosure was traced out, within which were rising the walls of a small church, while the noise of the mallet and chisel echoed back from the mountain side, and masons, white with stone- dust, swarmed around.

Across the bridge came a pilgrim, marked out as such by hat, wallet, and long staff, on which he leant heavily, stumbling along as if both halting and footsore, and bending as one bowed down by past toil and present fatigue. Pausing in the centre, he gazed round with a strange disconcerted air—at the castle on the terraced hillside, looking down with bright eyes of glass glittering in the sunshine, and lighting up even that grim old pile; at the banner hanging so lazily that the tinctures and bearings were hidden in the folds; then at the crags, rosy purple in evening glow, rising in broad step above step up to the Red Eyrie, bathed in sunset majesty of dark crimson; and above it the sweep of the descending eagle, discernible for a moment in the pearly light of the sky. The pilgrim's eye lighted up as he watched it; but then, looking down at bridge, and church, and trodden wheel-tracked path, he frowned with perplexity, and each painful step grew heavier and more uncertain.

Near the opposite side of the enclosure there waited a tall, rugged- looking, elderly man with two horses—one an aged mare, mane, tail, and all of the snowiest silvery white; the other a little shaggy dark mountain pony, with a pad-saddle. And close to the bank of the stream might be seen its owner, a little girl of some seven years, whose tight round lace cap had slipped back, as well as her blue silk hood, and exposed a profusion of loose flaxen hair, and a plump, innocent face, intent upon some private little bit of building of her own with some pebbles from the brook, and some mortar filched from the operations above, to the great detriment of her soft pinky fingers.

The pilgrim looked at her unperceived, and for a moment was about to address her; but then, with a strange air of repulsion, dragged himself on to the porch of the rising church, where, seated on a block of stone, he could look into the interior. All was unfinished, but the portion which had made the most progress was a chantry-chapel opposite to the porch, and containing what were evidently designed to be two monuments. One was merely blocked out, but it showed the outline of a warrior, bearing a shield on which a coiled serpent was rudely sketched in red chalk. The other, in a much more forward state, was actually under the hands of the sculptor, and represented a slender youth, almost a boy, though in the full armour of a knight, his hands clasped on his breast over a lute, an eagle on his shield, an eagle-crest on his helmet, and, under the arcade supporting the altar-tomb, shields alternately of eagles and doves.

But the strangest thing was that this young knight seemed to be sitting for his own effigy. The very same face, under the very same helmet, only with the varied, warm hues of life, instead of in cold white marble, was to be seen on the shoulders of a young man in a gray cloth dress, with a black scarf passing from shoulder to waist, crossed by a sword-belt. The hair was hidden by the helmet, whose raised visor showed keen, finely-cut features, and a pair of dark brown eyes, of somewhat grave and sad expression.

"Have a care, Lucas," he presently said; "I fear me you are chiselling away too much. It must be a softer, more rounded face than mine has become; and, above all, let it not catch any saddened look. Keep that air of solemn waiting in glad hope, as though he saw the dawn through his closed eyelids, and were about to take up his song again!"

"Verily, Herr Freiherr, now the likeness is so far forward, the actual sight of you may lead me to mar it rather than mend."

"So is it well that this should be the last sitting. I am to set forth for Genoa in another week. If I cannot get letters from the Kaisar, I shall go in search of him, that he may see that my lameness is no more an impediment."

The pilgrim passed his hand over his face, as though to dissipate a bewildering dream; and just then the little girl, all flushed and dabbled, flew rushing up from the stream, but came to a sudden standstill at sight of the stranger, who at length addressed her. "Little lady," he said, "is this the Debateable Ford?"

"No; now it is the Friendly Bridge," said the child.

The pilgrim started, as with a pang of recollection. "And what is yonder castle?" he further asked.

"Schloss Adlerstein," she said, proudly.

"And you are the little lady of Adlerstein Wildschloss?"

"Yes," again she answered; and then, gathering courage—"You are a holy pilgrim! Come up to the castle for supper and rest." And then, springing past him, she flew up to the knight, crying, "Herr Freiherr, here is a holy pilgrim, weary and hungry. Let us take him home to the mother."

"Did he take thee for a wild elf?" said the young man, with an elder- brotherly endeavour to right the little cap that had slidden under the chin, and to push back the unmanageable wealth of hair under it, ere he rose; and he came forward and spoke with kind courtesy, as he observed the wanderer's worn air and feeble step. "Dost need a night's lodging, holy palmer? My mother will make thee welcome, if thou canst climb as high as the castle yonder."

The pilgrim made an obeisance, but, instead of answering, demanded hastily, "See I yonder the bearing of Schlangenwald?"

"Even so. Schloss Schlangenwald is about a league further on, and thou wilt find a kind reception there, if thither thou art bent."

"Is that Graff Wolfgang's tomb?" still eagerly pursued the pilgrim; and receiving a sign in the affirmative, "What was his end?"

"He fell in a skirmish."

"By whose hand?"

"By mine."

"Ha!" and the pilgrim surveyed him with undisguised astonishment; then, without another word, took up his staff and limped out of the building, but not on the road to Schlangenwald. It was nearly a quarter of an hour afterwards that he was overtaken by the young knight and the little lady on their horses, just where the new road to the castle parted from the old way by the Eagle's Ladder. The knight reined up as he saw the poor man's slow, painful steps, and said, "So thou art not bound for Schlangenwald?"

"I would to the village, so please you—to the shrine of the Blessed Friedmund."

The Dove in the Eagle's Nest

"Nay, at this rate thou wilt not be there till midnight," said the young knight, springing off his horse; "thou canst never brook our sharp stones! See, Thekla, do thou ride on with Heinz to tell the mother I am bringing her a holy pilgrim to tend. And thou, good man, mount my old gray. Fear not; she is steady and sure-footed, and hath of late been used to a lame rider. Ah! that is well. Thou hast been in the saddle before."

To go afoot for the sake of giving a lift to a holy wayfarer was one of the most esteemed acts of piety of the Middle Age, so that no one durst object to it, and the palmer did no more than utter a suppressed murmur of acknowledgment as he seated himself on horseback, the young knight walking by his rein. "But what is this?" he exclaimed, almost with dismay. "A road to the castle up here!"

"Yes, we find it a great convenience. Thou art surely from these parts?" added the knight.

"I was a man-at-arms in the service of the Baron," was the answer, in an odd, muffled tone.

"What!—of my grandfather!" was the exclamation.

"No!" gruffly. "Of old Freiherr Eberhard. Not of any of the Wildschloss crew."

"But I am not a Wildschloss! I am grandson to Freiherr Eberhard! Oh, wast thou with him and my father when they were set upon in the hostel?" he cried, looking eagerly up to the pilgrim; but the man kept his broad-leaved hat slouched over his face, and only muttered, "The son of Christina!" the last word so low that Ebbo was not sure that he caught it, and the next moment the old warrior exclaimed exultingly, "And you have had vengeance on them! When—how—where?"

"Last harvest-tide—at the Debateable Strand," said Ebbo, never able to speak of the encounter without a weight at his heart, but drawn on by the earnestness of the old foe of Schlangenwald. "It was a meeting in full career—lances broken, sword-stroke on either hand. I was sore wounded, but my sword went through his collar-bone."

"Well struck! good stroke!" cried the pilgrim, in rapture. "And with that sword?"

"With this sword. Didst know it?" said Ebbo, drawing the weapon, and giving it to the old man, who held it for a few moments, weighed it affectionately, and with a long low sigh restored it, saying, "It is well. You and that blade have paid off the score. I should be content. Let me dismount. I know my way to the hermitage."

"Nay, what is this?" said Ebbo; "thou must have rest and food. The hermitage is empty, scarce habitable. My mother will not be balked of the care of thy bleeding feet."

"But let me go, ere I bring evil on you all. I can pray up there, and save my soul, but I cannot see it all."

"See what?" said Ebbo, again trying to see his guest's face. "There may be changes, but an old faithful follower of my father's must ever be welcome."

"Not when his wife has taken a new lord," growled the stranger, bitterly, "and he a Wildschloss! Young man, I could have pardoned aught else!"

"I know not who you may be who talk of pardoning my lady-mother," said Ebbo, "but new lord she has neither taken nor will take. She has refused every offer; and, now that Schlangenwald with his last breath confessed that he slew not my father, but sold him to the Turks, I have been only awaiting recovery from my wound to go in search of him."

"Who then is yonder child, who told me she was Wildschloss?"

"That child," said Ebbo, with half a smile and half a blush, "is my wife, the daughter of Wildschloss, who prayed me to espouse her thus early, that so my mother might bring her up."

By this time they had reached the castle court, now a well-kept, lordly-looking enclosure, where the pilgrim looked about him as one bewildered. He was so infirm that Ebbo carefully helped him up the stone stairs to the hall, where he already saw his mother prepared for the hospitable reception of the palmer. Leaving him at the entrance, Ebbo crossed the hall to say to her in a low voice, "This pilgrim is one of the old lanzknechts of my grandfather's time. I wonder whether you or Heinz will know him. One of the old sort— supremely discontented at change."

"And thou hast walked up, and wearied thyself!" exclaimed Christina, grieved to see her son's halting step.

"A rest will soon cure that," said Ebbo, seating himself as he spoke on a settle near the hall fire; but the next moment a strange wild low shriek from his mother made him start up and spring to her side. She stood with hands clasped, and wondering eyes. The pilgrim—his hat on the ground, his white head and rugged face displayed—was gazing as though devouring her with his eyes, murmuring, "Unchanged! unchanged!"

"What is this!" thundered the young Baron. "What are you doing to the lady?"

"Hush! hush, Ebbo!" exclaimed Christina. "It is thy father! On thy knees! Thy father is come! It is our son, my own lord. Oh, embrace him! Kneel to him, Ebbo!" she wildly cried.

"Hold, mother," said Ebbo, keeping his arm round her, though she struggled against him, for he felt some doubts as he looked back at his walk with the stranger, and remembered Heinz's want of recognition. "Is it certain that this is indeed my father?"

"Oh, Ebbo," was the cry of poor Christina, almost beside herself, "how could I not be sure? I know him! I feel it! Oh, my lord, bear with him. It is his wont to be so loving! Ebbo, cannot you see it is himself?"

"The young fellow is right," said the stranger, slowly. "I will answer all he may demand."

"Forgive me," said Ebbo, abashed, "forgive me;" and, as his mother broke from him, he fell upon his knee; but he only heard his father's cry, "Ah! Stine, Stine, thou alone art the same," and, looking up, saw her, with her face hidden in the white beard, quivering with a rapture such as he had never seen in her before. It seemed long to him ere she looked up again in her husband's face to sob on: "My son! Oh! my beautiful twins! Our son! Oh, see him, dear lord!" And the pilgrim turned to hear Ebbo's "Pardon, honoured father, and your blessing."

Almost bashfully the pilgrim laid his hand on the dark head, and murmured something; then said, "Up, then! The slayer of Schlangenwald kneeling! Ah! Stine, I knew thy little head was wondrous wise, but I little thought thou wouldst breed him up to avenge us on old Wolfgang! So slender a lad too! Ha! Schneiderlein, old rogue, I knew thee," holding out his hand. "So thou didst get home safe?"

"Ay, my lord; though, if I left you alive, never more will I call a man dead," said Heinz.

"Worse luck for me—till now," said Sir Eberhard, whose tones, rather than his looks, carried perfect conviction of his identity. It was the old homely accent, and gruff good-humoured voice, but with something subdued and broken in the tone. His features had grown like his father's, but he looked much older than ever the hale old mountaineer had done, or than his real age; so worn and lined was his face, his skin tanned, his eyelids and temples puckered by burning sun, his hair and beard white as the inane of his old mare, the proud Adlerstein port entirely gone. He stooped even more without his staff than with it; and, when he yielded himself with a sigh of repose to his wife's tendance, she found that he had not merely the ordinary hurts of travelling, but that there were old festering scars on his ankles. "The gyves," he said, as she looked up at him, with startled, pitying eyes. "Little deemed I that they would ever come under thy tender hands." As he almost timidly smoothed the braid of dark hair on her brow—"So they never burnt thee for a witch after all, little one? I thought my mother would never keep her hands off thee, and used to fancy I heard the crackling of the flame."

"She spared me for my children's sake," said Christina; "and truly Heaven has been very good to us, but never so much as now. My dear lord, will it weary thee too much to come to the castle chapel and give thanks?" she said, timidly.

"With all my heart," he answered, earnestly. "I would go even on my knees. We were not without masses even in Tunis; but, when Italian and Spaniard would be ransomed, and there was no mind of the German, I little thought I should ever sing Brother Lambert's psalm about turning our captivity as rivers in the south."

Ebbo was hovering round, supplying all that was needed for his father's comfort; but his parents were so completely absorbed in one another that he was scarcely noticed, and, what perhaps pained him more, there was no word about Friedel. He felt this almost an injustice to the brother who had been foremost in embracing the idea of the unknown father, and scarcely understood how his parents shrank from any sorrowful thought that might break in on their new-found joy, nor that he himself was so strange and new a being in his father's eyes, that to imagine him doubled was hardly possible to the tardy, dulled capacity, which as yet seemed unable to feel anything but that here was home, and Christina.

When the chapel bell rang, and the pair rose to offer their thanksgiving, Ebbo dutifully offered his support, but was absolutely unseen, so fondly was Sir Eberhard leaning on his wife; and her bright exulting smile and shake of the head gave an absolute pang to the son who had hitherto been all in all to her.

He followed, and, as they passed Friedmund's coffin, he thought his mother pointed to it, but even of this he was uncertain. The pair knelt side by side with hands locked together, while notes of praise rose from all voices; and meantime Ebbo, close to that coffin, strove to share the joy, and to lift up a heart that WOULD sink in the midst of self-reproach for undutifulness, and would dislike the thought of the rude untaught man, holding aloof from him, likely to view him with distrust and jealousy, and to undo all he had achieved, and further absorbing the mother, the mother who was to him all the world, and for whose sake he had given his best years to the child- wife, as yet nothing to him.

It was reversing the natural order of things that, after reigning from infancy, he should have to give up at eighteen to one of the last generation; and some such thought rankled in his mind when the whole household trooped joyfully out of the chapel to prepare a banquet for their old new lord, and their young old lord was left alone.

Alone with the coffin where the armour lay upon the white cross, Ebbo threw himself on his knees, and laid his head upon it, murmuring, "Ah, Friedel! Friedel! Would that we had changed places! Thou wouldst brook it better. At least thou didst never know what it is to be lonely."

"Herr Baron!" said a little voice.

His first movement was impatient. Thekla was apt to pursue him wherever he did not want her; but here he had least expected her, for she had a great fear of that coffin, and could hardly be brought to the chapel at prayer times, when she generally occupied herself with fancies that the empty helmet glared at her. But now Ebbo saw her standing as near as she durst, with a sweet wistfulness in her eyes, such as he had never seen there before.

"What is it, Thekla?" he said. "Art sent to call me?"

"No; only I saw that you stayed here all alone," she said, clasping her hands.

"Must I not be alone, child?" he said, bitterly. "Here lies my brother. My mother has her husband again!"

"But you have me!" cried Thekla; and, as he looked up between amusement and melancholy, he met such a loving eager little face, that he could not help holding out his arms, and letting her cling to him. "Indeed," she said, "I'll never be afraid

The Dove in the Eagle's Nest

of the helmet again, if only you will not lay down your head there, and say you are alone."

"Never, Thekla! while you are my little wife," said he; and, child as she was, there was strange solace to his heart in the eyes that, once vacant and wondering, had now gained a look of love and intelligence.

"What are you going to do?" she said, shuddering a little, as he rose and laid his hand on Friedel's sword.

"To make thee gird on thine own knight's sword," said Ebbo, unbuckling that which he had so long worn. "Friedel," he added, "thou wouldst give me thine. Let me take up thy temper with it, thine open-hearted love and humility."

He guided Thekla's happy little fingers to the fastening of the belt, and then, laying his hand on hers, said gravely, "Thekla, never speak of what I said just now—not even to the mother. Remember, it is thy husband's first secret."

And feeling no longer solitary when his hand was in the clasp of hers, he returned to the hall, where his father was installed in the baronial chair, in which Ebbo had been at home from babyhood. His mother's exclamation showed that her son had been wanting to her; and she looked fuller than ever of bliss when Ebbo gravely stood before his father, and presented him with the good old sword that he had sent to his unborn son.

"You are like to use it more than I,—nay, you have used it to some purpose," said he. "Yet must I keep mine old comrade at least a little while. Wife, son, sword, should make one feel the same man again, but it is all too wonderful!"

All that evening, and long after, his hand from time to time sought the hilt of his sword, as if that touch above all proved to him that he was again a free noble in his own castle.

The story he told was thus. The swoon in which Heinz had left him had probably saved his life by checking the gush of blood, and he had known no more till he found himself in a rough cart among the corpses. At Schlangenwald's castle he had been found still breathing, and had been flung into a dungeon, where he lay unattended, for how long he never knew, since all the early part of the time was lost in the clouds of fever. On coarse fare and scanty drink, in that dark vault, he had struggled by sheer obstinacy of vitality into recovery. In the very height of midsummer alone did the sun peep through the grating of his cell, and he had newly hailed this cheerful visitor when he was roughly summoned, placed on horseback with eyes and hands bound, and only allowed sight again to find himself among a herd of his fellow Germans in the Turkish camp. They were the prisoners of the terrible Turkish raid of 1475, when Georg von Schenk and fourteen other noblemen of Austria and Styria were all taken in one unhappy fight, and dragged away into captivity, with hundreds of lower rank.

To Sir Eberhard the change had been greatly for the better. The Turk had treated him much better than the Christian; and walking in the open air, chained to a German comrade, was far pleasanter than pining in his lonely dungeon. At Adrianople, an offer had been made to each of the captives, if they would become Moslems, of entering the Ottoman service as Spahis; but with one voice they had refused, and had then been draughted into different divisions. The fifteen nobles, who had been offered for ransom, were taken to Constantinople, to await its arrival, and they had promised Sir Eberhard to publish his fate on their return to their homes; and, though he knew the family resources too well to have many hopes, he was rather hurt to find that their promise had been unfulfilled.

"Alas! they had no opportunity," said Ebbo. "Gulden were scarce, or were all in Kaisar Friedrich's great chest; the ransoms could not be raised, and all died in captivity. I heard about it when I was at Wurms last month."

"The boy at Wurms?" almost gasped Sir Eberhard in amaze.

"I had to be there about matters concerning the Wildschloss lands and the bridge," said Ebbo; "and both Dankwart von Schlangenwald and I made special inquiries about that company in case you should have shared their fate. I hoped to have set forth at that time, but the Kaisar said I was still too lame, and refused me license, or letters to the Sultan."

The Dove in the Eagle's Nest

"You would not have found me," said his father, narrating how he with a large troop of captives had been driven down to the coast; where they were transferred to a Moorish slave-dealer, who shipped them off for Tunis. Here, after their first taste of the miseries of a sea life, the alternative of Islam or slavery was again put before them. "And, by the holy stone of Nicaea," said Sir Eberhard, "I thought by that time that the infidels had the advantage of us in good-will and friendliness; but, when they told me women had no souls at all, no more than a horse or dog, I knew it was but an empty dream of a religion; for did I not know that my little Ermentrude, and thou, Stine, had finer, clearer, wiser souls than ever a man I had known? 'Nay, nay,' quoth I, 'I'll cast in my lot where I may meet my wife hereafter, should I never see her here.'" He had then been allotted to a corsair, and had thenceforth been chained to the bench of rowers, between the two decks, where, in stifling heat and stench, in storm or calm, healthy or diseased, the wretched oarsmen were compelled to play the part of machinery in propelling the vessel, in order to capture Christian ships—making exertions to which only the perpetual lash of the galley-master could have urged their exhausted frames; often not desisting for twenty or thirty hours, and rowing still while sustenance was put into their mouths by their drivers. Many a man drew has last breath with his last stroke, and was at the first leisure moment hurled into the waves. It was the description that had so deeply moved Friedel long ago, and Christina wept over it, as she looked at the bowed form once so proud and free, and thought of the unhealed scars. But there, her husband added, he had been chained next to a holy friar of German blood, like himself a captive of the great Styrian raid; and, while some blasphemed in their misery, or wildly chid their patron saints, this good man strove to show that all was to work out good; he had a pious saying for all that befell, and adored the will of God in thus purifying him; "And, if it were thus with a saint like him, I thought, what must it be with a rough freebooting godless sinner such as I had been? See"—and he took out a rosary of strung bladders of seaweed; "that is what he left me when he died, and what I meant to have been telling for ever up in the hermitage."

"He died, then?"

"Ay—he died on the shore of Corsica, while most of the dogs were off harrying a village inland, and we had a sort of respite, or I trow he would have rowed till his last gasp. How he prayed for the poor wretches they were gone to attack!—ay, and for all of us—for me also—There's enough of it. Such talk skills not now."

It was plain that Sir Eberhard had learnt more Christianity in the hold of his Moorish pirate ship than ever in the Holy Roman Empire, and a weight was lifted off his son's mind by finding that he had vowed never to return to a life of violence, even though fancying a life of penance in a hermitage the only alternative.

Ebbo asked if the Genoese merchant, Ser Gian Battista dei Battiste, had indeed been one of his fellow-captives.

"Ha!—what?" and on the repetition, "Truly I knew him, Merchant Gian as we used to call him; but you twang off his name as they speak it in his own stately city."

Christina smiled. "Ebbo learnt the Italian tongue this winter from our chaplain, who had studied at Bologna. He was told it would aid in his quest of you."

"Tell me not!" said the traveller, holding up his hands in deprecation; "the Junker is worse than a priest! And yet he killed old Wolfgang! But what of Gian? Hold,—did not he, when I was with him at Genoa, tell me a story of being put into a dungeon in a mountain fortress in Germany, and released by a pair of young lads with eyes beaming in the sunrise, who vanished just as they brought him to a cloister? Nay, he deemed it a miracle of the saints, and hung up a votive picture thereof at the shrine of the holy Cosmo and Damian."

"He was not so far wrong in deeming ONE of the lads near of kin to the holy ones," said Christina, softly.

And Ebbo briefly narrated the adventure, when it evidently appeared that his having led at least one foray gave his father for the first time a fellow-feeling for him, and a sense that he was one of the true old stock; but, when he heard of the release, he growled, "So! How would a lad have fared who so acted in my time? My poor old mother! She must have been changed indeed not to have scourged him till he had no strength to cry out."

The Dove in the Eagle's Nest

"He was my prisoner!" said Ebbo, in his old defiant tone; "I had the right."

"Ah, well! the Junker has always been master here, and I never!" said the elder knight, looking round rather piteously; and Ebbo, with a sudden movement, exclaimed, "Nay, sir, you are the only lord and master, and I stand ready to be the first to obey you."

"You! A fine young book-learned scholar, already knighted, and with all these Wildschloss lands too!" said Sir Eberhard, gazing with a strange puzzled look at the delicate but spirited features of this strange perplexing son. "Reach hither your hand, boy."

And as he compared the slender, shapely hand of such finely-textured skin with the breadth of his own horny giant's paw, he tossed it from him, shaking his head with a gesture as if he had no commands for such feminine-looking fingers to execute, and mortifying Ebbo not a little. "Ah!" said Christina, apologetically, "it always grieved your mother that the boys would resemble me and mine. But, when daylight comes, Ebbo will show you that he has not lost the old German strength."

"No doubt—no doubt," said Sir Eberhard, hastily, "since he has slain Schlangenwald; and, if the former state of things be at an end, the less he takes after the ancient stock the better. But I am an old man now, Stine, though thou look'st fair and fresh as ever, and I do not know what to make of these things. White napery on the table; glass drinking things;—nay, were it not for thee and the Schneiderlein, I should not know I was at home."

He was led back to his narration, and it appeared that, after some years spent at the oar, certain bleedings from the lungs, the remains of his wound, had become so much more severe as to render him useless for naval purposes; and, as he escaped actually dying during a voyage, he was allowed to lie by on coming into port till he had in some degree recovered, and then had been set to labour at the fortifications, chained to another prisoner, and toiling between the burning sand and burning sun, but treated with less horrible severity than the necessities of the sea had occasioned on board ship, and experiencing the benefit of intercourse with the better class of captives, whom their miserable fate had thrown into the hands of the Moors.

It was a favourite almsdeed among the Provencals, Spaniards, and Italians to send money for the redemption of prisoners to the Moors, and there was a regular agency for ransoms through the Jews; but German captives were such an exception that no one thought of them, and many a time had the summons come for such and such a slave by name, or for five poor Sicilians, twenty Genoese, a dozen Marseillais, or the like, but still no word for the Swabian; till he had made up his mind that he should either leave his bones in the hot mud of the harbour, or be only set free by some gallant descent either of the brave King of Portugal, or of the Knights of Rhodes, of whom the captives were ever dreaming and whispering.

At length his own slave name was shouted; he was called up by the captain of his gang, and, while expecting some fresh punishment, or, maybe, to find himself sold into some domestic form of slavery, he was set before a Jewish agent, who, after examining him on his name, country, and station, and comparing his answers with a paper of instructions, informed him that he was ransomed, caused his fetters to be struck off, and shipped him off at once for Genoa, with orders to the captain to consign him to the merchant Signor del Battiste. By him Sir Eberhard had been received with the warmest hospitality, and treated as befitted his original station, but Battista disclaimed the merit of having ransomed him. He had but acted, he said, as the agent of an Austrian gentleman, from whom he had received orders to inquire after the Swabian baron who had been his fellow-captive, and, if he were still living, to pay his ransom, and bring him home.

"The name—the name!" eagerly asked Ebbo and his mother at once.

"The name? Gian was wont to make bad work of our honest German names, but I tried to learn this—being so beholden to him. I even caused it to be spelt over to me, but my letters long ago went from me. It seems to me that the man is a knight-errant, like those of thy ballads, Stine—one Ritter Theur—Theur—"

The Dove in the Eagle's Nest

"Theurdank!" cried Ebbo.

"Ay, Theurdank. What, you know him? There is nothing you and your mother don't know, I believe."

"Know him! Father, he is our greatest and noblest! He has been kind to me beyond description. He is the Kaisar! Now I see why he had that strange arch look which so vexed me when he forbade me on my allegiance to set forth till my lameness should be gone! Long ago had he asked me all about Gian Battista. To him he must have written."

"The Kaisar!" said Sir Eberhard. "Nay, the poor fellows I left in Turkey ever said he was too close of fist for them to have hope from him."

"Oh! that was old Kaisar Friedrich. This is our own gallant Maximilian—a knight as true and brave as ever was paladin," said Christina; "and most truly loving and prizing our Ebbo."

"And yet I wish—I wish," said Ebbo, "that he had let me win my father's liberty for myself."

"Yea, well," said his father, "there spoke the Adlerstein. We never were wont to be beholden to king or kaisar."

"Nay," say Ebbo, after a moment's recollection, colouring as he spoke; "it is true that I deserved it not. Nay, Sir Father, it is well. You owe your freedom in very truth to the son you have not known. It was he who treasured up the thought of the captive German described by the merchant, and even dreamt of it, while never doubting of your death; it was he who caught up Schlangenwald's first hint that you lived, while I, in my pride, passed it by as merely meant to perplex me; it was he who had formed an absolute purpose of obtaining some certainty; and at last, when my impetuosity had brought on the fatal battle, it was he who bought with his own life the avowal of your captivity. I had hoped to have fulfilled Friedel's trust, and to have redeemed my own backwardness; but it is not to be. While I was yet lying helpless on my bed, the Emperor has taken it out of my power. Mother, you receive him from Friedel's hands, after all."

"And well am I thankful that so it should be," said Christina. "Ah, Ebbo! sorely should I have pined with anxiety when thou wast gone. And thy father knows that thou hadst the full purpose."

"Yea, I know it," said the old man; "and, after all, small blame to him even if he had not. He never saw me, and light grieves the heart for what the eye hath not seen."

"But," added the wife, "since the Romish king freed you, dear lord, cared he not better for your journey than to let you come in this forlorn plight?"

This, it appeared, was far from being his deliverer's fault. Money had been supplied, and Sir Eberhard had travelled as far as Aosta with a party of Italian merchants; but no sooner had he parted with them than he was completely astray. His whole experience of life had been as a robber baron or as a slave, and he knew not how to take care of himself as a peaceful traveller; he suffered fresh extortions at every stage, and after a few days was plundered by his guides, beaten, and left devoid of all means of continuing the journey to which he could hardly hope for a cheerful end. He did not expect to find his mother living,—far less that his unowned wife could have survived the perils in which he had involved her; and he believed that his ancestral home would, if not a ruin, be held by his foes, or at best by the rival branch of the family, whose welcome of the outlawed heir would probably be to a dungeon, if not a halter. Yet the only magnet on earth for the lonely wanderer was his native mountain, where from some old peasant he might learn how his fair young bride had perished, and perhaps the sins of his youth might be expiated by continual prayer in the hermitage chapel where his sister lay buried, and whence he could see the crags for which his eye and heart had craved so long with the home-sickness of a mountaineer.

And now, when his own Christina had welcomed him with all the overflow of her loving heart, unchanged save that hers had become a tenderer yet more dignified loveliness; when his gallant son, in all the bloom of young manhood, received

The Dove in the Eagle's Nest

him with dutiful submission; when the castle, in a state of defence, prosperity, and comfort of which he had never dreamt, was again his own;—still the old man was bewildered, and sometimes oppressed almost to distress. He had, as it were, fallen asleep in one age of the world, and wakened in another, and it seemed as if he really wished to defer his wakening, or else that repose was an absolute novelty to him; for he sat dozing in his chair in the sun the whole of the next day, and scarcely spoke.

Ebbo, who felt it a necessity to come to an understanding of the terms on which they were to stand, tried to refer matters to him, and to explain the past, but he was met sometimes by a shake of the head, sometimes by a nod—not of assent, but of sleep; and his mother advised him not to harass the wearied traveller, but to leave him to himself at least for that day, and let him take his own time for exertion, letting things meantime go on as usual. Ebbo obeyed, but with a load at his heart, as he felt that all he was doing was but provisional, and that it would be his duty to resign all that he had planned, and partly executed, to this incompetent, ignorant rule. He could certainly, when not serving the Emperor, go and act for himself at Thekla's dower castle of Felsenbach, and his mother might save things from going to utter ruin at Adlerstein; but no reflection or self-reproach could make it otherwise than a bitter pill to any Telemachus to have to resign to one so unlike Ulysses in all but the length of his wanderings,—one, also, who seemed only half to like, and not at all to comprehend, his Telemachus.

Meantime Ebbo attended to such matters as were sure to come each day before the Herr Freiherr. Now it was a question whether the stone for the mill should be quarried where it would undermine a bit of grass land, or further on, where the road was rougher; now Berend's swine had got into Barthel's rye, and Barthel had severely hurt one of them—the Herr Freiherr's interference could alone prevent a hopeless quarrel; now a waggon with ironwork for the mill claimed exemption from toll as being for the Baron: and he must send down the toll, to obviate injustice towards Schlangenwald and Ulm. Old Ulrich's grandson, who had run away for a lanzknecht, had sent a letter home (written by a comrade), the Baron must read and answer it. Steinmark's son wanted to be a poor student: the Herr Freiherr must write him a letter of recommendation. Mother Grethel's ewe had fallen into a cleft; her son came to borrow a rope, and ask aid, and the Baron must superintend the hoisting the poor beast up again. Hans had found the track of a wolf, and knew the hole where a litter of cubs abode; the Freiherr, his wolf-hound, and his spear were wanted for their destruction. Dietrich could not tell how to manage his new arquebus: the Baron must teach him to take aim. Then there was a letter from Ulm to invite the Baron to consult on the tax demanded by the Emperor for his Italian war, and how far it should concern the profits of the bridge; and another letter from the Markgraf of Wurtemburg, as chief of the Swabian League, requesting the Lord of Adlerstein to be on the look-out for a band of robbers, who were reported to be in neighbouring hills, after being hunted out of some of their other lurking-places.

That very night, or rather nearly at the dawn of a summer morning, there was a yelling below the castle, and a flashing of torches, and tidings rang through it that a boor on the outskirts of the mountain had had his ricks fired and his cattle driven by the robbers, and his young daughters carried off. Old Sir Eberhard hobbled down to the hall in time to see weapons flashing as they were dealt out, to hear a clear decided voice giving orders, to listen to the tramp of horse, and watch more reitern pass out under the gateway than ever the castle had counted in his father's time. Then he went back to his bed, and when he came down in the morning, found all the womankind of the castle roasting and boiling. And, at noon, little Thekla came rushing down from the watch-tower with news that all were coming home up the Eagle's Steps, and she was sure HER baron had sent her, and waved to her. Soon after, HER baron in his glittering steel rode his cream-coloured charger (once Friedel's) into the castle court, followed by his exultant merrymen. They had overtaken the thieves in good time, made them captives, and recovered the spoil unhurt; and Heinz and Koppel made the castle ring with the deed of their young lord, who had forced the huge leader of the band to the earth, and kept him down by main strength till they could come to bind him.

"By main strength?" slowly asked Sir Eberhard, who had been stirred into excitement.

"He was a loose-limbed, awkward fellow," said Ebbo, "less strong than he looked."

144

The Dove in the Eagle's Nest

"Not only that, Sir," said Heinz, looking from his old master to his young one; "but old iron is not a whit stronger than new steel, though the one looks full of might, and you would think the other but a toy."

"And what have you done with the rogues' heads?" asked the old knight. "I looked to see them on your spears. Or have you hung them?"

"Not so, Sir," said Ebbo. "I sent the men off to Stuttgard with an escort. I dislike doing execution ourselves; it makes the men so lawless. Besides, this farmer was Schlangenwalder."

"And yet he came to you for redress?"

"Yes, for Sir Dankwart is at his commandery, and he and I agreed to look after each other's lands."

Sir Eberhard retired to his chair as if all had gone past his understanding, and thence he looked on while his son and wife hospitably regaled, and then dismissed, their auxiliaries in the rescue.

Afterwards Christina told her son that she thought his father was rested, and would be better able to attend to him, and Ebbo, with a painful swelling in his heart, approached him deferentially, with a request that he would say what was his pleasure with regard to the Emperor, to whom acknowledgments must in the first place be made for his release, and next would arise the whole question of homage and investiture.

"Look you here, fair son," said Sir Eberhard, rousing himself, "these things are all past me. I'll have none of them. You and your Kaisar understand one another, and your homage is paid. It boots not changing all for an old fellow that is but come home to die."

"Nay, father, it is in the order of things that you should be lord here."

"I never was lord here, and, what is more, I would not, and could not be. Son, I marked you yesterday. You are master as never was my poor father, with all the bawling and blows that used to rule the house, while these fellows mind you at a word, in a voice as quiet as your mother's. Besides, what should I do with all these mills and bridges of yours, and Diets, and Leagues, and councils enough to addle a man's brain? No, no; I could once slay a bear, or strike a fair stroke at a Schlangenwalder, but even they got the better of me, and I am good for nothing now but to save my soul. I had thought to do it as a hermit up there; but my little Christina thinks the saints will be just as well pleased if I tell my beads here, with her to help me, and I know that way I shall not make so many mistakes. So, young Sir, if you can give the old man a corner of the hearth while he lives, he will never interfere with you. And, maybe, if the castle were in jeopardy in your absence, with that new-fangled road up to it, he could tell the fellows how to hold it out."

"Sir—dear father," cried the ardent Ebbo, "this is not a fit state of things. I will spare you all trouble and care; only make me not undutiful; take your own place. Mother, convince him!"

"No, my son," said Sir Eberhard; "your mother sees what is best for me. I only want to be left to her to rest a little while, and repent of my sinful life. As Heinz says, the rusty old iron must lie by while the new steel does the work. It is quiet that I need. It is joy enough for me to see what she has made you, and all around. Ah! Stine, my white dove, I knew thine was a wise head; but when I left thee, gentle little frightened, fluttering thing, how little could I have thought that all alone, unaided, thou wouldst have kept that little head above water, and made thy son work out all these changes——thy doing—and so I know they are good and seemly. I see thou hast made him clerkly, quick-witted, and yet a good knight. Ah! thou didst tell me oft that our lonely pride was not high nor worthy fame. Stine, how didst do it?"

"I did it not, dear husband; God did it for me. He gave the boys the loving, true tempers that worked out the rest! He shielded them and me in our days of peril."

"Yes, father," added Ebbo, "Providence guarded us; but, above all, our chief blessing has been the mother who has made one of us a holy saint, and taught the other to seek after him! Father, I am glad you see how great has been the work of the Dove you brought to the Eagle's Nest."

CHAPTER XXV: THE STAR AND THE SPARK

The year 1531 has begun, and Schloss Adlerstein remains in its strength on the mountain side, but with a look of cultivation on its environs such as would have amazed Kunigunde. Vines run up trellises against the rocks; pot-herbs and flowers nestle in the nooks; outbuildings cluster round it; and even the grim old keep has a range of buildings connected with it, as if the household had entirely outgrown the capacities of the square tower.

Yet the old hall is still the chief place of assembly, and now that it has been wainscoted, with a screen of carved wood to shut off the draughty passages, and a stove of bright tiles to increase the warmth, it is far more cheerful. Moreover, a window has been opened showing the rich green meadow below, with the bridge over the Braunwasser, and the little church, with a spire of pierced lace- work, and white cottages peeping out of the retreating forest.

That is the window which the Lady Baroness loves. See her there, the lovely old lady of seventy-five—yes, lovelier than ever, for her sweet brown eyes have the same pensive, clear beauty, enhanced by the snowy whiteness of her hair, of which a soft braid shows over the pure pale brow beneath the white band, and sweeping black veil, that she has worn by right for twenty years. But the slight form is active and brisk, and there are ready smiles and looks of interest for the pretty fair-haired maidens, three in number, who run in and out from their household avocations to appeal to the "dear grandmother," mischievously to tell of the direful yawns proceeding from brothers Ebbo and Gottfried over their studies with their tutor, or to gaze from the window and wonder if the father, with the two brothers, Friedel Max and Kasimir, will return from Ulm in time for the "mid-day eating."

Ah! there they are. Quick-eyed Vittoria has seen the cavalcade first, and dances off to tell Ermentrude and Stine time enough to prepare their last batch of fritters for the new-comers; Ebbo and Gotz rush headlong down the hillside; and the Lady Baroness lays down her distaff, and gazes with eyes of satisfied content at the small party of horsemen climbing up the footpath. Then, when they have wound out of sight round a rock, she moves out towards the hall-door, with a light, quick step, for never yet has she resigned her great enjoyment, that of greeting her son on the steps of the porch—those steps where she once met such fearful news, but where that memory has been effaced by many a cheerful welcome.

There, then, she stands, amid the bright throng of grandchildren, while the Baron and his sons spring from their horses and come up to her. The Baron doffs his Spanish hat, bends the knee, kisses her hand, and receives her kiss on his brow, with the fervour of a life- devotion, before he turns to accept the salutation of his daughters, and then takes her hand, with pretty affectionate ceremony, to hand her back to her seat. A few words pass between them. "No, motherling," he says, "I signed it not; I will tell you all by and by."

And then the mid-day meal is served for the whole household, as of old, with the salt-cellar in the middle, but with a far larger company above it than when first we saw it. The seven young folks preserve a decorous silence, save when Fraulein Ermentrude's cookeries are good-naturedly complimented by her father, or when Baron Friedmund Maximilianus breaks out with some wonderful fact about new armour seen at Ulm. He is a handsome, fair, flaxen-haired young man—like the old Adlersteins, say the elder people—and full of honest gaiety and good nature, the special pride of his sisters; and no sooner is the meal over, than, with a formal entreaty for dismissal, all the seven, and all the dogs, move off together, to that favourite gathering-place round the stove, where all their merry tongues are let loose together.

To them, the Herr Vater and the Frau Grossmutter seem nearly of the same age, and of the same generation; and verily the eighteen years between the mother and son have dwindled into a very small difference even in appearance, and a lesser one in feeling. She is a youthful, beautiful old lady; he a grave, spare, worn, elderly man, in his full strength, but with many a trace of care and thought, and far more of silver than of brown in his thin hair and pointed beard, and with a melancholy thoughtfulness in his clear brown eyes—all well corresponding with the gravity of the dress in which he has been meeting the burghers of Ulm; a black velvet suit—only relieved by his small white lace ruff, and the ribbon and jewel of the Golden Fleece, the only other approach to ornament that he wears being that ring long ago twisted off the Emperor Maximilian's chain. But now, as he has bowed off the chaplain to his study, and excused himself from aiding his two gentlemen-squires in consuming their krug of beer, and hands his mother to her favourite nook in the sunny window, taking his seat by her side, his features assume an expression of repose and relaxation as if here indeed were his true home. He has chosen his seat in full view of a picture that hangs on the wainscoted wall, near his mother—a picture whose pure ethereal tinting, of colour limpid as the rainbow, yet rich as the most glowing flower-beds; and its soft lovely pose, and rounded outlines, prove it to be no produce even of one of the great German artists of the time, but to have been wrought, under an Italian sky, by such a hand as left us the marvellous smile of Mona Lisa. It represents two figures, one unmistakably himself when in the prime of life, his brow and cheeks unfurrowed, and his hair still thick, shining brown, but with the same grave earnestness of the dark eye that came with the early sense of responsibility, and with the first sorrow of his youth. The other figure, one on which the painter evidently loved to dwell, is of a lady, so young that she might almost pass for his daughter, except for the peculiar, tender sweetness that could only become the wife and mother. Fair she is as snow, with scarce a deepening of the rose on cheek, or even lip, fragile and transparent as a spiritual form, and with a light in the blue eyes, and a grace in the soft fugitive smile, that scarce seems to belong to earth; a beauty not exactly of feature, but rather the pathetic loveliness of calm fading away—as if she were already melting into the clear blue sky with the horizon of golden light, that the wondrous power of art has made to harmonize with, but not efface, her blue dress, golden hair, white coif, and fair skin. It is as if she belonged to that sky, and only tarried as unable to detach herself from the clasp of the strong hand round and in which both her hands are twined; and though the light in her face may be from heaven, yet the whole countenance is fixed in one absorbed, almost worshipping gaze of her husband, with a wistful simplicity and innocence on devotion, like the absorption of a loving animal, to whom its master's presence is bliss and sunshine. It is a picture to make light in a dark place, and that sweet face receives a loving glance, nay, an absolutely reverent bend of the knightly head, as the Baron seats himself.

"So it was as we feared, and this Schmalkaldic League did not suit thy sense of loyalty, my son?" she asks, reading his features anxiously.

"No, mother. I ever feared that further pressure would drive our friends beyond the line where begin schism and rebellion; and it seems to me that the moment is come when I must hold me still, or transgress mine own sense of duty. I must endure the displeasure of many I love and respect."

"Surely, my son, they have known you too long and too well not to respect your motives, and know that conscience is first with you."

"Scarce may such confidence be looked for, mother, from the most part, who esteem every man a traitor to the cause if he defend it not precisely in the fashion of their own party. But I hear that the King of France has offered himself as an ally, and that Dr. Luther, together with others of our best divines, have thereby been startled into doubts of the lawfulness of the League."

"And what think you of doing, my son?"

"I shall endeavour to wait until such time as the much-needed General Council may proclaim the ancient truth, and enable us to avouch it without disunion. Into schism I WILL not be drawn. I have held truth all my life in the Church, nor will I part from her now. If intrigues again should prevail, then, Heaven help us! Meantime, mother, the best we can, as has ever been your war-cry."

"And much has been won for us. Here are the little maidens, who, save Vittoria, would never have been scholars, reading the Holy Word daily in their own tongue."

"Ach, I had not told you, mother! I have the Court Secretary's answer this day about that command in the Kaisar's guards that my dear old master had promised to his godson."

"Another put-off with Flemish courtesy, I see by thy face, Ebbo."

"Not quite that, mother. The command is ready for the Baron Friedmund Maximilianus von Adlerstein Wildschloss, and all the rest of it, on the understanding that he has been bred up free from all taint of the new doctrine."

"New? Nay, it is the oldest of all doctrine."

"Even so. As I ever said, Dr. Luther hath been setting forth in greater clearness and fulness what our blessed Friedel and I learnt at your knee, and my young ones have learnt from babyhood of the true Catholic doctrine. Yet I may not call my son's faith such as the Kaisar's Spanish conscience-keepers would have it, and so the boy must e'en tarry at home till there be work for his stout arm to do."

"He seems little disappointed. His laugh comes ringing the loudest of all."

"The Junker is more of a boy at two-and-twenty than I ever recollect myself! He lacks not sense nor wit, but a fray or a feast, a chase or a dance, seem to suffice him at an age when I had long been dwelling on matters of moment."

"Thou wast left to be thine own pilot; he is but one of thy gay crew, and thus even these stirring times touch him not so deeply as thou wert affected by thine own choice in life between disorderly freedom and honourable restraint."

"I thought of that choice to-day, mother, as I crossed the bridge and looked at the church; and more than ever thankful did I feel that our blessed Friedel, having aided me over that one decisive pass, was laid to rest, his tender spirit unvexed by the shocks and divisions that have wrenched me hither and thither."

"Nay; not hither and thither. Ever hadst thou a resolute purpose and aim."

"Ever failed in by my own error or that of others—What, thou nestling here, my little Vittoria, away from all yonder prattle?"

"Dear father, if I may, I love far best to hear you and the grandmother talk."

"Hear the child! She alone hath your face, mother, or Friedel's eyes! Is it that thou wouldst be like thy noble Roman godmother, the Marchesa di Pescara, that makes thee seek our grave company, little one?"

"I always long to hear you talk of her, and of the Italian days, dear father, and how you won this noble jewel of yours."

"Ah, child, that was before those times! It was the gift of good Kaisar Max at his godson's christening, when he filled your sweet mother with pretty spite by persuading her that it was a little golden bear-skin."

"Tell her how you had gained it, my son."

"By vapouring, child; and by the dull pride of my neighbours. Heard'st thou never of the siege of Padua, when we had Bayard, the best knight in Europe, and 500 Frenchmen for our allies? Our artillery had made a breach, and the Kaisar requested the French knights to lead the storm, whereto they answered, Well and good, but our German nobles must share the assault, and not leave them to fight with no better backers than the hired lanzknechts. All in reason, quoth I, and more shame for us not to have been foremost in our Kaisar's own cause; but what said the rest of our misproud chivalry? They would never condescend to climb a wall on foot in company with lanzknechts! On horseback must their worships fight, or not at all; and when to shame them I called myself a mountaineer, more used to climb than to ride, and vowed that I should esteem it an honour to follow such a knight as Bayard, were it on all fours, then cast they my burgher blood in my teeth. Never saw I the Kaisar so enraged; he swore that all the common sense in the empire was in the burgher blood, and that he would make me a knight of the noblest order in Europe to show how he esteemed it. And next morning he was gone! So ashamed was he of his own army that he rode off in the night, and sent orders to break up the siege. I could have torn my hair, for I had just lashed up a few of our nobles to a better sense of honour, and we would yet have redeemed our name! And after all, the Chapter of proud Flemings would never have admitted me had not the heralds hunted up that the Sorels were gentlemen of blood and coat armour long ago at Liege. I am glad my father lived to see that proved, mother. He could not honour thee more than he did, but he would have been sorely grieved had I been rejected. He often thought me a mechanical burgher, as it was."

"Not quite so, my son. He never failed to be proud of thy deeds, even when he did not understand them; but this, and the grandson's birth, were the crowning joys of his life."

"Yes, those were glad triumphant years, take them all in all, ere the Emperor sent me to act ambassador in Rome, and we left you the two elder little girls and the boy to take care of. My dear little Thekla! She had a foreboding that she might never see those children more, yet would she have pined her heart away more surely had I left her at home! I never was absent a week but I found her wasted with watching for me."

"It was those weary seven years of Italy that changed thee most, my son."

"Apart from you, mother, and knowing you now indeed to be widowed, and with on the one hand such contradictory commands from the Emperor as made me sorely ashamed of myself, of my nation, and of the man whom I loved and esteemed personally the most on earth, yet bound there by his express command, while I saw my tender wife's health wasting in the climate day by day! Yet still, while most she gasped for a breath of Swabian hills, she ever declared it would kill her outright to send her from me. And thus it went on till I laid her in the stately church of her own patroness. Then how it would have fared with me and the helpless little ones I know not, but for thy noble godmother, my Vittoria, the wise and ready helper of all in trouble, the only friend thy mother had made at Rome, and who had been able, from all her heights of learning and accomplishment, to value my Thekla's golden soul in its simplicity. Even then, when too late, came one of the Kaisar's kindest letters, recalling me,—a letter whose every word I would have paid for with a drop of my own blood six weeks before! and which he had only failed to send because his head was running on the plan of that gorgeous tomb where he is not buried! Well, at least it brought us home to you again once more, mother, and, where you are, comfort never has been utterly absent from me. And then, coming from the wilful gloom of Pope Leo's court into our Germany, streamed over by the rays of Luther's light, it was as if a new world of hope were dawning, as if truth would no longer be muffled, and the young would grow up to a world far better and purer than the old had ever seen. What trumpet−calls those were, and how welcome was the voice of the true Catholic faith no longer stifled! And my dear old Kaisar, with his clear eyes, his unfettered mind—he felt the power and truth of those theses. He bade the Elector of Saxony well to guard the monk Luther as a treasure. Ah! had he been a younger man, or had he been more firm and resolute, able to act as well as think for himself, things might have gone otherwise with the Church. He could think, but could not act; and now we have a man who acts, but WILL not think. It may have been a good day for our German reputation among foreign princes when Charles V. put on the crown; but only two days in my life have been as mournful to me as that when I stood by Kaisar Max's death−bed at Wells, and knew that generous, loving, fitful spirit was passing away from the earth! Never owned I friend I loved so well as Kaisar Max! Nor has any Emperor done so much for this our dear land."

"The young Emperor never loved thee."

"He might have treated me as one who could be useful, but he never forgave me for shaking hands with Luther at the Diet of Worms. I knew it was all over with my court favour after I had joined in escorting the Doctor out of the city. And the next thing was that Georg of Freundsberg and his friends proclaimed me a bigoted Papist because I did my utmost to keep my troop out of the devil's holiday at the sack of Rome! It has ever been my lot to be in disgrace with one side or the other! Here is my daughter's marriage hindered on the one hand, my son's promotion checked on the other, because I have a conscience of my own, and not of other people's! Heaven knows the right is no easy matter to find; but, when one thinks one sees it, there is nothing to be done but to guide oneself by it, even if the rest of the world will not view it in the same light."

"Nothing else! I doubt me whether it be ever easy to see the veritably right course while still struggling in the midst. That is for after ages, which behold things afar off; but each man must needs follow his own principle in an honest and good heart, and assuredly God will guide him to work out some good end, or hinder some evil one."

"Ay, mother. Each party may guard one side or other of the truth in all honesty and faithfulness; he who cannot with his whole heart cast in his lot with either,—he is apt to serve no purpose, and to be scorned."

"Nay, Ebbo, may he not be a witness to the higher and more perfect truth than either party have conceived? Nor is inaction always needful. That which is right towards either side still reveals itself at the due moment, whether it be to act or to hold still. And verily, Ebbo, what thou didst say even now has set me on a strange thought of mine own dream, that which heralded the birth of thyself and thy brother. As thou knowest, it seemed to me that I was watching two sparkles from the extinguished Needfire wheel. One rose aloft and shone as a star!"

"My guiding–star!"

"The other fulfilled those words of the Wise Man. It shone and ran to and fro in the grass. And surely, my Ebbo, thy mother may feel that, in all these dark days of perplexity and trial, the spark of light hath ever shone and drawn its trail of brightness in the gloom, even though the way was long, and seemed uncertain."

"The mother who ever fondled me WILL think so, it may be! But, ah! she had better pray that the light be clearer, and that I may not fall utterly short of the star!"

Travellers in Wurtemburg may perhaps turn aside from glorious old Ulm, and the memories of the battlefields around it, to the romantic country round the Swabian mountains, through which descend the tributaries of the Danube. Here they may think themselves fortunate if they come upon a green valley, with a bright mountain torrent dashing through it, fresh from the lofty mountain, with terraced sides that rise sheer above. An old bridge, a mill, and a neat German village lie clustered in the valley; a seignorial mansion peeps out of the forest glades; and a lovely church, of rather late Gothic, but beautifully designed, attracts the eye so soon as it can be persuaded to quit the romantic outline of the ruined baronial castle high up on one of the mountain ledges. Report declares that there are tombs in the church well worth inspection. You seek out an old venerable blue–coated peasant who has charge of the church.

"What is yonder castle?"

"It is the castle of Adlerstein."

"Are the family still extant?"

"Yea, yea; they built yonder house when the Schloss became ruinous. They have always been here."

The church is very beautiful in its details, the carved work of the east end and pulpit especially so, but nothing is so attractive as the altar tomb in the chantry chapel. It is a double one, holding not, as usual, the recumbent effigies of a husband and wife, but of two knights in armour.

"Who are these, good friend?"

"They are the good Barons Ebbo and Friedel."

The Dove in the Eagle's Nest

Father and son they appear to be, killed at the same time in some fatal battle, for the white marble face of one is round with youth, no hair on lip nor chin, and with a lovely peaceful solemnity, almost cheerfulness, in the expression. The other, a bearded man, has the glory of old age in his worn features, beautiful and restful, but it is as if one had gone to sleep in the light of dawn, the other in the last glow of sunset. Their armour and their crests are alike, but the young one bears the eagle shield alone, while the elder has the same bearing repeated upon an escutcheon of pretence; the young man's hands are clasped over a harp, those of the other over a Bible, and the elder wears the insignia of the order of the Golden Fleece. They are surely father and son, a maiden knight and tried warrior who fell together?

"No," the guide shakes his head; "they are twin brothers, the good Barons Ebbo and Friedel, who were born when their father had been taken captive by the Saracens while on a crusade. Baron Friedel was slain by the Turks at the bridge foot, and his brother built the church in his memory. He first planted vines upon the mountains, and freed the peasants from the lord's dues on their flax. And it is true that the two brothers may still be seen hovering on the mountain-side in the mist at sunset, sometimes one, sometimes both."

You turn with a smile to the inscription, sure that those windows, those porches, that armour, never were of crusading date, and ready to refute the old peasant. You spell out the upright Gothic letters around the cornice of the tomb, and you read, in mediaeval Latin,

"Orate pro Anima Friedmundis Equitis Baronis Adlersteini. A. D. mccccxciii"

Then turn to the other side and read –

"Hic jacet Eberardus Eques Baro Adlersteini. A.D. mdxliii. Demum"

Yes, the guide is right. They are brothers, with well-nigh a lifetime between their deaths. Is that the meaning of that strange Demum?

Few of the other tombs are worth attention, each lapsing further into the bad taste of later ages; yet there is one still deserving admiration, placed close to the head of that of the two Barons. It is the effigy of a lady, aged and serene, with a delicately-carved face beneath her stiff head-gear. Surely this monument was erected somewhat later, for the inscription is in German. Stiff, contracted, hard to read, but this is the rendering of it

"Here lies Christina Sorel, wife of Eberhard, xxth Baron von Adlerstein, and mother of the Barons Eberhard and Friedmund. She fell asleep two days before her son, on the feast of St. John, mdxliii.

"Her children shall rise up and call her blessed.

"Erected with full hearts by her grandson, Baron Friedmund Maximilianus, and his brothers and sisters. Farewell."

CPSIA information can be obtained
at www.ICGtesting.com
Printed in the USA
LVHW060938140523
746948LV00004B/99